LIES COME EASY
The Twenty-third Posadas County Mystery

"Master of mystery Steven F. Havill accomplishes that rare and remarkable feat of making each book in his compelling series even better than the one that came before it. With meticulous attention to detail and a warm storytelling style, Havill transforms ordinary people into extraordinary. Evildoers, no matter how twisted and complex, don't stand a chance against hard-working Estella Reyes-Guzman and her legendary mentor Bill Gastner. If you haven't yet discovered these wonderful mysteries, you are in for a treat!"

—Anne Hillerman, *New York Times* bestselling author

"Havill's irresistible 23rd mystery set in tiny Posadas County, N.Mex. combines a police procedural with a complex family saga.... Havill's inviting world welcomes newcomers and keeps fans happily coming back for more."

—*Publishers Weekly*

EASY ERRORS
The Twenty-second Posadas County Mystery

"Fans of the long-running series will be drawn to the backstory here, which fills in gaps in the stories of both Torrez and Gastner. They will also respond to the qualities that have made this series so appealing over the years: meticulous plotting, multidimensional characters, sharp dialogue, and a vivid sense of place. This is one of the very best entries in a consistently excellent series."

—Wes Lukowsky, *Booklist* (starred review)

"Havill keeps his relentless hold on readers with bits of wisdom from veteran Gastner, creating a powerful sense of place in his portrayal of the bucolic southwestern New Mexico community."

—*Publishers Weekly*

"In this prequel to *One Perfect Shot*, Undersheriff Bill Gastner is first at the scene of a fatal car crash; two of the victims turn out to be the siblings of his new deputy, Robert Torrez, fresh out of the police academy. Were the three teens being pursued, and where is the fourth passenger? Fans and first-time readers will follow the case step by step in this compelling procedural, which leads from the accident to a remote New Mexican canyon and another death."

—*Library Journal*

COME DARK
The Twenty-first Posadas County Mystery

"The twenty-first Posadas mystery is a compelling mix of dusty small-town ambiance, complex plotting, and an authorial voice imbued with compassionate humanity. Each of the Posadas novels plumbs the collective heartbeat of a community. Those beating hearts belong to characters who range from despicable to saintly, but together they make up one of the most vivid worlds in mystery fiction."

—Booklist

"Series regulars, including former undersheriff Bill Gastner, interact with a number of intriguing new characters, including Miles Waddell, the owner and sole funder of NightZone. Newcomers will enjoy this entry as much as longtime fans."

—Publishers Weekly

BLOOD SWEEP
The Twentieth Posadas County Mystery

"Havill, in his twentieth Posadas County mystery, will keep readers guessing. He'll also have longtime readers holding their collective breath to learn the fate of the series' original protagonist, Bill Gastner, now 76, who shatters a hip in a fall. The Posadas County mysteries are carefully plotted, subtly written, and populated by an endearing, evolving cast of characters. A worthy entry in a fine series that appeals equally to procedural fans and to those who favor mysteries with a small-town setting."

—*Booklist*

"The family-secrets angle makes this leisurely episode most likely to appeal to fans less invested in the nominal mystery than in the long narrative arc supplied by the extended family of Posadas County, in which everyone seems to be related to everyone else by blood or spirit."

—*Kirkus Reviews*

"The story line is satisfyingly complex, but the novel's great strength is its well-rendered setting, from the opening description of a silent, motionless antelope to the evocation of a dry riverbed. The concluding note of empathy for the many people trying to cross the border is moving without being heavy-handed."

—*Publishers Weekly* (starred review)

NIGHTZONE
The Nineteenth Posadas County Mystery

"The nineteenth Posadas County mystery places the focus back on the retired Gastner after a few episodes in which the mysteries revolved around his successor. No matter the protagonist, Havill's work is believable and well plotted, and never, ever includes a character who isn't a viable human being. Another fine book in a terrific series."

—*Booklist*

"Gastner's capabilities are plausible for a septuagenarian, and Havill peoples the book with believable characters."

—*Publishers Weekly* (starred review)

ONE PERFECT SHOT
The Eighteenth Posadas County Mystery

"Gastner and Reyes complement each other well in an entertaining preview of a decades-long partnership. A welcome entry in an always satisfying series."

—*Booklist*

"Undersheriff Bill Gastner of Posadas County, N.M., meets Estelle Reyes, the once-and-future undersheriff, in a welcome, well-wrought prequel...Gastner and Reyes charm from the get-go."

—*Kirkus Reviews*

"This solid installment is the perfect introduction for new readers."

—*Publishers Weekly*

"Grab this prequel to Havill's winning New Mexico-set series to learn how Undersheriff Bill Gastner first met his new deputy, Estelle Reyes."

—*Library Journal*

DOUBLE PREY
The Seventeenth Posadas County Mystery

"Havill is a master at using procedural details to expose the complexities of small-town relationships, but he also excels at drawing meaning from landscape. Like an archaeologist sifting history from the ground, Reyes-Guzman digs clues from the guano-splattered floor of the cave where the jaguar's skull was found. One of the stronger entries in an always-satisfying series."

—Bill Ott, *Booklist*

THE FOURTH TIME IS MURDER
The Sixteenth Posadas County Mystery

"The sixth Posadas County mystery featuring Reyes-Guzman—her predecessor, Bill Gastner, was featured in nine previous books—builds on the series' strengths. The plot is revealed slowly and imaginatively. Reyes-Guzman is both an ambitious professional and family woman, forever fretting that she's neglecting either the job or the family. And, as always, Havill insinuates small-town rhythms, prejudices, and concerns into the mix for a satisfying, intelligent mystery."

—Booklist

"The Posadas County Mystery series notches its sixteenth with all its signature virtues intact: good writing, an unerring sense of place and a protagonist it's a pleasure to root for."

—Kirkus Reviews (starred review)

"Havill is especially good at showing how connecting facts depends on recognizing relationships within a family or a neighborhood. Arid, harshly beautiful Posadas County turns out to be full of captivating stories."

—Publishers Weekly

FINAL PAYMENT
The Fifteenth Posadas County Mystery

"The action and suspense have been ratcheted up several notches here, but Havill's always-sensitive depictions of human relationships remain the backbone of the series. Successfully blending light and dark elements is the key for any crime author basing a series in ordinary life, and it looks as if Havill, by darkening the brew just a bit, has once again found the right shade."

—Booklist

"Havill takes the reader through an all-terrain investigation to an edge-of-your-seat finale."

—Publishers Weekly

STATUTE OF LIMITATIONS
The Fourteenth Posadas County Mystery

"The primary appeal of this series continues to be its evocation of daily life in a small New Mexico town."

—Booklist

"A series that still feels freshly minted."

—Kirkus Reviews

CONVENIENT DISPOSAL
The Thirteenth Posadas County Mystery

"...as intelligent, carefully plotted, and insightful as its predecessors. The original star of the series, former undersheriff Bill Gastner, drifts in and out of the action these days, but Havill has successfully switched the focus to Reyes-Guzman and her struggle to balance a young family and an all-consuming career. An outstanding series on all levels."

—*Booklist*

"Literate, lively, and sharply observed as ever. Mystery fans who haven't yet made the trip to Posadas County, consider yourselves deprived."

—*Kirkus Reviews*

"Longtime readers of the series will be happy to see that Havill's retired protagonist, Sheriff Bill Gastner, is still on the periphery, but the undersheriff has proved herself a worthy successor in this third novel since Havill turned the spotlight on her; she's young, smart and dedicated, and she has a nose for solving crimes. Of course, the real protagonist is Posadas County, a troubled but endearing locale that readers will want to visit time and again."

—*Publishers Weekly*

A DISCOUNT FOR DEATH
The Twelfth Posadas County Mystery

"Interpersonal issues, usually sequestered behind closed doors in insular Posadas County, take center stage in both cases, as Reyes-Guzman follows a trail that leads from troubled lives on the edge of despair to her own thriving family. Mystery series too often lose their way when the author attempts to replace an appealing hero. Hats off to Havill for making the transition work smoothly."

—*Booklist*

"Undersheriff Estelle Reyes-Guzman gets her second star turn here, and longtime fans of Posadas County, New Mexico, won't mind a bit...A first-rate police procedural, small-town division. And Estelle's a charmer."

—*Kirkus Reviews*

"In carving out a little corner of New Mexico near the Mexican border, Havill has created an absorbing and entertaining universe."

—*Publishers Weekly*

"New undersheriff Estelle Reyes-Guzman hunts for the body of a missing/presumed dead insurance salesman. Because he was about to be indicted for fraud, the man may have voluntarily disappeared. Another death, meanwhile, seems caused by a local cop gone haywire. For fans of Southwestern mysteries."

—*Library Journal*

SCAVENGERS
The Eleventh Posadas County Mystery

"Throughout this low-key, character-driven series, Havill has managed as well as anyone in the genre to balance the particulars of cop procedure with the often unspoken emotions at the core of small-town life. The focus on Reyes-Guzman and her family brings a different dynamic to the series, but the human drama remains equally satisfying."

—Booklist

"Skilled investigation, happenstance and cooperation mesh through every phase of the puzzle, ushering the reader along to one satisfying conclusion."

—Publishers Weekly

"Series star Bill Gastner has retired but still offers support to new County Sheriff Robert Torrez and Undersheriff Estelle Reyes-Guzman. Estelle subsequently juggles family problems while dealing with two murders in the nearby desert. Solid groundwork for a new series. For collections where Southwestern mysteries are popular."

—Library Journal

RED, GREEN, OR MURDER
The Tenth Posadas County Mystery

"Havill shows us yet again how random bad decisions spur unnecessary tragedy. As always, a fine mix of village drama and carefully rendered police work."

—Booklist

"Another highly entertaining entry that shows those unruly New Mexicans doing what they do best. Long may they stay homicidal."

—Kirkus Reviews

"Havill's characters have a depth and a clarity that's refined with every new book in the series. It's a pleasure to see them operate not merely as lawmen or suspects or witnesses but as members of a community where flaws and quirks are understood and accepted."

—Publishers Weekly

BAG LIMIT
The Ninth Posadas County Mystery

"The quiet pleasures of small-town life are again at the center of this appealing series, as Gastner reaffirms his belief that even the encroaching evils of the modern world can be endured with the help of friends, family, and a properly prepared green-chile burrito."

DEAD WEIGHT
The Eighth Posadas County Mystery

"Havill is every bit as good at evoking procedural detail as he is at capturing small-town ambience. This series continues to provide a vivid picture of change in rural America: small-town values under siege from within and without as a big-hearted sheriff tries to keep the peace one day at a time. Quiet yet powerful human drama resting comfortably within the procedural formula."

—Booklist

"Nice, easygoing, entirely literate prose, and if the approach is a bit too 'cozy' for some tastes, others will delight in dollops of local color and in Sheriff Bill, of course, who may well be the most endearing small-town lawman ever."

—Kirkus Reviews

OUT OF SEASON
The Seventh Posadas County Mystery

"Gastner's calm, experienced leadership guides his staff, as well as FAA officials, through several prickly conflicts with a couple of fiercely independent ranchers. For readers, his considerate, methodical approach will prove a welcome change from the angry, violent paths trod by so many cops in other novels. Full of bright local color and suffused with a compassionate understanding of human motivation, this intelligent, understated mystery deserves a wide and appreciative readership."

—*Publishers Weekly* (starred review)

PROLONGED EXPOSURE
The Sixth Posadas County Mystery

"...another excellent small-town caper in which common sense, compassion, loyalty, and decency are law enforcement's primary tools against an increasingly brutal world. It's a good thing Gastner has had his heart mended because it may be the biggest in contemporary crime fiction."

—*Booklist*

"Fine storytelling married to a spicy Southwestern setting marks the latest Bill Gastner mystery...Gastner remains a solid center, using his knowledge and experience to good effect as the various cases of burglary, kidnapping and murder play out."

—*Publishers Weekly*

"Crisp writing and clarity of focus make this a pleasure to read and essential for any collection."

—*Library Journal*

PRIVILEGED TO KILL
The Fifth Posadas County Mystery

"The fifth Gastner mystery is a crystalline gem of dusty atmosphere, small-town personalities, and razor-sharp plotting. It also raises questions regarding the law—especially small-town law—and its attitudes toward the indigent, the homeless, and the privileged. Toss in Gastner, one of the most endearing mentors in crime fiction, for a mystery that is disarmingly simple on the surface but ultimately reveals surprising depth."

—Booklist

"Havill's fifth quietly continues a project virtually unique in detective fiction: anchoring his tales of crime and punishment as closely as possible in the rhythms of small-town friends, routines, and calamities."

—Kirkus Reviews

"A strong sense of place and tough but compassionate characters distinguish this series."

—Publishers Weekly

BEFORE SHE DIES
The Fourth Posadas County Mystery

"The fourth Gastner case is easily the best, no small feat in a series as strong as this one. Gastner is compassionate, intelligent, bulldog tough, and painfully aware of all his limitations, both physical and emotional. The same inward eye that provides insight into his own soul can quickly swivel outward to discern others' hidden traits. And if what you're hiding is motive, Gastner will ferret it out and do what needs to be done. An outstanding mystery."

—*Booklist* (starred review)

TWICE BURIED
The Third Posadas County Mystery

"Gastner is an incisive investigator whose two most valuable qualities are compassion and insomnia. Unlike other fictional detectives who approach murder as a personal affront, Gastner sees himself as the victims' advocate, striving to even the scales of justice for those no longer able to do it themselves. This is definitely a series to watch."

—*Booklist*

"Bill and his hardscrabble neighbors—especially Estelle, who seems destined for a return to Posadas next time—are as modestly appealing as ever, and in his third outing, he does his best detective work yet."

—*Kirkus Reviews*

"Havill sensitively explores the area's Mexican-American culture in this increasingly estimable regional series."

—*Publishers Weekly*

BITTER RECOIL
The Second Posadas County Mystery

"This one's a winner all the way."

—*Washington Times*

"The authentic flavor of the New Mexico locale is so real you'll be tempted to check your shoes for fine red dust."

—*Mystery Scene Magazine*

"Havill delivers an evocative tale of hard lives on the edge of society. His portly detective is a genuine low-key pleasure."

—*Publishers Weekly*

HEARTSHOT
The First Posadas County Mystery

"Gastner is a unique and endearing protagonist who certainly deserves plenty of encores."

—*Booklist* (starred review)

"Septuagenarian undersheriff Bill Gastner of Posadas County, N.M., is the skeptical, endearing narrator of this mystery debut by a writer of Westerns...If the villain's identity is not surprising, readers still will enjoy this caper and look forward to future appearances of curmudgeonly charmer Gastner."

—*Publishers Weekly*

Lies Come
Easy

Books by Steven F. Havill

The Posadas County Mysteries
Heartshot
Bitter Recoil
Twice Buried
Before She Dies
Privileged to Kill
Prolonged Exposure
Out of Season
Dead Weight
Bag Limit
Red, Green, or Murder
Scavengers
A Discount for Death
Convenient Disposal
Statute of Limitations
Final Payment
The Fourth Time is Murder
Double Prey
One Perfect Shot
NightZone
Blood Sweep
Come Dark
Easy Errors
Lies Come Easy

The Dr. Thomas Parks Novels
Race for the Dying
Comes a Time for Burning

Other Novels
The Killer
The Worst Enemy
LeadFire
TimberBlood

Lies Come
Easy

A Posadas County Mystery

Steven F. Havill

Poisoned Pen Press

First Edition 2018

10 9 8 7 6 5 4 3 2 1

Library of Congress Control Number: 2018940946

ISBN: 9781464210310   Hardcover
ISBN: 9781464210334   Trade Paperback
ISBN: 9781464210341   Ebook

Poisoned Pen Press
4014 N. Goldwater Blvd., #201
Scottsdale, AZ 85251
www.poisonedpenpress.com
info@poisonedpenpress.com

Printed in the United States of America

For Kathleen

Acknowledgments

Special thanks to Laura Brush, James Hall,
Josh Havill, and Lif Strand.

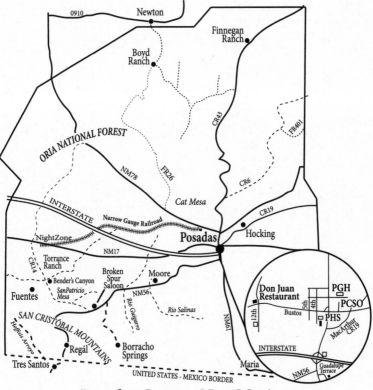

0910 Newton

Finnegan Ranch

Boyd Ranch

ORIA NATIONAL FOREST

CR43

FR401

NM78

FR26

Cat Mesa

CR6

INTERSTATE

Narrow Gauge Railroad

CR19

NightZone

Posadas

Hocking

NM17

CR14

Torrance Ranch

Broken Spur Saloon

Moore

Bender's Canyon

SanPatricio Mesa

NM56

Fuentes

Rio Guijarro

Rio Salinas

SAN CRISTOBAL MOUNTAINS

NM61

Regál

Borracho Springs

Tres Santos

Maria

UNITED STATES - MEXICO BORDER

NM56

Don Juan Restaurant

PGH

5th 4th

PCSO

12th

Bustos

PHS

MacArthur CR19

INTERSTATE

Guadalupe Terrace

Posadas County, New Mexico

Chapter One

"Three ten, PCS." Dispatcher Ernie Wheeler's voice sounded vaguely mechanical over the radio.

"Finally," Undersheriff Estelle Reyes-Guzman said aloud. The dash clock announced eleven forty-five p.m. on the Friday three days before Christmas. The last call she'd taken was a lost dog report at 8:08 that same evening, resolved fifteen minutes later—the aging, deaf, and half-blind Jack Russell mix was found snoozing on a neighbor's pillowed porch swing after dining on two bowls of cat food. The "daring rescue" had earned Estelle a smothering hug from the elderly dog's invalid owner, Florence Atencio.

The undersheriff had been sympathetic, since Fudgie the Jack Russell was Mrs. Atencio's truest companion. The Christmas season was hard enough on the lonely without a missing beloved pet.

The swing shift she had been covering for Lieutenant Jackie Taber would end in a few minutes, but Estelle wasn't tired. Deputy Tom Pasquale had come on duty a half hour earlier for the graveyard shift and Estelle was confident that tiny Posadas County, New Mexico, was in safe hands. Like Mrs. Atencio, though, she could admit to being a bit lonely, and had no inclination to go home to an empty house. To avoid that earlier, she had volunteered to cover Jackie's swing shift when Jackie had taken a couple of days of leave to visit *her* ailing mother in Kansas City.

Friday nights were potentially a showcase for less-than-attractive human behavior, but so far, the rare threat of snow that might bring a white Christmas had kept things quiet.

She keyed the mike in response. "PCS, three ten."

"Three ten, ten twenty-one, three oh four."

"Ten four." Estelle took a moment to wonder why Deputy Pasquale needed to communicate by phone, rather than a prompt and simple radio call. With no traffic, she slowed the Charger to a fast walk along State 61 and fished out her cell phone. Pasquale's number flashed on the screen and she keyed it in.

"Just one second," the deputy said by way of greeting. She could hear him talking to someone, and then he came back on the line. "Estelle, I'm about a hundred yards beyond mile marker twenty-one on State 56. I just picked up Derry Fisher. I think he's okay, and I got him all bundled up in a wool blanket. I don't have a child seat or nothin', and he's had some exposure, so I called out one of the EMT units. They're rolling now. They'll be with me in about a minute."

"Derry Fisher?"

"Yep. The little tyke. You know the folks. Penny and Darrell? I don't get it, but this time the little bugger was all by himself, tryin' to ride his Scamper along the shoulder of the road. How's that for strange? It looks to me like the kid got dumped. He isn't all that coherent, but I got 'dada' and 'truck' out of him and he pointed up the road toward town. It's snowin' like a son-of-a-gun right now. Just a little bit ago, Darrell Fisher passed me in his pickup goin' northbound, right by the intersection of 61. So if Daddy kicked him out of the truck, I figure the kid was outside for maybe five, six minutes. He's wearing a T-shirt and his wad of diapers, socks, and sneakers. I don't know what Dad was thinking."

"If at all. No sign of them? They didn't dump him out, drive a little ways, and then turn around to pick him up? Some version of the old fed-up parent's threat, 'If you don't stop that, you're going to walk home!'"

"My dad used to say that to me and my brother all the time. I don't remember him doin' that when I was two and half, though. And I haven't seen any hint of Darrell turning around to come back." He paused, and Estelle could hear motion. "Yeah. Come here. That's the way. You warm now?" The child said something incomprehensible, and Pasquale added, "Now he wants a hug. Oh, good. Here comes the ambulance. You're kind of stinky, little man."

"I'll meet you at the hospital, Thomas. I'm out past María, so it'll be a few minutes. No sign of Darrell returning yet? Or Penny? She works at the hospital, or did."

"Nope. You remember them gettin' into it a couple weeks ago at the Family Supermarket, and one of the clerks was going to file charges against Penny for assault? She clobbered Darrell in the head with a bag of frozen chicken. The clerk never filed, and Darrell let it slide."

"Is it possible to get photos at the spot where the boy was dropped off?"

"I'm going to try, but things are gettin' kind of white down this way."

"Do your best. I'll meet you at the hospital in a few minutes. I'll give Gayle a call. Children, Youth, and Families will be involved in this."

"Roger that. A Merry Christmas to all, huh?"

The snow was snaking across the state highway, looking for someplace to settle. Estelle's Charger, with rear-wheel drive and altogether too much power, wasn't happy on the slick asphalt, and she took her time, passing first through the tiny village of María and then out onto the great flat expanse of southern Posadas County. She flipped on the wipers and made a mental note to pick up Jackie's SUV after she'd finished at the hospital.

"Three ten, can you ten nineteen for a passenger?" This time, Ernie Wheeler's voice carried a faintly amused note.

"It'll be a few minutes. I need to swing by the hospital to

talk with some folks. I'll be stopping by the office to pick up a different vehicle in a bit. Ask him if that suits him."

"He's nodding yes."

The identity of the "he" was no mystery. Only one person asked for a ride-along in the middle of a cold, bleak December night.

Chapter Two

"I know it. I know it. I know it." Darrell Fisher sat on the blue molded plastic chair just outside the emergency room cubicle, hands clasped together between his knees. Exactly whom he was talking to was unclear, and he rocked back and forth as if in bladder agony. His jeans and T-shirt showed a thin body just on the soft side of wiry, as if he'd once weighed thirty pounds more and then dieted down faster than his skin could shrink. His long fair hair was frazzled over ears with lobes sporting the latest fad in self-mutilation, a pair of dime-sized holes rimmed with black plastic inserts. A thin mustache blended into a sparse chin tuft that did nothing for his long, pale face.

Outside in the unpredictable New Mexico weather, neither the little boy nor his father had been wearing a coat. *Like father, like son*, Estelle thought.

Deputy Tom Pasquale stood within quick, easy reach of Darrell Fisher. Pasquale looked heavenward in tired resignation as Estelle entered the waiting room, but Darrell kept his gaze concentrated on the floor tiles. "Amy's gettin' the boy all warmed up," the deputy said.

Estelle moved the cubicle's curtain far enough to one side that she could slip through. Inside the cubicle, Nurse Practitioner Amy Salinger had bundled little Derry Fisher in a heated blanket and was trying to interest the child in a covered child's thermal cup without much success.

"A good shot of brandy would be just the ticket," she remarked and glanced over at Estelle. "He's no worse for wear, though." She watched Estelle as the undersheriff bent and unwound the blanket just enough to examine the little boy's tiny feet. "All ten accounted for and working fine," Amy said. "I'm glad he was outside for just a few minutes."

"That's for sure." Estelle straightened up and snugged the warm blanket back around Derry's feet, and then pulled it close around the child's ears. "He—" A ruckus outside in the waiting room interrupted her, and she parted the curtain in time to see Deputy Pasquale envelope a large, beet-faced woman in a bear hug.

"You were down at Al's, weren't you?" the woman shouted. "I have to work late, and I can't trust you to stay home with the boy." Dressed in stretch slacks and a baggy sweat shirt that didn't complement her blocky body, Penny Fisher trembled with rage. "Let go of me, you big freak," she howled, twisting in Pasquale's restraining arms. She managed to raise one forearm and pointed a finger at her husband, who cringed back. "You went down to Al's, didn't you?"

"Just for a little bit," Darrell whimpered. "Really. Maria was there, too, playing with Derry."

"At midnight in the middle of a blizzard?" Penny twisted against the deputy's grip. "Are you going to let go of me, or am I going to have to—" She lashed out with a thick-soled work shoe, catching Pasquale on the side of the calf. One arm worked loose and smacked the deputy on the side of the head.

"Lady," Pasquale said, his voice full of calm resignation. With an expert twist, he spun her face-first against the wall with her nose pressed against the colorful poster explaining patient rights when unable to pay for medical care. The handcuffs snicked in place, securing first one wrist and then the other.

"What do you think...?" Penny bellowed. "Get these off of me."

"You're going to have to do some serious calming down," Pasquale said matter-of-factly.

"Calm? Are you kidding me?" She glared at Estelle, who had stepped between the husband and wife. Husband remained cowering in the chair. "And what do you want? What, Bobby is too busy to come out on a night like this?"

"Derry is fine," Estelle said, ignoring the distraught woman's snipe at Sheriff Robert Torrez. "I'm sure that's the first thing you'll want to know."

"I have to see him."

"In a few minutes. First you need to calm down and get a hold of yourself."

The woman huffed a deep breath, and tapped her forehead a couple of times against the wall, not hard enough to dent the sheetrock, but enough to jar the clock above her head. When she looked back at Estelle, a couple of tears were sliding down her cheeks. "This has to stop," she said. "This is it." Her gaze drifted over to her husband. "This worthless piece of shit…"

The ER door opened and Lester Gutierrez bustled in, almost as wide as he was tall, deep-set black eyes under heavy brows darting from person to person. The nylon jacket he wore over a crisp white shirt and black pants sported three-inch tall letters across the back that announced *Hospital Security*. He pointed the short antenna of his radio at Penny Fisher. "You're going to behave yourself, Miss Penny. I mean what's going on here? I could hear you all the way down the hall."

"It's just my former husband being stupid again," she said. "The hopeless son-of-a-bitch kicked our son out of the truck and was making him walk home through all this snow." She jerked her head back to indicate Deputy Pasquale. "And *I'm* the one in handcuffs. Go figure *that*."

"Former husband?" Darrell bleated.

Penny's face wrinkled into a sarcastic smile. "Yes, *former*. I've had enough of you and your dip-shit brother and *his* girlfriend of the moment and that whole dip-shit crowd of drug-heads down there."

Darrell squirmed sideways in his chair and said, just loud enough to be heard, "Well, you ain't such a grand catch yourself, woman."

Penny's muscles bunched, and Deputy Pasquale put one hand on the cuffs and one on her left shoulder. "Settle," he said.

"Look," she said, "will you *please* take these off? I'm not going to do anything other than maybe break a chair over his worthless head."

"Yep," Pasquale said. "So I think we'll leave 'em on for the time being. And kick me again and you'll be wearin' ankle wraps, too."

The ER door opened once again, and Gayle Torrez stepped into the room. Statuesque, with an angular face just shy of beautiful, Gayle had worked for the Sheriff's Department for years before marrying Sheriff Robert Torrez and then taking a job with the Children, Youth, and Families Division of the local Social Services. Seeing Gayle, Penny Fisher almost collapsed with relief.

"Oh, my God, Gayle...talk some sense into these people, *please*. That creature over there," and Penny nodded toward her husband, "put little Derry out of the truck, what, at just about midnight? In the *snow*? And what, he's supposed to ride his Scamper home in traffic? In his *diapers*?"

Gayle Torrez nodded at Deputy Pasquale. "How come the 'cuffs?"

"She kicked me, and hit me in the head. No big deal on that, but it appears she would really like to assault her husband."

Penny snorted. "Listen to this guy. And you bet your life I'd like to assault him."

Estelle stepped close to the woman, their faces inches apart. "Listen to me, Penny." She reached out and placed a hand on Penny's right shoulder. With Tom Pasquale keeping a hand on the cuffs, Penny was effectively blocked. Estelle lowered her voice.

"Derry is fine." She held up an index finger. "That's first. Now this is what's going to happen, Penny. Because your husband is facing charges of reckless endangerment of a child, possible child abuse, and several other counts, it's entirely possible that Judge Tate will want him to remain in custody overnight, at least until arraignment in the morning. That gives everybody a chance to cool down."

"Then how come…?"

Estelle shook Penny's shoulder, hard. "Be quiet and listen. *You're* in handcuffs because you struck one of my officers and were behaving in a thoughtless manner. *If* you behave in a reasonable fashion, *if* the deputy doesn't show physical signs of your assault, then maybe you'll go home tonight with your son, and have the night to think things over." She held up a hand when Penny looked as if she was preparing another blast.

"And then, if she's available and can arrange a Saturday session, you will meet with Gayle in the morning. First you with a deputy accompanying you, then your husband, then, if Gayle gives the all-clear, the two of you together. It will be the job of Family Services to determine the possible risk to Derry if he remains in that home environment." Estelle took a deep breath. "This is your chance, Penny." She turned and regarded Darrell, who was still trying to blend in with the furnishings. "And yours, Darrell." She looked back at Penny. "The two of you."

Gayle Torrez smiled at Amy Salinger as the nurse chose that moment to open the curtain around the bed. Derry sat looking like a little gnome under his cozy wrap, and when he saw his mother, he immediately began to squirm out of the blanket, his ear-splitting, high voice repeating "mama" as fast as he could.

"I have a little man here who would really like to go home to bed," Amy said, and as the nurse spoke, Estelle watched Penny Fisher's face. Softness touched the hard planes, and the woman's eyes riveted on her son.

"Are we all going to be smart about all this?" Estelle asked.

Penny nodded, the tears now flowing unchecked.

"We'll shoot for ten o'clock tomorrow morning," Gayle said.

"We'll start the ball rolling then. That'll give Judge Tate plenty of time for Mr. Fisher's arraignment."

With a deft twist, Deputy Pasquale released the handcuffs, and Penny immediately bolted across the room to her son, scooping him up as he stretched out both arms to her. Making a point to stand between the woman and her husband, Pasquale motioned for Darrell Fisher to rise. When the man cleared the chair, Pasquale turned him to face the wall and cuffed him. Darrell started to whine something, and Pasquale said, "Behave yourself. Sit."

"Do you have any questions?" Estelle asked Penny.

"I just want to take Derry home."

"That's where he belongs. You're all right driving? You have a good child seat in your vehicle?"

"Yes."

"Then we'll see you in the morning." She slipped one of her business cards in the pocket of Penny's jacket.

Bundling Derry close, Penny Fisher headed for the door, but stopped as she passed Deputy Pasquale. "I didn't hurt you, really…"

"Be careful out there," Pasquale said sternly. He reached out and ruffled Derry's hair. "You're the man," he said, and pushed open the door for them.

As the door closed behind them, Darrell Fisher slumped in his chair, trying to find a way to sit comfortably with his hands cuffed behind his back.

Estelle stood looking down at him until he began to fidget, unable to hold her gaze. "That stunt you pulled tonight is what makes police officers want to retire early," she said quietly. She turned to Pasquale. "Read him his rights and see if Tate will take care of this first thing in the morning."

As Pasquale hauled the young man to his feet, Estelle slipped another one of her cards into his hip pocket. "For future reference, Mr. Fisher. As of now, start being a whole lot smarter than you have been."

Chapter Three

Snow fringed the holiday decorations that brightened the otherwise somber Posadas downtown. Four inches' accumulation was promised by dawn, and if that happened, school kids would be delighted. A Saturday snow day wasn't much use during the regular school year, since it wouldn't prompt a cancellation. But during the Christmas break? Perfect. Complaints from motorists would fly as thickly as the snowballs. Snowmen would double the population of Posadas.

Farther south, the ragged San Cristóbals would be graced with a sparse white cap, extending low enough on the mountain to make the highway through Regál Pass treacherous. For a few moments come dawn, the white flocking would be glorious until the sun burned it off the mountain. With an overcast day, the snow might linger long enough to make Regál, the tiny village nestled on the Mexican border, look like something out of one of Lieutenant Jackie Taber's pastel Christmas card creations.

Estelle swung into the Public Safety Building's parking lot, and saw Deputy Thomas Pasquale over by the fuel island topping up his patrol vehicle. He lifted a hand in salute, and then pointed toward the office. Her ride-along didn't wait, and ignored the automatic doors at the front of the building. Instead he battered his aluminum walker out through the employees' entrance. Estelle parked the Charger and transferred her briefcase to Jackie

Taber's big SUV, but her ride didn't wait for her to start it and move closer to the building. He scooted his walker across the parking lot, leaving parallel tracks in the slush.

Bill Gastner, long-retired sheriff of Posadas County and a candidate for the American Insomniac Association's celebrity poster, yanked open the passenger-side back door, slapped his walker flat, and slid it onto the backseat. He closed the back door, and with a hand on the SUV's roof, opened the passenger door and maneuvered carefully before pulling himself up on the tall step. He settled into the front passenger seat.

"You had breakfast yet?" He slammed the door and she waited while he fussed with the seat belt. His bulky, multi-layered corduroy coat, its collar trimmed with lamb's wool, made the operation a tussle.

She palmed the mike. "PCS, three ten is ten eight, one in custody. We'll be central."

"Ten four, three ten."

"Ernie sounds as bored as I am," Gastner said. "And you haven't answered my question, Sweetheart. It's Friday. Well, no, it's not. It's well and truly Saturday now. The Don Juan is open until two or better. We have lots of time." He leaned forward and peered at the sky, a starless black void beyond the glare of the parking lot lights. "More snow on the way, they say. Then again, they tell stories most of the time."

She reached out and touched the windshield where a single flake had settled on the other side of the glass. Imitating the urgency of a television reporter trying to manufacture hot news on a dull day, she said, "And this is just *some* of the snow that's fallen tonight in the metro area."

"You laugh now," Gastner countered, and glanced around the interior of the SUV. "This is Taber's unit, no?"

"It is. The Charger doesn't like slippery. Jackie's in Kansas City for a day or two, so we'll ride in high style."

"Ah." He breathed deeply. "I detect her perfume lingering." He reached forward and touched the miniature potpourri bouquet affixed to the dash. "So what are you doing out and about at this hour? I heard all the jabber about the stranded kid, but you and Pasquale have that all cleaned up." He glanced over at her. "Francis is away at that damn conference all weekend?"

"He'll be home late tomorrow. And yes, I was at the hospital talking with the parents. It's going to be a rough Christmas for them."

"What fun, huh? But look, do you mind a ride-along, or were you headed home? I'm kind of barging in on you here."

"Absolutely not, I don't mind. And an early morning snack sounds good if they haven't locked the doors on us."

Deputy Pasquale pulled past them, sending a snappy salute their way as he did so.

"I crossed paths with young Thomas for the first time when he was twelve years old," Gastner mused. The Expedition fishtailed a little as Pasquale accelerated hard through a rime of slush. "And he hasn't slowed down since."

"His twins are in first grade now. He can't afford to slow down."

Gastner humphed an amused grunt. "And we can stop talking about things that remind me of how old I am." He pointed at the Don Juan as they approached, as if somehow Estelle might have forgotten their destination. She swung the Expedition into the spot immediately beside the handicapped slot by the front door. "And speaking of fates worse than death, Camille is coming down for a visit. Did I tell you that already?"

"No, you didn't. Anyway, sir, I *like* Camille. She's sweet." She lifted the mike. "PCS, three-ten is ten-ten, Don Juan."

"Not when she's trying to talk me into a home." Gastner maneuvered himself down to the running board and then the ground, both hands on the door. "That's her agenda this time, if I'm not mistaken. Doesn't *that* sound repulsive?"

"A home where? In Flint, you mean? Like a retirement home?"

Gastner's eldest daughter lived in Flint, Michigan, with her oral surgeon husband. Their four children were grown and gone, the youngest now in graduate school, the oldest practicing criminal law in Detroit.

"Grim, eh? It ain't gonna happen." He opened the back door and started to reach for the walker, but changed his mind and pushed the door shut. "To hell with it." Estelle knew better than to assist, but at one point when they had to maneuver around one of the parking lot bumpers, he reached out and snagged the tail of her jacket. She took the easiest route to the door, and he released his hold on her coattails only when he could transfer his hand to the door jamb.

"I saw an ad in one of those sporting magazines not long ago for a back country wheelchair...rifle scabbard, four-wheel drive, knobby tires. Designed by some guy up in Montana for handicapped vets, by the look of it. *That* looked like fun. I'm going to see about ordering one."

"Just the thing," Estelle said dryly, and held the restaurant's front door for him. "Give it to Pasquale for a couple days so he can re-engineer it for some real speed."

"Exactly." Gastner covered the six feet to the front counter and planted both hands on the polished glass. A recent second operation to tune up a hip damaged six years before had been successful, as had the old man's efforts to follow the surgeon's orders to shed weight. Not yet exactly svelte, he had managed to lose nearly forty pounds. In the process, he'd lost some of his old man's stoop, and looked ten years younger.

In a few moments they were seated in Gastner's favored booth, now overhung with a pungent juniper wreath flocked with something meant to resemble snow. The window provided them with a view out across the parking lot toward the southwest. At the moment, that view was fast disappearing as snow scudded down Bustos Avenue. Every now and then, wind rattled the glass.

"I'll need a menu," Gastner said, and Eileen Goodman, a

pudgy girl who'd been a waitress at the Don Juan long enough to learn her regular customers' habits, looked momentarily blank. Bill Gastner, whose customer status at the restaurant had become legendary, hadn't actually read a Don Juan menu in thirty years. "It's all part of the new me," he explained to the girl.

"Well, Merry Christmas, new you," Eileen bubbled.

"The new you is looking good, sir," Estelle added.

"Well, diligence is the name of the game." He accepted the menu from Eileen. "Although at eighty-four, I'm not sure I see the point of diligence."

"I'd like the taco salad with chicken," Estelle said. "With hot tea, please."

"Nope, nope, nope," Gastner mumbled as his finger drifted down the menu list. Finally he looked up at Eileen. "As long as you folks aren't too busy, can I make a special request?" He flopped the menu closed. "For about the hundredth time?"

"Anything." Eileen offered a fetching smile. "And I bet I can guess."

"I'd like," and he spread his hands six inches apart, "a junior-sized shredded beef burrito. Fernando will know what I mean. Not a grande, much as I'd like that. And no beans, no rice."

"Red or green, sir?"

He hesitated. "Oh, how about Christmas? A touch of both. And just a touch of guacamole and sour cream on the side would make my day."

"No problem. Coffee, black?"

"Absolutely." He watched the girl head toward the kitchen, his brows furrowed in thought. "I was out at the airport today," he said, and looked at Estelle. "Jim's thinking of retiring. Did you know that already?"

"I've heard that, but he's talked about it for ten years."

Jim Bergin's tenure as airport manager had spanned more than a quarter of a century. He'd seen the facility grow from a single, rarely used dusty strip to what Posadas Municipal Airport was today—both a paved eight-thousand-foot runway and a seven-thousand-two-hundred-foot cross-wind strip. The facility supported a modest conference center and airport hotel, both of which had been financed by Miles Waddell, owner of the rapidly expanding astronomy theme park *NightZone*, itself isolated on a mesa-top development twenty-five miles southwest of Posadas.

"At the last county commission meeting they were talking about putting out bids for the F.B.O. if Jim really did retire."

Gastner shook his head in wonder. "Remember when we had a single dirt strip? With that old government surplus storage unit as an office?"

Estelle smiled. "My memory goes back to a paved runway, a used mobile home as an office, and the pair of hangars that Consolidated Mining put in."

"Hell, that was just yesterday. Now look at us. Two runways, fancy taxiways, a helipad, and the hotel at the west end. And on top of that, we even have the station for Waddell's little narrow-gauge choo-choo out to his park. Absolutely amazing. Earlier this evening when I stopped by, Jim was shuffling stuff around in the west hangar to make room for another corporate jet."

"Yet another. Who has the deep pockets this time, did he say?"

"ViaJet, I think he said. A jet charter outfit." Gastner frowned, looked as if he might add something else, and instead said, "Jim says he's going to hit up Waddell for another hangar. There's plenty of room farther on down the taxiway to build whatever he wants."

"This whole development will rival Carlsbad Caverns if the Park Service follows through on all their plans," Estelle said. "But I think it's interesting that we've become such a Mecca for bird watchers. The word is that Miles has tied down an Audubon conference for late spring. They're after a migratory bird-count, coordinating with Mexico, among other things."

"He has *three* birding sites that he's developed along the narrow gauge," Gastner added. "Tourists can hop off the train at any one of them, and be picked up an hour or so later for the return trip. Who woulda thunk?" He shrugged. "Obviously, Miles Waddell thunk so. He's a go-getter, that guy. And speaking of go-getting, what's the latest with the boys? A little bit ago, you were worried that they might not be able to visit over Christmas?"

Estelle sat back to give the waitress room to land the servings. And sure enough, Gastner's burrito was far from *grande*. In past years, he would have fumed at such a diminutive serving. Still, it was a creative beauty, the colors of the cheese and two-tone chile blended just so across the top, the scattering of fresh greens fringing the sides.

Her own taco salad was enough for two meals, and she caught Eileen's eye and formed her fingers into a square. "A small take-home, please?"

When the girl had left, Estelle dabbed touches of sour cream on the half of the salad that she was planning to eat. "I don't think a visit is in the cards," she said. "Not at this late date, anyway. Carlos has a major project due at school, and then he accepted a work offer from one of his professors that's going to eat up his holiday break." She saw Gastner's eyebrow lift with curiosity. "And I don't know what it is. He was a little evasive."

Gastner chewed thoughtfully. "That's the trouble with these kids. They all of a sudden grow up and have lives of their own." He waved his fork in her direction. "They grow from 'Hey, Mom! Look at this!' to cutting you off, reduced to a need-to-know basis." He orchestrated another generous bite and watched the flow of melted cheese. "That's quite the truck Francisco found, by the way."

"Truck?"

The old man paused. "Ah." He looked contrite.

"What truck are we talking about?"

He ducked his head. "Out at the airport. But I probably wasn't supposed to say anything. A slip of the tongue. Pretend I didn't mention it."

"*Francisco* has a truck at the airport?" She put down her fork. "My *son* has a truck stored out there?"

"That's what Jim tells me. I didn't want to go walking through all of the junk that Jim is trying to reorganize, but from what I could see…" He nodded approval. "It brought back memories."

"How so?"

Gastner savored a dripping morsel. "There were still a lot of those trucks in service when I enlisted in '46. Little by little, they were phased out."

"*They* being…"

"The old military WC, a big old four-by-four pickup, most of 'em made by Dodge, I think. Others, too. Hell, the WC went way back, way before the war, in all shapes, sizes, and designations. This one's a WC Fifty-two, I think. Come later, the civilian version was based on the old war lineage, just dressed up a little. First civilian four-by-four marketed after the war. The old Power Wagon." Gastner squirmed a little in his seat, getting comfortable with his reminiscence.

"And you're saying that's what Francisco has?" *He's twenty-five. He can do what he wants*, she chided herself.

"I'm just guessing, but a quick glance leads me to believe that his is an older military workhorse." He watched the puzzled expression cloud Estelle's face. "Sorry. Maybe I wasn't supposed to say anything."

"No need to be sorry, *Padrino*. And don't be silly. If *hijo* wants to buy a truck, that's entirely up to him. He doesn't need Mom's approval or permission. And there are certainly worse impulsive behaviors."

"Impulsive is not a word that I ever associated with your oldest son, Sweetheart. Now Carlos? Maybe." For a moment, he chewed thoughtfully, eyes closed. With a little shake of the head, he finally surfaced from burrito-induced bliss.

"The concert venues are keeping Francisco busy?"

"It's incredible. Right now he's in the middle of a five-week series with the Berlin Philharmonic. It's a *Christmas Tribute to Beethoven*, or however that's said in German. They're two weeks into it, with rave reviews. They're recording it all, and planning a fancy DVD release. Our souvenir shelf is filling rapidly."

"Miss Trevino is with him?"

"She is. When the *Tribute* is finished in Berlin, he has an extended concert series in Buenos Aires. That starts in late January. The only thing I know about it is that if all goes well, he'll be performing a collection of four-handed pieces with Barenboim. He's excited about that."

Gastner puffed out his cheeks. "As he should be. What an amazing career. Is Miss Trevino participating?"

"In Germany, yes. I don't know about Argentina."

"What's the *maestro*'s next concert in the United States?" He grinned. "The grilling is never going to stop, you know. Us old duffers are nosey as hell."

"Francisco sent me an itinerary…and at the moment, it's pinned on the kitchen bulletin board."

"I'm surprised you don't keep a copy in your wallet."

"Like people who keep a photo gallery of the grandkids."

"Exactly."

She pushed the remains of the salad into the take-home box. "January twentieth in Aspen, Colorado. It's just before the festivities in Argentina, and coincides with another CD release. The early review of the CD in the *Wall Street Journal*, how do you say it? 'Heaped plaudits.'"

"Those are good things to heap. Congratulations to him. He's come a long way from that concert he gave in Posadas a number of years ago."

"Just an older version of the same kid."

Gastner laughed. "What a doting parent you are."

"I *do* dote."

"Yeah, quietly, I guess you do."

"I hope you'll go to Aspen with us. You and Camille, if you haven't driven her off by then."

"She'll be thrilled. Any excuse to stay and stay and stay. Hey, I'll be thrilled too. But this late, you're never going to get lodging. Not in Aspen. Not in January. And certainly not for *his* venue."

"Arrangements have already been made, *Padrino*. And see, here I am giving away secrets. It's his Christmas present to us. Francisco sent us a package deal. Four tickets for seats that he personally reserved, accommodations at the St. Regis, rental car…the whole thing. He's made arrangements so that we'll fly right out of Posadas Municipal, direct to Aspen." She smiled. "He sent four tickets because that's what the special package included, way back in July."

"Always thinking, the *maestro*. He was able to bribe an airline into stopping in Posadas?"

"I believe he's booked a charter."

Gastner's eyebrows shot up. "A charter! Damn, that's some bucks."

"I don't know, and I didn't ask. He's excited, and so are we. He said his agent took care of all the details."

"Always thinking, that kid."

"Or at least his agent is always thinking. He describes her as his 'doting, spinster aunt.'"

"More doting." He pushed his platter, almost empty, to one side and slid to the edge of the booth seat. "Ready to go?"

"Yep."

He accepted the offered elbow, and when he was firmly on his feet, he stood quietly for a moment. "I'm letting my joints settle," he said. He fished out his wallet, and despite her protest at his grabbing the check, dropped two twenties on the table. "Time to go home?"

"In a few minutes. I want to see this truck you were talking about. Can you stand that?"

He grinned. "Once a mom, always a mom."

"A doting mom," she corrected.

Chapter Four

Overhead, the powerful mercury vapor lights fixtures in the hangar ceiling sputtered and buzzed, the wash of light from them painfully bright.

"A Dodge WC-Fifty Two," Jim Bergin announced. "Made in nineteen forty-one." He pulled the hangar man-door closed, and nudged Gastner gently as he walked past. "A few years older'n me. You coulda played with it, though."

Estelle gripped the steering wheel and pulled herself into the cab, maneuvering around various pieces of plumbing as well as the huge spare tire that nestled on the running board. The interior had an interesting blend of aromas—old grease, oil, gasoline, and seventy-plus years of unaccountable smells that had soaked into the canvas top and seat. She held the black steering wheel with both hands, gazing out through the slab-flat windshield, out across the mammoth hood and flat fenders.

Thumping the palm of her left hand on an odd piece of heavy pipe framework that was welded to the doorframe near her left elbow, she looked quizzically at Bergin. "What's this?"

"That would be the mount for the machine gun platform." Bergin grinned. "Notice all the American Safety Council-approved safety padding."

She ran a finger along the hard steel edge of the ominous structure again. "Nice."

"With the canvas top pulled to one side or removed altogether, the gunner could stand right in the bed of the truck, just behind the driver, and chop things up with the fifty-caliber."

"Uh huh."

"The old girl is simple to start," Bergin offered. "Just purrs along. Want to take an early morning spin down the taxiway? It sure as hell doesn't care about a little snow."

"I'll wait," she said. "Francisco shipped this thing from somewhere, somehow? I mean, *he* didn't drive it."

"Oh, no. Oh, my achin' kidneys, no, thinking about driving this old rig across the country at thirty-five miles an hour! Nope, one of the classic vehicle transporters brought it in, tucked in the comfort of a semi. Francisco e-mailed me, and asked if I'd be willing to give the old girl a physical, and then drive 'er once in a while." He took a deep breath. "Sure happy to do that." He leaned over and peered at the floor by Estelle's feet. "Lookin' at the condition of the pedals and all else, I don't think she's got all that many miles. And, you know, I might even have good use sometime for that big old winch that's bolted on up front."

"So this is the female version?"

Bergin lifted his cap and ran a hand through his gray stubble. Small of stature and with one of those heavily creased faces that broke into a dozen interesting planes when he smiled, he stroked the windshield frame, then ran a finger along one of the long cracks in the glass. "Just a manner of speaking. It's easy to feel some affection for these old warriors."

"As Francisco obviously does."

"Yup. Well, he wants to rent space to keep it parked right here at the airport. I got no problem with that." He placed one boot on the running board. "So this is a surprise for you?"

"To put it mildly." She smiled with a touch of resignation. "Not the first, though."

"Well, I can tell you one thing. If he takes care of it, he'll never lose a penny on it, that's for sure. It's a good investment."

"He could carry his piano in the back," Gastner observed.

"You know, I was thinkin' that he could file the paperwork and for a couple hundred bucks to register with the feds, he could mount the fifty-caliber machine gun right back on that pedestal. Make a good rig for hunting prairie dogs."

"And I'm sure you'll suggest that next time you see him," Estelle scolded gently. "I look forward to seeing his little brother's face when Carlos sees this."

She ran her hands around the circumference of the big steering wheel and sighed. "The sheriff will be delighted."

"He saw it already. Let's see. It come in last Thursday week. Bobby watched 'em unload it."

No one was better at keeping secrets than Sheriff Robert Torrez, Estelle reflected. "What'd he say?"

"His exact words?"

"Yes."

"'I want one.'"

She laughed. "I could have guessed something like that."

Bergin stepped back to let her slide down. He turned to Gastner, who was resting his rump against one of the knobby front tires. "What year were you born?"

"I would have been thirteen when this old brute was built in forty-one. And if I could have stolen it, I would have."

Estelle's phone announced itself with a single, complex chord that she knew to be in E-flat minor, recorded for her by Francisco the last time he'd been home.

"Guzman."

"Ma'am, arraignment's set for nine o'clock," Deputy Pasquale said. "Darrell's trying to make himself comfortable in our second-floor suite."

"Where he'll be safe from various flying objects sent his way by Penny."

"Yep."

"You did a great job with them tonight, Thomas. Thanks."

"My pleasure."

As Estelle was occupied on the phone, Gastner made his way toward the SUV, accompanied by Jim Bergin, who walked with one hand an inch from the older man's elbow as they stepped from the dry concrete of the hangar floor to the quarter inch of fresh snow on the tarmac.

"Jim, thanks for all you've done," Estelle called. "You have a new tenant flying in?"

"Sometime Monday, they say."

She glanced up into the snow, now diagonal and strong from the southeast. "Good luck to 'em," she said, and ducked into the warmth of the Expedition.

"Why don't you just drop me off at the office?" Gastner said. "It's time for me to be getting out of your way. I'm fed and entertained. Now maybe I can get some sleep."

The SUV fishtailed a little as Estelle swung around the apron and headed for the airport gate. "Tough night for a two-year-old to be out, pushing his bike along the state highway, dressed in a T-shirt and diapers," Gastner mused. "That's one for your memoirs."

Chapter Five

The next-door neighbor's shepherd-lab cross greeted Estelle with a profusion of doggy opinion, but other than him, Twelfth Street was quiet at three a.m. when Estelle rolled the county Expedition to a stop in front of the Guzman home. Her own Toyota sat in the driveway, now covered with an inch of snow.

Standing for a moment on the front step of the modest brick ranch house that had been home to the Guzmans for more than twenty years, she listened to the sounds of the village. As usual, the Interstate to the south was a constant reminder that the rest of the world didn't sleep. Snow on the streets and the highway had turned to slush, and a few stars peeped through gaps in the clouds. Whether she could sleep or not was still open to question.

She put the small box containing the remains of her Don Juan salad in the refrigerator and turned the heat on under tea water. The hiss of the gas stove seemed loud in the empty house. No messages showed on the landline phone on the kitchen counter, and she stood by the kitchen table and regarded the laptop. She touched a key and it promptly awoke but displayed no new messages. "Ho hum," she said aloud, and turned to fix her green tea.

With the mugful in hand, she walked into the living room and pulled the piano bench out far enough so that she could perch on one corner. Opening the heavy keyboard lid, she regarded the black and whites, then gently touched middle C and listened to the sound swell and flow through the house. Idle for months, was the piano anywhere near tune? She had no idea, but Francisco had asked her not to have anyone else tune it. That would be his first task the next time he visited.

She smiled at the memory from earlier in the night. An army truck. From kindergarten onward, her two sons—one now twenty-five and the other soon to be twenty-two—had been one surprise after another

She played the middle C again, then stretched to the C above that, and again another octave above that. "He's in Germany now, and then Argentina after a quick stop in Aspen," Estelle said, speaking to the small rocking chair in the corner by the fireplace. Her mother's spirit probably already knew. "And he's bought himself an antique military truck. The kind the Mexican *policia* used before they discovered Toyota pickups." She touched the middle C once more, then A below, then G.

"Oh...and Carlos is working on some mysterious project at school, and doesn't think he'll be home for Christmas." She closed the piano lid. "I was thinking of having a good, noisy party here this year. Except the kids won't be home, and what fun is that?" *And would Francis have me committed if he could hear all this?*

The tea soothed and she rose to return to the kitchen. On the way, she nudged the thermostat upward a degree or two and heard the furnace light with its gentle *whump*. When she had first arrived home and shed several pounds of cop gear, she had planned to head for the shower. Now, she shivered at the thought of getting wet on such a blustery, rowdy winter night. She was tying the belt on her favorite fleecy robe when the phone rang. Instinctively, she glanced at the clock and frowned. Messages at 3:27 a.m. were rarely good news.

One of the landline phones was on the nightstand beside the bed, and she sprawled across on her side, stretching to pick up.

"Guzman."

A couple of seconds passed as digital bits flew from Earth

to satellite and back to Earth again, with several other skips in between.

"Hey, Ma."

Those two syllables sent a surge of electricity through Estelle so powerful that her heart pounded against her ribs. In recent years, as her sons matured, she found it a challenge to differentiate between Carlos and Francisco on the telephone, but the hesitation of circuits said this wasn't a simple call from the West Coast.

"*Hijo!* What a surprise!"

"A good one, I hope. I called the S.O. just now, and Ernie said you'd just gone home, so you'd likely still be up."

"I am, as a matter of fact. The cup of tea thing." She sat upright on the bed. "Oh, *hijo*, it's so good to hear your voice."

"My father the doctor isn't home from Vera Cruz yet, right?"

"Tomorrow, we hope. Your father the doctor is just too busy. He promises to be home Sunday...tomorrow, I think."

"So you're rattling around the house all by your lonesome."

"That's exactly right. *Padrino* came out to ride with me for a little while and we stopped off at the Don Juan for a snack. So that helped. Angie is well?"

"She is. We'll be going to lunch in a few minutes."

"A discreet little bistro hidden on a narrow side street."

The transatlantic pause made it sound as if Francisco had to think about that. He laughed. "No, actually it's a luncheon at the *maestro*'s country estate just south of Berlin. Outside of Mittenwalde, I think. Thirty k's or so. We'll go eat ourselves sick, and then have a short late afternoon rehearsal to get polished for tonight."

"All goes well with the festival?"

"Well, I think so, and the audience still is enthusiastic, so..."

"Four weeks is a lot of Beethoven."

"*Sin duda*. And it's *five* weeks. To keep everyone excited and coming back, the programs also include music by everyone who ever knew the composer, I think. Even a series of smaller pieces composed by some of the amateur musicians who were students of his. One of the real treats so far is playing the *Music of the Royalty*. Turns out that several of Beethoven's ardent supporters, like Count Lichnowsky and some of his friends, tried their hands at composing. Just *finding* the manuscripts was quite a challenge. Playing the music is something else."

"I would have liked to have heard some of those."

"Some. Others, maybe not. Some of them were so bad that the audience laughs in all the wrong places."

"*Ay.*"

"We have a wonderful narrator, though. She clues in the audience and gives just a taste of background. Not a lecture. Just stage quips. Somebody put in a *lot* of work researching this whole thing. I've learned that Beethoven had a far greater sense of humor than most give him credit for. Than I gave him credit for."

"You never see a portrait or sculpture of him smiling, *hijo.*"

"True. He probably had bad teeth."

Estelle sighed. "It is so good to hear your voice. You have a couple of weeks left in Berlin, and then on to Aspen…and then Argentina. I talked to *Padrino* about it earlier tonight—we're excited about the trip north."

"I'm glad you would make it. Who's using the other ticket?"

"*Padrino* invited his daughter Camille, it turns out. She's planning to come out for a visit."

"Wonderful. How's the old *tejón* getting along?"

"Just fine. I appreciated his company tonight."

"I hope you gave him my best."

"I did. Your ears are probably still burning, we talked about you so much. And by the way, we stopped by the airport to have a chat with Jim Bergin. I had a chance to sit in the truck."

The silence was just long enough that Estelle thought Francisco might not have heard, but in a moment, with voice tinged with amusement, he said, "It's really hard to keep secrets from you, you know that?"

"It's a small county, *hijo*. And in that hangar with all those sleek, shiny airplanes, your old brute kind of stands out. Jim Bergin is in love with it."

"I guess it would stand out, but that seemed like such a good place for it."

"I can't take credit for finding it, though. *Padrino* saw it first. He let the cat out of the bag. That's why we went out there."

Francisco chuckled. "I'm going to have to talk to that guy. But I'm going to promise—try to promise, anyway—no more secrets. You know...just a second." She heard muffled voices in the background, then her son said, "Sure, that would work. Give me a couple minutes." He came back on the line. "Rush, rush, rush. That's my life at the moment, Ma."

"As long as it's your passion, *hijo*."

"As long as. Anyway...the reason I called you at three in the morning your time...will you and Dad be home on Monday?"

"The day after tomorrow, you mean? As far as I know, sure."

"We have three days off—I won't need to be back here until Thursday early afternoon. Angie and I are going to zip over to Posadas for a visit. Among other things, I need to meet with Carlos."

"Whoa. Run all that by me again."

Francisco did, and Estelle could hardly hear him, her pulse was pounding so hard. "Carlos told us that he's hung up with a project at Stanford—something with one of the professors."

"Well, I'm going to *unhang* him. We'll pick him up on the way in. He's already made arrangements to come with us."

Estelle groped for the right words. "You'll be here Christmas Eve, Christmas, and then leave the day after? Twenty-four, twenty-five, and twenty-six? Is that what you're saying?"

"That's it. ViaJet shrinks the globe, Ma. It's the same outfit that will fly you all to Aspen next month. Very professional, very safe."

"So you fly first to California, pick up Carlos, and then you all fly here on the twenty-fourth?"

"Yep."

"*¡Ay, caramba, hijo!* That's good news. But that's a lot of hours to spend on an airplane."

"Not so bad, 'cause there aren't any airport holdups. I think we stop in New York just long enough to take on fuel. That's it. It's a Grumman Gulfstream IV, and we'll have the whole plane to ourselves. Probably all the fancy food we can eat."

"You can't imagine how happy this makes us all, *hijo*."

"Well, I would have told you earlier, *should* have, but we hadn't worked out all the details yet." He paused. "And I have a favor to ask."

"Whatever you need, *hijo*."

"Can we schedule a free day on Christmas? On Christmas Day on Tuesday? Like all day? No parties, no company, no interviews, no *nada*? Just us, and *Padrino*, of course, if he'll come."

"I will dig out my magic wand, but there are lots of people who will be disappointed not to see you."

"Not this trip, please, Ma. With the schedules you guys keep, that magic wand might be necessary," Francisco said. "But if we can do that, it'd be great."

"You sound as if you're cooking up something."

"I just need time to decompress, Ma. Just the family."

"We can do that."

"*Perfecto*." He laughed. "And you can go to bed now."

"Oh, sure! My mind's swirling with all this. But, *hijo*, thanks for finding me. This means a lot."

"I remember the time years ago, when Angie and I made that surprise visit to Posadas, driving cross-country in her new birthday Corvette. I was…what?…sixteen at the time. You didn't scold me for making the trip, but you *did* lecture me for not understanding the joys of anticipation. So that's why the heads-up this time."

"I don't know what to say, *hijo*, except you guys take the time to travel safely, and we'll see you Monday sometime. And, *hijo*, I know the world loves you, but not the way we do."

"Thanks, Ma. Give our favorite doctor a hug for us, okay?"

When the telephone circuits closed, Estelle sat on the bed for a long time, phone in hand, numbed by the news. Life could go from zero to sixty in a heartbeat.

Chapter Six

"I've heard about a lot of stupid stunts in my time." Judge Ralph Tate glared at Darrell Fisher, who still stood as if his spine had the consistency of overcooked spaghetti. "You had no idea of the danger your actions might pose to that youngster?"

Fisher mumbled something, and Judge Tate rapped his gavel hard. "For God's sake, speak up, young man."

"I didn't think that…"

"You didn't think. The understatement of the year."

"I mean, there wasn't nobody out on the roads, and I was just going to just let him walk a little bit. You know."

"No, I don't know. The deputy," and he nodded at Tom Pasquale, who, along with Undersheriff Estelle Reyes-Guzman, sat directly behind Fisher, "found your son struggling along the highway." He picked up the police report and peered at it through his gold half-glasses. "'The child was pushing a Scamper,'" he read, and his busy eyebrows lifted in question. "What's a Scamper, Deputy?"

Pasquale rose. "Your Honor, it's a child's bike with no pedals and no cranks. They can learn to balance without getting their little feet tied up in the pedals. No training wheels, either."

"Along a state highway," Tate said with considerable acid. "At night. In the snow. In diapers." The judge shifted his glare back to Darrell Fisher. "How did you know that the child had been taken to the hospital, Mr. Fisher?"

"The deputy saw me."

"Explain that."

"I mean, I was goin' back out to pick up Derry, and there goes the ambulance by toward town, with the deputy behind. He sees me and right away turns around and stops me. Tells me to get my ass over to the hospital, 'cause that's where they're takin' the boy."

"Just brilliant." Tate leaned back in his chair and tossed his glasses on the blotter in front of him. "Let me see if I understand the logistics of all this." He held his hands up as if in supplication, eyes closed—even though he'd read and reread the concise deposition that Deputy Pasquale had provided him and clearly knew the details. "You dropped your son off—you kicked him out of the truck—because you were fed up with his using the inside of your pickup truck as a rumpus room. No child seat, of course." He didn't wait for a response. "Then you drove off, leaving him, let's see, just a few yards short of mile marker twenty-one." He peered across at Pasquale. "Where exactly is that, Deputy?"

"Your Honor, twenty-one is just northeast of the Rio Salinas arroyo bridge."

Tate's eyebrows shot up. "Oh, an icy concrete bridge. *That's* a good place for a two-year-old in diapers to be pushing a Scamper." He folded his hands. "What were you doing down there at that hour of the morning?"

"I...I was visiting with my brother, Al."

"Brother Al. That's Albert Fisher?"

"Yes, sir."

"At midnight?"

"Well, I didn't...I mean, you know. We was there earlier, and I guess time got away from us."

"Just having a beer or three?"

"Well, yeah."

"So the boy gets rambunctious, and you ran out of patience and dropped him off. That's about it?"

"Yes, sir. I mean it was just going to be for a minute."

"Kicked him out of the truck."

"I guess so."

"And you unloaded the Scamper and gave it to him? Is that how it worked?"

"Yes. It's his favorite thing in the whole world right now."

"And then you drove off."

"Yes. But I wasn't goin' far, Your Honor."

"I bet not. Just for a minute or two."

"Just kind of out of sight, so he'd get the message."

"A two-year-old."

"Well, two-and-a-half."

Tate nodded judiciously. "Ah, that explains it, then. Damn, the lad is almost ready to vote." He heaved a mighty sigh. "So you drive on, and next thing you know, here comes an ambulance?"

Darrell Fisher ducked his head, trying his best to control the tears. "No. The deputy went by first. Just like maybe a couple of minutes after I dropped him off."

"Oh. So now we're up to 'a couple of minutes,' and the ambulance still isn't there. You know Deputy Pasquale personally?"

"Yeah." He glanced up at Pasquale. "We went to high school together."

"So he drives by. But you keep going."

"Yes, sir."

The judge leaned forward. "Now why would you do that?"

"I don't know, sir." Fisher's voice was a whisper.

"You don't know. Didn't it seem likely to you that the deputy would stop when he saw the little boy slogging along the side of the road?"

"I didn't want no trouble with him."

"I see. Well, that certainly makes as much sense as any of this. And, you know, we still haven't accounted for the time that it took for the ambulance to respond to the call, then drive down there to the scene."

Darrell blanched and hung his head a little lower, if that were possible.

"So assuming the ambulance crew was ready to roll…" Tate pushed the deposition papers away and folded his hands, his head shaking in resignation. "Mr. Fisher, let's cut to the heart of this mess. Do you actually want your family?"

"Do I *want* them?" When the judge declined to answer, Fisher looked helplessly at the judge, and then at Deputy Pasquale, whose impassive face gave Darrell no clues about how he should respond. "Course I want 'em." His Adam's apple bobbed. "They're all I got."

Tate picked up the paperwork again in disgust. "You've been arrested and charged with one count each, reckless endangerment of a child and child abuse. You blew a .07 with the breathalyzer, so you were sober enough to understand what you were doing. As this mess winds its way through the legal channels, my recommendation to you is that you remain completely sober, Mr. Fisher. What I'd really like to do is incarcerate you for the rest of your pathetic life, but I suppose I can't do that. Where do you work, Mr. Fisher?"

"Work?"

"The word is foreign to you?"

"No, I mean, I work over at the junior high, in maintenance."

"Ah. On Christmas break now."

"Well, we ain't. We work all the time."

"Ah. And your wife? Where does she work?"

"She works nights at the hospital. She's one of their custodians."

"So little Derry is in day-care most of the time?"

"Yes, sir. On days, when I'm working. Over at Little Nippers."

Tate pursed his lips and regarded Fisher thoughtfully. "Bail is set at five thousand dollars, cash only. We'll accept the ten percent up front." He banged the gavel. "Deputy, any questions?"

"No, sir." Pasquale looked pleased.

"Undersheriff, did you have anything you wanted to add to these proceedings?"

"No, sir. Thank you." Estelle watched Pasquale snap the handcuffs in place on Darrell Fisher's thin wrists. If possible, the man's shoulders slumped a little more.

Chapter Seven

The rest of that Saturday settled into inexorable slow motion. Last-minute shoppers behaved themselves. Motorists behaved themselves. Folks put a lid on domestic disputes.

It was possible that a peace of sorts had even settled over the Fisher household. Penny Fisher somehow had scraped five hundred dollars together for bail, and Darrell Fisher went home. Had he looked out the window during the rest of that Saturday afternoon, he would likely have noticed a Posadas County Sheriff's Department patrol unit passing by the Fisher residence now and then, as if their lane was of particular interest.

Estelle tried to pressure the clock forward by immersing herself in the mundane business of polishing her home on Twelfth Street, fluffing pillows, checking sheets, and scrubbing bathrooms that didn't need it. In the living room she hesitated in front of the rocking chair that had been her mother's comfort spot for the final years of her extraordinarily long life. She'd made it to her 103rd year before announcing one spring morning, "It's time." Two days later, she quietly slipped away. The afghan that had warmed her bony frame was still folded over the back of the chair.

Estelle refolded the afghan neatly and replaced it with a couple of small Mexican pillows, then moved the chair a bit farther from the fireplace. She paused, reflecting that they had not enjoyed a blaze in the fireplace since Teresa had died. Estelle's younger son,

Carlos, was the artistic fire-builder, constructing the kindling and piñon rick just so, his fires never failing. He wouldn't be inside the home for five minutes before he gravitated to the fireplace to work some magic.

And even while Carlos did that, Francisco would be edging toward the piano bench, so absorbed by his music that a day away from the keyboard was agony for him.

No matter how immaculate their once-a-week housekeeper kept the home, the black ebony finish of the Steinway attracted the gentle settling of dust. Left untended long enough, the piano adopted a grayish cast as the dust motes found it. Methodically dusting and polishing, working her way up the keyboard, Estelle enjoyed the competing notes as the micro-fiber cloth stroked the black and whites.

"Cleaning Symphony in C," she said aloud. Finished polishing the keys, she closed the piano's keyboard lid and sat quietly for a long moment, eyes roaming the modest living room. What was missing was a holiday aroma. She left the piano and headed for the kitchen where she made a quick shopping list. She had all day Sunday, plenty of time to restock the larder.

When her husband Francis telephoned at six-thirty that Saturday evening, she was in the process of pinching the decorative borders around the crusts for a pumpkin and a sour cherry pie.

"*Querido!*" she exclaimed when she heard his calm voice. "I am *sooooo* glad you called. Do you wrap up tomorrow?"

"Actually, we finished late this afternoon," the physician said. "My flight out is at eight-fifteen in the morning, if I can haul my carcass out of bed."

"Long sessions?"

"Wellllll, yes. Dr. Luis Fernando was here from Mérida, and if something can be said in five words, he uses thirty-five."

"But progress?"

"*Mucho.* How about you?"

"*Ay*. The usual, but then *Padrino* decided to be a creature of the night. He came out at his usual midnight hour, and then did a short ride-along with me. I was covering for Jackie. She's visiting her mother. But guess who called."

"Uh oh. Good news or bad?"

"The best. Francisco called from Berlin, *Oso*. The concert series is a wild success, but he's got a few days off when they take a break for the holiday. He's coming for Christmas. Just a couple of days. He and Angie." Before her husband could work in a word edgewise, she added, "And then…" she took a deep breath. "He's stopping in California to pick up Carlos on the way in! All of 'em, *Oso*. They'll all three be here Monday afternoon!"

"So much for a quiet holiday with just the two of us snuggled in bed," Francis groused in mock disappointment. His tone brightened with the excitement that she knew her husband felt. "How's he managing all this?"

"Private jet. He's been using ViaJet…the same folks who will fly us up to Aspen next month. This time, it's nonstop from Berlin to New York, I think he said, then on to San José to fetch Carlos, then back to Posadas."

"Wow." Francis chuckled. "Whatever happened to his goal of being a starving artist living in a fifth-floor walk-up, subsisting on crackers and water?"

"I don't think that's going to work for him, *Oso*. And I think I'm very glad that it's not."

"And Carlos?"

"I'm going to call him later this evening. He has a private project he's working on with one of his professors."

"I knew about that."

"But we don't know *what* it is, *Oso*. Somehow he managed to wrangle some time off, though. I'm about to bust with excitement. *¡Caramba!*"

"Well, lemme get home, and I'll bust with you, *Querida*."

She turned at the whirring noise from the kitchen counter

in time to see her cell phone turning itself in a slow circle just as the first orchestral chord sounded.

"Is that your cell?"

"Yes. I can ignore it."

"Three ten, PCS." The hand-held radio that she had turned loose from her belt sat in the middle of the kitchen table.

"I can't ignore that, though," she said. "*Oso*, I need to go. Dispatch knows where I am and they wouldn't call if it wasn't important."

"Go to it. Be careful, and remember that I love you more than any of this *puro cuento* that keeps us so busy."

"*Y tu, mi solo mio*." She stood for a moment, holding the old black phone that was their landline.

"Three ten, PCS," the dispatcher said again, and her cell phone persisted with its circular dance. She chose the radio.

"PCS, three ten. Go ahead." At the same time, she retrieved her cell phone and snapped it open as she glanced at the kitchen clock. At 7:02 p.m., it had been pitch dark for more than an hour. She saw the number on the phone. Only Sheriff Robert Torrez was patient enough to let a phone ring twenty or thirty times.

"Three ten, contact three oh eight."

"I'm on it." She activated the cell. "What's up, Bobby?"

"Nine oh five Larson," the sheriff said without greeting. "What's your ETA?" She paused, trying to place Larson. "Just off County 19, across from the trailer park," he prompted. "Fishers' place."

Her heart sank. "About six minutes." She snapped the phone shut and froze in place for a moment. "What do I do with you guys?" she said aloud to the two waiting piecrusts. With a quick peel and tear, she drew out enough plastic wrap, bundled up the crusts, and slid the pans into the refrigerator.

In two more minutes, she was out the door. The snow had stopped, the wind died, and stars lit the clearing heavens. It would be a glorious holiday evening for somebody.

Chapter Eight

County Road 19 began grandly as Camino del Sol, one of those names that developers loved as a reflection of the Southwestern motif, right up there with howling coyotes sporting colorful bandannas around their necks. The illusion lasted to the postal cluster box just beyond Baldridge Mobile Home Park, and then the paved and potholed Camino del Sol gave way to County Road 19, narrow, graveled, and dusty most of the time.

After jouncing onto the gravel, Estelle slowed the county Expedition for the right-hand turn onto Larson, an irregularly graded cul-de-sac that at one time had been home to a dozen or more trailers, but now supported only three—and one of those had stood empty for several years.

Sheriff Robert Torrez' pickup was parked one lot before 905, and Tom Pasquale's county unit was turned crosswise in the road just beyond the Fishers' driveway. Estelle saw the flashing lights of one of the county's EMS units coming up behind her. Sheriff Torrez, looking immense in his Carhartt hooded parka, gestured for her to stop in the middle of the street. Behind him, Deputy Pasquale had attached a yellow boundary tape to the far corner of the mobile home and was reeling it out across the front yard toward the antelope-catcher on the front of Torrez' truck.

Darrell Fisher's pickup sat in the driveway, behind a battered Chevy Cavalier whose wheel-less right rear suspension rested on a concrete block. Just off the small front porch, a six-by-eight metal storage shed missing one of its doors rested under a quarter-inch of melting snow. A small Christmas wreath with a dozen lights graced the front door of the trailer, and another string of lights had been hung from the roof gutter.

"He's in the truck," the sheriff said as Estelle approached.

"Where's Derry?"

"Don't know." Torrez glanced at his watch. "I ain't been in the house yet. I got dispatch lookin' to see if Penny is at work." He looked down at Estelle. "This don't look good."

"So what do we have?"

"Darrell Fisher is in the truck behind the steering wheel, dead and just startin' to cool down."

"Ay, what happened to him, do we know?"

"Don't know. I'm guessing shot, by the looks of it. Driver's window is down."

"Who called this in?"

"Pasquale was doin' a routine drive-by, 'cause of what went on earlier. He saw 'im in the truck. Here's Linda."

Department photographer Linda Real Pasquale guided her red Honda to a stop behind Torrez' pickup. It somehow fit the ebullient department photographer that a bright holiday wreath was wired to the grill of her tiny car.

Estelle scuffed at the wet gravel underfoot. "It would have been nice if the snow had stayed around."

"Yeah, well," Torrez said laconically, "we get what we get." They moved into the scene behind Linda, letting her rip one photo after another before anything in the immediate area around Darrell Fisher's truck was disturbed. Less than a minute later, Estelle's cell phone came to life.

"Guzman."

"Estelle," dispatcher Ernie Wheeler said, "Penny Fisher is working tonight at the hospital. The lieutenant just got home from Kansas City, and I sent her over to get Penny. They should be there any minute."

"Thanks, Ernie."

"*The way you treat a domestic dispute when you first respond will determine what you have to deal with on the second visit.*" Former Sheriff Bill Gastner's words from decades ago were a grim reminder now. Everything that the officers had done, everything that Gayle Torrez had accomplished on behalf of Children, Youth, and Families, everything Judge Tate had tried to guide—all of it was trashed. Out on bail, in all likelihood facing the loss of job and income, Darrell Fisher had had lots of grief heaped on his plate.

Estelle touched Torrez' elbow. "I need to check inside for the little boy."

"If the door ain't open, have Pasquale kick it for you."

"You bet."

The door was unlocked, and Estelle opened it cautiously. The entry opened immediately into the living room, where the television was on, volume turned low. Keeping far to the side in the hallway, she moved back toward the bedrooms. The first one on the left, just beyond the bathroom, was small—as was its occupant.

In his crib, Derry Fisher slept deeply, on his stomach with his butt hiked into the air like a caterpillar caught in mid-stride. Estelle had seen her own younger son sleeping in the same position. She stroked a light finger down the little boy's cheek as she watched his even breathing. "That's one favor, at least," she whispered. A quick check revealed that the other rooms were unoccupied.

The country lane had become a fair-sized parking lot by the time Estelle left the house. Torrez beckoned to her. "Perrone is hung up with something down in Deming, and there's no assistant available for a little while. We got the coroner comin' out of Grant County." He pointed with his chin to a gathering spot across the road. Lieutenant Jackie Taber, who wouldn't even have had time to stretch her legs after her trip, was standing beside Penny Fisher, with Tom Pasquale flanking the woman on the other side.

"Give me a minute," Estelle said, and Torrez nodded toward the cab's occupant.

"He ain't goin' nowheres."

"No one heard anything?"

"Neighbor right over there." He pointed at the trailer on the opposite side of the street, the cul-de-sac's only other resident. "He thinks he heard a gunshot."

"And that's it?"

"That's it." Torrez almost smiled. "He was worried, with the Fishers fighting most of the time. And he used to be a hunter. A single shot like that...means the target got nailed. No follow-up."

"But he didn't see anything?"

"Nope."

"We'll talk with him again in a bit. I need to go talk with Penny. And the boy is sleeping, but she needs to be with him when he wakes up."

Even as Estelle approached Penny Fisher, the woman's right index finger rose as if fixing to issue commands, at the same time as she tried to jerk her elbow out of Lieutenant Taber's grip.

"My son's in there," she raged, and Estelle held up a hand.

"Mrs. Fisher, Derry is just fine. He's sound asleep in his crib, and we'd like to keep it that way."

"Well, this circus...what's Darrell done now?" She squinted at the truck, but the angle was such that she couldn't see Darrell Fisher's body slumped low against the steering wheel.

"It's not a circus, ma'am. We're waiting on the coroner. I regret to tell you that your husband is dead. I'm sorry."

"What?" Her eyes grew big as the light from Linda Pasquale's strobe broke the darkness again and again. Without warning, Penny lost her balance and fell straight down, as if someone had kicked her knees out from under her. Both deputies knelt with her.

"Oh, now what am I going to do?" Penny wailed. She choked back another sob. "In the truck? What's he doing in the truck?"

"We don't have any answers for you yet, Penny. What we…"

"No. I need to…" Penny Fisher said, and struggled to her feet.

"Mrs. Fisher, the first thing I want you to do is go in the house and be with your son. With all this commotion, it's likely he'll awaken. You need to be with him."

"Yes." With that purpose guiding her, she burst into an awkward trot toward the house with Lieutenant Taber close behind. She never looked in the pickup's direction.

"You were just cruising by?" Estelle asked Tom Pasquale.

The deputy nodded. "You know how domestics go. I kinda had a feeling, after meeting with the judge when the bail came in, that Darrell was going home to some hard times. That woman…" He shook his head in resignation. "I don't know. But she was at work, though. Kinda bizarre."

"All right. I want Jackie to stay with the mother." She nodded at the fire engine that had idled up behind the EMTs' rig. "We have a good road block, anyway." A State Police cruiser pulled onto Larson. "Dull night for everybody else."

"I think we're ready," Linda Pasquale said as Estelle walked back to the pickup. Estelle didn't need to ask Linda if she had taken establishing shots of the scene in general. A magician with the camera, Linda would have covered every angle.

"Let's take the driver's door first," the undersheriff said. Torrez waited until Linda was in position, then touched the seam between door and truck body with one gloved index finger, holding it there while Linda worked the camera.

"Door isn't latched hard," he said, and the flash punctuated his comment.

The door opened with a screech of misaligned metal as if sometime in the past it had been forced beyond its limits. Darrell Fisher slumped in the seat, his upper body fallen forward, his head turned so that his left cheek rested on the steering wheel.

He wasn't dressed for a formal Christmas party—an old pair of loafers with the backs broken down from being used as house slippers, blue jeans with rips above both knees, and a T-shirt that once had been white many launderings ago. His hands were cupped loosely in his lap. A heavy revolver lay on the floor between his feet.

The back of his T-shirt was blood-soaked starting a scant hand's-width down from the neck line, and some of the splatter had covered the driver's side of the back window, marking the empty rifle rack that hung there.

"Linda, take one now, but we'll want a close-up of this after the body has been removed." Estelle pointed at the frame around the window where the tough rolled metal was deeply scarred and torn. "The bullet is still in there, I think."

Torrez stepped away from the truck and swung his flashlight beam across the exterior of the cab above the bed. "Yep," he said. "No exit."

Only a modest amount of blood had burst from the front of Darrell Fisher's body, enough to puddle around the revolver on the floor and soak the T-shirt, the crotch of his jeans, and the seat fabric. A medical examiner's ruling wasn't necessary to tell them that the young man's heart had been shredded by the gunshot.

There was so much to record photographically that they worked in silence for some time, occasionally hearing conversation from the other officers gathered by the EMS vehicle, or from inside the house where Penny's sobs and lamentations were loud enough for all to hear.

A large BMW turned into Larson, and the driver doused his lights. One of the officers bent down to talk to the driver, then pointed ahead toward Estelle's car. The sleek sedan eased forward.

"He made it after all," Estelle said in wonder. Medical Examiner Alan Perrone stepped out of the Beemer and stood rooted in place, surveying the neighborhood. Collegiate tie always neatly in place, he had traded a suitcoat for a tan quilted jacket. Estelle had never seen Alan Perrone with a hat or cap. Instead, his long blond hair was combed straight back and heavily Brylcreemed so that it resembled a shiny helmet.

Estelle caught his attention and indicated a direct line to reach the truck, avoiding any further footprints to contaminate the scene. What little snow there had been was confined to faint windrows along the road and driveway. Footing was wet gravel—a hopeless matrix for shoe or boot prints.

"I thought you were stuck in Deming." She shook Dr. Alan Perrone's hand.

"For a while it looked like I would be." He didn't explain, but grimaced at the scene through the open truck door. "Who be he?"

"His name is Darrell Fisher. He was twenty-six, worked over at the school in the physical plant. He and his wife and two-year-old son live here."

"The wife is all right?"

"Yes. She works at the hospital as a night shift custodian. She's here now. One of the officers brought her home just a few minutes ago. Their boy was asleep in the bedroom."

He took a step to one side and rested a hand for support on the silent Torrez' shoulder, leaning into the truck's cab. "Ah. That's the handgun involved, probably."

"Could be," Torrez said.

"*Could.* You have reason to think that it isn't?"

"Nope. Not yet."

"Well, let's see then." Disturbing the position of the body as little as possible, he worked his way through the scene, narrating to himself. Finally, he looked up at Linda. "How are you doing, young lady?"

"I'd rather be home, wrapped around a warm husband."

"Well, I bet. Except he's working, too, right?"

"Such is life in the fast lane, Doctor. And Merry Christmas to one and all."

He smiled at her. "Can you scrunch in from the other side and get a photo of this?" He eased the body away from the steering wheel. "Bobby?"

The sheriff obliged and reached in, holding the body in place with a hand on the left shoulder. Perrone eased the T-shirt up and held it away from the chest wound long enough for Linda to shoot a series. "Now the back," he said. "Let him ease forward again." He paused. "No rigor yet. It'll be interesting to see the body temp. You have a time for this?"

"Nope. Not yet." The sheriff made no effort to elaborate, but Perrone was used to his taciturn personality.

With the shirt hiked up in the back, the exit wound was revealed as almost half-dollar size and ragged, having blown through the body of one of the heavy upper thoracic vertebrae. Perrone looked hard at the back window frame where the bullet had lodged after driving through both body and seat.

"Huh," he said. "Well, all right." He took a moment to run his gloved fingers around Fisher's skull, probing here and there. Then he picked up each hand in turn, turning them this way and that. "Tox is going to be interesting." He let the hands return to their original position and straightened up. "The smell of marijuana is strong. And beer. And who knows what else. Did this young man have a narcotics history with you folks?"

"Nope," the sheriff replied.

Eventually Perrone stood back. "Let's get him out of the truck first. Take a body temp, check for other wounds or injuries, and go from there."

Sheriff Torrez pulled his hand-held radio off his belt and turned toward the ambulance. He pressed the transmit and said, "Gurney." Someone popped the transmit button a couple of times in reply. In a moment, two EMTs appeared and lugged the gurney across.

"Merry Christmas." EMT Matty Finnegan Sheehan favored everyone with one of her kilowatt smiles. "This is Bruce Cutler. He just started with us." Bruce glanced at the corpse, and his face turned a shade paler in the glare of ambulance lights.

"Bruce, welcome aboard," Estelle said. "This gentleman needs to be off-loaded." She turned to Alan Perrone, and he nodded agreement. "But before you do, Thomas?"

She waited as Pasquale stepped past the sheriff and approached the truck. "Thomas, secure the handgun first. I'll want it in a suspension box. There's one in the back of Taber's unit if you don't have one. And use the larger dowel to fit the barrel. It's a forty-four."

Pasquale returned with the gun cradle, nothing but a sturdy cardboard box with a network of support cords made from forty-pound test monofilament fishing line. The others watched silently as he slipped a stout dowel down the muzzle of the blood-caked revolver and lifted it out of the truck. He looked at it closely.

"Still loaded with five more."

"Huh," Torrez grunted.

"Be sure to indicate that on the box," Estelle reminded the deputy. "Tag it clearly as loaded."

"I don't know this young man," Dr. Perrone said. "Is there reason to think he might have been suicidal? There's a record of that?"

"Oh, yeah," Torrez replied.

Estelle touched Perrone's sleeve. "A domestic earlier yesterday, arraignment this morning on charges of endangerment and child abuse, continuing fight with his wife. Low-paying job in maintenance at the junior high. And the holiday season on top of all of that. So, yes. He had lots of reason to think that life had handed him a raw deal."

"Sad." Perrone stepped out of the way as the two EMTs worked first Fisher's feet and legs out of the truck, and then his upper torso. With helping hands from Torrez and Pasquale, they positioned the corpse on the body bag that had been spread on the gurney. "As long as it's handy, let's get a preliminary temp." He pulled up the T-shirt again, and ever so gently slipped the long probe of a thermometer into the gunshot wound. He frowned as he waited. "That's interesting. Thirty-five point two." He glanced at Estelle and made a face as he calculated. "That's ninety-six point four or so Fahrenheit. So…in this weather, in a cool truck, with the victim being slender of build, and he's wearing only a T-shirt—I'm guessing this didn't happen very long ago."

"The deputy's discovery call came into dispatch at six fifty-five."

"And I got here at what, about eight? He hasn't dropped much core temp. I'm guessing he was shot just moments before Pasquale came on the scene. Would that be about right?"

"Just about."

"And no witnesses."

Torrez turned and chinned toward the mobile home across the cul-de-sac. "Over there. Old man might have heard the shot. He said that he didn't look."

"He heard, but didn't see what happened?"

"Nope. That's Ollie Escobedo. He's eighty-two and legally blind."

"But he knows a gunshot when he hears it? And a muffled gun shot, at that?"

"Well, a forty-four magnum toots pretty loud, Doc."

"Apparently so."

Perrone reached out a gloved finger and touched the wound. "You can see the pattern of the front sight above the entry wound," he said. "That kind of imprint is not unusual in suicides…that and the star-shaped wound that's characteristic of blowback from a powerful weapon. The victim holds the gun with a nervous death grip, pulling it into himself. That's what he did here. He pulled it in hard enough to dig a gouge in his skin. So often, that's why the victim removes his clothes, so there's nothing in the way."

"One layer of thin cotton ain't going to stop much," Torrez remarked.

"But that's a layer, nevertheless." Perrone tapped his own fore-head. "It's all up here. In their perception. If they were thinking

straight, they wouldn't be suicides in the first place." He beckoned Linda, who had been waiting expectantly. "You'll want to
bag his hands," Perrone said, but Estelle already had the plastic
bags ready.

Perrone straightened up and turned to Torrez. "We'll see," he
said, and the sheriff nodded. "If the revolver is his, that removes
a little more of the doubt." He watched as Matty Sheehan zipped
up the body bag. "Not an unusual scenario going here. He waits
for mom to be out of the house and for the kid to be sound
asleep, then slips outside and takes care of business."

"Maybe so."

The physician shot a quick glance at Torrez. "I'm planning
the post for two tomorrow afternoon, if one or both of you can
make it."

"We appreciate you being so prompt," Estelle said.

"With something like this, time matters," Perrone said. His
expression brightened a little. "Well, onward. When's your hubby
due home?"

"What day is this?" Estelle smiled. "He'll fly in Sunday midday
to El Paso, so late afternoon if all goes well. Tomorrow."

"His meetings went well?"

"He thinks so."

"Good for him. I look forward to hearing about them."

Her smile grew a little wider. "And the boys are flying in on
Monday."

"Oh, wow. Even better for the both of you. Is there a concert
planned? Did I miss hearing about that?"

"I'm afraid not," Estelle said. "Not this visit."

The physician shrugged philosophically. "I guess the *maestro*
deserves a holiday too, right?" He shook hands all around and
headed for his BMW.

"That's it?" Matty asked before touching the gurney.

"That's it," Torrez said.

Chapter Nine

For the past several minutes, the home at 905 Larson had been silent, and Estelle rapped on the front door and entered to find Lieutenant Taber sitting on the couch with Penny Fisher. Bright-eyed and wide awake, little Derry sat in Penny's lap, and when Estelle entered the room, he pointed a sharp little index finger toward her and said something incomprehensible.

Penny had obviously been crying, with dark circles under her eyes. Derry squirmed, but she hugged him close.

"Mrs. Fisher, I'm so sorry for your loss." The words sounded hollow to Estelle as she said them, and no doubt sounded totally empty to the widow.

"The lieutenant tells me that we may never really know what he was thinking. What pushed him to do this," Penny Fisher said. She lowered her head and snuffled against the little boy's neck.

"That's true." Estelle left it at that. "Can you answer a couple questions for me, Mrs. Fisher?"

"If you'll call me Penny, Sheriff."

"Penny. We need to know about the handgun. The Ruger Redhawk. Was that his?"

Penny clenched her eyes tight for a moment. "Yes. He bought it up in Albuquerque. That was another one of our legendary fights. I was *so* angry with him when he did that. I mean, we don't earn a whole lot of money, Sheriff. And here he goes and spends eight hundred dollars on that thing. He was going to hunt with it, but he never did. His brother borrows it now and then. Al likes to go pig hunting over in Texas. As least we've been getting some meat out of that."

"Had your husband ever hinted at taking his own life? Did he talk about that?"

"Once he did. Last year, after things piled up on him." Penny stopped abruptly and drew in a long, ragged breath. "Sheriff, I know I'm not the easiest person to live with. Well, neither was he, you know. There were times…there were times when I thought I had two two-year-olds in the house." She finally let Derry slide down to the floor, and he stumped over to an enormous, fleecy bear. First he hugged it, then seized it by one foot and dragged it down the hall.

"He won't even remember his daddy, will he? When he's grown up, I mean."

"The young can be pretty resilient," Estelle said. "Penny, I'll ask Gayle Torrez to stop by later today. Her department has all kinds of resources for you to draw upon."

"I want to keep my job. I really do. I love working at the hospital."

"And you should. Gayle can help you make arrangements for comprehensive sitter services for your son, and she'll find out what other kinds of assistance the county and state can offer you. Maybe the hospital can transfer you to working days. Penny, it's important that you accept all the help that's out there. No one expects you to handle this alone."

Tears flooded the woman's eyes and she buried her face in a thick wad of tissue.

"Undersheriff." The voice behind Estelle was quiet, and she turned to see Linda Pasquale standing in the doorway. "The sheriff needs to talk with you if you have a moment."

Or even if I don't, Estelle thought. She reached out and took one of Penny Fisher's hands in hers. "Call us if we can help."

"I'm sure there's nothing you can do," the woman said, almost wistfully. She cleared her throat. "I know I'm probably as much to blame as anyone for what happened. That's something I'll have to figure out how to live with."

Estelle pushed herself upright and transferred her grip to a traditional handshake. "Call me whenever you need to, Penny." Estelle handed her a business card. "Call me whenever you think I can be of help."

Outside, she saw that the sheriff was occupied at the passenger side of the pickup, and when he saw her, he beckoned impatiently.

"She going to be all right?" he asked as she approached.

"I think so."

He nodded once. "Tell me what you think of this." Stepping to one side, he cleared the truck's door so she could squeeze past him. He aimed his flashlight at the truck's floor mat.

"Still wet," Estelle said after a moment. "A good partial boot print. Linda recorded it?"

"Yep. About a hundred times."

"Digital film is cheap, Bobby." The sheriff snorted something that could have been a chuckle at the well-worn joke.

"And right there." He directed the flash beam upward to a spot on the dashboard just above the radio console.

Estelle pulled out her own flashlight and took her time examining the surface. "Good eyes," she said. Drawing out her pen, she brought it up just short of touching the surface where a smudge—what could be imagined to be a palm print—marked the dust on the dashboard. She pointed at three small points of dried blood. "This looks like some blood splatter. Not much, maybe not enough even to type."

"Only one guy bleedin' in this truck," Torrez said. "And splatter can go a long ways."

"But the handprint is on *top* of the blood splatter. On *top* of it." She looked around at the sheriff, and he nodded slightly. He watched as she held her hand out, fingers spread just above the evidence without touching, trying to match the faint print on the dusty dashboard's surface. "Thumb is down, fingers pointing off toward the steering wheel, toward the driver. It's a right hand, like the owner needed to push back against something for support."

Linda Pasquale was waiting patiently behind Torrez. "Linda?"

"Yes, ma'am."

"Are you confident that you captured this as clearly as possible?"

The girl held out her camera, and Estelle took it, bringing up the series of photos on the preview screen. She took her time, looking at each one. Finally, she said, "Someone was in the truck besides Darrell Fisher."

"Yep."

"And somebody was turned sideways in the cab, and had his foot over in one corner, and his gloved hand stretched out for support."

"Yep."

"Linda Wizard, how large can we print back at the office? On the new computer and printer."

"Fourteen-by-eighteen or so, I think."

"I'd like to see that, one for each. The best of the handprint, the best of the boot."

"It likely won't be detailed enough to stand up in court," Linda said.

"And it might not have to. Sometimes, just showing a print to someone is enough to loosen their tongue. And messy pixels or not, the photo *will* show that the handprint is on *top* of the blood spatter."

"'Messy pixels.' I like that." Linda grinned at Torrez.

"Remember the PM is at two. You need to be there," Estelle reminded her.

"Yuck time," Linda said. "Anything else here?"

"We're gonna go through it one more time," Torrez said. "Don't go runnin' off."

"That's what I was about to do, all right," Linda said. "I do that a lot, run off."

The sheriff's deep-set eyes regarded Linda. He had never quite gotten used to her casual manner and almost insubordinate, flip attitude, but she blasted him with one of her huge grins, and reached over to dig a knuckle into his ribs. "Lots of film left," she said.

Chapter Ten

"I'm not calling that creep," Penny Fisher snapped at one point. Estelle had gone back in the house and sure enough…Lieutenant Jackie Taber's notebook was ballooning with tidbits she'd gleaned from commiserating with the widow. "If I don't ever see him again, it's too soon."

"We'll need to touch bases with him," Estelle said. That earned a slight nod from Jackie, who thumbed through the little notebook.

"Penny tells me that Al was going on a pig hunt over in Texas this weekend," Jackie said.

"He was tryin' to get Darrell to go with him, but I said, 'Oh no. I have to work, and you need to spend some time with this one.'" Derry and his bear had returned to the couch, and she nestled the snoozing boy closer. "We can't afford it anyways. I mean, all they'll do is drink beer for a weekend. And who's going to mind Derry while they're gone and I'm workin'?"

It wasn't the responsibility of the Sheriff's Department to contact all of the Fisher next of kin, but Estelle had dispatched Deputy Thomas Pasquale to Regál to talk to Darrell's brother, Al, before Penny relented and changed her mind, calling relatives to alert them of the tragedy.

Pasquale offered a ride-along to Tanner Garcia. Tanner, the department's most recent hire, was accumulating ride-along hours before attending the spring session of the Law Enforcement Academy. A former resident of the South Valley in Albuquerque, the thirty-two-year-old Garcia was fresh out of a marriage, and equally tired of the traffic congestion, smog, and noise of city life. It didn't hurt that he was one of Thomas Pasquale's first cousins.

When she was sure that the scene at 905 Larson had nothing more to add to the meager assortment of evidence, Estelle returned to the office to browse through Linda's first round of photographic offerings. The Seth Thomas wall clock clicked to twenty minutes after midnight—she'd spent the last five hours of that Saturday at the Fishers', as if the rest of the world had been put on hold.

Refusing to be denied, the rest of the world was responsible for a small stack of Post-its that accumulated in the in-box beside Estelle's telephone console, Post-its written by the dispatcher for incoming calls when the caller didn't want to have the message routed to Estelle's voicemail. For contacts who embraced technology, the little amber light on the phone's answering machine winked patiently. That was as close to immediate contact as Estelle wished to get. The idea of walking about with an i-gadget demanding constant attention was repugnant. A simple cell phone was enough. Sometimes she agreed with former sheriff Bill Gastner's gruff opinion that "telephones should be black and hang on the wall."

"You have...twenty-two messages," her phone extension announced when she tapped the button. The message log, from most recent to those a day or two old, scrolled up the small green screen. Posadas County Manager Leona Spears wanted to talk with her. One of the Post-its was from, or referred to, Leona as well. Estelle was surprised that the ebullient Leona hadn't appeared out at the scene on Larson. The manager hadn't called Estelle's personal cell phone, but that could be expected shortly.

Frank Dayan, owner, publisher, and energetic reporter for the *Posadas Register*, had called both dispatch and Estelle's extension, and no doubt when she booted her computer she'd find an e-mail from him as well.

Estelle scanned down the list of callers, seeing little to pique her interest. Craig Stout, one of the few law enforcement officers employed by the U.S. Forest Service, had called twice, the last effort at close to eleven p.m. Saturday—an odd time to be trying to contact her—four-thirty was the magic hour for government agencies to quit for the day. That was reason enough to return the call, and she tapped in the Arizona number and waited for the circuits to connect.

"Craig Stout with Coronado National Forest. I'm not in right now, but…" She waited for the message to finish, and at the tone said, "Craig, Undersheriff Reyes-Guzman from Posadas County…" That was as far as she got before Stout picked up.

"Hey, you caught me in mid-yawn," Stout said. "Dispatch says you've been busy."

"Yes."

He laughed at her cryptic answer. "Well, look, I won't keep you. To make a long story short, we're missing one of our range techs, along with his unit. Last we knew, he was headed out to Stinkin' Springs to check on one of the permitees who's building a fence where he's not supposed to."

"Your Stinkin' Springs, or ours?"

He laughed again. "That's right. Everybody's got a Stinkin' Springs, don't they? No, the one off Forest Road 113, over near Three Peaks."

"That's a long way from us, Craig."

"I know it is. But we don't have any report of him showing up there. See, you gotta know that this is Myron Fitzwater, and he marches to his own drummer. He has this habit of getting a wild hair at the last minute and going off somewhere without telling anybody."

"We have a few of those."

"Doesn't everybody. Anyway, I'm doing a quick call-around.

He hasn't answered his radio or his cell. 'Course, he could be in a dead zone. Lots of land out there without cell towers."

Estelle leaned back and swiveled her chair so she could see the wall map behind her desk. Stout's office in Douglas, Arizona, was a long drive from Posadas, but as the ravens flew, it was just next door.

"When was last contact?"

"He talked to one of our other range techs on Friday, a little before lunch. Larry said that they talked about a project where they're building some erosion control structures north of here, around the Alejandro area. Fitz said he had some errands to run, and that's the last we saw of him."

"He has a government truck?"

"Yep."

"The unit has a radio?"

"As a matter of fact, it doesn't. Just kind of a utility rig, you know. Have to depend on either cell or handheld radio."

"Is it the usual procedure to bring the unit back to your office at the end of the day, or do some of the techs take their ride home for the weekend?"

"No, they always bring the vehicle back to the boneyard."

"Okay. Is there any particular reason for you to think that Fitzwater might have come this way?"

"He's got a girlfriend, for one thing." He said the word "girl" as if it has about six r's. "He hasn't been able to talk her out of that little corner of New Mexico that you guys boast over there."

"You called her?"

"If she has a phone, it's a cell, and there's no cell service down there.

"'Down there' meaning...?"

"Little crossroads named Regál. Now I *know* you know all about that place."

"Indeed we do. What's the girl's name? Do you know?"

"*I* don't, but wait a sec. Maybe Glenda does. She's worked

here forever and knows everything about everybody. She's a night owl, too. She'll be home, so let me give her a quick buzz. I'm putting you on hold. Don't go away."

While she waited and listened to the silence on the phone line, Estelle stood up and stepped closer to the map. She imagined that the whole corner of the state was a territorial nightmare for the Forest Service. Stout's home office was in Douglas, Arizona, but a wing of the Coronado National Forest touched Posadas County, wrapping around the west end of the San Cristóbal Mountains and blanketing the country around Regál, as well as coming within a few miles of sharing a boundary with the Oria National Forest to the north and parts of the Apache-Sitgreaves to the west. Like most federal law enforcement officers, Stout would have an enormous area to cover, with little assistance.

He was back on the line in a moment. "Okay. I survived that encounter. Connie Suarez, Glenda tells me. *Constance* Suarez."

"Sure."

"You know her?"

"Yes. A nice girl. She still lives with her mother, as far as I know. Or did, anyway. The last time I talked to her was some months ago, at the Catron County fair over in Reserve. She and her mom make about the best peach preserves in the entire universe."

"So, there you go. Look, do you have anybody down that way at the moment?"

"As a matter of fact, at the moment, I do. Two of the deputies went down that way on another matter. I'll have them swing by Connie's place and see if your wayward range tech is there. Maybe the two of them got tired of the commute and eloped."

"Right now lying on a beach in Bermuda, probably."

"Probably."

"Undersheriff, thank you. I appreciate it. This is one of those incidents when the weekend got in the way. Fitzwater forgot to check in, and we didn't follow up. Everybody's in such a hurry to get out the door on a Friday afternoon. All this came about because his name is on the crew list to head up to Flag on Monday for a reconstruction conference after *their* fire. But he's gone, truck's gone…so they dump Mr. Fitzwater and his escapades in my lap."

"I'll get back to you asap. Or Deputy Pasquale will. I'll have him call you one way or another."

"Let me give you my cell. No one's going to be in the office by then."

"You got it."

He rattled off the number, then said, "The truck he's driving is a standard issue 2016 Ford F-150 crew, color government white. Last time I saw it, he had about six rolls of barbed wire and fifty or so steel posts in the back. Chrome locking toolbox across the bed."

"Maybe it was just more convenient for him to keep it over the weekend rather than driving back to the boneyard in Douglas. Especially if he's decided to spend the weekend over here with Connie."

"No doubt. Just so long as he didn't drive it head-first into some arroyo and ended up spending the night looking up at the stars."

"We'll check for you."

"Everything else going all right over there?"

"Sure, depending on what your definition of 'all right' is."

"I hear that."

"I have to ask, though. What are you doing working in the middle of the night, Craig?"

"Ah, like I said, we had a little fire. Maybe a hundred acres, but it's about burned itself out. One of the firefighters came up with a good tip about who started it. We made a good arrest, but of course the magistrate let 'em go 'cause there was no property damage, other than a campground restroom. Same old, same old. Apparently a hundred acres of prime timber doesn't count for much."

"And so it goes. Look, if Fitzwater's truck is down at Connie's, I'll have the deputy wake him up and call in. If he's not there, I'll make sure the road deputies are on the look-out for government license A-163100."

When Estelle hung up, she made a couple of quick notes to herself and then left her office, stopping briefly at the dispatch island. "Pasquale is ten eight?"

"Yes, ma'am." Ernie Wheeler ran a pencil down the log, then rested a fist on the mike's old-fashioned transmit bar. "Three oh four, PCS. Ten twenty."

Pasquale's response was immediate. "Three oh four is just coming down off the pass into Regál, mile marker thirty-nine."

She explained the brief note to Wheeler, who frowned and transmitted. "Three oh four, BOLO a U.S. Forest Service truck, tag Alpha 163100. White 2016 Ford F-150. Should be operated by a Milton Fitzwater, range tech out of Douglas."

"Ten four."

"Check at the Suarez residence. If the truck is there, give Fitzwater the message to call USFS Law Enforcement ASAP." Wheeler read off Stout's cell number.

Pasquale acknowledged. Wheeler looked amused.

"Do you want to be notified if this guy Fitzwater is in Regál?"

Estelle stifled a yawn. "No. If he locates him, Tommy needs to tell Fitzwater to call Craig Stout in Douglas for a heads-up. The rest is up to them. This one's not my child."

"I hear ya."

Nothing else on her list warranted a return call in the middle of the night, and Estelle left the office in Ernie Wheeler's capable hands, with the county under Deputy Thomas Pasquale's watchful eye, and with soon-to-be-deputy Tanner Garcia to keep Thomas awake. When he was finished in Regál, Pasquale would stay central, since the county Sheriff's Department also provided coverage for the village of Posadas—its own police department one of the victims of economic collapse with the closing of the area mines.

With such scant coverage, the best to hope for was a quiet rest of the night, with everyone keeping their domestic squabbles behind closed doors.

Chapter Eleven

"Hey."

Not "good morning," or "are you coming to work today?" or "how did it go last night?" The classical music of her cell phone followed by Sheriff Robert Torrez' monosyllabic greeting finished the job that Estelle's alarm had tried to do an hour before.

"Good morning, Robert." Her voice was husky from too-deep sleep, and with her free hand, she chopped a trough through her pillow so she could see the clock.

"Are you going to be able to see Perrone this afternoon?"

"Yes," she managed, and coughed hard, once. "Excuse me," she added. *There's just nothing I'd rather do than gag through an autopsy.* But if Dr. Alan Perrone was willing to spend his Sunday afternoon in the morgue to advance their case, she would support him in any way she could.

"You sound like shit," Torrez said, about as close to sympathy as he ever came.

"Too much sleep." Maybe Bill Gastner had discovered something with his persistent insomnia, she thought—never having to wake up feeling as if clubbed into submission the night before.

"It ain't no surprise," the sheriff continued. "The bullet I recovered from the cab of Fisher's pickup came from the gun found lyin' between his feet. That's all preliminary, but I'm sure it's right."

"We expected that, didn't we?"

"Yep. And the gun is his. The wife found the paperwork for it from Rio Grande Shooting Sports stuffed in the back of his reloading journal."

"She told me that he'd bought it—she wasn't too pleased about that. In fact, it sparked another knock down, drag out. Anyway, the bullet came from his own gun. A tough nut for her to face. She said her husband had talked about suicide once before."

"Taber thinks that what he did to the little boy triggered it," Torrez said. He sounded almost sympathetic. "That and knowin' that he might be facing some jail time."

"Not likely in this day and age." Estelle rolled onto her back and watched the morning sun patterns on the closet door. "Remorse can sometimes be a powerful thing, Bobby."

"More likely that if he was all that sorry about makin' the kid hike, he'd just try to make up for it. Buy the kid a new bike or something."

"Most likely. But he didn't do that."

"Nope. Hey, Craig Stout called a few minutes ago. That deal from last night? They found their guy's truck up north of Newton. Grant County's lookin' into it."

"*Found* it? Where?"

"You know where County Road 0910 comes into Newton from the west?"

"Sure."

"Just about five miles west of there. Where the road dips down into that set of arroyos comin' out of the Oria. Truck was pulled into that area that used to be a campground. Ain't nothin' there now. Ground's too hard for tracks to tell 'em anything."

"But no Myron Fitzwater?"

"Nope. A load of fencing shit in the back. Wire, posts, stuff like that."

"His radio or phone?"

"Don't think so. Deputy Miles Clark is the local contact, if you want to talk with him. Him or Stuart, either one."

"Stout didn't say whether or not Fitzwater was supposed to be working on something up there."

"He says not."

"I'm sure the Forest Service is capable of handling things," Estelle said. "And Grant County will assist. There's no connection with us."

"Just his girlfriend in Regál, but Pasquale didn't contact her last night. She wasn't home. Her car was, but the trailer was dark. Maybe off visiting for the holidays. Her mom don't live there anymore...in some kind of home up in Albuquerque."

"Maybe Fitzwater hiked in a ways from the truck. That's big fossil country in that area. Maybe he took a header in one of those arroyo cuts."

"They're checkin' all that. Didn't get any snow up that way, so it's like workin' with shoe prints on concrete. Tough country. It don't look good."

"The Feds are mounting a search?"

"Lookin' that way. I'm sendin' Mears and Garcia up there for whatever help they can give, make sure they take a hard look at that vehicle and the area around where it was parked."

"Do we have a good photo of Fitzwater coming?"

"Yep. Got both his ID photo and a snapshot blow-up...him sittin' on the tailgate of his truck, talkin' with his girlfriend. Stout faxed me those this morning."

"Was the truck locked?"

"Nope. And no keys."

"Disabled? Could they tell?"

"Don't think so. Mears'll find out for sure. He's going to talk with Deputy Clark."

"If it was disabled, Fitzwater could have just walked back to Newton if his phone and radio didn't work out there. There's not a lot of traffic out that way, but Hippie Dan still lives in Newton. He would have helped."

"Maybe so."

"Something like this, an air search might be productive, Bobby. Were you going to touch bases with Jim Bergin?"

"Yep. They'll be in the air here in a few minutes. Pasquale's ridin' with him."

"Did you have a chance to talk with the Fishers' neighbor, by the way? Mr. Escobedo?"

"Yep."

"And?"

"He said he heard one loud kind of *whump* noise. Like someone hittin' a mattress with a baseball bat."

"That's an interesting observation."

"Yeah, but nothin' else. By the time he got out of his chair and used his walker to move over to the front window, there was nothin' to see, even if he coulda. Or hear, for that matter. He *thinks* he might have heard a vehicle drive by, but he wasn't sure. He said couldn't really see if Fisher's truck was in the driveway or not."

"But he could tell that Penny Fisher's car was gone?"

"So he says, and he didn't see anyone walkin' around, or hear anybody talkin'. Never did figure out what caused the noise."

"No other traffic?"

"Maybe not payin' attention to it, if there was."

"Maybe he heard the truck door slam when Fisher climbed inside."

"Nothin' he was payin' attention to," Torrez said. "Right now, it's *lookin'* like Fisher did just what it seems like. Climbed in that truck, thought about it for a minute or two, then did it."

Estelle heard the skepticism in the sheriff's voice. "Maybe so. Except for the matter of the scuffed handprint on the dash, and the maybe footprint on the passenger side."

"Tell me what you're thinkin'." That request came as a surprise.

"As long as Alan Perrone has questions, *I* have questions. I trust his judgment."

"Yep. I can't see him leavin' the kid all alone in the house while he takes the easy way out."

"Remember that this is the same idiot who put his son out of the truck in the middle of a snowstorm," Estelle said. "Anything goes with this guy. I'll see you at two, then, if not before."

After switching off, Estelle lay quietly, phone resting on her stomach.

Quick and easy, she thought. A simple, uncomplicated ruling by Dr. Alan Perrone, coupled with finding range tech Myron Fitzwater safe and sound. Then Estelle's husband would be home, and her sons and Francisco's fiancée would jet in, and all would be perfect for a quiet Christmas. She groaned as she sat upright, and massaged the heavy scar that rippled diagonally from right armpit to almost the center of her torso below her right breast. Despite eight years of healing time, her battered ribs and muscles still protested the damage done by a nine-millimeter hollow-point bullet and the hours of surgery that followed.

After letting the shower's hot water beat on her for ten minutes, she stepped out and wrapped herself in the huge white towel, preparing to do a series of careful stretch exercises before rescuing the two piecrusts that waited in the refrigerator. The piano chord interrupted her, and she turned to see her cell phone walking circles on the bureau top.

Chapter Twelve

The voice was muted and distant, as if the speaker was holding his cell phone well away from his mouth. He responded to her initial greeting with a question.

"Is this Sheriff Guzman?"

"This is Undersheriff Guzman. Who's calling, please?"

"I didn't know if I should call or not." The man's voice was soft, but with the hint of a west Texas twang. "Anyways, I figured I should."

"Who's calling, please?"

"Oh. Sorry. This is Al Fisher?"

"Darrell's brother."

"Yes, ma'am." He started to add something else, but choked. After some snuffing and heavy breathing, he said, "I just thought I should call."

"We're sorry for your family's loss, Mr. Fisher. Did Deputy Pasquale speak with you?"

"No, ma'am. My girl...that's Maria? She said he stopped by. But I wasn't back from Texas yet. I got home late yesterday and heard what happened. God almighty, I don't believe this. I mean, Darrell? I'm all...everyone else is okay?"

"His wife wasn't home, and the little boy was asleep."

"Derry didn't see it happen, did he?"

"No, sir. He was asleep at the time. You talked with Penny?"

"No, ma'am. Well, I tried to, but me and her, well you know how it can be."

"Where are you now, Mr. Fisher?"

"I'm at home."

"I need to meet with you, sir. It takes forty-five minutes to drive from Regál to our office in Posadas." She turned and looked at the wall clock over the kitchen range. "It's ten thirty-five now. I'd like to meet with you at eleven-thirty, in my office. Is that possible for you?"

"Well, I…"

"Good. Eleven-thirty."

"Yes, ma'am." He didn't sound enthusiastic. "Is there something special I can tell you? I mean, my brother, he…" That's as far as he got before choking into silence.

"There are probably lots of things you can tell us. Lots of things that you can help us with. And we'll appreciate any help you can give us, Mr. Fisher. So eleven-thirty." Estelle hung up and looked at the wall calendar. Friday night, when he'd been arrested, Darrell Fisher said that he'd been in Regál, visiting his brother. Possible. And then Al had driven over to Texas bright and early Saturday morning for a pig hunt. A very brief pig hunt—home again by Saturday night. That was also possible.

She dialed Bob Torrez' number and the sheriff's robot picked up on the fourth ring. "You have reached Sheriff Robert Torrez. I can't come to the phone right now, but…" And the robot was chopped off at the knees. "Yup."

"Bobby, I'm going to be talking with Al Fisher here in an hour or so. I thought you might want to sit in on that."

Silence followed that for a moment. "What are you thinkin?"

"I don't know. But there are just too many dark spots in this picture."

"What time with Fisher?" Estelle could hear little voices in the background, and Gabe came close to his father's phone, jabbering nonstop.

"Eleven-thirty."

"I'll be there. Say goodbye, Gabe."

"Bye!" the five-year-old shouted.

"That's one of the dark spots, Bobby," Estelle said, and his grunt of agreement told her that he knew what she meant.

An hour and ten minutes later, Al Fisher walked into the Public Safety Building. He saw Estelle standing behind the dispatch island and tried to pull his shoulders back a little. Two years older than his brother, four inches shorter and thirty pounds heavier, Al looked as if he hadn't slept much in the past forty-eight hours.

"Couldn't help it," he said by way of greeting. "Dang truck wouldn't start. And Maria wanted to come, but I wouldn't let her."

Estelle shook hands. His grip was limp. "And why is that, Mr. Fisher?"

"Well, 'cause. This is a family deal, right?" He followed Estelle into her small office, and stopped short when he saw Sheriff Robert Torrez sitting relaxed in one of the three vinyl padded chairs, leaning it back until it rested on the plastered concrete blocks of the wall. The sheriff didn't get up, or offer his hand.

"Have a seat, Mr. Fisher," Estelle said. He slumped into the chair on the opposite side of the room from the sheriff. For a moment he couldn't find a spot to rest his hands, and finally crossed his arms over his chest, resting them on his comfortable belly. "I'm sorry your family is facing this tragedy," she added. Pushing a small tape recorder toward Al's side of the desk, she added, "We need to record this conversation. It's standard record-keeping."

Al ducked his head—the same defensive expression Darrell Fisher had relied upon to field insults from life. "My brother had his problems, see. That's what I wanted to talk to you about. I mean, it ain't an *excuse*, but I'm offering it up to you so maybe it'd make things a little easier to understand."

"We appreciate that. And I'm sure your brother appreciated your coming up with his bail so promptly after his hearing."

Al shook his head vehemently. "Ain't right. The judge was wrong on that one. Puttin' my brother in jail only makes things worse." He glanced sideways at Torrez. "Even I know that. I had to get him out. I told Penny she had to take the money before things got any worse. She didn't want to, 'cause she doesn't like me, but she needed it."

"Worse how?"

Al smiled crookedly, a sly expression that said that he understood more about the situation than anyone else. "I don't suppose you've spent much time in prison, have you?"

"No. And it's not a 'prison.' It's a modest little county lock-up."

"Yeah, well, just the same. I couldn't let him stay there. You know, when we was drinkin', sometimes—" and Al stopped and shut his eyes. "He talked about maybe doin' something crazy."

"You mean something crazy like suicide?"

Al nodded. "I'd try to tell him, 'Now look, Darrell, you got a good wife, and you got Derry. He's the best, you know what I mean?' Yeah, he and Penny fought like cats and dogs, but it didn't mean nothin'. I mean, that Penny—she could be a real witch when she wanted to be, you know? Damn bully is what she is." He tried to smile. "I mean, once she was goin' on and on and on about me and Darrell going on an elk hunt trip up into the Datil country. Just for a *day*, for God's sakes. No big deal. I know one of the guides up there. We even invited her along…her and Derry. And *that* set her off, I don't know why. And I got mad and said, 'Jeez, why are you such a bully?' and I thought sure as hell she was going to hit me. I mean, she don't like me much."

"And why do you think that was?"

He shook his head slowly. "I don't know. I mean, I *know* that she doesn't like Maria much, either. Couldn't tell you why, 'cause my girl is as sweet as they come. I don't know. Maybe she just don't like Mexicans, if you'll pardon me for sayin' so. But that Penny, she's got a mouth on her, you know? The way she goes on, you'd think that she don't like a single soul she's ever met 'cept Derry. She's as sweet with him…" He shook his head. "Go figure. Now I know for a fact that she don't mean half of what she says, but just the same, you know, Darrell would tell me that one of these days," and he made a swishing chop with one hand, "he'd be gone. He said he was just going to walk out on her…except for the boy, you know. He loved that kid like there was no tomorrow."

"Tell me about the handgun, Al."

"What handgun?" He looked genuinely quizzical.

She slid a photograph across to him, showing the big Ruger in its evidence bag. He flinched but looked hard at the photo. "Is that the one…?"

"We think so," Estelle nodded.

He leaned back in his chair abruptly. "Well, that's another fight they had. She didn't want that thing in the house. But I mean, what's the danger? Derry couldn't even pick it up, even if he did find where Darrell kept it."

"So you knew about it."

"Well, sure. Darrell, he loaned it to me a couple times to take pig hunting. That brushy river country over north of Tahoka? And once…" he stopped abruptly and ducked his head again, staring at the floor. "Once, he asked me to keep it for him for a while. He was feelin' kind of down, you know what I mean? That scared the crap out of me. So I had it for two, three weeks. Until he said things were okay." He shook his head slowly. "Should never have gave it back."

"How long ago was this?"

"Oh, last year sometime."

"You two hunted a lot together?"

"Some. Not as much as I'd like."

"Was the forty-four the only gun Darrell owned?"

He nodded quickly. "Far as I know. He'd borrow something from me if he needed it for a hunt. I got this old Winchester that he likes to use." He dabbed at his left eye. "If I'd known he was serious—I mean if I'd known he was going to blow his brains out—I never would have given that gun back to him."

"But you didn't borrow the gun for this most recent pig hunt that you went on Saturday…yesterday?"

"No, ma'am. He offered it, but I'm not all that good with it, if you want the truth."

The room fell silent for a moment. "So, Mr. Fisher, tell me what it was that you wanted to talk to me about…that you thought I should know."

"Look…"He struggled to find the words. "I *knew* my brother was havin' thoughts about…about maybe doin' something stupid. Maybe something that he thought would hurt Penny a good one. He'd have these moods, what do you call 'em? *Black* moods that he had a hard time climbing out of. But he'd been that way since he was a kid. But I never thought that he'd…" Al stopped and cocked a finger against his own skull. "And I know it don't sound good, but I blame Penny. She sure as hell pushed him to it. That's what I think."

Estelle took a deep breath and turned toward Torrez. "Sheriff Torrez, do you have any questions for Mr. Fisher?"

"Nope."

She nudged the business card that Fisher earlier had ignored. "Mr. Fisher, did your brother come down to your place in Regál on Friday night?"

"Yes, ma'am. He did."

"What time did he arrive?"

Al Fisher's forehead puckered. "I'm thinkin' right around four or five o'clock. Maybe a little later."

"He had Derry with him?"

"Yes, ma'am. Maria, she was lookin' forward to spending some playtime with that little bugger. She thinks a lot of that boy."

"And what did you and your brother do during that time?"

"Well, for one thing, I was tryin' to talk him into going

hunting with me. Just a quick run over into that brush country. I mean, you should see some of them hogs, Sheriff. Buddy of mine nailed one last month that went seven hundred pounds. *That*, my friends, is a lot of ham and bacon."

"But he didn't want to go?"

"Wasn't a question of not *wanting* to. He and Penny had just had a fight, I guess. Darrell wants...wanted...a new truck, one with four doors and a backseat. Penny said no way, José. No way they could afford that kind of money."

"Talking about a pig hunt kept you busy all evening?"

"Well, not just that. He was helpin' me out in the greenhouse."

Sheriff Torrez made a gentle scoffing sound but said nothing. Estelle knew what the sheriff was most likely thinking—greenhouses and the agricultural crops frequently grown in them. Darrell Fisher's clothing and the atmosphere in his truck had smelled of marijuana—and he certainly didn't grow it at his small lot on Larson.

"No, he was," Al persisted. "I got this new little pump, and he was helping me get it all hooked up. He's really good with stuff like that."

"What time did he leave that night?"

"Well, dang." He frowned. "It was late, I know that. And the weather was going all to hell. I know *that*. I guess they took off sometime around eleven. A little later, maybe. I told him that he needed to clear the Pass before it got any worse."

Estelle leafed through several pages of her small notebook. "Derry was asleep when they left?"

"Nah. He was fussing some. Kinda cranky. He napped some earlier, but by then, it was past his bedtime, you know? Then Maria had him all wadded up in a heavy quilt...couldn't even tell he was in there, just about."

"Hard to put him in the child seat that way."

"Darrell won't use one. He claims to know a kid got burned up in one. Car lit up, and they couldn't get him loose in time."

Al shook his head vehemently. "Just more of Darrell's bullshit. I mean, I know who *he* knows, and I haven't ever heard of something like that. But he won't use one. Just lazy, is what it is."

"They had a bike along with them. One of those little ones without pedals? Why was that?"

Al laughed. "You try and separate that little Derry from his Scamper bike, and you'll see a tantrum, for sure. If they'd let him sleep with it, he would. I got this path through the orchard that Derry likes to ride. Not with snow on it, he don't. And jeez, not at night, you know? Just easier to throw it in the back of the truck than argue about it, I guess." He shook his head in amusement. "Some kids got their teddy bear, some got their baba. Derry, he's got his Scamper bike. Go figure."

"Mr. Fisher, thanks for coming in." She picked up the business card that he had so studiously ignored and handed it to him. "If you think of anything else we should know, I encourage you to call. Twenty-four, seven." He accepted the card without looking at it and slid it into his shirt pocket. "Thanks for taking the time, Mr. Fisher."

He hesitated. "We're going to miss that guy."

"Of course. I'm truly sorry."

"I mean, really. Penny don't know it, maybe, but his passing leaves a big hole in our family."

"I think she knows that, Mr. Fisher."

He rose quickly, as if the chair had suddenly become uncomfortable. "I just thought I should, you know? Come in and tell you the way it was."

Estelle shook his hand once more and watched him hustle out of the room.

"What think you?" she asked Torrez.

The big man stretched and rubbed his face, not a picture of deep sympathy. "I don't think his brother shot himself in the head, for one thing. And I was just wondering…"

"About the bail money?"

"Yep."

"Maybe he figured out in advance that his brother was going to need it," Estelle said. "Maybe he gave Penny a down payment on bail early Saturday sometime, before he left for Texas."

Torrez looked at her skeptically.

"That's okay, Bobby. I don't believe it happened that way either."

Chapter Thirteen

Darrell Fisher's sheeted corpse lay on the polished stainless steel table, and Dr. Alan Perrone was busy typing on a laptop when Estelle arrived. Sheriff Torrez looked huge and silly in the surgical gown, waiting not so patiently as Linda Pasquale secured the gown's ties behind his back.

"I'm using square knots," Linda quipped. "We don't want this coming loose."

"You are so helpful," Torrez said.

"Here's the thing," Perrone said as he rose from his desk. He greeted Estelle with a nod, his otherwise smooth face lined with concern. He turned the laptop so it faced them. Six images were crowded on the screen.

"These were taken after various incidents over the years, from various jurisdictions, and only one of them was a suicide. In each one of these, you can clearly see the imprint of the firearm's muzzle where contact was made with the body as the shot was fired. It's like an instant, violent tattoo as the hot gasses escape the muzzle of the gun immediately behind the bullet." His index moved across the screen. "Two temple shots, a forehead, one under the chin, and two chest wounds. In each case, the imprint is a contact one, and the impression is so clear that a match-up, a comparison, can be made with the weapon used."

He stepped away from the computer and pulled the sheet

down to the waist to reveal Fisher's pathetic, pale corpse. Estelle was startled at how thin, almost wasted, the victim appeared. "Deflated" was a term Bill Gastner used to use, and it certainly fit. Without the vitality of blood pumping through the muscles, the tissues lay flat and featureless against the bones.

"Between you, me, and the lamppost, I can't think of a single reason why we would take up a Sunday to.conduct an autopsy for a suicide victim." He rested a gloved hand on the corpse's left shoulder as if they were the best of buddies. "But I would be willing to bet that Darrell Fisher did *not* commit suicide."

"This," and he turned to the counter behind him, "is the Ruger Redhawk revolver found at the scene. "I'm sure the fingerprints on it, or lack thereof, could tell an interesting story all by themselves. But what interests me are the two wounds left behind by the front sight." He smoothed the plastic of the evidence bag so the muzzle of the revolver was clearly visible. With his pen, he touched the front sight through the plastic.

"Notice the serrated front sight ramp, with a red plastic insert. The sight base itself is set back a couple of millimeters from the revolver's muzzle, and the actual *blade* of the sight is dovetailed into the base. But the blade is set back even farther." He looked at each of the three spectators in turn. "Keep the image of this front sight in mind, the way it actually sits back a considerable distance from the muzzle. Sergeant Mears is working up the print profiles from the gun, and he doesn't miss a thing. So." He stood looking down at Darrell Fisher's corpse.

"The first of the two obvious wounds is a contact entry wound centered right below the xyphoid process, right on the very distal tip of the sternum. He was wearing a T-shirt, and you can see…" He walked over to a whiteboard on which was clipped the bloodied, scorched clothing. "A corona of burned and unburned powder, blowback flesh and blood, charred cotton fibers. Lots to compare there."

He returned to the table, bent down, and again used his pen

as a pointer. "You can clearly see the scorched imprint of the revolver's barrel around the wound. But what I find interesting is the imprint of that prominent front sight blade. Remember, that blade sits back from the muzzle. So we're talking a scenario where the gun is *rammed* into the victim's body, high in the solar plexus, immediately below the xyphoid. Not just held, not just touching. *Rammed.* So hard that the sight blade actually *cut* the skin through the thin cloth of the T-shirt." He looked up. "Linda, you'll want to pay special attention to that when you photo document."

"It'd be good to hold the revolver barrel right beside the wound. Then the match-up will be obvious," she replied.

"Absolutely right." Offering a large hand lens to Estelle, Perrone narrated the injury's characteristics as she peered closely. "Notice that the front sight blade…the very top of it, the tip… is actually a considerable distance, in the neighborhood of a centimeter, above the outside curvature of the barrel's muzzle. The bruising and laceration at that point is caused by the sight blade, not by damage as the bullet passes through, and not by blowback of gasses." He waited while Estelle offered the lens to Torrez, but he waved it off impatiently.

"You going to be able to get that?" the sheriff asked.

"Absolutely," Linda said.

"All set?" Perrone said when they were finished with the hand lens. "The exit wound," and with Torrez' help rolled the corpse on its side, "is directly through the body of the third thoracic vertebra. The projectile, already expanding, would have simply exploded the body of the vertebra. The alignment of the two wounds, entry and exit, suggest to me that the victim was bent over slightly at the time." He relaxed the body back on its back. "If you think about it, that would be expected if something—in this case, the gun—had been rammed into his midsection. I'll know more after we do a detailed examination when we open him up. But that's what I'm betting right now, a preliminary for you to go on. The wound trajectory has to be upward through the chest cavity, unless we find surprises inside."

The physician turned the corpse's head to one side, and lifted the jaw. With his index finger, he traced a deeply bruised scratch that began beside the middle of the Adam's apple and extended upward to the base of the jaw below the right ear. "This wound interests me. A nasty gouge. The skin is broken where whatever the object was raked along his jawline." He traced the bruised wound with his fingertip.

"That would have hurt like hell," Perrone added. "And what's the natural reaction? Say someone took something hard and fairly sharp and rammed it toward your throat."

"Like a gun barrel," Torrez muttered. "The front sight blade rammed into his jaw."

"I can't imagine a suicide doing that," Estelle said. "Pull the barrel in close, maybe. Even likely. Hug it there while he works up the courage to pull the trigger. But this looks like someone rammed him in the throat with something. I think Bobby's right. That something was most likely the gun."

The physician nodded and continued. "And if that happens, what's next? The victim's hands come up in defense. It's natural. He wants to push it away. But then what? The gun is yanked back out of his grip and rammed a second time into the center mass of the body, unprotected for a brief second because the victim's hands might still be raised."

"Alan, did you tell Sergeant Mears all this?"

The physician nodded. "He's going to be particularly interested in any fingerprints he found facing backward on that gun." He regarded the body. "No other defensive injuries. Lots of powder residue on the hands, including," and he lifted the bagged right hand, "serious scorch marks on the palm of the right hand."

"Could have tried to grab the gun around its cylinder," Torrez said. "All revolvers have some blow-by between the cylinder and the barrel, some more'n others."

"That I leave to you to work with," Perrone said. "Last night we made some guesses about the bullet's path. After passing through the victim, it burst through the upper portion of the seat and lodged in the rim of the rear window's lower frame. It seems to me that's consistent with the angle up through the body. And the damage to the seat and then the window, off to the driver's left a bit, implies to me that he was turned slightly to the right. To *his* right."

The room fell silent, and all four of them regarded the remains of Darrell Fisher. "He *could* have gotten his act together," Estelle said after a moment. "Such a waste."

Never one to spend much time with sentiment, Torrez said, "So when he goes out to the truck, who'd he go out to see? He walks out, climbs in the driver's seat like maybe he's going to go somewhere. And then?"

"And he does that carrying that big revolver," Estelle said. "Why would he do that? What's the perceived threat? Or the alternative—he wasn't meeting with anyone. He takes the gun out to his truck and just sits there for a while, thinking things through."

"I see the rake across his neck sayin' otherwise," Torrez said.

"A defensive wound, rather than a wound of hesitation," Estelle added.

"If Darrell was having an argument with somebody, and if Derry slept right through everything, it wasn't much of a shouting match," Linda said. She turned on the preview window and handed the camera to Estelle so the undersheriff could scroll through the pictures. "Anything else you need before I bundle back home?"

Estelle took her time as the slide show slid by on the camera's little viewing screen. Even the displayed T-shirt with the prominent, burned and bloodied hole in the center was featured in ten photos from five angles, front and back. "And the truck will be secured in the county impound, so we can go back to it if we need to."

"Toxicology will take a little longer," Perrone offered. "But I can tell you that the preliminary blood alcohol came in at zero-seven. He'd had a few. And a moderate level of both marijuana and tobacco aroma on his clothes."

"What are you plannin' to do?" Sheriff Torrez asked Estelle.

"I want to talk with Maria Apodaca."

"What's she going to know?"

"For one thing, Bobby, it's hard to imagine her being all that happy about those two blockheads being out half the night with a two-year-old in tow. She would have been after Darrell to take the boy home, especially with the weather threatening."

"Yep." Torrez nodded. "Take somebody with ya."

"I don't think—"

"Just do it," the sheriff interrupted. Estelle looked at him in surprise. Bobby Torrez so rarely fell back into command mode, especially with her, that on those rare occasions when he did, she knew that something was on his mind. In due time, he might tell her.

Chapter Fourteen

Where the sun could reach, no trace of the winter scud remained. New Mexico 56 was clear and dry, the sunshine turning roadside grasses into swaths of gold. Each runty piñon or juniper shaded its own little shrinking souvenir patch of snow.

Lieutenant Jackie Taber kept the Expedition cruising at a lazy fifty-five as they started the long, winding route up the north side of the San Cristóbals. She drove with her left hand locked on the wheel at twelve o'clock, right elbow propped on the lid of the center console, right hand free to manage radio, computer, or phone.

"You doing okay?" Taber looked across at Estelle, who had been shifting uncomfortably in the seat, trying for a position that didn't aggravate the ache in her right side.

"Hard seats," she replied. "When you talked with Penny, what did she have to say about Al Fisher and his girlfriend?"

Taber slowed for the first tight switchback. "A little jealousy there, I think. I got the impression that she doesn't much care for Maria Apodaca. Penny thinks that Darrell spent too much time down there, 'playing with his brother.' Either too much brotherly love, or too much enjoying the company of the girl-friend. Take your pick."

She made a philosophical grimace. "Sometimes it works, sometimes it's a nightmare—husband and wife working at opposite ends of the day, a little kid caught in the middle. Day care takes a big bite out of their budget." She shrugged. "And Penny doesn't strike me as the sort of person who handles even a little bit of friction very well. She doesn't think before she engages the mouth—at least not where her husband was concerned. And who knows? Maybe he *liked* being bullied."

They rode in silence for a moment. "Both husband and wife have entry-level jobs," Taber mused. "Not a lot of income there. And now along with everything else, add a high energy young-ster to the mix. Where were they going to come up with five hundred in cash to bail hubby out of the clink after his stupid mistake? So older brother pays the bail, and dollars to donuts says *that* created even more friction. Penny doesn't like feeling beholden to her brother-in-law and, being the motor-mouth that she is, makes sure that hubby feels even worse about being such a worthless loser."

Ahead of them, the highway sign announced Regál Pass, elevation 8,817 feet. Even here, mere traces of snow reached out from patches of shade. The storm had been more bluster than production. Below them, woodsmoke blanketed the village, an inversion holding the smudge close to the ground. From just beyond the pass, the highway jogged around a towering limestone buttress, and from that vantage point, Estelle could see the tiny Mexican village of Tres Santos, six miles south, along the ser-pentine, tree-lined avenue of the sometimes stream, the grandly named Rio Plegado…a *rio* only a couple of weeks each year.

Late afternoon sun cast hard, long shadows, and the border fence's barbed wire winked. Estelle could remember when the fence had first been just four strands of wire, more just a demar-cation than a prohibitive boundary. Her late Great-uncle Reuben had told her about the days when there had been no wire at all at the crossing. Now the port of entry, a squat featureless block structure, squatted on the border just yards beyond the adobe church. The Mexican counterpart, tan adobe with bright blue trim and a host of Mexican flags, guarded the two-lane dirt road that ran toward Tres Santos and then Janos, twenty-five miles farther south.

The latest census had revealed that thirty-seven people still populated Regál. Estelle knew that living there required a certain stubborn streak of patience, since the village had changed little in the past hundred years...maybe even less than the undersheriff's birthplace across the border, tiny Tres Santos.

In Regál, there was no gas station, no bank, no convenience store, no school. Just the obligatory church, the whitewashed Iglesia de Nuestra Señora that was more a simple chapel, or *capilla*, than a full service church. The nearest grocery shopping was down south in Janos, with all the complications the officious border crossing forced on folks. Or thirty-eight miles northeast, in Posadas. The nearest clinics were Francis Guzman's clinic in Posadas, and his partner's satellite clinic in Janos.

Most of the time, the distance and the seclusion didn't matter to the residents of Regál—most of them, most of the time, saw their isolation from the crazy modern world as a blessing to be treasured. A few had embraced satellite-bounced internet, and the UPS driver was on a first-name basis with all of the internet shoppers.

When there were enough participants to warrant more than a front porch gathering, the Iglesia de Nuestera Señora was the community epicenter for bake, produce, yard, and rummage sales, with its generous graveled parking lot right along the well-traveled highway.

The border fence, ugly chain-link with a roll of razor wire on top, passed within a hundred fifty yards of Maria Apodaca's family compound, situated on the western border of Regál just below the first jumble of rocks skirting the base of the San Cristóbal foothills. "Compound" was the operative word. Solomon Apodaca, Maria's father, was an artist with cement, and over the years his perimeter wall, five feet high and gaudily decorated with a veritable museum of artifacts, had grown to enclose almost an acre of lush gardens where he, his wife, Isabel, and daughter, Maria, nurtured the growth of enough food to feed an army. The wall that Solomon had built kept deer out of the corn, beans, and squash, and was the subject of continuing border wall jokes among the village residents.

Solomon's passion grew along the inside perimeter of the garden wall, where with its artistic serpentine form, any combination of sun and shade was possible. His collection of cabernet sauvignon wine grape varieties, now at twenty-one specimen vines and counting, was a vintner's delight—cabernet sauvignon petite, lafite, petite Bouschet, vidure, Breton, noir...on and on they went, and Solomon Apodaca delighted in the role of tour guide.

The Apodaca grapes grew abundantly with his constant nurturing, producing sufficient crops to make small batches of the dark, fragrant, and mostly undrinkable wines that only Solomon loved.

The solid wooden gate, intricately carved and festooned with winter-dead squash vines, yawned open. Solomon Apodaca stood with one hand on the heavy wooden latch as if he'd been carved there. Short and burly, he favored suspenders rather than a belt to hold up his jeans, and his white shirt was bright enough to be hard on the eyes.

He pushed back his black baseball cap and stepped close to the Expedition as Taber eased it to a stop.

"I saw you coming down the hill," he said. "I figured you'd be coming this way." His voice was a gruff baritone, raspy from too much unfiltered pipe smoke. He leaned down and peered across at Estelle. "Good to see you again, Señora Guzman. We don't see so much of you since Reuben is passed."

"It's my loss, Señor Apodaca."

"Life has a way of intruding," Apodaca said. "And who's this?" He touched Jackie Taber's shoulder.

"Solomon, meet Lieutenant Jackie Taber. She's been with us for nine years now."

Solomon looked puzzled. "Nine? And all that time…" He shook his head sadly as he shook Jackie's hand. "But listen. I know you have work to do."

"We need to speak with Maria," Estelle said.

"I'm pretty sure she's home. She and that boyfriend of hers, they bought the old Chavez place across the way." He ducked his head at Estelle. "You know the one. It's that place built right into the rocks, just across the way."

"I knew they were living there. I didn't know that they had purchased it."

"Just this fall, they did that. You know how kids are these days. They want a place of their own." He made a face. "I keep telling Maria that she should make herself an honest woman and marry that kid, but these days? And why *that* place, I don't know. They're so close to the rocks, there's no good ground for a garden or anything." His weathered face brightened. "Maybe they can raise goats or something."

His face wrinkled, and he gazed off into the distance toward Mexico. "A terrible thing about the boy's brother. I just heard that from Maria today." He shook his head slowly, and then looked down at Estelle. "It's a sad thing when a young man decides that's the only way out, you know."

"Yes, it is."

Solomon nodded judiciously. "It runs in families, you know. That's what I've heard." He held up an index finger. "But you should have a glass of wine before you go. The noir was abundant this year, and sugared early. My wife says it's the only wine I've ever made that's drinkable. How about that?" He grinned. "But if they don't like it, it's more for me, you know."

"We're going to have to take a rain check, Solomon."

"Take a bottle with you and share it with your husband the doctor. He'll agree with me."

"Next time, maybe." Jackie Taber let the car drift forward a little, and Solomon Apodaca stepped back.

"You two come back soon, and you'll see. The noir is spec-TAC-u-lar this year." He beamed a smile of colorfully stained enamel, and slapped the window sill near Jackie Taber's shoulder. He waved toward the village. "Maria is home now, I think."

"Thank you, Señor."

"Just across the way" was actually nearly two hundred yards, past Madrid Alonzo's mobile home and hound dog runs, and coming up on the spreading junk yard that hid Lupe Gabaldon's ancient adobe. The "old Chavez place," now home to Al Fisher and Maria Apodaca, was a tidy little adobe which, like several other homes in Regál, had incorporated some of the bus-sized boulders that gravity had sprung loose from the mountain behind the village. Convinced that his boulder of choice would roll no further, old man Chavez had used it as the back wall of the house, extending outward with adobe blocks.

The house had stood empty for half a dozen years after Aaron Chavez missed a corner up on Regál pass, he and his wife taking flight in their aging Oldsmobile. By the time Al Fisher had acquired the place from a uninterested daughter who'd long since found life to her liking in Tucson, the adobe cottage was home to packrats, banner-tailed kangaroo rats, lizards, jackrabbits, and at least one gigantic bull snake who enforced peace and quiet among the inhabitants.

Jackie Taber maneuvered the Expedition through the ramshackle stockade fence and stopped behind Fisher's diesel Ram pickup. A large, white plastic water tank dominated the truck's bed, a few gallons still visible inside it. The upper fill line indicated a three-hundred-gallon capacity.

"A pint's a pound. A lot of weight when that thing's filled," Taber observed.

Somewhere deep in the house, a small dog yapped and as the two officers stepped through the open yard gate, Maria Apodaca appeared in the front door, deftly keeping the little dog inside with one foot.

"Hi!" she greeted with a broad and beautiful smile. Estelle knew that Maria had certainly seen her thirtieth birthday, but had the undersheriff not known, sixteen or seventeen would have been a good guess. "Al is somewhere up the hill," she said, and then looked deeply sympathetic. "Losing his brother has been hard for him. *Really* hard. It would be for anybody, huh? I mean, it just makes me sick."

She smoothed an errant shock of black hair away from her thin face. Taken singly, Maria Apodaca's features wouldn't have won any beauty contests. Her eyes were set too closely together, separated by a proud aquiline prow of a nose. One eye drifted slightly to the left when she looked straight ahead. Her mouth, with full lips that curved in a delightful S-shape, one end up, one down when she smiled, housed a full compliment of teeth, none of them particularly straight, but all of them Hollywood white.

Slender with perfect posture, shoulders so square that a drill sergeant would have coveted them, and just enough body curves to no doubt set young Al Fisher's heart pounding, Maria Apodaca combined fetching looks with a honeyed voice. She beckoned them toward the door. "Did you want me to jog up the hill and find Al for you?"

"No, thanks. Actually, we came to talk with you, Maria."

"Oh." She looked uncertain. "Well, come inside out of the sun. I saw your car over at Dad's. He didn't try to poison you with his wine, did he?"

"He did," Estelle laughed. "We resisted."

"On the other hand," Maria said, "I have some wonderful iced tea. How about that?"

"Perfect." They followed her into the cool home, and the tiny dog, a cross between a Chihuahua and something much smaller—a chipmunk, perhaps—decided not to bark, since she had nowhere to hide. She settled for her doggie bed in the kitchen, guarding a handful of doggie biscuits.

The tiny house had only one partition, serving to offer some bathroom privacy. All the rest of the area, including living room, dining room, and bedroom, were an open commons. A queen-sized bed was charming with a vintage quilt, and snugged against the nearest wall was an antique rolltop desk that was open to reveal a laptop computer. Cables led to a printer on its own tiny table beside the desk.

A large wood stove dominated one wall that appeared to be continuous, solid boulder, and Estelle could feel the gentle heat that radiated from the cast-iron stove. To one side of the outside door, a modest Christmas tree had been decorated on the wall farthest from the stove. The overall effect of the home was one of cozy intimacy.

In a moment, Maria brought them each a glass of dark iced tea, with a sprig of wild mint on the edge. She didn't offer sugar or other additives. "Are you warm enough? We let the fire go out because it gets *so* warm in here, *so* fast. It has to be just about a blizzard outside for us to keep the stove going all day. For a little while yesterday, we thought we were going to catch it. But the storm pooped out."

"That's a beautiful set-up," Jackie Taber said. She ran a hand across the boulder's surface near the stove. She turned and smiled at Estelle. "Still warm and cozy."

"I think Mr. Chavez built the house around that rock."

"Good thing he didn't have to move it far." Taber held a hand close to the stove, then tapped the cast iron. "Holds heat a long time."

"Maria, we need to talk with you about Friday," Estelle said. "Friday night, in particular, when Darrell Fisher visited here."

"Yes, ma'am." Maria set her own glass down carefully, and then she turned to face Estelle expectantly, settling onto a straight-backed chair near the bed.

"About what time was that?"

"He came right about five-thirty. It was already dark, especially with the snow coming. He came just in time for dinner." She smiled self-consciously. "That's sort of a family joke. We say that Darrell can smell my Mexican food from thirty miles away."

"Who was with him, if anyone?"

"He had little Derry with him. See, Penny works nights at the hospital, and they can't afford a sitter all the time. So, wherever Darrell goes when he's not tied up with work, so goes Derry." She smiled. "He's a doll, isn't he?" She twisted and pointed at a two-cushion love seat not far from the stove. "He played for a little with White Fang, and then they both curled up there to snooze. I mean," and she grimaced, "it got kinda late."

"White Fang is…"

"The dog." She nodded in the tiny creature's direction. "She's afraid of everything and everyone, except Derry, I think."

"What time did they leave?"

"Oh, gosh. It was right around midnight, maybe a little before. Maybe around eleven-thirty. Derry woke up, kinda cranky like little kids get. You know. I was a little short with the boys for not paying attention. I mean, Darrell still had to drive back to town, and the weather wasn't all that great."

"Did you see Darrell at any time after that? After he and Derry finally left?"

"No." Maria sighed. "Al got up early on Saturday—I don't know how he does it after being up half the night. Anyway, he said that he was going pig hunting over in Texas. He's got a favorite spot just over the border, in the breaks along the Red River. See, he wanted Darrell to go, too, but Darrell said he couldn't."

"That's why Darrell came over Friday night? To tell his brother that he couldn't go along?"

She nodded quickly. "Pretty much. He brought over some gun that Al wanted to borrow for the hunt." She looked pained, then her expressive face cycled through a number of expressions before settling on resigned sympathy. "I think it's so sad when someone gets to a point where nothing is worth living for. I mean to leave that little boy…"

Boot falls on the wooden porch interrupted her. The door opened and Al Fisher stepped inside. He closed the door carefully, not releasing the latch, as if unsure whether to stay or leave.

As she had been during Al's visit to the Sheriff's Office, Estelle was struck by the family resemblance, even though Al was several inches shorter than his brother, with a well-padded, stocky build. A baseball cap was crammed down on his skull, with his longish brown hair pulled back into a careless ponytail.

"Saw your rig." He released the door latch and stepped across to Estelle, who stood and extended her hand. His hand was rough, his grip perfunctory. "Mr. Fisher, this is Lieutenant Jackie Taber."

"Hi." He didn't offer his hand.

"Mr. Fisher, there are one or two things we'd like to ask if you have a few minutes." *Or even if you don't.* "Things we didn't cover when you stopped by the office earlier."

Maria rose quickly and lifted her jacket off a peg by the door. "I have some things to check in the greenhouse. I'll do that so you have some privacy." As she passed Al, she stroked a hand affectionately down his left arm. At the door, she hesitated and looked back at Estelle. "Do you have anything else for me?"

"Not at the moment. Thank you, Maria."

"So." Al stepped closer to the wood stove, opened the door and peered inside. Apparently satisfied, he clanged the door closed and straightened up.

"First of all, I appreciate your contacting us, Mr. Fisher."

"That's okay. And it's Al. Call me Al."

"There are some questions remaining concerning the handgun that your brother apparently used to take his life."

The young man grimaced as he turned and sat down heavily on the love seat near the Christmas tree. He shook his head slowly, the oscillation continuing as he said, "I don't know why he felt he needed to do that." He looked up first at Estelle, then Jackie Taber. "I've been thinkin' and thinkin' about that all day, and

I can't come up with a thing. I mean, why wouldn't he want to watch Derry grow up? There's got to be joy in that, doesn't there?"

"It's hard for us to judge what he was going through," Estelle replied. "When Darrell came down here Friday night…he brought the handgun with him?"

Fisher hesitated. "Yeah. He did."

Estelle regarded the man for a long moment. "Earlier, when you came down to the office, you told me that you *didn't* take the gun on the hunt."

The young man leaned forward, both hands holding his forehead as if he expected his skull to pop. "Look, he *did* bring that gun down with him. And, yeah, I had it in the truck with me Saturday goin' over to the hunt. But I never used it. It just stayed in the truck, in one of those zip-up cases. And then I dropped it off at his house when I got home."

"What time was that?"

"Oh, Christ, I don't know. Maybe five o'clock. It was just startin' to get dark."

"And then you left his house to come home?"

Fisher nodded. "Weather wasn't all that great."

"Did you get a pig?"

The question took him by surprise, and his face brightened. "Yeah, I got one. I couldn't believe it. I parked the truck, and I *heard* 'em over in the brush. I walked like fifty paces, and there he was."

"So," and Estelle paused, her gaze roaming the vast surface of the Fishers' living room boulder. "That's quite a drive, no?"

"I guess I make it in three hours or a little more. Just shoot over to Artesia and Hobbs, and then cut off north a ways."

Lieutenant Taber smiled, almost good-naturedly. "You broke a few speed limits to make *that* drive in a little more than three hours."

Al Fisher looked surprised, and then cunning. "Well," he said, "maybe once or twice."

"You left here pretty early, then. Saturday morning, I mean."

"*Way* early."

"How did you hear about your brother's troubles the previous night?"

"Penny called me on my cell on Saturday and told me what happened. What the judge had said, and about bail and everything. I couldn't get a word in edgewise, she was so hoppin' mad. Anyways, I called Maria right away, and told her to run a check up to Posadas for Darrell's bail."

"Darrell didn't call you, then. He spent the night before his hearing with Judge Tate in jail, but he didn't call you?"

"No, ma'am."

"But sometime later—when you were on the road bound for a pig hunt—Penny was able to reach you."

"That's how it was."

"And with all this trouble at home, you continued on with the hunt?"

"By the time she called me, I was already in Texas." He shrugged. "And I mean, what else could I do?"

"What time was that?"

"What time was what?"

"When Penny was able to reach you. When the two of you discussed the bail issue."

"Right around eleven or so. Maybe a little later."

"Eleven our time, or Texas time?"

Al laughed good-naturedly. "What is this, the Spanish Inquisition?"

"A cop's habit," Lieutenant Taber said pleasantly. "How much did the pig weigh?"

"The pig…"

"Your hunting trophy."

"Oh, how much did he *weigh*?" He frowned and closed one eye, figuring. "Right at five-hundred-twenty."

"Wow."

"Well, yeah, but there's hogs rippin' up that country that weigh a whole lot more'n that. We're not talkin' those little javelinas here."

"So what do you do with a quarter ton of pig carcass?" Taber had been jotting notes, but now folded up her notebook and slid it in her pocket, as if her questions were just chit-chat.

"It goes to a game locker. I got a guy that butchers and wraps for me. Even with payin' for that, it's still a good deal."

"I would think so," Jackie said. "Which processor do you use?"

"Phil Lockley, up in Glenwood. Well, just south of Glenwood. Like down in Pleasanton. Do you hunt?" Estelle said nothing, but pictured the route to Glenwood—a north-south highway connecting Silver City and Reserve, with Glenwood in between. Other than a few rough roads up into the Mogollon Mountains, there were no east-west roads until NM 12 left Reserve and curved northeast to Datil. Al Fisher had been smoking asphalt.

"I've been known to try for elk," Jackie Taber said. "When I'm lucky enough to draw the license."

"I hear you there. I've been tryin' to draw for a bull elk tag for years, man. No luck yet."

"It'll come when you least expect it," the lieutenant said. "Just about the time you have a dozen other things to do, even in a tiny town like Regál. You used to work for the gas company, didn't you?"

"Used to. I'm on my own now." He smiled, obviously proud of himself. "A world of opportunity on e-Bay, Lieutenant."

"Al, do you know Connie Suarez?" Estelle's question clearly caught Al Fisher by surprise.

"Connie…"

"Suarez. She lives over behind Lupe Gabaldon's place, just where you pull off north of the church, Betty Contreras' road."

"Well, sure. Everybody in Regál knows everybody else." He grinned. "If you ever forget what you're doin', just ask anybody. They'll tell you."

"Strangers stand out, don't they?" Jackie interjected.

"Oh, yeah." Al nodded vehemently.

"Then you probably know Myron Fitzwater."

Fisher frowned. "Is that the guy who hangs with Connie? That the one?"

"That's the one."

"Then I don't know him." Fisher waved his hands as he mentally backpedaled. "I mean, I know who he *is*. I've seen him a time or two. But I don't know him. I think he works over in Arizona most of the time. That's what I've heard, anyways. Connie works at the school, otherwise she's home. Like now, I mean, with Christmas vacation and all. You can ask her."

Lieutenant Jackie Taber had stepped close to a huge windowsill trellis that was dotted with cherry tomatoes. "I can't grow these to save my life." She stroked the underside of one of the leaf clusters. "What's your secret?"

"TLC from Maria, mostly," Fisher replied. "She does really, really well. Both of her thumbs are green."

"I'd like to tour your greenhouse sometime."

Fisher laughed, then settled into the cunning, squinty-eyed expression that Estelle had already decided she didn't like very much. "Well, you want to tour as a cop, or a gardener?" he asked.

"Oh? It makes a difference?"

"Yeah. One you need a warrant for, the other you don't."

"Ah," Jackie said, nodding. "I understand." She touched one of the little ripe tomatoes with an index finger. "May I?"

"'Course you can. Help yourself."

She plucked the tiny fruit and rolled it around the palm of her hand as if she'd never actually seen a cherry tomato before, then popped it into her mouth, chewing thoughtfully. "Oh, wow."

"Three or four of us get together with a produce sale over at the church on Saturdays. Maria is always there. Rotten as the weather's been, she was even there for a little while yesterday. It's a good deal. I mean, nothing like we have in the summer, when all the fruit comes in, but there's enough greenhouse produce to make it worthwhile. You should stop by next week. We start at nine in the morning."

"Except when you're pig hunting." Taber smiled. "But I'll do that. Thanks for the tip."

"Interesting," Estelle said a few minutes later as they climbed back into the Expedition. "For a guy who just lost his only brother, Al Fisher seems pretty upbeat."

"Operating with a magical clock will do that for you," Taber said.

"A magical clock…"

"Leave before dawn and drive all the way over into the Texas boonies, jump out of his truck, shoot the hog that's conveniently standing right there waiting for his turn to be slaughtered, then drive all the way back to Glenwood to drop off the carcass for butchering? Come on. And who helped him do all of this? A five-hundred-pound hog, for cryin' out loud. How'd he even get the carcass into the back of his truck, even if it was field-dressed? And still be home in time to return his brother's gun? Why would he do that, anyway? He could have returned it any old time."

All the while she was talking, Jackie Taber was thumbing her phone. "No Phil Lockley listed for Glenwood. There's Custom Meat Processing a little south of there, in Buckhorn. Maybe our man Phil works there." She glanced sideways at Estelle. "Or not."

"Al Fisher impresses me as the sort of guy who once he starts spinning a story, just keeps spinning away, getting more and more creative as he goes. He likes to hear himself talk. Is a phone contact given for the processor in Buckhorn?"

"There is. Two strikes against us, though. It's Sunday, and nobody is apt to be working. And cell service down here is rotten. We need a landline. Or give dispatch something to do."

"And while we're down here, I want to take a few minutes and talk with Connie Suarez."

"About?"

"About nothing in particular. Just to touch bases with her. See what she's heard from her boyfriend. He's gone missing, and I'm curious about that. If he doesn't show up soon, she's going to be hosting visitors from the Feds. When one of their own goes missing, they won't just sit on it. They'll expect all the cooperation we can give them. I'd like to be up to speed. She can tell us when she saw her boyfriend last." They thumped along the rough two-track, skirting an apple orchard and a collapsed adobe barn. "You know where Connie lives? That trailer just across the road from Lupe Gabaldon's place?"

"I do."

"Let's see if Al Fisher is right. Let's see what Connie has heard…see how the Regál grapevine works."

The Suarez mobile home, one of those creations that designers thought fashionable in the sixties with its silly tack-on fins and garish tri-color paint job, was sandwiched into a small site dominated by winter-naked dwarf fruit trees, a small shed, and a fading Oliver tractor once owned by Connie's father, Nick. The tractor hadn't been started in more than thirty years. All four tires were sun-split and flat. When she'd been a teenager, Estelle had seen Nick Suarez on the Oliver, the brush hog trailing and clattering, as he thrashed weeds along the roadside. Connie's late-model Subaru Outback was parked in the open shed.

Despite its age, the mobile home was tidy. Estelle stepped out of the Expedition and then stood quietly, surveying the homestead. She waited until Jackie Taber had finished checking in with dispatch, and then crossed the yard to the small metal front steps. She pushed the doorbell button with one knuckle and heard the simple, two-tone gong inside. The trailer remained quiet.

"I'll check around back," Taber said.

"She probably walked over to a neighbor's house for Sunday tea," Estelle said. What passed for a "street" in Regál snaked along the side of the rock falls, past the adobe that had belonged to Lupe Gabaldon back when Estelle was growing up, and whose adobe walls no longer rose true and trim from the stone foundation. Lupe had hauled in a new home, but could look out an east window and watch time take care of the old adobe. The roof had collapsed, allowing the rain to dissolve the adobe wall bricks. In another decade or two, it would be just a ragged remnant, the blocks rounded smooth.

Through a grove of elms, she could see the roofline of Betty Contreras' tidy home to the east, just off the paved state highway. Betty's husband had passed away the year before, too crippled to walk, too short of breath to try. Betty still commuted to Posadas Elementary School every day, determined to get in her fifty years before retiring.

"Or Connie's with Myron Fitzwater, eloped to Jamaica," Jackie replied, and disappeared around the corner of the trailer, passing under the angled dining nook windows. She reappeared thirty seconds later and beckoned to Estelle. "She didn't elope."

The curtains of both bedroom windows were open, and would have afforded a spectacular view of the ocean of rocks and boulders on the face of the San Cristóbal Mountains behind Regál.

"*Por Dios*," Estelle breathed. Connie Suarez lay in full view on the floor, her face turned toward the window, the bottom end of the bed obscuring her lower body. What wasn't obscured was the massive flow of blood, now caked to a dull brown, that surrounded the young woman's head.

Taber retraced her steps back to the front of the trailer and climbed into the Expedition. She backed the truck along her route out of the driveway, taking care that her tires cut no new tracks, then parked to block the drive. Estelle could hear her on the radio. In this far-flung corner of the county, it would take a minimum of half an hour for the team to arrive, even flogging the horses. The victim's half-open, glazed eyes and the brown puddle promised that there was no hurry on her account.

Chapter Fifteen

The Suarez trailer's front door was closed but not locked, but when Estelle tested it tentatively with gloved hands, she saw that the latch rocked in the jamb, opening new cracks in the wood. The metal trim, so thin that she could bend it with her fingers, was deformed and misaligned.

Using her upper arm and shoulder, she put steady pressure on the door and turned the knob gently. The deadbolt, although it clearly had torn out of the wood at some point, along with the knob latch, was retracted. Someone had closed the shattered door, taking care to keep the pieces together.

A quick glance around the living room showed nothing amiss, and Estelle walked carefully down the narrow hallway, keeping close to the wall. In the master bedroom, she circled the body, then knelt and touched Connie Suarez' neck with two fingers. The girl's skin was cool, with rigor well developed.

Estelle squatted, balanced on her toes with her arms folded across her knees, hands clasped in front of her mouth. The victim had apparently either been standing beside the bed, or perhaps even sitting on the corner of it, before falling in a crumpled heap. In addition to the lake of blood on the floor around the victim's head, the blood spatter stretched across the queen-sized bed and marked the wall beyond. Estelle's gaze followed the pattern to where a bullet hole was punched through glass and screen near the top of the window, just below the hem of the valance.

Drawing a ballpoint pen from her pocket, Estelle reached across the body and lifted the skirt of the bed's comforter. A semi-automatic pistol lay just beyond the girl's right hand, the black rubber grips a scant quarter inch beyond the tips of her slender, almost slight, fingers.

Without changing her position, Estelle pulled her handheld from her belt.

"We're going to need the whole crew, Jackie," she said, keeping her voice down.

"Ten four. The troops are rolling."

"We have the one victim in the master bedroom. I'll check across the hall." Estelle forced herself to move slowly, senses taking in every detail. By the time she covered the few steps to the door of the back bedroom, her heart was hammering, her sore ribs complaining at the tension. She took a deep breath. When Jackie Taber came back on the air, the radio sounded harsh and loud in the silence of the trailer.

"Linda said she's only twenty minutes out."

Estelle clicked the transmit bar in response. The two bathrooms and the remaining bedroom held no obvious secrets. The double bed was made, the comforter tight and smooth. The bathrooms included the usual accoutrements, including obvious evidence of a man's continued presence. Estelle stood in the bathroom doorway, waiting for something to shout at her. The battered front door of the mobile home suggested an intruder, but there had been no apparent struggle after that—no overturned furniture, nothing out of place.

Estelle retraced her steps to the front door. The mobile home, although clean and neat, had been manufactured before the stringent standards and regulations of the mid-1970s. Flimsy at best, the doorframe was not as stout as the composite door itself. A determined kick would shatter the door jamb and the thin wood around the strikers. Something as innocent as a miscalculation while delivering a new appliance through the front door could result in the same damage.

Connie Suarez had made it to the sanctuary of her bedroom before what appeared to be a single bullet struck her in the neck. She'd tumbled to the floor and bled out, but the blood from that catastrophic wound appeared to be limited to the bedroom.

Estelle stood in the bedroom doorway, letting the images offer up possibilities. Connie Suarez might have been holding the heavy automatic herself. She might have jammed it under her jaw and pulled the trigger, collapsing without taking an additional step, the gun spilling from her hand. And sure enough, the front door might have been broken earlier, and be entirely unrelated to Connie's misfortune.

Might.

Jackie Taber waited for her, standing on the gravel at the bottom of the front steps.

"Just the one victim here. We need to reach Craig Stout ASAP."

"He's on the road our way, ETA probably an hour at best," Jackie replied. "Gunshot?"

"It would appear so." She didn't elaborate, and Jackie didn't ask. "Let's get this taped-off before the hordes arrive." She looked east across the road and through a small field of cornstalks. A woman stood on the front porch of a tiny adobe, almost entirely obscured by the towering brown remains of a hollyhock planting. She was more than a hundred yards away, out of earshot. "And then we'll find out who heard what." She stopped and turned back to the trailer. "We're going to need all the help we can get. Is someone coming from the State Police?"

"Officer Hector Dominguez was on the interstate just west of Posadas. He's headed this way."

"A rookie."

"That, he is."

"We're going to need their mobile crime lab before this is over."

"I'll get started with that, and he'll help."

Estelle held her index fingers pressed to either side of her head. "Myron Fitzwater isn't just a curiosity out of the Arizona

National Forest anymore, Jackie. We need to find him." She brought her hands down and pointed in stereo at her lieutenant's utility belt, where Jackie's own automatic rode in a black holster. "A Glock 17 is lying in there on the floor, close to Connie's right hand, soaking in a pool of blood. Maybe we're supposed to think that she used it, and maybe she really did. Or maybe it's a throw-down piece."

She took a deep breath. "*Ay*, this could go so many ways."

Far in the distance, they heard the shriek of sirens, and in a moment the tiny black and white beetle flashing through the trees up on the mountainside morphed into a State Police car. Tires squalled as the driver had to brake hard for the first of several hairpins.

"If Officer Dominguez makes it here without piling into a tree, have him control the sign in. He needs to block the lane, and they can use his squad car as a checkpoint. Nobody gets past him until we invite 'em in."

She stepped to Taber's vehicle and removed her own camera from the briefcase. "I want some outside photos before the crowds get here," she said.

"I saw just the one bullet hole through the back window," Taber said. "If that's fresh damage from this incident, it's going to be hell finding the slug."

Estelle's phone played its tune. "Guzman."

"Sheriff, Craig Stout. Are you at the scene?"

"I am."

"One fatality?"

"Yes."

"You're sure of the I.D.? It's Connie Suarez?"

"Yes. I'm sure."

"Damn it." In the background she could hear the roar of his truck. "Signs of a struggle? Anything like that?"

"No…at least not at first glance. The victim is lying on the bedroom floor, beside the bed. Nothing else in the house appears to be disturbed."

A moment of silence followed. "Look, I'm just coming into Lordsburg. That puts me about forty-five minutes out. What are you going to need?"

"The medical examiner is on the way and after that, I'll know more. The gun that *might* have been used appears to be a Glock 17. I'd be interested to know if Fitzwater owned one. That's standard issue for several agencies."

Again Craig Stout fell silent. "Damn," he said at last. "As a range tech, he's not allowed to carry a gun, or even have one with him in the government truck. He certainly wasn't *issued* one. We just don't do that." He took a breath. "But, having said that…I know that Myron has at least one letter of reprimand in his file for doing just that. I know, because I wrote it. Just a second."

Estelle watched Jackie Taber confer with the young state policeman who was now standing beside his unit, nodding as she spoke. Dominguez' body language said clearly that he wanted to stride into the scene and take over. Lieutenant Taber's said he wasn't going to. A tough young woman, Taber nevertheless had a light touch when necessary. She understood the turf wars that were possible between agencies like the State Police and the Sheriff's Department.

"Sheriff?" Craig Stout came back on the line.

"Our team is just starting to arrive," Estelle said.

"Good. Look, I just sent a text back to the office. I know that in the original report I wrote on Fitzwater's firearms incident last year, I included the make, model, and serial number of his weapon, in case we had a repeat incident. We'll have that report in a few minutes, certainly by the time I reach your location."

"Was there any indication of conflict between the two of them? Between Myron and Connie? Had you heard of anything like that?"

"Not a thing, but I'd probably be the last one to know, Sheriff."

"What was the nature of the firearms complaint with Fitzwater?"

"He was hard-nosing some campers about their campfire pit. As it turns out, Smokey Bear himself would have awarded them a medal for proper compliance. Apparently Fitzwater thought the fire was too big. Some of his language was inappropriate, and the folks filed a complaint. He's a range tech, for crissakes. He builds fences, installs erosion control structures, cuts a few trees, checks on seed plots. That's what he does. He's not law enforcement. He's a GS-seven laborer. That's it."

"A BOLO will go out in a few minutes," Estelle said. "The fact that Fitzwater has been among the missing since Friday complicates matters for all of us."

"How long has the girl been dead, can you tell?"

"At least a day, maybe more. Craig, you reported that Fitzwater's Forest Service truck was found up by Newton. He had a project going on up there?"

"Not that I'm aware of. I talked with his supervisor, the district range manager, and there was nothing up in that country that he's aware of, either."

"Then we'll see you as soon as you can get here." She switched off and walked across to where Jackie and Hector Dominguez were unrolling the yellow ribbon. "BOLO for Myron Fitzwater," she said. Jackie nodded, handed the spool to Dominguez, and turned toward her vehicle. The young state trooper looked hard at Estelle as if he expected that she was holding something back.

"That's the guy whose truck they found up north?"

"That's the guy."

"I'll lay money that he's already deep in Mexico."

"Maybe so." She reached out and touched his left jacket sleeve. "Thanks for being here, Hector. We appreciate your help in all this."

Estelle turned and surveyed the small mobile home, trying to fit the pieces of the puzzle together in her mind. Fitzwater's Forest Service pickup was abandoned west of Newton. That was fifty or so miles to the north, with only one direct route—County

Road 14—winding its way up there. Connie Suarez' Subaru was parked in the shed beside the house. Maybe she'd met him up there after he'd abandoned the government truck. Maybe. Maybe the young couple had argued. Maybe over the busted door. That was known to happen. But none of the details fit.

The Mexican border was just yards away, and it would have been easy for Fitzwater to skirt the fence. Thousands had done it before him—most of them headed north rather than south. But the notion of a felon skipping *into* Mexico to avoid the cops was just that…a romantic notion from the days of the Old West, with help from Hollywood…ride your horse across a cooperative Rio Grande, and you're home free. But the Rio Grande and the border it marked were far to the east. South of Regál stretched thousands of square miles of hostile Chihuahuan Desert. Despite the vast distances, though, the days of the frontier were over. Computers, a perfectly able Mexican police force, and the strands of modern communication made going "south of the border" not such a viable alternative, especially for a conspicuous gringo.

Chapter Sixteen

"Fifty-four inches from heel to chin," Dr. Alan Perrone said. "More or less." He looked over at the damaged window. "And that's if she was standing up straight when struck, as opposed to struggling or ducking or a hundred other variables."

Linda Pasquale's big digital camera clicked again, capturing the medical examiner posed and pointing. Perrone ignored her, or appeared to. But a couple of fingers strayed up to his carefully slicked blond hair to make sure every last strand was in place.

"Is it likely that when she was shot, she collapsed in her tracks?" Estelle's question formed more as a thought to herself, rather than directed to the medical examiner, but Perrone frowned as he considered the possibilities.

"You have one gunshot wound that entered under the left side of her jawbone, just anterior to the curve of the mandible. It exited on the right side of her skull, through the mastoid, on a slightly upward path." He nodded at the spray of blood, tissue, and bone fragments across the bedding, wall, and even a portion of the ceiling. "What's obvious is that she was *not* shot somewhere else and dragged here. Now, how she twisted around, how she struggled—who's to say? And I'm guessing from the blood spatter that she was standing beside the bed, not sitting on it."

He mimed with his hands, and Linda's camera captured the performance. "Picture her head here, the bullet passing straight through on a slightly upward path. To answer your question, my guess is that the bullet path suggests lights out, like that." He snapped his fingers. "Chop off the brain stem, and you chop off the body's control center."

Sweeping his pen in a wide arc to include the puddle of drying blood, he added, "Her *heart* soldiered on by itself for a little while, for a few seconds, maybe even a minute or two, and she bled out. But that puddle hasn't been disturbed or smeared. I don't think she struggled." He grimaced. "So, to answer your question, no, I don't think she moved much after the shot was fired. I think she went down like a puppet with its strings cut. The blood flowed out and around the gun."

The physician let out a loud breath. "I would be very surprised to learn that this head wound was caused by a nine millimeter. I mean, I suppose it *could* be. The entry wound is small enough, but there appears to be a lot of expansion there at the exit. Explosive, even. If you can find the bullet, that'd be a plus. We'd know for sure. There's some fancy nine millimeter ammo on the market… home defense stuff that's loaded hot, with extreme hollowpoint bullets. They could do this."

He knelt quickly and pointed at the victim's jawline. "*Most* interesting, this, and Linda, make sure it's well documented. The gun was pushed hard against her neck, right under the jawline. So hard, there's a scrape and bruise there, along with the burn corona." He looked up, first at Robert Torrez, who had arrived unannounced and had been standing in the bedroom doorway, silent and grim-faced. "*Déjà vu*, all over again, as the man said. Where have we all seen *that* before?"

When neither Estelle nor the sheriff offered comment, Perrone added, "I think it's really unlikely that this was self-inflicted. Not on the underside of the chin like that." He looked hard at Estelle. "I'm not saying that it's impossible. Just unlikely." He rubbed his own smooth chin, and his latex glove squeaked. "I'm judging that the trauma inflicted by the gun barrel is in some ways similar to the young man's death yesterday. For the sake of argument, say that this young woman is right-handed." He picked up the evidence bag that now contained the Glock. "It's possible to hold this weapon, bend the wrist, and turn the head to present the left upper neck as a target. Awkward, but possible. If what I remember about these Glocks is correct, there's no separate safety to think about…no fancy grip safety the shooter has to pay attention to. In that respect they're like an old-fashioned double-action revolver. If you can pull the trigger, whether it be with a finger, a pencil, or a toe, I don't care what, then the gun goes off. Am I right?"

He directed the question to Torrez, who nodded silently.

"All right, then. So she could twist her arm around, and *bang*. Maybe easier if you put your thumb on the trigger, instead of the conventional grip. That's also awkward." He shrugged. "But why would she do that? Why not just press it against her right temple?"

"Her watch is on her right wrist. What looks like an engagement ring is on her right hand," Estelle said. "If she was left-handed…"

"Then it's easier, sure enough," Perrone said. "But, still, why would she do that? Why not against her *left* temple, then? You've responded to a depressing number of suicides over the years, both of you. What's the most common method used when a firearm is involved?"

"Temple, or by the ear," Sheriff Torrez muttered, more to himself than to Perrone. "That or suck on the end of the barrel."

"And what we saw yesterday with the young man is maybe a little ways farther down the list of favorites. It's hard to miss with center mass, but there have been lots of cases where folks do."

"This ain't suicide," Torrez said quickly. "She ain't going to ram a handgun under her lower jaw so hard the front sight tears the skin. And Darrell Fisher wasn't going to jam the gun so hard into his own gut that it folded him over."

"She's nervous, apprehensive, desperate?" Perrone offered.

"Not likely." Torrez regarded the bed and the stains that shot across it to the far window wall. "String," he said cryptically. "String and tripod. That might get us a little closer."

The physician looked dubious. "Tough call, with both ends of the string unknown. You have a hole through glass, and that looks like *all* you have. You don't know how she was standing, how the gun was held. You'd be guessing at trajectory." He shook his head. "No word on the boyfriend?"

"Not a thing. We have his truck, abandoned up outside of Newton."

"Newton?" the physician asked. "That's a nowhere place, for sure."

"Maybe so. That's where it was left. No trace of him." Estelle nodded at the bagged gun. "The law enforcement officer from the Forest Service district is on his way. There's some reason to believe that this might be Myron Fitzwater's gun."

"That's starting to paint an ugly scenario for you," Perrone said.

"Maybe so," she said again. "Paint by numbers. Stay inside the lines."

Perrone looked at her sympathetically. "I wish I could give you more to go on. The sheriff is right. You find that slug, it might answer some questions. And there's likely more of them still loaded in the Glock. Who's to say the gun's magazine didn't hold an assortment, though? Finding the fired projectile is going to be a trick, I don't care how much string you use. The bullet went out the window, and that's a hell of a thing to deal with." He looked at his watch. "On the other hand, we might just end up with more questions. I'll get you what answers I can, just as quickly as I can. Right now I'm so tired I think my eyes are crossed. That won't be any good for you. Maybe by tomorrow morning."

"Whatever and whenever you can."

"Francis is due back today?"

"Any minute."

"Then the two of us can put our heads together first thing in the morning." He looked up sharply as Lieutenant Taber appeared in the bedroom doorway.

"Sheriff, Officer Stout is here from the Forest Service. He and District Ranger Robert Tulley."

"I'm finished here," Perrone said. "The EMTs can move the body whenever you're ready." He stopped and looked down at the victim once more. "Somebody must have heard something, in a tiny place like this."

"Depends how and when," Estelle said. "A single gunshot, muffled in a back room? Television sets blaring, all the other noises of a small community? The nearest neighbor is a hundred yards away. Even though everyone knows everyone else's business, it's amazing what you can get away with. It's every bit as bad as the problems we ran into up in Darrell Fisher's neighborhood."

Chapter Seventeen

"There are no fragments on the carpet by the front door." Lieutenant Taber had waited until Estelle finished on the phone. She held up a small magnifying glass. "I used my Sherlock Holmes gadget. If the door was damaged by an intruder, he took the time to clean up thoroughly. If there's anything in the carpet fibers, it's microscopic."

"I don't think so," Estelle said. "I think the door was broken some other time, some other way."

"That's a possibility. There are a few scrub marks on the door itself. If the state is coming down here, we might want them to take a look at those. And we're set with the sight line. I was thinking we could use a red dot laser. It might be more accurate than the string."

"You can see the red dot outside?"

"If we're oh-so-lucky, maybe. It's dark enough now, that I'd think it would be visible. Boss man has one we can use."

Estelle looked skeptical. "Alan is right, I think. Even a fraction of an inch," and she held up her hands, left hand forming an "O" to represent the hole through the window glass, right-hand thumb and index finger pointing like a gun. "Move the gun position up or down a fraction, and the trajectory of the bullet varies wildly. See how high on the windowpane that hole is? In all likelihood, the gun barrel was pointed up. The bullet's trajectory goes through the girl's skull and then up to the windowpane, and then on out." She shook her head in resignation. "We'd be searching a *huge* area for a small bullet fragment. For all we know, it struck somewhere up on the hill, and then ricocheted who-knows-where. Some packrat will find it and add it to his nest collection of strange human souvenirs."

"It's worth a try, though."

"Sure enough, it's worth a try."

"Estelle?" The sheriff's disembodied voice was little more than a whisper over her radio.

"Go ahead."

"The Forest Service guys are here. And Pasquale has a neighbor rounded up who might have seen something. I'm going to talk to 'em."

Opening the front door gingerly, Estelle saw that even tiny Regál could produce crowds of spectators. Outside the yellow tape, she saw Betty Contreras, bundled up against the dropping temperatures as the afternoon wore on, in conversation with Maria Apodaca. Elwood Sanchez and one of his older sons had strolled over, as had half a dozen others—including Al Fisher, who was in animated discussions with one of the Border Patrol officers and another State Policeman.

Craig Stout was a tall, overly thin young man whose shoulders hunched as if he were self-conscious of his six-foot-five height. Although he and his companion had ducked under the yellow tape, they did not cross the front yard. He thrust out a hand as Estelle approached.

"Undersheriff? Have you met Robert Tully, our district ranger?"

Tully's smile was pained, and he had a hard time taking his eyes off the mobile home behind Estelle.

"Good to know you," he said softly. Unlike Stout, whose specialty was law enforcement, Tully was unarmed. He had the soft look of a desk-bound administrator, and after a long look, he turned so that his back was to the trailer.

"It's Ms. Suarez? The identification was positive?"

"Yes, sir. The medical examiner has attended, and we're waiting on the State Police team before we go any further."

"They're going to bring the van down here?"

"We've requested their assistance."

"All right." Tully took a deep breath, and shook his head in frustration. "So what do we actually *know*, at this point?"

"We know," and Estelle turned to view the small mobile home, "that Connie Suarez is in the bedroom of this residence, shot once through the neck and lower skull. The bullet entered under the left side of the jaw, ranged slightly upward, and exited through the right mastoid process, exploding a large portion of the skull as it did so." Tully looked even more deeply pained. "We know that death was more or less instantaneous, and that the body was not moved afterward. A Glock 17 was found near the body, and its position recorded photographically as well as carefully measured. One spent nine-millimeter shell casing, headstamped from Federal, was found lying against the southeast baseboard trim." She took a deep breath, but Tully nodded for her to continue the recitation.

"The bullet passed through the victim, and appears to have then punched a hole in the upper bedroom window."

"You recovered it?"

"No. I'm guessing that the chances of that are very slim. As much damage as a nine-millimeter bullet can do, it's still a comparatively small object."

Tully grimaced some more. "When was the last time that Fitzwater was here? Do we know that?"

"Not yet."

"Did she live alone? Parents, siblings, anyone like that?"

"She lived alone, as far as we know—except when Myron was visiting. Her mother used to live with her, but for health reasons, moved to Albuquerque."

"But we're reasonably sure that Myron Fitzwater visited her on a regular basis?"

"It appears that way, sir. Enough that one of the staff in your offices knew of the relationship, and provided us with Ms. Suarez' name."

Tully put his hands on his hips and turned a slow circle, viewing the little village. "And other folks around here would know as well."

"We're working on that at the moment."

"Why the long wait for the State Police van?"

"As you know, they're busy folks with limited resources, sir, and it's a large state." Estelle said. "It was my decision to call them in before the body is removed. I suspect that DNA evidence, along with blood, fibers, and so forth, are going to be important in establishing who was in this building Friday and through the weekend."

"TOD?"

"The medical examiner thinks that sometime Friday is likely."

"The day that Fitzwater didn't return to the office."

Stout retrieved a small notebook from his shirt pocket. "Were you able to record the serial number of the Glock?"

"We were." She waited until he found the notebook page he was looking for, and then recited the number from memory. Stout repeated it back.

"That's Fitzwater's weapon." He held up a hand quickly. "Not issued by us. As I told you on the phone, he was not authorized to carry a weapon while on duty, or in a government vehicle even if off-duty. No firearm has been issued to him by the Forest Service."

"Has Fitzwater's truck been moved from where it was found?" Tully asked.

"Not yet. I know that in light of this investigation, Sheriff Torrez," and Estelle pointed at the big man as he approached up the two-track in company with Deputy Tom Pasquale, "is going to request that Grant County allow us to impound the vehicle in our yard until the investigation is complete."

"Okay, but I want to see the location before that happens."

"I know where it is," Stout said. "About an hour or more north of here."

"An hour." Tully looked at the ground, his brow furrowed. "Spectacular timing, all this. But we don't want to wait until dawn, do we?"

"No, we don't," Estelle said. "I'll make whatever arrangements are necessary. The truck won't be moved until you have a chance to see it."

"I mean, I don't know what I'm looking for," Tully said, "but just to see. To get the whole scenario in my mind. So..." He regarded Torrez, and a slight smile touched his bland face as he extended a hand. "Sheriff, good to see you again, although not in these circumstances." Torrez was dressed in jeans that looked as if he'd worn them to work on his vintage truck. To counter that image, he wore one of the black nylon jackets with PCSO in five-inch letters across the back, the sheriff's badge embossed over the left breast, and his name tag over the right.

"Your guy was here Friday," Torrez announced without any preliminary greeting. He looked at Thomas Pasquale as if prompting him.

"I talked with Flora Gabaldon, the neighbor over there across the way, and she remembers seeing the Forest Service truck here," Pasquale said. "She says Fitzwater was here most of the day, from mid-morning on."

"She recognized him?"

"Well, I don't know if she recognized *him*, for sure, or if it was the truck. She says she sees the white Ford with the government plates fairly regularly. She did say that Connie—Flora knows her really well—was arguing with Fitzwater about something. They were at the front door, and she thought that they were maybe trying to adjust it or something. She said that the guy was kneeling down in front of the door, messing with the lock."

"Good vision when she needs it," Stout said.

"So Fitzwater most likely was here midday Friday. And then

his truck ends up near Newton sometime over the weekend. Tell me how any of that makes sense."

"Where was Fitzwater *supposed* to be working last week?" Estelle asked.

"He was building some test plot enclosures on a grazing allotment over west of Horsehead Springs. He and Bret Freeman. Freeman didn't work Friday, so Myron was by himself."

"And decided that Regál was more attractive than Horsehead Springs."

"Lots of places are more attractive than the Horsehead," Stout said.

"Is it possible that later in the day on Friday, he figured that he needed to make an appearance at his scheduled job, and drove up to Horsehead Springs to put the finishing touches on his test plots?" Estelle asked.

"That's possible, although that's still a good ways from where his truck was found." Stout nodded eastward, toward the state highway. The heavy mutter of a braking diesel engine drifted to them, and Estelle saw the black hulk of a large RV trundling down from the pass. The State Police mobile crime scene unit slowed to a crawl, and Officer Dominguez walked east on the two-track, as if a few feet would make his radio communications clearer. After a pause, the state RV turned right and jounced off the highway, and for a moment it looked as if it were going to drive through the middle of Betty Contreras' home. The lane was narrow, with orchards and front porches encroaching, but the trooper driving the van did a masterful job. In a few moments, the RV rounded the last, pinched curve past Lupe and Flora Gabaldon's home and sighed to a stop.

Estelle saw a ripple of interest pass through the various little knots of spectators. Such a sideshow wasn't usual in the tiny village. Of particular interest to her was the little gaggle that included Lupe and Flora Gabaldon, Al Fisher, and Maria Apodaca. Lupe, short, stocky, and bandy-legged, was obviously holding court. His hands waved as he narrated his version of events, or posed all the questions that might be swirling around in his old, gray-topped head.

"Maybe some answers now," Estelle said. Sheriff Torrez looked skeptical.

Chapter Eighteen

He had reason to be skeptical. As winter-early darkness deepened, the sun in a hurry to sink behind the crest of the San Cristóbals, it became evident that only the most unimaginable luck would recover the bullet that had crashed through the window. That slug, even spent, could be almost anywhere, at almost any distance. It might have buried itself in one of the shrub groves, or skipped off rocks until it fell into hiding.

The more officers scoured the hillside, their size twelves disturbing the ground and scuffing the rocks, the more unlikely the recovery of the treasure became. A metal detector found nothing. Still, officers hope that their flashlight beams might wink a reflection from a brass jacket fragment.

Inside the modest little trailer, other than a very clear and gory photo of the Luminol-enhanced blood splatter in Connie Suarez' bedroom, nothing unusual presented itself. There were plenty of hairs and fibers that would prove Myron Fitzwater's presence in the trailer, but that was to be expected. His fingerprints would be on almost any surface, including the Glock's slab sides, and, indeed, there was a cluster around the front-doorjamb.

A profile of prints was lifted from the pickup truck near Newton, all belonging to Myron Fitzwater.

Connie's Subaru was locked, but the car's keys hung on a hook in the kitchen, and when it was unlocked, the open vehicle revealed nothing other than prints on the driver's side belonging to Connie, with Myron's on the passenger side .

It was pitch-dark when Lieutenant Gil Sandusky of the New Mexico State Police approached Estelle Reyes-Guzman and Robert Torrez. He shook his head in frustration, and pushed his black uniform cap far back on his closely shaved skull. His cheek muscles twitched as if he wanted to bite someone's head off.

"We're not getting anything," he confessed. "I'm beginning to think that maybe, yeah, she walks into the bedroom, thinks about it for a minute, then pops herself. Sure as hell no sign of a struggle—unless Perrone finds something in the post." He shrugged. "He's good at that. But I just don't know." He looked down at Estelle, who was sitting on the second step of the front door stoop. "You look beat."

"I am," Estelle said.

"The gun," Torrez said. "That don't make sense."

"That's a problem, isn't it?" Sandusky nodded. "It'll make sense if she's the one who pulled the trigger. I'll get with Perrone and make sure we run every test in the book. If she fired it, it'll show up. She's left-handed, I'm told, so an entry on the left side of her neck is certainly a possibility, but you already figured that out." He shrugged. "We've taken samples from the scuffing on the door, but I doubt that's going to tell us anything." He thumped his fist on the flimsy porch railing. "I wish I could be more optimistic. We need to find Fitzwater—that's what we need."

"And I wish I could be optimistic about *that*," Estelle said. She pushed herself to her feet, but one shoe slipped on the edge of the bottom step, and she lurched and twisted to keep her balance. She stifled a gasp as pain lanced across her right side. "*Ay*, I'm walking in my sleep." She shook her head at Sandusky's quick response with a helping hand.

With both feet flat on the ground, she pulled out her phone and checked that the text message was still there. It was. *I'm home, and the tea water is on.* And a long row of X's and LOL's for punctuation.

"You have coverage here for tonight?" Sandusky asked.

"We do. Deputy Sutherland is going to close patrol the village tonight."

The state officer regarded the silent Torrez. "Anything else we can do for you, Sheriff?"

"Nope, thanks."

"We'll follow through with Perrone," Sandusky said. "Mears is the one putting the print profiles together from both this site and up north?"

"Yes."

Sandusky nodded. "He's a good man, Sergeant Mears is." He grinned. "It's about time he went to work for us."

Estelle punched him lightly in the gut. "Don't even think about it, L.T."

"Come dawn, then. We'll see what we've got. Maybe daylight will loosen up some tongues." He nodded toward the little gaggle of villagers who had become no more than dark shapes silhouetted against the distant arc lights of the border fence. "Hard to believe all this went down on the sly." He touched the brim of his cap. "Lemme know."

"Thanks, L.T." She turned to Torrez, but he spoke first.

"Go home," he said abruptly. "I got things here."

She pulled in a long tentative breath, and felt the muscles complain. "I'll see you in the morning."

"Yep."

She walked back to Jackie Taber's Expedition and leaned against its broad flank. *I'm on the way*, she texted to her husband. She sensed more than heard Lieutenant Taber loom out of the darkness beside her. "I'm stealing your unit," Estelle said. "I need to go home."

"Get a good price for it."

"When you finish up here, take Pasquale's ride. He can hitch a ride back with the Sheriff."

"He'll love that. Sutherland's coming into the village for the night, though."

"Yes. I'll be back in the morning. We'll see what other folks have to say."

"You bet. Maybe by then, Mr. Fitzwater will make an appearance."

"Don't hold your breath, Jackie. Nothing about any of this adds up to him ditching his truck and taking off on foot."

Taber looked hard at her. "So you're starting to think the same as I am. That he's lying out there somewhere with a bullet in his head?" She didn't wait for Estelle to answer, but added, "Get some rest. And have that husband of yours check up on what's hurtin' you. Then tomorrow we'll decide which way to go."

Estelle smiled in spite of herself. Lieutenant Jackie Taber didn't miss much.

Chapter Nineteen

"Gastneritis," Dr. Francis Guzman said. Estelle's left eyebrow lifted.

"Gastritis?"

"No. *Gastneritis*." He held up an admonishing finger. "You spend enough time, at all hours, without decent food or rest, and sooner or later, something in the system is going to shout out a complaint. It's a work ethic that I think you picked up over the years from *Padrino*, and now it's payback time." He sat back on the edge of the bed and regarded her sympathetically.

"It worked when you were a kid, but now that you're proudly past the half century mark? Payback time." He spun his finger in a circle. "You don't get enough sleep, you don't pay attention to diet…" He reached out and cradled her head in both hands as he looked deep into her eyes. "Let me play doctor. Shed the robe and lie down on your left side."

The long, hot shower had beaten some of the weariness out, and she'd ended the sauna session only when the hot water heater had no longer been able to keep up. The bedroom now felt delightfully cool, and her husband's strong hands warm and smooth.

She did as she was told, amused but grateful.

"Raise your right arm up as if you were going to scratch the top of your head," he instructed. "These rib cage muscles are notoriously slow to heal." His hands worked their way from behind her armpit, following both the delineations of her ribs and the pattern of heavy scars that tracked them. At one point, where the eighth rib curved anteriorly to blend with the heavy cartilage that in turn swept upward to join the sternum, she flinched in anticipation.

"That's tender?"

"A little."

"This," and his fingers traced the eighth rib with a butterfly's touch, "is where the bullet shattered the rib upon exit. So about an inch of rib and associated cartilage was just blown away. And that's not taking into account all the damage surgeons inflicted tackling the repair job. Does it make you uneasy to talk about this?"

"I like hearing you talk, *Oso*."

"Ease over onto your tummy now."

He examined her back, where the major scar curved around to the margin of her shoulder blade. "The first goal in surgery like this is to stop the bleeding, *querida*. That one little slug did a *lot* of damage on the way through, and the repair job is going to be just about as bad, with all those hands rummaging around inside your chest, snipping and stitching and sponging."

"Rummaging."

"Yes, rummaging. So after all of that, healing takes time when there's so much damage. It's been what…going on eight years or more since you were hurt? I know that seems like long enough, but obviously it's not. Patience is the answer. Painkillers are most definitely *not* the answer. Maybe a little arnica gel. Lots of long, slow hot showers. Lots of sleep. Lots of *very* careful exercises. The ideal therapy for all this might be a nice heated swimming pool. Maybe one of those long, narrow pools for lap swimmers."

Estelle murmured something that might have been a "yes," but the urge to slip deep into slumber as those warm hands worked was overpowering.

"All that lattice-work of muscles had to mend. Bone and cartilage had to grow. The nerves have to settle down. As long ago as they were, I'm sure you remember all the physical therapy sessions."

"Ugg."

"Yep, but you did good, *querida*. The ribs have to mend, grow new bone. And just about the slowest to repair are the intercostal connections—muscles, ligaments, cartilage. All of that can ache and hurt and twang for centuries, it sometimes seems. It's entirely possible that when you celebrate your eightieth birthday, you'll *still* have some occasional discomfort. You can't be hurt as badly as you were and not pay the piper on down the road." He stroked her sides, then worked down the muscles of her back.

"I'm sure you've heard of folks who blow out a knee, and forever afterward, that knee acts as a weather forecaster. Or they cut off a finger, and forever after, they claim they can still feel the amputated digit?"

"Ummph."

"Exactly. Rest works wonders, *querida*, along with careful therapy to build strength and flexibility. Sitting for hours scrunched up in a patrol car is just about the *worst* thing you can do. Or sedentary at your desk. Not *the* worst, of course. Breaking up bar fights, like you and Jackie Taber had to do last month? That's probably the worst."

Estelle lifted her head out of the pillow. "The two guys going at it laughed and gave up when we walked in, *Oso*. There was nothing we had to do other than put on the cuffs." She turned slightly to look at him. "And they both held out their wrists for us. 'Please, take me!' the one guy says."

He patted her bottom. "Roll over on your back, tough guy."

She did so.

"When you take a deep breath, where does it ache?"

"Right where your hand is."

He stroked upward along the scar. "Nowhere else?"

"No."

"Does the pain make you cough?"

"No."

"Still got an appetite?"

"Too much of one."

He stroked her flat, muscular belly. "I can see that. Look at all that blubber. Hurts to twist, though?"

"Sometimes. Not always. It's always unexpected."

"Intercostal neuralgia is a persistent little demon." He bent over and kissed the hollow of her neck. With the toes of her right foot, she caught the hem of his robe and tugged.

"You keep this up, and you know where we're headed, *Oso*."

"I sincerely hope so, if we can figure out a way not to strain all those battered and bruised muscles any more than they already are." He sat up, perched on the edge of the bed. "The kids are really coming in *tomorrow?*"

"That's what Francisco promises."

He looked at her with frank admiration, tinged with a physician's interest in her collection of scars. Then he leaned across and pulled her robe closer so she could reach it if she wanted to. "One little pink track doesn't make you any less of a gorgeous woman, *querida*."

"We won't have much privacy once the hordes descend."

"Nope."

"So we'd better get a head start."

Chapter Twenty

Unsure whether it was the phone or the tire hiss of a passing car, she awakened only once during the early pre-dawn hours. For a long time she lay quietly, enjoying the closeness of her husband's warm body, trying to focus only on that, her thoughts enriched by the impending arrival of her two children on this Christmas Eve. But the bloody images of the mobile home down in Regál intruded.

The three-inch numerals on the bedside clock announced 4:45. The first hints of dawn were still an hour away from tracing the edges of the horizon. Regál, shielded by the craggy rise of the San Cristóbals and the crown of scrub and remnant timber, wouldn't see the sun for another four hours or more. She could picture, in her mind's eye, the tiny community that hugged the border, the way the sun would touch each house in turn when it finally broke over the mountain crest in mid-morning.

Connie Suarez' trailer would be among the last to feel the morning sunshine, huddled in the shade of the boulder slide until nearly eleven o'clock. It would be after that before the sun ever touched the black water tank up at the spring behind the village.

Reality turned effortlessly into a dream world as she drifted off. From an impossible vantage point on the highway over the pass, she watched as four youngsters pushed the black water tank off its base and sent it tumbling down the hill like an enormous beach ball, bouncing wildly from boulder to boulder, spewing water in great geysers. That dream morphed into a kaleidoscope of silly images, until a final episode featured her elder son, Francisco, explaining how his U.S. Army vintage WC-52 was such a good buy for "only thirty-two thousand dollars."

Estelle awoke with a start. This time, it was for sure the telephone that intruded. The clock read 8:05, and then she heard her husband's quiet voice out in the kitchen.

"Let me see," he said.

She heard his feet padding on the hardwood floor and he appeared in the bedroom doorway.

"I'm up," she said.

"It's the high sheriff, and he sounds impatient."

"Bobby is *always* impatient, *Oso*." She reached out for the bedside extension.

"I'm making a therapeutic breakfast, so don't be heading off anywhere until you've eaten, *querida*."

She smiled at him, and picked up the phone.

"Good morning, *Roberto*."

"Hey," Torrez said. "You need wheels?"

Estelle pulled the east curtains to one side and flinched against the blast of sunshine. "I don't think so, Bobby. Unless we're headed off into the boonies somewhere."

"We got to get rid of that unit," the sheriff grumbled, referring to the Charger that preferred pavement to two-tracks. "Anyway, Sutherland and Taber need us ASAP down south. You free?"

I can't. The kids are coming today, she wanted to say, but instead settled for, "Yes. What's the deal?"

"Taber said she'd meet us at Betty's place. Her and Brent were scouting around behind Suarez' trailer and found some interesting stuff."

"Stuff? Like what?"

"Well, blood, for one thing. They taped the area off. Taber called Linda back."

"All right. You're headed down that way now?"

"Yup."

"I'll be there as soon as I can." She hung up and two minutes later was out of the shower. A quick shake or two of the head put her hair in place, and she dressed in jeans, sweatshirt, and running shoes. The aroma from the kitchen was overpowering, and Francis slid a plate loaded with an omelet and slathered English muffins in front of her as she sat down.

"Scarf that down," he instructed. "Coffee this morning?"

"Sure. Thanks."

"What's Bobby got for us this fine Christmas Eve?" Francis plated his own omelet and joined her at the table. He reached across and gripped her shoulder gently, rocking her from side to side. "And where's your vest?"

"In the car. I'll put it on when I go out, *Oso*."

"Out to where this morning?"

"Jackie and Brent found a site somewhere near Contreras' place in Regál this morning. Probably blood. Animal or human, we don't know yet."

"Seems as if there's been enough human blood spread around to last us quite a while," Francis said. "Alan asked if I'd stop in today to consult on a couple of autopsies he's got going."

"Maybe suicides, maybe not," Estelle said. "We'd like your opinion on them."

"This bit this morning…related somehow?"

"I'm not much of a believer in coincidence, *Oso*." She touched her napkin to her nose. The green chile was piquant and the bacon crisp and finely diced. "This is perfect," she said.

His large, furry face took on his best serious physician's expression. "Carlos instructed me a couple of years ago on how an omelet should be done properly."

"He'll probably start baking something wonderful two minutes after he walks through the door."

"If he waits *that* long."

She tackled the rest of the omelet and stood up, the second half of the muffin in hand. He reached out and locked one large hand around her wrist.

"Aches and pains this morning?"

She moved sideways so that she could lean against him. "Much better, *Oso*. With you away, with the kids away, the house was a little quieter than I would have liked. I was glad to be rescued by *Padrino*, even if it was in the middle of the night." She looked down at him. "And now all is well. You're here, and they're on their way."

He released her wrist and stroked her under the chin. "Vest, *querida*."

"Yes, yes, yes." She kissed him hard, and the urge was powerful to simply sink into his lap and let things progress as they might.

Chapter Twenty-one

A large flatbed trailer towed behind a pickup truck had pulled into the church parking lot, and Estelle counted six people gathered around it, all working methodically to scoop sand into brown paper bags and then nestle short votive candles inside. The *luminarias* would line the highway approaching the *Iglesia*, mark the parking lot itself and the front steps of the church. Lit just at sundown, they would light the way during Christmas Eve services.

The faces of the six workers were grim. As she approached, Estelle lowered the driver's side window and slowed to a walk. Betty Contreras looked up, said something to a coworker, and brushed off her hands as she approached Estelle's car.

"Nobody has much heart in it," she said. A tidy lady, maybe an inch or two over five feet, she had taught elementary school for years in Posadas, making the daily drive over the pass. Regál hadn't censused sufficient children for an elementary school in years, and no children had joined the adults to prepare the Christmas *luminarias*.

With both hands, Betty adjusted the large bun of steel-gray hair on her head.

"Sad, sad day. You know," and she looked hard at Estelle, "that Connie was a teacher's aide in three of our classrooms."

"She will be sorely missed, Betty."

"And one on top of the other. I feel so sorry for Penny Fisher and the little boy." She leaned closer. "I don't tell many people what I really think, of course."

"What do you really think?"

"For Darrell Fisher—and I knew him really well, you know, from the time he was in my second grade classroom—suicide is such a cowardly, thoughtless thing to do. Such a *weak* thing to do, Estelle." She patted the windowsill of the Charger. "Sure, sure, I know that things hadn't been going his way recently, but to choose to leave his wife and little boy like that? *Cowardly*, is what I call it."

"Have you had the chance to talk with Al or Maria?"

She grimaced. "Just to say 'I'm sorry.' I had Al in class, too, you know." She grimaced again. "I've taught just *forever*, haven't I? I'm planning to retire in two more years…and there I go with fifty-one years in the classroom. And I'll tell you, I'd rather have a dozen Al Fishers in my classroom than another Darrell, let me tell you. Al was all full of piss and vinegar, and I could never be sure what tall tale he was going to tell me next." She nodded with satisfaction. "That's the way a kid should be, as far as I'm concerned. Now, Darrell—he was like trying to teach one of those bags of sand over there. Mopey most of the time. Down in the dumps. Just *unpleasant* to be around.

"I thought that maybe, when he married that fireball Penny Dooley, that she'd wake him up." She leaned close again. "I had *her* in second grade, too, you know."

She pensively dusted her hands off again. "So sad, huh?"

"Very," Estelle said.

"I saw the sheriff and some other traffic just a bit ago. They're up on the hill, I think. And let me tell you what *I* think. There is *no way*, no way on God's green Earth, that Connie Suarez would shoot herself. No way."

Estelle regarded Betty Contreras with curiosity. "Where are you on the grapevine, Betty?"

"What do you mean?"

"Who told you that Connie shot herself?"

"Oh, well," and she didn't look the least bit uncomfortable at the question. "From where we were standing last night, over near where that group of troopers was waiting for something to do, we could hear *their* comments. And Lupe Gabaldon heard them, too. So, no mystery. I mean, everyone in town knows. That's what I told your lieutenant. That Jackie Taber, what a delightful young lady *she* is."

"Yes, she is. And by the way, have you seen Myron Fitzwater around lately?"

"Oh, now don't go blaming him for anything. Such a nice young man. I don't think there is a square inch of these mountains that he and Connie haven't hiked. I mean, I'd see them coming down off the rocks, laughing and carrying on." She lowered her voice again. "Sound carries, you know. Well, of course you would know." She reached in and patted Estelle's left shoulder.

"You never heard him…or *them*…arguing with anyone? Talking with anyone? Hiking with company?"

"Well, everybody knows everybody, and you know…neighborhood chitchat is a way of life in a little town like this. So, sure…Myron would stop and talk with Lupe Gabaldon. Now what about, I don't know. And they both, I mean Myron and Connie, liked to visit with the Apodacas. Maybe they liked his wine."

"So Myron was something of a regular around here?"

"That's fair to say. In fact, you know the last time I saw him, I mean other than when his truck was at Connie's, was when he was up on the pass, stopped and talking with one of the state troopers. I *think* one of the hunting seasons was going on. I remember that Myron had a big pair of binoculars slung around his neck. I guess that's not so strange, but I don't know for sure what he did for the Forest Service."

"Do you recall which trooper?"

Betty shook her head. "I don't know him. Great big fellow. He was leaning against his SUV and made it look like a sports car, he's so big."

"That would be Charlie Austin. When was this, do you remember?"

Betty frowned. "This is an official question, isn't it?" When Estelle nodded, she added, "So I can't just make something up that sounds good."

"I'd rather you didn't, Betty."

The woman took a deep breath and stared up into the heavens. "It was after Thanksgiving, I remember that. I couldn't tell you *why* I remember that, but it seems reasonable. Sometime in early December, is my best shot."

"All right. So not just in the past day or two."

"Oh…no. Not that recently."

"At any time in recent history…" Estelle began, and then stopped when her cell phone concertized. "Guzman."

"You comin' up?"

She glanced toward the flank of the mountain, even though it would be impossible to actually see Bob Torrez as more than a dot, even if he were perched on a boulder.

"Directly," she said. Torrez switched off without additional comment.

"So, all the times you've seen Myron Fitzwater around the village, was he wearing a gun? A handgun?" She ducked her head to look at the workers at the *luminarias* trailer. "And this is just between you and me."

"You don't think that he…do you think that there's a possibility of that?"

"Of what, Betty?"

"That he might have…"

Estelle smiled at the woman. "I bet you didn't allow sentence fragments from your students."

"From second-graders, I'd take anything. But listen. Most

of the time, when I saw Myron out of his truck…which wasn't all that often, I have to say…he was wearing a handgun." She pulled both hands across her waist. "On one of those wide belts that all you folks wear. Handgun, and once I saw a pair of handcuffs." She looked hard at Estelle again. "But he would, after all, wouldn't he?"

"When you saw him with Trooper Austin up on the pass—was he wearing a handgun then?"

"I honestly didn't notice, Estelle." She reached out a hand and touched the undersheriff on the shoulder. "Have you been able to talk with Myron?"

"Not yet." She dug a card out of the center console, but Betty waved it off.

"Oh, I have half a hundred of those. Don't waste another one."

"Good. If you should happen to see Mr. Fitzwater, call me asap, would you? Any time, twenty-four seven. Even if it's just a glimpse of him driving by."

"Absolutely, I will. And you know, the last person I saw talking with Myron was Lupe Gabaldon. That was just earlier in the week. You might want to check with him, if your officers haven't already."

"I'll follow up with him. Thanks, Betty." She pulled the Dodge into gear. "I need to meet with the others. Thanks for the information."

"Such a sad thing," Betty said, stepping away from the car.

"Let's hope that it doesn't get any sadder," the undersheriff said.

Chapter Twenty-two

As she had experienced just the night before, the trail up to the water tank high above the village was the site of bad dream fodder. She had once chased three illegals up toward the tank after they'd made their way through half of the backyards in Regál, and been reported by four different citizens. Lupe Gabaldon had taken a shot at them, but number nine birdshot at a hundred yards was less effective than a swarm of no-see-ums.

The arrest of the three, all of them winded, terrified, and thankful to be caught, had been uneventful, but the location had worked itself into Estelle's subconscious dream center for frequent replay.

She parked just behind Betty's house alongside the two department SUVs, and then walked up the rough, circuitous path—it was hardly a road or even a two-track—until she reached the U.S. Forest Service boundary fence. The trail reached a people pass-through, one of those Y-shaped structures that cattle couldn't figure out, and wouldn't fit through even if they did, and which nimble deer just vaulted. Estelle walked another hundred yards, the trail ascending steeply, dodging around house-sized boulders, a couple talus slides, and long-dead juniper stumps that still showed black char from a fire a century before.

From this raven's eye view, the village looked like something out of a finely crafted HO gauge train layout. She could look to each roofline and know by name the occupants of the house. So steep was the hillside that someone with a good throwing arm could pitch a stone, and after a couple of ricochets and bounces, it might even reach the back wall of Connie Suarez' trailer.

The water tank was a three-thousand-gallon unit, eight feet in diameter and as many tall. It rested on a pad built with railroad ties by one of the Forest Service summer youth work crews. They had snuggled it tightly against a buttress of rock, and an inch-diameter fill pipe ran off the rocks behind the tank to the black polyvinyl dome of its top.

Loaded with water, the tank would weigh more than twelve tons—not something that a handful of vandals could tumble off its base. They could use it for target practice, and for the fun of watching water squirt out through the bullet holes. Sure enough, a few screw-in repair plugs dotted its black sides.

Estelle stopped at the yellow ribbon that crossed the trail, secured from bush to tree.

"Thought you'd got stuck down there," Bob Torrez said. She glanced down the hill and could see the ant-figures working at the *luminarias* trailer.

"Some of the locals trying to work up some holiday spirit."

"Well, yeah. Good luck with that." He beckoned to Jackie Taber.

"L.T., come fill 'er in."

"You probably remember when this unit was put in," Taber said, and Estelle nodded. "The spring that feeds it is right up there." She nodded uphill, beyond the shelf of boulders. "Because it's so high up, they were able to route the fill pipe straight over to the top of the tank. A really convenient location. It's not much of a flow, but it runs all the time, and the tank overflow pipe is over there, on the south side of the tank. The tank is hooked up to a wildlife drinker."

"Why the tank?" Estelle asked. "Why not just let the spring fill a little pond without using all the hardware?"

"I suppose the cattle and other critters, the elk especially, would walk all over it until it was just a mucky wallow." Jackie looked over at the sheriff, who nodded.

"The spring worked just fine for thousands of years, just as is, without no tank or drinker. It don't matter how it works," Torrez said.

"Well, Sheriff, actually it does matter." Undaunted, Taber walked westward around the tank. "Over here, on the downhill side…" and she stopped when Estelle's phone rang.

"Help!" Linda Pasquale's yelp was audible even to those not holding the phone. "Where the heck are you guys?"

"Turn off the highway where you see three units parked behind Betty Contreras' home. The trail up here is behind her house. You'll see it."

"Arrgg. I'm supposed to schlep everything all the way up there?"

"Yes. Your Honda won't fit through the gate."

Her sigh was audible. "Here I come."

Estelle switched off the phone. "Linda, feeling put upon," she said. "Go ahead, Jackie."

"On the downhill side of the tank is a wildlife drinker. Pretty nifty. Small enough that hopefully the elk won't step in it and punch holes through it, but big enough to hold several gallons of water. Another nifty valve keeps it full." She stood with her hands on her hips and looked at Estelle. "I won't swear to it, but this unit—tank, valves, pipe, all of it—isn't designed to supply the village down there. There's not that big a flow. The idea of the tank is that three thousand gallons is too large to freeze solid, with enough reserve to serve the critters during an extended drought. And the black plastic of the tank acts like a trombé, keeping the valves from freezing most of the time. They're further protected by being below ground in a valve box."

Estelle followed her around the tank and looked down at the plumbing.

"So, no piping down to the village. This doesn't supply any homes down there?"

"No. Strictly designed for wildlife habitat. That's the intent, anyway."

"And this?" Estelle touched a piece of white PVC pipe one inch in diameter that lay exposed several feet below the tank where it joined with black polyvinyl pipe that appeared to wind down the slope through the rocks.

"Like I said, intent. Someone's taking advantage of the source, is my guess. I'm betting that the pipe runs down the hill to someone's home. Or garden. Or something."

Estelle knelt and examined the pipe. It had been buried neatly at one point, perhaps all the way to the valve box, where it had been hard-plumbed into the existing piping. All but two feet of it had been covered, and the marks where the dirt had been first swept aside, but then replaced, were obvious.

"Okay. This kept a plumber busy for a little bit."

"Yes. But then it gets interesting. This way." Fifty feet west of the tank, in a spot encircled by yet another yellow ribbon, Taber stopped. She leaned against a boulder and used her hands to draw a valley in the air—the ground protected between two collections of boulders. The blood that had soaked the soil and even splashed on the rocks was clear.

"Oh, here we are," Linda Pasquale said cheerfully as she joined the others. "Party time. And this is gross. Who is it?"

"More like a what, girl," Jackie Taber said. "The remains of hide, the guts, the skull, the spine—they're all widely scattered, but close by."

Linda nodded. "When fully assembled, what was it?"

"A muley. Mule deer. A little buck."

"Mountain lion, you think? No, scratch that. If it were a lion at work, we all wouldn't care, right?" Linda looked around at Sheriff Torrez.

"Soooooo right." Torrez managed a faint smile.

"Well, yuck."

"The yuck part starts over there," Taber said, pointing downhill, beyond the tank. "I wish I could claim finding this, but Sharp-Eyes Sutherland did the good work. Follow in my footsteps, please."

Walking past the tank, they angled downhill for thirty or forty feet. "The deputy was headed downslope this way because he wanted to see where the pipe led." In a moment she stopped where two evidence flags were pushed into the ground. "The piece of scrub oak is what's interesting."

Standing back as if the stick that lay on the ground was a rattlesnake about to strike, Estelle then knelt slowly. "Why am I guessing that's not mule deer blood? Or mule deer fur." About four feet in length and two inches in diameter, the wood was seasoned long enough that all the bark was gone, the wood smoothed with age. "Oak," she added. "Tough stuff."

"I wouldn't think that a lot of hunters nowadays use cudgels to beat up on their game," Linda said helpfully.

Estelle pulled out her phone, and sorted through three numbers before her husband answered.

"*Oso*, Alan is hiding out somewhere, but we need a blood sample typed and another preserved for DNA analysis. Can… *will*…you do that typing for us? We need to know if it's human, and then if it is, what type."

"As in now, *querida?*"

"Yes. I'll have one of the deputies run it up."

"You're back down south?"

"Yes."

"Am I going to end up in court testifying with all this?"

She laughed. "Always thinking ahead, you are. We can only hope so, *Oso*. It adds legitimacy to your assistant deputy medical examiner status with Alan."

"*That's* just what I need. By the way, Francisco called. They're about two hours out. He'll call again when they're closer. Are you going to be able to meet and greet at the airport? Otherwise, we can call *Padrino* and have him head out there."

"*Ay.* I will do my best. But the blood sample is *primero, Oso.*"

"Tell the deputy to bring the samples to the clinic. I can do all the preliminary work right here. I'm tied up at the moment with a twelve-year-old who owns a really nasty, infected ingrown toenail. Just a grand thing to have on Christmas Eve. You're going to give me a few minutes?"

"Just a few. We love you, *Oso*, me most of all." She consulted her phone again, then stoked the appropriate panels. The phone on the other end rang five times before Craig Stout answered.

"Craig, this is Undersheriff Guzman. What's your twenty?"

The Forest Service Law Enforcement officer sounded tired. "We're back up in the Newton area. Your folks are just coming in to collect Fitzwater's truck. Any word down there?"

"We're up on the hill behind the village. You recall the wildlife tank you folks have up on the hill?"

"Vaguely. We have wildlife drinker tanks like that in several places in the district. It's sometimes a cooperative venture between us and the permitee for cattle. That one, though—I think it's primarily for wildlife. I think that one was a project with the YCC kids a few summers ago. I'd have to check, but I'm not sure that we have a permitee on that mountain right now."

"We found evidence of a wildlife kill, but more important, we recovered what may be a weapon. *Maybe.* There's blood and some hair that needs to be tested."

"You're thinking human samples?"

"I don't know for sure, but the hair looks so. My husband is going to process it as soon as we can deliver it to him."

"That's a hell of a lot faster than what I'd have to do when things like that are found on federal property," Stout said. "Go ahead with the sample, and I'll pretend you didn't tell me about it."

"Lots of questions for you when you return."

"We're on our way. If Fitzwater doesn't show his face today, I'm going to contact the FBI. We could use their help."

"Any assistance is welcome," Estelle said. "Sooner rather than later." She closed the phone and nodded in appreciation at Jackie. "Anything else?"

"Not unless Deputy Sutherland found something during his hike down the hill."

"He's following the pipeline?"

"We'll find out who's siphoning off spring water."

"That would be earth-shaking news that we should all be vitally interested in at this point," Linda snorted.

"It'll shake our earth if that's human blood and hair on that club," Jackie replied. "People have been known to get pretty riled over a few gallons of water." She looked back toward the evidence flag. "Lots and lots of pictures before we move it, please."

"And how that might be related to a butchered muley, we may never know," Estelle said. "But it's a start."

Chapter Twenty-three

United States Forest Service Law Enforcement Officer Craig Stout stood quietly, his hands deep in his pockets. District Ranger Tully sucked on a canteen, as if the moderate hike uphill to the water tank was his whole week's exercise.

"This is fairly recent," Stout said, feeling the need to verbally inventory the obvious. He twitched both pant legs up and knelt, just outside of the splash of dried, brown blood and what little remained of the deer carcass. "Makes sense that he dropped 'er right here, rather than dragging it in from somewhere." Still kneeling, he twisted and peered downhill to the evidence marker that had replaced the blood-soaked oak limb.

Without being asked, Linda offered her camera, and both Stout and Tully stroked through the photos she had taken of the bloody oak cudgel before it was removed and shipped north to the lab. "It's what…" Stout said, "about four feet long or so?"

"Just under," Estelle said. "Forty-one and five-eighths."

Stout peered closely at the best photo that showed the whole length of the stick. "Whittled on?"

"No. Both ends look naturally broken, and well aged."

"So just a handy walking-stick sort of thing."

Tully looked vexed. "I don't get it. Sheriff, what are you thinking?"

Torrez shook his head slowly. "We're waitin' on the M.E.'s results."

"If that's deer's blood on the tree branch, then what?"

"Then that's that," Torrez said. "Maybe the hunter used it…or was gonna use it…to prop open the carcass, or to prop the hind legs apart. He finishes up with the guttin' and tosses the stick."

"And why would he do that?" Tully persisted.

Torrez looked puzzled. "Why keep the stick? He's done with it, and tosses it."

"And if it's human blood and human hair on there, not from the deer?"

"Then we find out who it belongs to."

Tully frowned and looked across at Stout. "These two events might not even be related, then." He nodded first at the site where the carcass had been butchered, and then over his left shoulder at the spot where the stick had been found. "How long until the M.E. gets back to us?"

"As soon as he can," Estelle replied. "The deputy left with it," and she looked at her watch, "about forty minutes ago. The M.E. has it now and, other patients depending, he'll get right to it."

"Other patients?"

"Live ones come first, Ranger Tully."

Her formal tone wasn't lost on him. He nodded impatiently. "And what's this? We have the whole town on the visitors' list?"

Estelle turned to see Lupe Gabaldon and Al Fisher, along with Maria and her father, Solomon Apodaca, making their way up the trail from the village, escorted by Lieutenant Taber. Gabaldon and Apodaca looked as if they might be brothers—short, barrel-chested, bandy-legged, and walking with arms stretched out to the sides for balance, as if their ankles were about to sprain on the uneven ground. Al Fisher was walking with one hand lightly on his girlfriend's elbow, the two of them in deep conversation.

Taber halted them at the yellow ribbon. Al reached out and lifted the police line marker as if he planned to duck under, but Jackie stopped him short. He took a deep, exasperated breath and let the yellow tape drop.

"Gentlemen, Maria, thanks for coming up, but we need to keep people out of this area for a little while," Estelle said.

"What happened?" Lupe Gabaldon said. "Did I leave too much of that deer carcass behind?"

"It ain't much of a trophy," Torrez said. "I wrapped the head, though. I'll dispose of it for you."

"Well, sure. I was going to collect that, but didn't get around to it. It looked like the critters had dragged it off some."

"They were workin' on it."

"He ain't much of a buck, but he don't have to be for good eating," Gabaldon offered. "He was just a little spike, you know. 'Course, if you picked up the head, you know all that."

"What did you bag him with?" The old man shifted under Torrez's unblinking gaze.

"That old thirty-thirty Marlin of mine. Good gun. One shot ruined the heart, and down he goes."

Torrez nodded thoughtfully, but it was Jackie Taber who interjected, "That's quite a haul down to your house."

"I got me this neighbor guy to help me with it," the old man said.

Estelle looked at Al Fisher, who was grinning. "You're this 'neighbor guy,' Mr. Fisher?"

"That be me."

"When was the hunt?" Tully asked. "For this area, I mean?"

"Closed out end of last week," Torrez said. "Lupe, you have the tag down at your house?"

"Oh, sure." He managed to make it sound like "no," complete with a shake of the head.

Tully took a step forward, squaring his shoulders as if he expected someone to throw a punch at him. "You want to explain to us where all the piping goes?"

Lupe Gabaldon smiled and turned to look at both Al Fisher and Solomon Apodaca to make sure they were sharing the humor. "I guess you could dig up that pipe if you wanted," he said. "It's on your land, so I guess you could do that."

"That's not what I asked," Tully snapped.

Lupe's mouth formed a surprised "O"—surprised, but in no way intimidated by Tully's confrontational tone.

"Gentlemen," Sheriff Torrez interrupted, his patience wearing thin, "it don't make no difference where that water pipe goes, or who put it there." He turned to Tully. "We got a man missing and a woman down the hill shot to death. *That's* what we're supposed to be thinkin' about, not some damned water line."

"Amen, Sheriff," Solomon Apodaca said fervently. "A tragedy like this, right in our midst. Don't know how it could happen."

"Lupe, forget the damn pipe," Torrez said. "Have you seen Myron Fitzwater around the village in the past few days?"

"Well, yeah, I've seen him. Sure. He visits here quite a bit. Or did."

"When's the last time you saw him?"

Lupe looked askance at Torrez. "You're askin' what *day*?"

"Yep."

Something at his feet fascinated the old man, and he stared down for a full minute. "Saw him Friday morning. Pretty early."

"Where?"

"Over at Connie's place."

"What was he doing?"

"Him and Connie was arguing about the front door. I don't know what about it. At one point he hit the door with his shoulder, like he was trying to break in. The door swung open, and they argued some more." He shrugged. "That's it."

"When did you see him next?"

"Didn't, I don't suppose. I had things to do, and I guess they did too."

"Was Fitzwater up here? When you shot the deer?" Estelle asked.

Gabaldon looked puzzled. "Now why would that be? Why would he have been up here?"

"That's the next question, then," Estelle said.

"Well, he wasn't. Last time I saw him, he was on Connie's porch, and he and the girl were arguing about something. Like I said."

"How about you?" Estelle looked at both Al Fisher and Solomon Apodaca. "When was the last time you saw him?"

"Couldn't tell you. It's been a while, actually," Al said. "I've had family troubles of my own."

"I saw him one day when I went over to get the mail at the cluster box a couple weeks ago," Solomon Apodaca said. "Been that long. I asked him if he and Connie would like a nice bottle or two of Merlot, and he said sure. He swung by and picked 'em up. But that's been two, three weeks ago." Solomon shrugged. "I thought the young couple might like it for Christmas dinner, you know. Guess that ain't going to happen. Damned shame."

Lupe Gabaldon resettled his cap. "Now, you know this country as well as most." He regarded Bob Torrez with interest. "You've hunted here often enough, you got maybe a relative or two living here…are you any closer to figuring out what happened down below in that trailer?"

"'Spose so," Torrez said.

"Maria?" Estelle reached out a hand and touched Maria Apodaca on the arm. "Walk with me for a minute?"

The girl glanced at her boyfriend, but Al just shrugged, then nodded. Walking as if she had all day and nowhere to go, Estelle led the girl beyond the tank, beyond the remains of the deer carcass. When she spoke, she kept her voice low and confidential, and chose a spot where the tank loomed between them and the others.

"In a tiny village like this one, you must have known Connie Suarez better than most. She was about your age, no?"

Maria's voice was husky. "I knew her, sure."

"Friends?"

The girl hesitated. "I wouldn't say that."

"What would you say?"

Maria turned this way and that, her feet shuffling as if they couldn't decide whether to take her back to the group of villagers. "I didn't see Connie or her boyfriend much," she said finally.

"All you guys live within a hundred yards of each other, and you didn't see them on a regular basis?"

"No. I mean, she was busy with school and all. And when her boyfriend was here…"

"By 'her boyfriend,' you mean Myron Fitzwater."

Maria nodded. Estelle watched the girl's dark face intently, and saw the trace of tears in her deep-set eyes.

"As far as you know, did the two of them get along? Was there any friction there that you as a neighbor would have noticed?"

"No. Just that he wanted her to move. I know that."

"Just move out of that old trailer, or move away from Regál, you mean?"

"Away."

"But she wouldn't agree to that?"

"No. She grew up here. She loved it."

"You knew that for sure?"

"Yes." It looked as if she wanted to say something else, and Estelle waited patiently. "We talked about that once—we were at the parish market that we have on most Saturdays. We got to talking. It was kind of funny. She didn't want to move, and neither did I. Her boyfriend wanted her to move, and sometimes Al talks about it, too. She and I were in the same boat that way. We're happy where we are, with boyfriends who want something more."

She looked up and smiled brightly, tears still lurking. "That's what we decided. There are two kinds of people who live here—those who love it and would never leave and those who hate the solitude. I mean, I understand what they're saying. Sometimes it seems like this old mountain blocks out the rest of the world on one side, and that border fence blocks to the south." She cupped her hands together. "I can understand that someone might feel trapped."

"But you don't."

"No, ma'am. I love it. I love having my parents just next door. I love the holidays." She pivoted and looked up the hill, toward the patches of scrub and brush that managed to find toeholds among the rocks, toward the remnant conifers higher up on the slope. "I feel…protected." She heaved a great sigh. "And so did Connie Suarez. She told me that."

If only she had been, Estelle thought. "Tell me about Penny."

Maria looked up sharply, caught off-guard at the sudden change of subject. After a long moment of thought, she whispered, "I blame her. I might as well say it, Sheriff. I blame her a *lot*."

"You mean for Darrell's death?"

"Well, maybe she didn't pull the *trigger*, but…"

"But what?"

"It always seemed like there was nothing that Darrell could do that was right, you know? She was on his case all the time. Every little thing. I guess that's just the way she is, maybe." She shook her head sadly. "You know that old saying about putting brain in gear before engaging mouth? That was written for Penny, I think."

"And Darrell just put up with it?"

"Well, yeah. I mean, what else could he do?" She shrugged. "I guess there were all kinds of things he *could* have done, now that we look back on it. I thought that when they had Derry, things would get better." She wiped her eyes. "They didn't. And then…and then," she cleared her throat. "And Al tried his best to help Darrell along, you know. He liked to have him down here, *especially* with Derry. He liked to take him hunting. And all of that," she stopped abruptly, as if not wanting to interrupt the tear that had sprung loose and tracked down her cheek. "That made things worse. Penny didn't like me, and she *sure* didn't like Al. And Al, he tried to be obliging with Penny, but she's a hard case."

"I'm sure Al wishes that he'd found some way he could have helped."

Maria laughed hopelessly. "Yeah, well. He always said that what Darrell needed was a spine, and I guess he got that right. Maybe unkind, but true enough. Now me," and she held up both hands, "I tried to stay out of it." She rested a hand on her chest. "My job is to make life good for Al. That's my job, to make a nice home for him. So I didn't complain when he and his brother drank too much, or when Darrell stayed too late, or when they'd drop everything and take off hunting. I worried about Derry, but it wasn't my place…"

"Penny has visited down here?"

"Once. Just after Derry was born."

With a hand on her elbow, Estelle led Maria back around the tank. As soon as Al saw her, his face lit up in a bright smile.

With Deputy Brent Sutherland returned from his evidence delivery, Sheriff Torrez posted Sutherland downhill at the Suarez trailer, with rookie Deputy Tanner Garcia called in to sit the second site by the water tank.

"Cut away for a while," Torrez instructed Estelle as the others filed off downhill. "Go meet the celebrity at the airport." He came close to smiling. "And tell him I want to buy that truck of his when he gets tired of it." His face turned serious. "We got to put all this together, somehow. I got a couple of things I want to do, and I'll want to meet with you maybe this evening." He nodded at the retreating backs of the two Forest Service officers. "Stout and Tully are staying in town until something breaks."

"That could be a while."

"Maybe. I'm thinkin' not." He didn't tell her what he had in mind, but that was vintage Torrez. He kept his cards close, and Estelle had long ago learned to work with that.

Chapter Twenty-four

It would have been easy to let herself be distracted by her family's pending visit, but on the drive back to Posadas, Estelle forced herself to focus on the puzzle pieces that still floated in limbo. Coincidence was the gremlin, as *Padrino* had often said. There was no absolute proof that Darrell Fisher's death was a suicide—and ample reason to believe that it wasn't. The second death, this time in Regál, *might* have been a suicide, if credibility were stretched to the breaking point.

Everyone involved knew everyone else, and any psychologist would testify that suicides were epidemic. Once one person solved his problems with a bullet, then someone else near the brink might follow suit. But the scenario didn't fit the profile. The same psychologist might testify that Connie Suarez *might* have used her boyfriend's handgun to commit suicide—a hopelessly final way to lash back at Myron Fitzwater for some perceived slight.

No, she wouldn't, Estelle mused, unable to imagine Connie choosing the big Glock over another holiday spent in the sleepy little village.

The Broken Spur saloon flashed by, and Estelle glanced down at the speedometer. It hovered near ninety, and she backed off. A few minutes later, she swung into the Sheriff's Department parking lot in Posadas for a moment, and manipulated her cell phone, stroking down to select her son's number.

"Hey, Ma." Francisco sounded amused, then serious. "Dad says you've got a real mess going. I woulda called you, but I didn't want to interrupt something."

"Merry Christmas, but not for everybody, *hijo*."

"I'm sorry to hear that. Are you going to have time to visit with us? Is Big Bad Bobby going to let you take a day off? "

"I'll *make* time." *Easily said*, she thought.

"Or we could all ride along in the Beast with you."

"Are you talking about my car, or your truck?"

"Your beastly car. But either one will do."

She laughed. "That'll happen."

"I bet. Anyway, I think that's Lordsburg down below our left wingtip, so we'll be on final for Posadas International here in just a few minutes."

"I'm headed to the airport right now."

"Nifty. We have this whole thing figured out, so not to worry."

"Worry is not in my nature, *hijo*."

"I'll remember you said that, Ma. See you in a bit."

"Love you all, *hijo*. You and Carlos and Angie…"

"And Tasha. She's on the list now, too. But wait about six minutes for an introduction. I can see Cat Mesa now off in the distance, so we're close."

"Tasha?"

He laughed, and she could hear voices in the background. "You don't get to hear all the secrets, Ma. Be patient."

As she drove north out of Posadas, she kept glancing to the west, trying for that first glimpse of the incoming jet. The wind was from the southwest, which meant their final approach after they over-flew Posadas would be coming in from the east, down the narrow avenue between Cat Mesa to the north and the village of Posadas to the south. She heard the rumbling whistle of the jet engines before she saw the aircraft, and then it flashed over the highway, its graceful winglets raked high.

By the time the jet was ambling back along the taxiway, Estelle had pulled into the airport and parked beside her husband's SUV and Jim Bergin's aging Dodge Durango.

Bergin trotted out on the apron, two orange wands in hand, and directed the Gulfstream to an isolated spot on the tarmac convenient for the fuel truck. Even as its wheels stopped turning and the engines spooled down, the door hinged open and the small stairway extended.

Dr. Francis Guzman's hand slipped through her elbow, and she snuggled against him. "Can you believe this?"

"In this crazy day and age, I'll believe anything," he replied. "How are the aches?"

"I feel better already just being here." She hugged him even harder.

"And I called Bobby already," Francis said. "Not to spoil the moment," he quickly added.

She stopped abruptly, her hands lifting to both sides of his face. "And told him what? About the blood?"

"It's human, and it's O-positive. Statistically the most common type. Now file that away and enjoy this moment." He grinned widely and waved. "And here they are."

Francisco, looking impossibly handsome in blue jeans and a dark blue polo shirt under a lightweight black jacket, stepped out of the plane and turned, reaching back to offer his hand to Angie Trevino, who moved with great care on the narrow steps. With one hand holding the doorframe, she flashed a radiant smile and a wave as Estelle and Francis approached. When they were both safely down on the tarmac, Francisco linked his arm through Angie's.

When Estelle had last seen Angie Trevino, the girl had been so thin that at first Estelle had feared incipient anorexia. But it had become clear as Estelle came to know the girl that her svelte, model's figure was the result of work, hard work, and even more hard work as Angie kept up with a brutal concert career. Now, as she spread both arms wide to envelope first Estelle and then

Francis, the modest swell of her belly was unmistakable beneath her embroidered blouse.

"It is so good to be on the ground," Angie said, "and so good to see you folks again. What a wonderful holiday!"

"A bit of clear air turbulence over Arizona," Francisco explained. "I think both Angie and Tasha would rather have walked." Pulling her son close, Estelle breathed in the smell of him, feeling the power of his body, the depth and weight of his shoulder muscles, the strength of his hands.

"I can't believe you're here," she whispered, and hugged him all the harder.

He laughed ruefully. "For about thirty-six hours," he said. "That's better than nothing, I guess." He reached across and pumped his father's hand, and Francis flinched in mock pain.

"God, let me see that paw." The physician took Francisco's right wrist in one hand, spreading his hand wide with the other. "You've been lifting finger weights, or what?"

"Just hours and hours of five-flat, five octave scales," the young man explained. He turned toward the airplane and shouted, "Carlos! We're here, you know!" He turned to accept another fierce hug from his mother. "He's always busy with something, my brother. He and Tasha have this project going…" He turned his mother toward the aircraft's stairway as if about to make a formal presentation. "And it turns out that flying isn't her favorite thing to do, anyway. And the bumpy ride cinched the deal."

One of the flight crew appeared in the doorway, reached back and accepted a heavy flight bag from someone. She was nimble on the steps, and smiled broadly at Estelle and Francis as she extended a free hand.

"I'm First Officer Mary Steinbrenner. A picturesque little town you have here." Her accent carried the lilt of Scandinavia.

"It is that," Francis said. "Welcome. This is quite a surprise."

"Our stock and trade," Steinbrenner said. "We like to deliver surprises." She watched as Estelle transferred the hug from Francisco to an encore with Angie Trevino.

"A long flight for you," Estelle said.

"Time for *lots* of sleep," Angie said. "Compared to the past couple of weeks, the flight was almost a treat. *Almost.* Dr. Guzman, it's great to see you again, too." She wrapped him in a hug and as she did so, Francisco held up a finger signaling patience and then accompanied the agile Mary Steinbrenner back up into the aircraft.

When he reappeared at the top of the steps, it looked for a moment as if he'd somehow replicated himself, a double image. But it was Carlos, who leaned forward through the doorway, a hand on each side of the bulkhead. He raised his voice just enough to be heard. "Merry Christmas, and give us a minute, please." He turned and said something private to Francisco, and disappeared back into the airplane.

The older boy rejoined the group on the ground. "Tasha needs a moment or two to clean up a little." He grinned sheepishly at his father. "We didn't pop the Dramamine soon enough. I didn't realize that this was her first ride in a small jet. And what a ride." He turned and admired the sleek aircraft. "And bumps in the road at thirty-eight thousand feet. Can you believe that?"

He encircled his mother with an arm around her shoulders and reached out with the other hand to draw in his father. "So, how have you two been? Other than way too busy?"

"Way too busy," the physician replied. "I just returned from a confab in Mexico, so *that* put me behind. And your mother is trying her best to work twenty-six, eight." He reached out and hugged Estelle close.

"Well," Francisco said brightly, "let's just all pop back on board, and have Ms. Steinbrenner, Captain Oakes, and Second Officer Dave Lloyd hijack us someplace quiet and wonderful for a couple of days."

"You keep thinking," Angie muttered. "I like the idea of a quiet rocking chair in front of a roaring fire, and I bet I know where there might be both of those just a short drive from here."

"Are you doing okay?" Estelle asked.

"Actually I am, thanks—now that we're sure." She patted her belly. "There's a wonderful obstetrician in Berlin…probably several dozen of them, I'm sure. But Dr. Stein is special. I wish I could wave a magic wand and transport her to the states when the festival is finished."

"Magic wand." Francisco nodded toward the jet.

"Yeah. Well, we'll see." She beamed at Estelle. "Anyway, all is well, we're delighted, and after all the music the baby's heard these first two months, and has yet to hear over the next seven, he'll probably wind up being a NASCAR driver. Who knows?"

"A boy, though?"

"Oh, we don't know. And I don't want to know. It's just easier than calling him 'he, she, or it.'"

"I like the sound of NASCAR driver," Francisco said. "I vote for boy."

"And Danica will cut your chauvinistic throat, dude," Angie said.

Myriad questions swirled through Estelle Reyes-Guzman's head, but she shunted them all off to one side, content just to bask in the presence of these young world travelers.

"Ah," Francisco said as his brother reappeared, this time accompanying Tasha, with First Officer Mary Steinbrenner immediately behind. The young couple descended to the tarmac, and Tasha stopped, extending both arms in a broad salute. Her smile was radiant, and then she bent at the knees, dropping down so that she could pat the ground with both hands. Steinbrenner stepped close, perhaps thinking that the young woman had started to collapse, then smiled with relief. She angled off toward the fuel truck to engage Jim Bergin in conversation.

"May I present my brother and his better half, Natasha Abdullahi Qarshe? Tasha, this is our father, Dr. Francis Guzman, and our mother, Estelle Reyes-Guzman, undersheriff of Posadas County, upon whose firm ground you are now safely standing." Francisco ended his introduction with a stiff bow.

Better half, Estelle thought. *What exactly does that mean?* Ms. Qarshe matched Carlos's five-ten, with a willowy body, black hair secured in a casual ponytail, and skin the color of burned toast.

"It took me a moment to dig out a clean blouse," Tasha said. "How to embarrass myself." She extended both hands in greeting, and her grip was strong. Estelle found herself looking into a pair of deep-set eyes so dark that the irises were invisible, surrounded by exotic facial features—slightly aquiline nose, high and prominent cheekbones, and a generous, full-lipped mouth.

"Welcome, welcome," Estelle said.

The wide, brilliantly white smile returned. "Your son warned me that I would be meeting the most beautiful woman in the world. And here I thought he was exaggerating." She released her right hand and reached for Dr. Guzman's. "And here you are, Doctor." She looked from one to the other, and then back again. "An astonishing couple."

"So, let's boogie," Francisco said. "The flight crew needs to get us out of their hair, and have made a slight change of plans. Instead of staying in Posadas, they're going to deadhead up to their hub in Denver. They tell me that they have a little electronic issue that needs to be resolved before they tackle trans-Atlantic again the day after tomorrow."

Aft of the Gulfstream, First Officer Steinbrenner continued to engage Jim Bergin, who nodded patiently.

"There isn't a chance you all might be marooned in Posadas for a week or so?" Dr. Guzman asked. "We'd like that."

"I'm afraid not," Francisco said, but Carlos didn't sound so optimistic.

"When they end up giving a concert while marooned in Tahiti," the younger brother said, "you'll know the mechanics didn't get the instruments repaired just right."

Chapter Twenty-five

With enough luggage stowed in the back of Francis Guzman's SUV to provide for a week's marooning, Francisco waved off a side trip to the hangar and a visit with his vintage truck. "Maybe later," he said. "Right now, we all need home." Estelle marveled at his restraint, and then at his thoughtfulness for the comfort of the other weary travelers.

"He bought it sight unseen, except for a few photos," Angie said. "One of those Internet wonders."

"So it's a surprise for you too, *hijo*."

Francisco shrugged as if they'd been discussing picking up a dozen eggs on the way home. "We have better surprises coming up," he said.

"Speaking of which," Estelle said, "if Tasha rides in the front with Francis, you two guys can crowd into the back. Angie can ride with me. That might be the easiest arrangement for tender tummies."

By the time Estelle settled into her car, the fuel truck had pulled clear of the Gulfstream, and the jet's engines began their shriek.

"It's good to be on the ground," Angie repeated fervently. "And *so* good to see you folks." She shifted in the seat, angling her knees away from the racked shotgun, the computer terminal, and the emergency equipment control panel.

"Have you had the chance to talk with your mother recently?" Estelle asked.

"I called her last night. You knew that she moved to New York?"

Estelle nodded. "I was sorry to hear about your father."

"A tough summer, all around. Then my mom got her act back together and moved to the apartment of her dreams in Manhattan." Angie smiled. "Turns out that Kansas just wasn't her most favorite place to live, after all."

"An acquired taste, perhaps. Some folks swear by it."

"Or swear at it, in her case. My father loved it, she just put up with it for his sake. Shortly after my father's death, she put the house on the market and the agent called her *the next day* with a solid cash offer."

"Then she made the right move," Estelle said.

"And the next wonderful news is that she's joining us in Berlin for New Year's. We're so pleased about that, because this trip we just don't have the time to include New York."

They turned out of the airport's driveway onto State 76. As she turned to check for traffic, Estelle saw that Angie was gazing at her.

"Are you okay with this?" The girl rested her hand on her belly.

"Am *I* okay? I'm delighted, as long as you both are. I'm glad you found a physician you can trust."

"She's wonderful. I guess what I meant was are you okay that your son and I aren't married?" She flashed a huge smile. "Yet."

Estelle's phone played its E-flat chord, and she groaned as she slid the instrument out of her pocket. "Life goes on," she said. "Guzman."

"Hey."

"So, O-positive on the bloody stick," she prompted the sheriff, not adding that Dr. Guzman already had given her a heads-up on the blood.

"Yup. And Stout says that agrees with Fitzwater's personnel

file. The guy donates blood twice a year." When Estelle didn't respond, Bob Torrez added, "Yeah, I know. O-pos is the most common type…about four out of ten have it, or something like that."

"That doesn't narrow it much."

"Nope. And O-pos is more common in Hispanics than in Anglos, by a small margin."

"And that doesn't narrow it much, either."

"Nope. I talked to Posey just now."

"What's he tell us?" Doug Posey, one of the district officers for New Mexico Game and Fish, had been notified about the deer taken near the Regál water tank, but as far as Estelle knew, had not yet visited the site. A single deer, whether taken legally or poached, wasn't cause for much excitement.

"I told him about the bloody stick. He said that they did a little study last year after a poaching deal. As far as they could tell, muleys all have the same blood type, at least within the herd. It may be different from white-tail blood, or different races of muleys over a wide area."

"Why were you checking that?"

"Just curious. The blood on the stick is O-pos human. We're sure of that. It wasn't deer blood. And the type matches Fitzwater."

"And the hair? Most likely not deer hair, either, then."

"We haven't seen a hair comparison yet, but it's hair, not fur, if you know what I mean. Kind of blondish hair."

"So…who clobbered whom?"

"That's the question, ain't it? That and one other little thing."

"And that is?"

"We ain't got shit that says the three incidents are related—the dead deer and Fitzwater's blood up there and Connie Suarez lyin' dead down in the trailer. Or how Fitzwater's Glock come to kill Connie. *If* the Glock is the murder weapon. If it wasn't just dropped."

"Have you taken the deer carcass apart yet? The skull?"

"That's next. Posey is going to be in town later tonight. Him and me were going to go down and talk with Lupe again after we dig the slugs out of the skull."

"Slugs, plural?"

"Lookin' like two, and a third maybe grazed. The two didn't exit. And not lookin' a bit like a high-powered rifle, either."

"Lupe said…"

"Yeah, I know what he said. That he bagged that deer with one shot from his Marlin thirty-thirty? It ain't lookin' like that's the case."

Estelle fell silent, thinking about Lupe Gabaldon and elderly, matronly Flora, the couple living in their cozy little place out of the hustle and bustle. "I'll be home for a while, if you need me."

"Yup. Tell the kid that if he's ready to sell that truck, he's got an eager buyer."

"They just landed, and Francisco didn't even look at it, Bobby. How's that for self-control?"

Torrez grunted something incomprehensible and switched off.

"Wow," Angie said in wonder. "I couldn't help hearing some of your end. Somebody is shooting deer out of season? I thought game wardens dealt with that sort of thing."

"It's a mess, Angie. One big unhappy mess. And I wish it was just deer that they're shooting."

Chapter Twenty-six

The living room of the Guzman home had gone from achingly empty to bursting at the seams, the kitchen from a pair of unfinished pies to a wealth of food, a large portion of which was the younger brother's creation, kibitzed to completion by Tasha Qarshe's affectionate encouragement. The two piecrusts that Estelle had made and then stowed in the fridge were rescued and completed by Carlos, with two more sour cherry pies added to the inventory.

To add to the hubbub, Bill Gastner arrived ten minutes after the first lasagna went into the oven, and the new flurry of introductions and explanations swirled through the group. Never particularly reserved, Gastner regarded Tasha with interest as the girl re-entered the living room after a foray into the kitchen. She stopped beside Estelle, who had settled in the rocker. Tasha bent and draped a long arm across Estelle's shoulders, turning to whisper something in her ear.

"Kitchen is his favorite word," Estelle replied with a laugh to whatever the girl had said.

Gastner held up a hand to catch the young woman's attention and then gestured toward the couch. "So, young lady. Sit still for a moment and tell me about yourself."

Tasha looked quizzical. "Myself?"

"How did you happen to meet our chef of the moment? Let's start there."

"Ah, that." She straightened up and moved to the end of the couch. "Truly the 'Small World' department, sir. You see, I attended a concert in Palo Alto—well, at Stanford—by Rafael Duprés, the classical guitarist? Perhaps you've heard him play?"

"And perhaps not," Gastner said agreeably. "He hasn't come to Posadas yet."

"Well, someday, perhaps. He's magnificent. At any rate, this was in September. Before the concert, I was out in the lobby, looking at one of the posters advertising upcoming artist performances. Perhaps you can guess who was featured for an October recital." She looked across at Francisco, who sat sideways on the piano bench. "Here is this huge photo of the artist sitting at the piano, right hand resting on the music rack, left hand on the keys, eyes closed, this *soulful* expression on his handsome face." She laughed as Francisco struck the pose.

"You have to catch naps when you can," he said.

"Just enchanting. Then I sensed this presence directly behind me, and I turned." She paused and sucked in a breath, one slender hand going to her mouth dramatically. "And there he was."

"Except he wasn't," Carlos added from the kitchen doorway.

"No, *he* wasn't. But this young man who bore a striking resemblance to the *maestro* smiled at me as if we'd known each other for decades, as if we had agreed previously to meet at the concert. 'Would you like to go?' he asked. And I pointed at the "Sold Out" banner across the poster. He dismissed it. 'I have tickets.' I was speechless, but I managed to say something really intelligent, like 'you do?'"

"I do," Carlos interjected. "I *did*." He leaned against the kitchen archway.

"To make a very long story short, we went to the Duprés concert and managed to finagle seats together. Afterward, he let it slip. He said something innocent, like, 'So, will you go to my brother's concert with me?' His *brother*."

"And that's when you refused to go..." Francisco interrupted helpfully.

She made a contrite face. "By the time the concert came around, Carlos had been living in my apartment for two weeks." She held her shoulders up in an enormous shrug. "What was I to do?"

Gastner frowned, but his eyes twinkled. "So he's a free-loader, to boot."

"Absolutely."

"It must be serious if you'll even go so far as to get airsick for him."

"It's his culinary skills, sir."

"Ah. Understandable, then." Gastner's face softened a little. "I have lots more questions, you'll be delighted to know."

"I don't mind."

"You may, by the time I'm done. Interrogation comes easy to us old has-been cops."

She folded her hands primly between her knees, back ramrod straight, and looked expectant.

"Home is…"

"Where Carlos is." Her answer was so immediate that Francisco clutched his chest in mock romantic agony, and Gastner twisted around to grin at Estelle.

"She's sharp. How about B.C., then? *Before* Carlos."

"I was born in Boston, and lived there until three years ago, when I enrolled at Stanford. My mother is first-generation Irish, my dad still cherishes his Somali citizenship. He and my mom are partners in McKinney, Qarshe, and O'Hanrahan in Boston." She flashed a smile. "My mom is the O'Hanrahan part. Their firm specializes in design and engineering of container ship load-handling equipment—elevators, cranes, waterproof hatches, that sort of thing."

Gastner raised an eyebrow. "Congratulations on choosing your parents well, young lady."

"Thank you, sir."

"And if we can enjoy the rest of the evening without your calling me 'sir,' I'll be delighted."

Carlos appeared again. "*Maestro*, the lasagna will be ready to serve in fifteen minutes. Is there a chance for a short thematic piece to set the mood? And, Ma, I forgot where you hide the candles."

Gastner rose from the heavy straight-backed chair he had appropriated and moved to the end of the piano where he settled a hand on the raised lid. "You charter a jet to fly all the way over from Germany to play for a damn dinner party. How special is that?" He rapped a knuckle on the ebony finish. "You and your brother and the young ladies have made this a special Christmas, Bud. Thanks for that."

Chapter Twenty-seven

"How long have you known Lupe Gabaldon?" The question came at 9:35 that Christmas Eve, after enough food, laughter, music, and banter that Estelle Reyes-Guzman had almost begun to think that life couldn't be any better. Five minutes before, a sleepy Bill Gastner had excused himself, gladly accepting a steadying hand from Francisco as he made his way out to his SUV. Estelle watched as they stood for a few moments on the sidewalk, the eighty-four-year-old and his twenty-five-year-old godson, engaged in quiet consultation—about what, only they knew.

Then, just as Francisco came back inside, her cell phone had begun to spin circles on the polished surface of the piano where she'd placed it, its audio silenced—just in case.

For a moment, coming as it did without so much as a simple "hello" of greeting, Sheriff Robert Torrez' question about Lupe Gabaldon formed in Estelle's brain an enormous clot, a classic non-sequitur stall.

"You there?" Torrez prompted.

"I'm tempted to say 'no'." Estelle walked past Francisco, out of the room and down the hallway to their bedroom. "But, yes—I've known Lupe all my life. At least it seems that way. As long as I can remember."

"He's something of a bandit."

"Well, by today's standards, I suppose. Like my Great Uncle Reuben. Or Soloman Apodaca. Or any of those *viejos*. They've lived long enough to see lots of changes in their world."

"You remember what he told us up on the hill, though, about the deer?"

"Yes. He said he took it with his thirty-thirty."

"Yup. Claimed one shot through the heart."

"'Ruined' the heart is what I remember him saying."

"That ain't what happened, though."

Estelle reached out and closed the bedroom door. "What did you find out?"

"I recovered the spent bullets from the deer's skull. Two of 'em, anyways. The third just grazed the soft skin behind the ears."

"So he shot several times?"

"Nope. He ain't no Rifleman. And the slugs I recovered were twenty-twos, nothin' heavier."

Estelle fell silent. After a moment, she asked, "So what do you think?"

"I don't think any of this happened the way Lupe says it did."

She took a long, deep breath of resignation. "You're down at the office?"

"Yup. I got Linda comin' in after a little bit to document the skull. I want nice clear eight-by-tens when we go down to chat with Lupe." Torrez made a little snorting sound as if a laugh was bubbling to the surface. "And him bein' the old-timer that he is, I'm bettin' that the deer heart is wrapped up in his freezer. And I'm bettin' that it ain't got a hole blown through it by a thirty-thirty."

"What's Posey think?"

"He's kinda curious."

"I bet he is. He's going down with you in the morning?"

"I was thinkin' first thing. Before Lupe has a chance for his second cup of coffee."

"Or now, while he's too tired to think straight."

Torrez scoffed gently. "That would be you, I'm guessin'. Look, I need some time to get the pichures in order, and Posey was out all last night, so *he* ain't too excited about it. Look, I know it's Christmas, but how about six tomorrow morning?" He paused, giving Estelle time to think, then added, "Your company ain't going to be out of bed by then, anyways. We can scoot down and do our business, and get you back home."

"You should spend Christmas morning with Gayle, Gabe, and little Sophie, Bobby. And your folks, and a hundred other relatives. Bullets in a deer's skull can wait. Lupe's not going anywhere."

"Maybe not. But the longer we sit on this, the harder it's going to be. You know that, and I know that. Your guys are stayin' all day tomorrow? Jettin' out Wednesday early?"

"I think that's the plan, Bobby." She clearly understood by his tone where this was heading. Robert Torrez was hunting.

"That'll work, then. See you at six. You want I should pick you up, or what?"

"I'll meet you at Betty's at six. Right at the intersection."

"You got it."

"Give my love to Gayle and the kids. Enjoy Christmas Eve, at least."

"Yup."

She stood for a moment, silent phone in hand. Robert Torrez was eager to be on the hunt. When that happened, holidays and company didn't matter much.

Chapter Twenty-eight

When Estelle left the bedroom and returned to the kitchen, the dishes were cleared, washed, and stashed away. Half of one of the sour cherry pies—its finely pinched crust the work of her son's culinary talents—was wrapped in kitchen film. The others had vanished.

A large architectural rendering covered part of the dining room table, along with a series of smaller drawings, and Estelle instantly recognized the building, and the country reflected by the large map and the various printouts from the computer's satellite imagery.

"Is everything all right?" her husband asked.

"We're not sure." Estelle only half-heard the question, so transfixed was she by the works spread before her. "This is *Mamá's* old place in Tres Santos." Her voice was scarcely a whisper.

"The Rio Plegado," Francisco said. He leaned over the table and ran his index finger along the watercourse. "The old school, and higher up here on the bench, the new school. The old church is gone, but the new one shows up pretty well. Your mother's original house is this little speck, just high enough above the river to be safe." He tapped the array of buildings to the northeast of Teresa Reyes' small cottage. "The Diaz family's hacienda. Ramón is eighty now, *Mamá*, but both he and Marta are doing well—spry and hard at it. And what I think is neat is that seven of the eight Diaz children live in this little mini-village here."

"Federico and his wife moved to Mexico City some years ago," Estelle said. "They lived in *Mamá's* house for a while, then they moved."

Francisco reached out and pulled a small rendering across the table. "This is Teresa's place."

"Yes." She felt a twinge. "That," and she lightly touched the drawing, "is the tree stump into which Pancho Villa supposedly carved his name in 1913." She picked up the drawing as if it were rendered on the thinnest tracing paper rather than the heavy artist's stock that had been used. "This is amazing." She turned it slightly and looked at the signature.

"The fastest pencil in the West," Francisco said.

"When did you do this?"

"Last week," Carlos said. "A rush job."

"You remembered the place well, *hijo*."

"Well, Ma, there isn't a whole lot of detail to remember. Your mom's house is a small box, with some vigas, stuff like that."

"And this," Francisco said, "is what we're thinking about." He turned a larger rendering so that it faced Estelle. She involuntarily took a step backward. She recognized Carlos' work—the meticulous architectural printing, the deft touches of shading here and there to highlight corners and overhangs, even the faint pencil-stroke images of three ravens far in the distance, riding the air waves over the mesa.

It didn't surprise Estelle that her younger son, in only his first year at Stanford, already had such masterful drafting skills—he'd been designing and drawing since he'd been old enough to walk and find paper and pencil. He'd taken every mechanical drawing and drafting class that Posadas Public Schools had offered. And finally, before transferring to Stanford, he'd experimented with two years in the state university at Las Cruces, exploring their curriculum.

"I think we'll be experimenting with lots of changes in this concept," Francisco said eagerly. "Right now," and he shifted another paper, "the entire original structure of Teresa's four-room adobe has blended with the new structure, and accommodates a proposed music room off the southeast wing of the house."

"Whoa," his father said. "I'm missing something."

"Ay, missing something is right." Estelle pointed with her chin at the legend in the lower right corner. "'Teresa Reyes Adobe Renovation, Tres Santos, Mexico.' So this, and she touched the original rendering of her mother's former home, "is Teresa's original adobe. And now someone is having you design this *massive* project on the same property, Carlos? And somehow including the original little house?"

"Someone," Carlos agreed, and nodded at his brother.

"Exactly," Francisco said. "That's what we're thinking about."

"*We?*"

Francisco sat down and looked up at his mother. "Angie and I, and we're going to need all kinds of help, including the services of the most talented architect I know."

"Start at the beginning, *hijo*."

"Well, last year we decided, Angie and I, we need a quiet retreat somewhere when we're not on the road. We're in agreement on that. Angie has a rigorous practice and composing schedule, and so do I. We've discovered that when we're 'in the zone,' as they say, we both tend to sort of implode. We don't want the sound of traffic, or barking dogs, or sirens, or jets taking off...so, tell me that you know of a place more serene, quieter, than Tres Santos."

She turned and regarded her son thoughtfully. In the lines of his face, she could still see the little boy he had once been, the eagerness, the "anything is possible" expression. "You're not kidding."

"No. And now, Posadas is just a forty-five-minute drive north of this property. With a newly resuscitated airport that can handle jets, no less. We can fly in from anywhere in the world, just as we did today, grab the car, and be home here," and he rapped the table beside the rendering, "in minutes." He watched her face intently. "You think we're nuts."

"Yes. Not for wanting peace and quiet, *hijo*. I understand *that*. And not for building an elegant, spacious home with facilities for your music. Most people—not everyone, certainly—but most people need an anchor, a place to be when they're not traveling. I understand that. I understand that you would want that." She stopped abruptly.

"But…" Francisco prompted.

"But I'm not sure you two have thought this through. Now, am I assuming correctly that you somehow plan to purchase the property from the Diaz family?"

"Yes. We've investigated that already, primarily through the help of Colonel Naranjo's wife. Eloisa handles many real estate transactions, and said that this one would be no problem for her."

"Even though the property is in what the Mexican government calls the restricted zone? You've explored that issue? Tres Santos is close enough to the border to be affected by that… all the restrictions on ownership by foreigners that the Mexican government has imposed."

Francisco nodded slowly. "Eloisa Naranjo is familiar with the complications of establishing the real estate trust, the *fideicomiso*, on our behalf. She also said that she can enlist the aid of an attorney friend in Janos, where a likely lending bank is. As you are aware, Ma, in the restricted zone, it's the bank that actually ends up owning the property, and establishing the real estate trust for us."

"Yes. But, *hijo*, I can't imagine you have time for all of this."

"I don't. That's why the experts are involved. To make sure our interests are considered fully, and also the third party's interests."

She glanced at her husband, who was slouched back in his chair, feet extended under the kitchen table. He raised an eyebrow at her, but said nothing.

"I'm almost afraid to ask. A 'third party'? Who might that be?"

"You remember Mateo Diaz? He's the second-oldest of the Diaz children." He smiled. "No child anymore, of course. He's forty, at least."

"Yes."

"If we do all this, he would like the opportunity to live in an included apartment on the property. A sort of caretaker for us, if you will."

"He's the son who's so badly crippled. Arthritis in his spine."

"Yes, he is. In fact, he tells me that he's been to see the good doctor more than once." Francisco grinned at his father. "He already uses a walker to help him maintain his balance. But his hands—his ability to carve the most wondrous things—those skills are undiminished."

"He has never gotten married."

"No. Of the eight Diaz children, he is the only one who is not."

Estelle walked slowly around the table and took a chair immediately beside her husband.

"You've given a lot of thought to this adventure."

"Oh, yes. And lots more thought to come."

"And when you're home, and working at the piano eight hours a day, or Angie is locked in to the cello, Mateo is going to be able to put up with your practice and composing schedules?"

"Won't hear a note, Ma," Carlos said. "Acoustical engineering being what it is, their music room will be like being locked in a bank vault. Mateo won't hear them, and they won't hear his woodshop next door."

The two young women, Angie and Tasha, leaned on the kitchen counter, overseeing the gathering. Estelle nodded at Angie. "And you? What do you think about all of this?" She leaned forward and clasped her hands tightly on top of the rendering. "With a baby coming in six months? With trips back and forth across the border in these times? With a wealth of construction facing you?"

"I think that these days, it's all in who we hire, Estelle. Mateo has told Francisco that he'll gladly oversee construction—it is, after all, his home too. Or will be."

"And he's already suffering health problems of his own."

"It's interesting, Ma," Francisco said. "He's more concerned with his elderly parents than he is with himself. The other siblings may come and go...in fact Tinita and her new husband are in the process of moving to Mexico City."

"I didn't know that."

"Yep. That's where Federico has a family outlet store. And who knows what the others might do over the years? For us, Mateo is the stabilizing factor. He has no visions of leaving Tres Santos. He makes a good living from his carving and his guitars. He and his brothers Juan and Federico are making exquisite instruments now. Very upper end, concert quality."

A ghost of a smile touched Estelle's face. "I always imagined you ending up living in some place like St. Moritz, or Los Angeles, or Manhattan."

"Save me, please." The young man's face was sober. "When I stand and look out the front door...or the back door...what I *don't* want to see is traffic. Or tourists. Or neon lights."

The room fell silent. "And in five or six years, when your child is ready for school? She's going to travel with you, with all the upsets, the frantic schedules, all the *strangers*? How are you going to manage that?"

"Others have in the past," Francisco said. "Others have found a way." He grinned. "When I was little, I remember our own *Nana*. You were often busy at all hours, and *Papá's* patients didn't always schedule themselves conveniently. Irma was a jewel, wasn't she?"

"She was. Irma Sedillos was a rare jewel."

"Perhaps there is another Irma Sedillos out there, just waiting. One thing I know for sure. The child will have a doting grandmother."

Estelle knew exactly what her son meant, but she quickly corrected him. "*Two* doting grandmothers."

Francisco and Angie both laughed. "One at each end of the country," Angie said. "We're covered."

An hour later, exhausted from an impossible day, Estelle snuggled against Francis, luxuriating in the warmth of his hand on her sore ribs. "Do you think they know what they're in for?"

"Of course not. That's what makes it fun."

"You're a big help."

"I'm serious," Francis said. "The only thing that really makes me pause is that little Mexican village that stands to have its serenity disturbed. Tres Santos has enjoyed anonymity for hundreds of years. It's not on the way to anywhere, and it's not a destination. Now imagine who moves in, right off the cover of *Rolling Stone*." His hand paused just under her right breast. "You've got a knot right there."

"A tender knot." She sighed and stretched a little. "And you're right. Is that tiny village ready for *them*? That's something that they haven't considered. But…"

"But?"

"But I like the tentative house plan Carlos has going. I like the way it blends in with the features of the land. Sprawling as it is, it still makes use of the river's gallaria to blend and hide. It's high enough above the riverbed to be out of harm's way during a flood, but still benefit from the vegetation."

"They'll make a convert of you yet. And, you know, having a little one around will be a joy. You can be that doting grandma."

"And grandpa." She wiggled closer. "I like the sound of that."

"And not to bring up a less pleasant subject, what did Bobby want earlier? I heard something about six o'clock."

"That's what time we're meeting in Regál. We're going to ruin Lupe Gabaldon's Christmas Day."

"Lupe? *Viejo* Lupe?"

"The very same."

"How's he involved?"

"We aren't sure. But he lied to us, *Oso*. For no good reason.

He told us that he shot the deer. And Bobby is sure that's not the way it happened."

"The kids are wanting to go to Tres Santos tomorrow."

"I think so, yes. I'll try to be back in time. Or maybe meet them down at the border. And *Oso*, please…a big favor. Let them use my Toyota. Or if you're going down too, let them ride with you. Don't let them take that damn Army truck that he's got in the hangar at the airport."

"It's not licensed, is it?"

"No. A minor detail. But it has no top, no seat belts, no nothing."

"Maybe Bobby can confiscate it."

"An *excellent* idea, *Oso*. I'll mention it to him."

Chapter Twenty-nine

She tossed and turned, too much rich food on top of too much to think about. She forced herself to wait until the digital clock recorded four-thirty a.m., and shrugged off the bedding.

"Merry Christmas." Her husband's voice was muffled. He turned his head slightly out of the pillow. "And eat something," he added.

"I was thinking of a couple scrambled eggs and a piece of cherry pie. Can I fix you some?"

"Yuck. No."

She bent down and whispered with her lips touching his ear. "Merry Christmas, *Oso*. I'm still finding it hard to believe the kids and their girls are all here. That makes it the best Christmas ever."

"Francisco and Angie were up talking half the night," Francis said. "They're going to be pooped."

She patted his shoulder as she turned away. "The energy of youth."

"Hey?"

"Yes?"

"Wear your vest."

"I always do, *Oso*."

"No, you don't."

She turned and looked down at him, scrunched in a tight ball under the comforter, head half-buried in the pillow. "Hibernate some more, *querido*," she whispered.

The second egg had just started sizzling when she felt an arm around her shoulders. She turned to see a tousle-headed Francisco, eyes heavy with sleep. Her son shut his eyes and let his head sag to her shoulder.

"Merry Christmas, *hijo*."

"I think so. My screwed up internal clock says it's already mid-afternoon."

"Berlin time, I suppose that it is. You guys really have to fly out tomorrow?"

"Unfortunately so."

"I'm sorry we didn't have a big Christmas shebang for you."

"Thank God for small favors. Tell you what, I'll stop somewhere today and buy a half dozen sweaters. Then we can trade them back and forth. Anyway, you have the tree, and that's all that counts, as far as I'm concerned." The "tree" was a tiny thing that stood on the living room windowsill behind the piano, hand-crafted out of various colors and textures of paper, with a small string of mini-lights giving it cheer. Irma Sedillos and Carlos had constructed it during one holiday a dozen years before. It generally remained on the windowsill, its delicate illumination bouncing off the polished ebony surface of the piano, until mid-April, when Estelle forced herself to tuck it away.

"It looks like you're headed out this morning?"

"I'm afraid so, for a little bit, anyway. I'm meeting Bobby down in Regál in a few minutes."

"They don't give you Christmas Day off?"

"They? Nope, 'they' don't. The holidays are when family disputes are often at their worst. Christmas isn't as bad as New Year's Eve, thankfully." She plated the scrambled eggs and cut a slice of cherry pie. "Festive colors," she observed. "You're sure you don't want something?"

"Coffee." He jerked his hands up like a spastic robot, and turned to the coffeemaker. "Must have coffee." For a couple of minutes, she leaned against the counter and ate as he fussed with the coffeemaker. "Do you have any idea how *Padrino* found out about our project with Teresa's property?" he asked finally, satisfied that the drip was on the way.

"*Padrino* knows?"

"He does. Not in any great detail, but the gist of it, he knows." He half-turned away from the gadget. "Not that I mind, not that it matters. I mean, he obviously didn't tell *you*, right?"

"No, he didn't."

"I mean, he's about the most tight-lipped old cuss that I know. Maybe my brother has been in contact with him."

"That wouldn't surprise me. Maybe he had questions about construction that includes old adobe. *Padrino*'s lived with that for decades now. His place was old before he bought it way back in the day. He added on to it, changed this and that. Both Carlos and you have spent lots of time over there."

"It's a grand place," Francisco said pensively. "That big sunken living room could be easily modified to make a great home for the Steinway."

"You spoke with him last night?"

Francisco looked up quickly. "Just for a few minutes, out at his truck, when he was getting ready to go home." He nodded and poured a cup of coffee. Still thinking hard, he sipped, then sipped again. "He had two pieces of advice. And you know *Padrino*." Francisco smiled. "He doesn't pull punches."

Estelle slid her empty plate into the sink. "What did he suggest?"

"First, that we, especially Angie, would *hate* Tres Santos. 'Good-hearted neighbors will barge into your lives, whether you welcome them or not.' That was his first admonition."

"How true." She could picture the elderly Marta Diaz bustling next door after Angie's baby arrived, sure in her ancient wisdom that Angie would need *something*, without ever considering that what the young mother might need was peace and quiet.

"And he said, 'You don't want the border as a part of your lives. Maybe back in 1950, but not now.'"

"He's right about that. Things have changed with the border," Estelle said. "And not for the better." Despite the validity of the old man's advice, she felt a keen sense of disappointment, a looming of St. Moritz, or Paris, or New York in the future.

"And then he offered us his home."

"What do you mean, 'offered'?"

"He offered to give it to us, with a caveat." He waited for Estelle's reaction, and when no comment was forthcoming, said, "He wants to live there until he can't any longer."

"*Ay.*"

"Negotiating with him will be a challenge."

"How so?"

"He wants to *give* it to us, for a dollar."

"Well…"

"How can I do that? Come on."

"Because that's what he wants? That's his way. He gave your father's new clinic almost four acres."

"That's right. I remember that. But still, what's the market value of that place? Three, four hundred thousand? Maybe more?"

"*Hijo*, probably the last thing *Padrino* needs, or wants, is more money. I'm sure he offered his home to you because he loves you unconditionally, because he *believes* in your career, because he *knows* that this could be a wonderful, secluded spot for you, away from the world." She smiled. "For those odd few moments when you'll be home."

"You think I…*we*…should consider the offer?"

"For many reasons, I think that you and Angie should give it serious thought."

"Well, as one of my favorite people on all of earth is fond of saying, '*Ay*'."

"We'll talk about it this afternoon, or tonight. Whenever."

"He invited us to stop over today to tour the place. You know—with an eye toward a possibility."

She waited until he set the coffee cup down, then hugged

him hard. "I need to get dressed." She looked up at him. "That would be some Christmas gift, you have to admit."

"Oh, my."

"We'll talk about it tonight." She slapped both his upper arms simultaneously, hard, and glared at him with mock ferocity. "And don't be driving that old unlicensed truck on the highway, *hijo*." The ferocity vanished in an amused grin. "Bobby Torrez would *love* to confiscate it."

Chapter Thirty

By dint of breaking a few speed limits herself, Estelle arrived at Betty Contreras' driveway at 5:58 a.m. Two minutes later, the sheriff's aging pickup—what he called his "undercover unit," rumbled down the hill into Regál, swung in a wide loop, and pulled up driver-to-driver beside Estelle's unit, a pungent odor of burned oil arriving with it.

"I was guessin' you'd sleep in," he greeted.

"I could have. Bobby, this is the only day I have with the kids, so I'm kinda antsy."

"Yeah, well."

Mr. Sympathy, she thought.

Without further comment, he handed a folder across. Estelle turned on the interior reading light and swiveled it to shine down on the pages. She leafed through the images. Linda Real had done a masterful job. The illustrated rifle slugs were clear against a black background, enlarged to fill an eight-by-ten sheet.

"Twenty-two for sure?" The projectiles appeared to be solid lead, and the scale laid across the bottom of the photos showed slightly more than an exact twenty-two caliber. The legend box in the corner announced that both projectiles were .224 inches base diameter.

"The third one just cut the fur on the back of the neck behind the ears," Torrez said. "These two entered just behind the eyeball, punched into the brain through that thin orbit bone. Didn't make it out the other side."

She slid the photos apart. "Who'd you bribe at the hospital?" The X-ray image of the small skull was equally sharp, showing the two slugs in situ, less than an inch apart. In the final photo, the two small holes were difficult to see clearly in the fur covering the deer's skull, but again, a ruler had been carefully placed. The holes were slightly less than half an inch apart.

"They kinda wondered," Torrez said evasively, perhaps a little reluctant to implicate a cousin.

"Heck of a double tap," Estelle observed.

"If the deer hadn't been runnin', the third one might have been with the group," Torrez said. "As it was, it's only a couple inches out."

"Pretty fancy shooting."

Torrez shrugged, unimpressed. "Good semi-auto, good low-power scope, kinda short range—no big deal. But the shooter sure didn't get buck fever. I'll give him that." He pointed and Estelle looked in her rearview mirror. The state Game and Fish truck pulled up behind her charger. Lieutenant Doug Posey took his time getting out and then closed the driver's side door as if it might shatter if he pushed it too hard. Estelle unbuckled from the Charger and met Posey by the back fender. His twenty-seven years with the Game and Fish Department had apparently agreed with him—as tall as Torrez but thin as a rail, he still looked much younger than he was, until he removed his Stetson and revealed a polished, hair-free dome.

"Merry Christmas," he said. "I hear your two urchins flew in yesterday."

"Merry Christmas, and yes, they did." And once more, Estelle marveled at the tenacious tendrils of the community grapevine.

"Well, if *I* had a wife and kids, I'd want to be home for the holiday, too." He extended a hand to Torrez. "Long time no see, Robert."

"Yep," the sheriff said, and drew his hand back into the truck. "Let's go do it."

Estelle handed Posey the folder containing the photos. "This is what was recovered from the skull."

"Huh." Posey turned the prints this way and that, holding them down so the headlights of his truck played over the glossy paper. "Okay. And just to make sure I'm up to speed, Lupe claims he shot the deer with a thirty-thirty."

"Yep."

"These are all filed away in an evidence bag for me?"

"Sure."

"But we don't really care about the deer, do we?" He grimaced. "Listen to me saying that. But that's the direction this is all going. If Lupe shot the deer the way he says he did during season, and has a tag for it, then that's that. I guess based on this evidence, I could write him a ticket for use of an illegal gun, but I don't think that's going to happen. Anyway, let's clear this up and I can go home to my imaginary wife and kids."

"He didn't take it with one shot through the heart with a thirty-thirty, guaranteed," Torrez said. "You ready?"

"Let's wake people up," Estelle replied.

Lupe Gabaldon didn't need waking. He stood on the small front porch of his home, coffee mug in one hand, cigarette in the other. He watched the three vehicles maneuver for a spot to park, with Torrez nosing his pickup into the Suarez' driveway across the lane.

"You want some coffee?" he greeted, lifting his cup.

"Is Flora up and at 'em?" Lieutenant Posey asked.

"Oh, long since," Lupe said. "She went over to have breakfast with Betty. One of their Christmas morning traditions after Betty's husband died." He pointed at Torrez with his cup. "When Bobby here called me last night and said he wanted to stop by this early in the morning…" He didn't finish the thought, but instead said, "Two old maids together on Christmas morning." He chuckled. "You need to talk with her too?"

"Maybe. But if she was in bed, I didn't want to disturb her."

"Oh, no. She's down the road. Come on in." He held the door for the trio. The adobe was snug and fragrant, the woodstove on the west wall alive with a bright fire.

"Why don't you sit here?" Lupe touched Estelle's elbow and indicated a slender, straight-backed chair near the kitchen door. "If Bobby sits on it, he'll break it." He turned to Torrez. "Coffee?"

"Sure."

"Mr. Lieutenant?"

"Absolutely," Posey said. "Black, please."

Estelle's gaze roamed the room, taking in the impressive collection of carved creatures. Lupe returned with two mugs filled, and saw Estelle examining one of the carvings, a museum-quality rendition of a cow elk with twins in trail.

"That's the work of one of the Diaz boys. Juan, the youngest boy. He did that." He pointed across the room at a mountain lion creeping down a snag. "That's one of Roberto's." He looked back at Estelle. "You know them all, I guess. The Diaz boys?"

"Certainly. They're a talented family."

Lupe sighed with satisfaction. "I go down there, maybe once a month, to see what they have. Sometimes I'm lucky. They sell fast, you know. If I don't get there first…"

Sheriff Torrez, growing impatient with small talk, rapped the manila folder of photographs against his thigh. "We got to talk about your deer, Lupe."

"Well, okay." The old man looked expectant, but not the least bit apprehensive or worried.

"What day did you bag him?" Posey asked.

"I got to think about that." He moved to the old sofa and sank down, careful not to spill his coffee. "What day did I tell you?"

"That's what I'm asking." Posey grinned, at ease with having to hear the tall tales fishermen and hunters were so adept at spinning.

"I think it was Thursday. Thursday in the afternoon. Not late. I'd say just about one o'clock."

"You hunt up around the water tank often, I imagine."

"Not so much now." Lupe shrugged. "It's a long hike and a steep hill." He huffed a deep breath. "I was winded yesterday after that hike to see what you guys were doing up there."

"So how did it happen this time?"

"How did what happen?"

"You and the deer on Thursday."

"Oh. Well, I see them." He pointed at the northeast window, past the carved mountain lion. "Right through here?" He pulled the sheer curtain. "You can see Betty's roof. The Contreras place? And just up the hill a little ways is that old path, right where we were yesterday. Part of that path is in the open, but you know that, 'cause you hiked it too. Now, those darn deer, they just walk around here, you know? Like they own the place. I look out the window and see them moving through the trees, and I'm thinking, well now, this is easy."

"So you got your gun and stalked up there."

Lupe nodded proudly. "They all ran up through the rocks, but this little buck, he thinks he's not afraid of anything." He held his hands up high in front of his mouth, miming being sneaky. "I'm real quiet. And he lets me get close enough. I use the water tank for cover, sure. I keep it between me and him."

"So one shot with your trusty thirty-thirty and down he goes." Posey looked impressed. "Right through the heart."

"That's the way it was."

"Who helped you drag the carcass down?" Estelle asked, and Lupe looked at her as if seeing her for the first time.

"I took my time. It took me three trips. He wasn't so big, but then again," and the corners of his eyes crinkled, "I'm a little older than I was." Estelle felt uneasy, knowing that Lupe Gabaldon was inventing a different story than the one he'd spun up on the hillside. Had he forgotten?

"Mr. Gabaldon, I need to see the license tag you filled out when you harvested the animal," Posey said. "You have that handy?"

"Sure I do." He frowned. "I got to think where I put it."

"It's supposed to be with the carcass."

"Then that's where it is." He pushed himself off the sofa with a loud cracking of joints, steadied himself, and pointed toward the kitchen. "You want a refill while I look?"

"No, thanks."

Estelle watched him leave the room, imagining him hobbling up through the woods, trying to be both stealthy and sure on his feet. Torrez rose and followed him to the kitchen. "While you're diggin' in the freezer, find me the heart, Lupe. I need to see that."

"What, you're checking for heartworm?"

"Oh, yeah." Torrez was actually amused.

Gabaldon muttered something further in response, but by then both men were out beyond the kitchen, headed toward the utility room.

"Have you ever dealt with Lupe on game violations before?" Estelle asked Posey.

"Never. I don't think he hunts much anymore." He looked heavenward. "Or didn't until he had a chance at an easy kill." He rose. "Let's see what Bobby's found."

The kitchen was pleasant, with a back door leading to a utility and mud room where the freezer was stored. The freezer's contents were neatly wrapped and organized, and Lupe had to root for only a moment before he straightened up with a shoebox-sized package labeled "HT/Liv/12-18."

"You do your own butchering, Lupe?" Posey asked.

"Well, sure I do. I use that little shed out back." He handed the package to Torrez, then reached out to the inside lid of the chest-style freezer and peeled off a game tag. "And there's that." He handed the tag to Posey. Turning back to the freezer, he rummaged some more, and patted several smaller packages. "I like the sausage. I make a lot of that."

Torrez retreated to the kitchen and crossed to the counter by the sink. He unwrapped the package carefully, and at one point glanced at Estelle. "You got your camera?"

"Sure."

He nodded and exposed the frozen organs. "A thirty-thirty makes a pretty good hole," he said, and turned the frozen heart this way and that. "So, Lupe. Come here a minute."

The old man thudded the freezer lid down and made his way out to the kitchen. Torrez handed him an envelope. "That's our warrant, Lupe. To search for and confiscate any illegal game you might have."

Gabaldon looked at the paper as if it might bite him. "A warrant?"

"Yep. Keeps us fair and square."

"I don't understand you sometimes. I invited you into my home. You want to dig through my freezer, you just go right ahead. You don't need no damn warrant. And I don't have no illegal game. You got the tag right there."

"'Preciate that." Torrez retrieved the warrant, removed it from the manila envelope, and placed it on the counter. "So show me the bullet damage."

The heart, other than being neatly detached from its surroundings, appeared to be in perfect condition. Lupe said nothing. Torrez turned the frozen heart over, peering closely. "What do you think?" he prompted.

"Well, you know."

"Maybe through the liver?"

Lupe seemed to deflate. "All I know is that I took one shot, and down he went."

"Through the head, maybe?"

"You took that."

"Yep." Torrez took the folder of photos that Estelle had been holding, and leafed out the over-sized one, an X-ray view of the entire skull. He reached out and held the X-ray up against one of the kitchen windowpanes. "What do you make of that?" Lupe peered at the X-ray, and then at the enlarged photos of the twin bullets, first one and then the other. "How far do you figure that deer managed to run with two bullets in the brain?" Torrez' voice was calm, almost a whisper.

"I don't know what you're trying to tell me," Lupe said. "How do I know that this is the same deer?"

"'Cause I'm tellin' you it is." The sheriff managed to avoid any belligerent tone, and added almost kindly, "And I'm tellin' you that the deer kill didn't happen just the way you said it did. Do you own a twenty-two, *Viejo?*"

"Sure, I own one. It belonged to my grandfather. He got it when he was a kid. I still got it."

"I'd like to see it."

For a long moment, Lupe stood motionless, eyeing Torrez expressionlessly. The sheriff was well-practiced at waiting, and he returned Lupe's glare unblinkingly. He did nothing to remind Lupe of the warrant so conspicuous on the counter.

"Okay. It's out in the living room closet, last I saw it." He made no move to turn toward the living room.

"That'd be good," Torrez said.

"Okay, then." He glanced over at the stove clock on his way out of the kitchen. "Flora should be back soon."

A tall, narrow closet, finished in rough-cut knotty pine, had been built beside the door. Lupe opened the door and stood back. "You can get it out if you want to. Be careful. It's loaded. Always loaded."

The closet was only fourteen inches wide or so, Estelle saw—about right for a broom and dustpan, maybe a pair of snow boots, and a couple of jackets. The rifle stood in the corner among a collection of walking sticks.

Torrez examined the closet for a moment before reaching in and removing the tiny rifle. He looked at it for a long moment, then pulled it back to half cock and thumbed open the tiny breech. A cartridge gleamed, and he stroked it out of the chamber.

"Is this little Remington the only twenty-two you own, Lupe?"

"That's a good gun. It still shoots…" and he made a straight line motion with his hand while he avoided answering the question. "My grandfather won that rifle in 1906, in El Paso." He smiled. "It could tell stories."

Posey held out his hand and Torrez passed the gun. "A Remington Number Six," the Game and Fish officer said. "A kid used to be able to get himself one of those by selling enough newspaper subscriptions."

Posey looked at Lupe in amusement. "Heck of a deer rifle, sir."

Lupe Gabaldon wouldn't have made much of a poker player, Estelle decided. His face screwed up in a coy, smug expression, but he didn't say anything.

"Are you saying you shot that little buck with this?" Posey asked.

"I didn't say that. This young man," and he nodded at Torrez, "asked to see it. So there it is."

"Well, I wouldn't think you did. For one thing, twenty-twos aren't legal for large game, and you would know that, being the law-abiding hunter you are. And this is a single shot rifle. It would have had to have been a *really* patient deer to wait for you to crank out three shots with this little guy." He worked the breechblock back and forth.

"I didn't say I did that."

"Nope," Torrez said, taking the little Remington back. "You said you used your Marlin thirty-thirty."

"You want to see that, now?"

"Sure. Why not?" He carefully replaced the little twenty-two in the closet and dropped the single cartridge in his pocket.

"It's in the bedroom."

Torrez followed him, staying within easy grab reach. A little thumping in a back closet, and Lupe said, "There. You watch out, 'cause it's loaded too."

The sheriff straightened up, holding the rifle, then turned and levered out seven rounds, each cartridge landing on the bedspread with a dull thump. Satisfied it was empty, he stuck his little finger in the action so the mellow light from the overhead bulb would bounce off his fingernail. He peered down the bore. Then he sniffed the barrel.

"This old dog ain't seen a whole lot of action," he said, and handed the gun to Posey.

"So this is the one?" Posey asked. When that brought no response, he looked sharply at Lupe. "This is the one? You shot the deer with this?"

Lupe rubbed his chin and made a disgusted face, and took his time figuring out what to say. "I guess you know I didn't," he said finally. He looked at Estelle as if embarrassed to admit such a thing in front of her. "You know, your great-uncle borrowed that little twenty-two from me a couple of times. Said he liked it because it was so small and handy."

"I don't doubt it. But who went hunting with you this time, Lupe?" She looked pointedly at his hands, his knuckles large and crooked with arthritis. "Someone used a fast-shooting twenty-two to kill that deer. Not this rifle, and not your old antique from the El Paso days."

He turned abruptly and left them in the bedroom. Out by the stove, he sat down heavily, hands on his knees.

"That hike up the hill yesterday wore me out," he said quietly. He fell silent for a moment, then said, "The only way I'd shoot a deer now is if he came down and helped himself to the flower beds out behind the kitchen. I got a license, you know that. I buy one every year." He shrugged. "I don't know why, now. But I do." He waved a hand toward Posey. "His department could use the money, maybe."

"Someone else shot the deer and asked to use your tag?" Posey asked. Lupe nodded. "But you weren't with him when the deer was taken?"

The old man shook his head. "I didn't know anything about it."

"Up by the tank?"

"That's what I think. But I wasn't there."

"But you didn't hear the shots? A twenty-two doesn't make much of a bark, but the way sounds roll around these hills…"

"No. I didn't hear it."

"And your tag—the one you filled out and is taped to the freezer door—it says the deer was harvested Friday, not Thursday."

The crow's-feet around Lupe's eyes deepened with amusement. "You young bucks just wait until you're eighty-four years old. You just wait and see how good you remember things."

"Sure enough, that's how life goes, Lupe. So who was this? Who bagged the deer for you?"

"Just…" He rubbed both hands on the top of his skull, through the bristle of gray hair. "Just give me the ticket. I mean, I got most of the deer right there in my freezer. I didn't have to take it when he offered it to me, so it's my own fault. No, I didn't shoot the deer, but I butchered it and wrapped it, and into my freezer it goes." He held up both hands in surrender. "So just start writing that ticket, Mr. Game and Fish guy, and that's it."

Doug Posey sighed and looked across first at Bob Torrez and then at Estelle.

"Lupe," Torrez said, "it ain't about the deer in your freezer. If it was up to me, I'd say let you keep it and enjoy it. You got one tag, you got one deer. It evens out. But there's other complications in all this. We need to know who shot it."

"Maybe you do."

"And?"

"All I know is that I got the meat frozen in there." He shrugged again. "That's what I know. And now you know I didn't shoot it."

"Who did?"

"That's just going to be the way it is."

"Why did he give it to you? Why didn't he keep it for himself?"

"Don't know. He was in kind of a hurry, is all I know."

"Somebody local? Somebody who knew you would help?"

Lupe Gabaldon looked at the floor.

"I guess we can go door to door," Torrez said, and when he looked at Lupe, Estelle thought she saw the faintest trace of sympathy in Torrez' dark eyes.

"Lupe," Estelle said, "yesterday up on the hill, you told us that you shot the deer, then you said that Al Fisher helped you carry the carcass down."

He almost smiled and looked cagey. "You know, I didn't say that Al helped me. I said I got a *neighbor* to help me."

"And Al agreed that he was the neighbor in question."

This time, Lupe's grin was so wide it looked as if his eyes were closed. "Now there's nothing wrong with *your* memory, is there, young lady?"

Chapter Thirty-one

The sun hadn't yet risen above the San Cristóbals, and Estelle was glad for the suggestion that they all bundle into Doug Posey's four-door pickup. A shaft of Christmas morning sunlight slipped through the dip that was Regál pass and tinged the foothills far to the west of the village. Farther south, sunshine was waking up the Mexican desert. Regál itself was still sleeping, without a single child in residence to spark excitement over a full stocking.

"So now," Posey said, "let me see if I follow your way of thinking, Sheriff. Somebody kills a little buck, somebody without the proper, legal firearm, *and* without a license. Bam, bam, bam, a triple tap to the skull with a twenty-two. Two connect, the third grazes and goes off somewhere. So the shooter field-dresses it, leaving for the critters the skull, spine, and whatever else isn't edible, and asks Lupe to take the carcass and butcher and wrap it. Lupe, the obliging old soul that he is, does that, using his own big game tag in the process."

"So far, so good," Torrez grumbled. He shifted, trying to make a comfortable spot for his bulk.

"But I think I'm right in that the Sheriff's Department could give a flyin' rip about the whole incident. That's where Myron Fitzwater fits in, am I right?"

"Yep."

"The bloody oak stick—club, staff, whatever you want to call it—says that someone with type O-positive blood got whacked, maybe murdered, within feet of where that deer went down. Am I still on track?"

"Yep."

"And according to Forest Service records, Myron Fitzwater had type O-positive."

"Yep."

"So how does it happen? A guy bags an illegal deer. From down below Myron hears the shots, and being the nosy young bastard that he is, he strolls up the hill. There's a confrontation, and Myron is whacked over the head hard enough to put him down."

"Timing is everything in this," Estelle pointed out. "Let's say that Lupe admits to accepting the deer on *Friday*. He says that he shot it, we know he didn't, and Al Fisher volunteers that he carried the carcass down to Lupe's kitchen. We also know that on Friday, Myron skipped work, true enough. So odds are good that he was here in Regál. It's obvious that Lupe wants to protect the shooter. Maybe he knows what happened, maybe he doesn't. He's a pretty crafty old guy."

"A lyin' old bastard is what he is." Torrez vehemence surprised Estelle. "First of all, Lupe knows exactly what happened. He's protectin' somebody. One thing's for sure…when this is all over, some Grand Jury is going to have a field day with him. Conspiracy, aiding and abetting, tampering with evidence," and he looked hard at Posey. "And you'll have your own list to add to that menu."

"You know the one constant in all this," Posey mused. "Connie Suarez was killed with one shot from a 9 millimeter…*probably*. You don't have the slug, but I wouldn't be surprised if the gun you found at the scene, Myron Fitzwater's Glock, is the weapon in question. You have one shell casing found at the scene that might match it. It's Fitzwater's blood…*probably*, on the oak staff. His hair, *probably*, too."

"That's a lot of probably," Estelle said. "Al Fisher claims that he helped carry the carcass down the hill for Lupe. There's every possibility that Alt did the shooting, too—Lupe is just playing coy to protect a neighbor. That's all possible."

"It is. Find Fitzwater and some of 'em might clear up."

"This is where I'm goin'," Torrez said. "If Fitzwater is layin' out there somewhere with his skull cracked open, who knows if we'll ever find him. Maybe somebody will stumble across his bones twenty or thirty years from now. And how did his truck end up north, up by Newton? We don't know that, either. But starin' us in the face is somethin' a little simpler. We find who put three into that deer, if we can. *That* can clear a whole big corner of the puzzle. Find out who Lupe is protecting, and why. Maybe it's Al, like you say. Maybe not."

"There's a shortcut or two for that," Estelle said.

"We make Lupe's life miserable, for one thing." Torrez opened the truck door and slid out, then turned to face them. "It ain't going to be hard to figure out who *didn't* go huntin' up on that hill. That'll narrow it down some. Pretty short list."

"I was thinking another route, Bobby. Right about now, a cup of hot tea would taste good. No one serves better than Betty Contreras. I need to talk with her. I think she trusts me. She and the other member of the waffle club."

"You want company?"

"It'd be better not. Seems a little less official with me by my lonesome."

"That'd be good." Torrez squinted into the distance. "While you're doin' that, me and Doug can go down and talk with Danny Rivera. He ain't workin' today."

She glanced at her watch. "Suppose I meet you in the church parking lot right at ten? Then I really need to go home for a bit."

"Has Francisco decided about that old truck yet?"

Estelle laughed. "Bobby, if you want to buy that thing, *you* talk to Francisco. Or, if you happen to catch him driving on the highway without license, registration, or insurance, you can confiscate it. That would suit me just fine."

The sheriff actually smiled.

Betty Contreras smiled too, when she opened the door to greet Estelle. Tiny bells on the door's Christmas wreath jingled. "Well, Merry Christmas and look who's here. Flora and I were just having a final cup of coffee to settle all the food." She wrapped an arm around Estelle's shoulders to usher her inside. "How about yourself? I can tell you never take time to eat enough. How about a nice waffle with walnut syrup?"

Estelle tried not to gag at the thought. "No, thank you, Betty. A cup of tea would be nice, if it's no trouble."

"Oh, pshaw. Trouble. Flora, look who's here."

Flora Gabaldon peered out from the kitchen, looking a little apprehensive. "We didn't see you at the Christmas Eve services last night," she greeted. A round little woman with a cherubic face just beginning to show a few wrinkles and canyons, Flora was facing an eightieth birthday soon, Estelle knew—but she looked and moved as if she were a solid fifty.

"Guilty," Estelle replied, and Flora waited a couple heart-beats expectantly, hoping for tidbits. But being absent from church didn't compare with the other gossip that was rife around town, and Flora Gabaldon switched quickly enough. "So awful about that sweet girl, don't you think?" Flora advanced from the kitchen. "I mean, we've known her since she was this high." She held her hand two feet off the floor. "Just awful."

Before Estelle had a chance to agree or amplify, Flora held up a hand and glanced toward the door as if to assure herself that a band of fellow officers wasn't lurking outside the door.

"We saw the parade yesterday and again this morning," she said, then her face sank into an expression of contrition that suggested that, if no one else, she was certainly guilty of something. Her voice dropped to a whisper. "It's that illegal deer, isn't it?"

"Believe me, the deer is just about the least of our worries, Flora."

"Well, I saw you all talking with Lupe this morning…"

"And we're glad to see you both doing so well. Lupe is getting around just fine now, isn't he?"

"Well," and she hesitated while Betty handed Estelle the brimming cup of tea.

"The new hip at the end of the summer made such a difference. I won't exaggerate and say that he's a kid again, but *such* a difference. I mean, you saw him walk up that mountain yesterday with the whole gang."

"Good that Al Fisher stayed close to his elbow, though—just in case."

"Oh, my, he's been such a help this year, Al has. You know, with Lupe's hip surgery and all, Al made sure we had enough firewood, fine split and stacked, to last the whole winter, and then some. And then when the transfer case in Lupe's old truck went south, Al took it over to Danny's and they fixed it up. Al borrows it once in a while, you know. That truck's hauled more wood than you can shake a stick at." She smiled at her joke. "Or however that saying goes."

"This is Danny Rivera you're talking about?"

"Sure. You know him. Down in his grandparents' old place. In all of Regál, he's the closest to the border. His squash roots burrow out of the garden and get flattened by the Border Patrol when they drive by, running the fence."

"Who's the hunter in the group?"

"The hunter?" Flora looked over at Betty, then back at Estelle. "You mean other than Lupe? I wouldn't call him much of a hunter, not after his hip. An ambusher, maybe, when the deer come into the yard." She made a face. "Poor things. They like to eat the apples and pears, you know. Then they sleep in the backyard. Lupe says they think we're running a bed-and-breakfast just for them."

Estelle took a sip of tea and savored the complex flavors. "Al Fisher impresses me as the hunter in the group."

"Now *his* specialty is rattlesnakes, and more power to him, I say."

"Yuck," Betty added. "Those nasty little green things. *Mojave greens*, I think they call them. He dries the skins and makes hat bands out of 'em. And every once in a while he gets one of those Western diamondbacks, the really big ones." She shivered dramatically. "Big enough to make a belt for a fat lady."

"But not deer?"

"Who, Al? Well, see—" Flora stopped, an action that was obviously hard for her.

"He killed *three* greens on my little back patio last summer," Betty interrupted. "*Three.* They scare me to death."

"But not deer? He doesn't hunt deer?"

"I think he hunts anything that moves," Betty said. "I see him with that little gun of his, hiking the hills. You know, on a couple of occasions, I've given him a lift home. He'll hike up to the pass, and sometimes he'd walk back along the road. If I see him, I'd always stop. Hiking up to the pass is one heck of a deal." She grimaced at the memory. "One time I picked him up, he had that darn canvas bag with him. That's the way he carries the snakes, you know. They're all dead, of course, but still…yuck."

"Flora, did Al shoot this most recent deer? The one taken up by the water tank? The one that Lupe butchered and wrapped?"

Flora didn't hesitate a heartbeat, and Estelle had the impression that the woman knew the question was coming. "What did Lupe tell you guys?"

"He said he shot it with his thirty-thirty. That obviously isn't the case."

"I would think," Flora said slowly, measuring each word, "that you people would put more energy into dealing with Connie Suarez' death than worrying about who shot or didn't shoot one sorry little deer."

"Exactly," Estelle said. "Just between you and me," and she saw the light of anticipation in both women's eyes, "we have ample evidence that more went on up at that water tank than a simple case of deer poaching." She shrugged. "Al bags a tempting deer, and asks your husband to use his license tag and then butcher and wrap the meat. That's simple enough, and it's no big deal, at least to me. And I'm not investigating that. We're working on Myron Fitzwater's disappearance. Flora, *that* may very well be tied with Connie Suarez' death."

"So you *do* think Myron might be responsible?" Betty asked.

"Now *I* thought that Connie killed herself," Flora said. "It's hard to believe, I know."

"It *is* hard to believe," Estelle echoed.

"Right on the heels of Al's brother? Now, *he* was just down here on Friday, I know. We saw his truck over at Al's. And then all this." She shook her head sadly. "Young people these days."

"Did Al bring the deer carcass over to Lupe's by himself, or did his brother help him?"

"I just don't know," Flora said. "I was busy over at Isabel Apodaca's most of that day. She and Maria and I were molding the last of the candles for the Christmas Eve mass."

"But you do know that Al shot the deer."

This time, Flora Gabaldon did hesitate before saying meekly, "Yes."

"And how do you know that, if you were busy over at Isabel's?"

"Lupe told me that evening, when I got home."

Betty reached over and took Estelle's empty cup. "You're thinking that there's a connection, aren't you? Between Darrell Fisher's death and Connie's."

"We're investigating that."

"And Myron Fitzwater's disappearance."

"Yes."

Betty Contreras' face looked stern, the same expression she would have used to freeze a recalcitrant second-grader in his tracks. "And somehow Al is right in the middle of it. You know…" She paused to take a deep breath. "Al and Myron didn't get along all that well. They certainly weren't the best of buddies, I know that. I'd talk with Al now and then, and he didn't have much good to say about young Mr. Fitzwater. I always thought that it was a jealousy thing, myself. Al had a fondness for Connie, I know that. Despite living under the same roof with the sweetest girl in the world, sometimes that's not enough to stop a young man's roving eye."

"Only that?"

"Well, Myron had a way about him. You know how a young man who's full of himself sort of *struts*? Myron loved working for the Forest Service, I'm sure. He liked driving that fancy truck; he didn't have to wear a uniform, but he made his work clothes *look* sharp."

"He wore a gun from time to time?"

"I've seen him with one." Betty looked at Flora, who nodded. "I don't think he was supposed to, but he did from time to time, especially if he was by himself."

"Can you tell me what time of day Al and Darrell visited Lupe and dropped off the deer carcass?"

Flora shook her head. "Lupe could tell you, of course." *Or he could make up a good story*, Estelle almost said. "Now, if I had to *guess*, I'd say sometime in late afternoon. Well, it was coming on to dark, so *very* late. I say that because when I left Isabel's, it was five-thirty. I looked at the clock, and knew that Lupe would be getting antsy for his dinner. When I got home, he was just finishing up with the meat wrapping. When he does that, you know—when he butchers, he gets right to it. He keeps all his equipment spotless, and wants the game processed promptly."

Betty reached out and laid a slender hand on Estelle's wrist. "And this is such an awful way for you to be spending Christmas Day. The youngsters are able to visit?"

"Yes, both of them. That's where I'm heading right now."

"Well, yes. Don't let us keep you. Maybe you'll be able to bring them down for the ten o'clock service this morning."

"Unlikely, but you never know." Estelle rose and extended a hand to Flora and then Betty. "If you happen to think of anything else that I should know, you'll call?"

The women nodded, and Estelle was sure what the topic of conversation would be after she left. The list of what they probably knew, but hadn't told her, was most likely a lengthy one.

Chapter Thirty-two

"Posey with you?" Al Fisher twisted to see past Estelle and Torrez.

"Nope," Torrez said, and let it go at that.

"So Merry Christmas and all that. And yeah." His smile was smug. "I shot that deer. And then gave it to Lupe and he put his tag on it. He can't hunt no more, so there ain't nothin' wrong with that."

"Sort of like a designated hitter," Torrez said.

Al laughed. "That's a good one. But yeah, that's the way it is. Exactly."

"You own a twenty-two rifle?"

"Sure I own one. That's what I shot the deer with. Lupe, he was just playing with your minds, you know. Havin' some fun. He's quite the storyteller."

"You're quite the snake hunter, too, I'm hearing," Estelle offered, and Al's eyes squinted momentarily. "Is that just another village story, too?"

"I done my share."

"You get a good price for the skins?"

"Good enough. So what was it you guys wanted, anyways?"

"I'd like to see that rifle, Mr. Fisher," Torrez said.

"Well, *Mister* Sheriff, you can, easy enough, but aren't you supposed to have a warrant? I mean, this is my home. You can't just barge in and take stuff."

Torrez frowned and looked at his surroundings. He was standing on the stone front porch of the modest home tucked among the boulders. "Barge in? What'd I miss?"

"You know what I mean," Al Fisher puffed. By standing on the top step, he could look eye to eye with Torrez.

"Suit yourself, then. A deputy will be here with a warrant within the hour," Torrez said. "I just thought I'd save us some time. I'm just curious, is all. A triple tap like you used on that deer is pretty darn good marksmanship."

"Well, at twenty-five feet and with a scope, it ain't hard, guy."

"A few game law violations, though. A twenty-two ain't legal for deer, even if you had a license...which you didn't."

"You enforcing game laws now, Sheriff?"

"Can, if need be."

Al Fisher laughed again, a short knowing chuckle, as he shook his head. "You're somethin' else, guy."

"So you shot the deer on Friday, were up half the night with your brother and little nephew, then turned around and went pig hunting on Saturday," Estelle said.

"So? Winter's comin' on. It'd be nice to have something in the pantry, don't you think? Or are you guys taking on the feral pig controversy over in Texas now, too?"

"When you got the pig, why didn't you take *that* carcass over to Lupe for processing, too?"

Fisher's eyes narrowed again, an odd, not especially attractive quirk, Estelle thought.

"Carcass is too heavy for Lupe," he said. "A little deer cut into quarters is one thing—and I tell you, he ain't going to be able to do that much longer, either. Pig's too big, too much of a struggle for him."

"That's thoughtful of you."

"Yeah, well." He sighed and looked behind him, back into the house. "Tell you what, me being the thoughtful person that you think I am...if I show you that little gun, then you can go away and have a Merry Christmas? Hell of an overtime bill you're rackin' up." Torrez said nothing in response to that jibe, and after a moment, Al nodded. "Hang tight a minute."

Torrez glanced at his watch, and sure enough, it was scarcely a minute before Al Fisher returned, a plastic rifle case under his arm. "Come on in for a minute." He held the door for them, then entered and rested the case on the arms of a rocker near the door. He snapped it open.

"I put this one together, and I gotta admit, I'm kinda proud of it." He lifted it gently out of the case, removed the long magazine that was heavy with ammo, and racked back the bolt, popping a round out of the chamber. He handed the rifle to Torrez, who examined it from one end to the other.

"You do the stock work?" The sheriff slid his hand into place, thumb comfortable through the thumbhole stock.

"Yes, sir. It'll be a little short for you."

Lowering the rifle, Torrez examined the muzzle, where half an inch of fine threads capped the barrel.

"Suppressor?"

"Could be, someday. I ain't got one now." He grinned. "That would be another law to bust, am I right?"

"Be patient, and before long, they'll be legal anyway," the sheriff said.

He handed the rifle back and watched silently as Al put it back in the case. "Walk up to the tank with us?"

"Up the hill again?" He shrugged. "Sure, why not? But what for?"

"I got a few questions, a couple things to clear up."

"Yeah, I guess. Lemme get my jacket and leave a note for Maria." He ducked back into the house.

"You have time for this?"

"I think it's better if we both go." She lowered her voice. "I don't really trust him. Not even a little bit."

The route Al Fisher took up to the water tank was a challenge.

They cut up into the rocks just west of Suarez' mobile home, and he zigzagged this way and that until they broke into the small clearing with the tank to the east. Pausing on the flat, Estelle sucked in deep lungfuls, trying to get her breath back. Torrez, half a dozen years older and now carrying some extra weight, thanks to his wife's bountiful cooking, still breathed as if he'd taken a short stroll on a level sidewalk.

"Now you know why Lupe don't hunt much anymore. 'Course, the dumb deer come right into the village, so who needs to chase 'em up here?"

"But you did," Estelle managed between breaths.

"I was comin' up here anyways. That's why I had that twenty-two. If I'd been deer hunting for real, I'd have had the 308."

"Why did you come up here?"

"I wanted to check on the tank. Actually, I wanted to check on the valve. When Lupe put it in, he put in about the cheapest discount store junk he could find. It's leaked since day one. I was going to get a good one, but I couldn't remember what size the stem was comin' out of the bottom of the tank. It's a jerry-rigged piece of shit. Actually," and he grinned, pleased with himself, "it's a *Lupe*-rigged piece of shit. Lemme show you."

They skirted the tank, and he stopped and pointed at the wooden valve box. "The guts are in here." He lifted the lid and with a stick raked away the black widow cobwebs. The glossy black widow huddled in one corner. Al pointed at the black nylon bulkhead that projected from the bottom of the tank. "See, that bulkhead's two inches. And then it steps down, like twice more, until it joins up with the three-quarter-inch line that runs down the hill. That," and he reached out with the stick, "is a three-quarter-inch valve, a little dinky thing. And he's got it threaded onto a coupling, rather than just glued. One thing and another. So it leaks." He bent down and stroked under the valve, and held up a wet finger. "Only thing it'll do is get worse."

His face fell, sadness pulling the corners of his mouth down.

"Darrell was going to help me with this, but he didn't come down early enough on Friday afternoon. He's got...he *had*... all kinds of fixtures, valves, and that kind of shit." He shook his head in bewilderment and sat down with a spine-jarring thud, as if someone had pulled his legs out from under him. "I just don't believe it. What he did, I mean. And I ain't ashamed to say it...what Penny probably drove him to do."

"You think that's the way it was?"

His accusatory squint was immediate. "Yeah, that's what I think."

"So where was the deer?"

Al pushed himself to his feet, pushed the wooden lid back in place and took a step back, away from the plumbing. He leaned over, peering around the tank, mimicking his earlier hunting experience. "I caught movement out of the corner of my eye, and here he comes, makin' his way up the slope. I waited. See that double rock over there? That's where he stopped. The wind was right, I guess, 'cause he hadn't smelled me. I was pressed up against the tank, kinda thinking that maybe I shouldn't take the shot, and then again, maybe I should." He grinned crookedly. "The shoulds won out."

"So you shot right from here."

"Yep. Eased the gun up, then eased around the tank in slow motion. Bam, bam, bam, just like that." He snapped his fingers three times. "And down he went. I field-dressed him right over there, and scattered the guts and stuff. He wasn't some big old stud, and gettin' the carcass down the hill wasn't a big deal. Lupe was surprised."

"Lupe was?"

"Yeah. He knew I didn't have no license, and he knew usin' a twenty-two was illegal. But he helped me anyways."

"So what time did you pull the trigger?"

Al laughed. "Like I punch in with a time card, right?"

"About what time?" Torrez asked patiently.

"Probably about four o'clock or so. It wasn't gettin' dark quite yet, but by the time I field-dressed the carcass, even workin' fast, the cold was settin' in and it sure as hell looked like it might snow. So, yeah, about four."

"And what time did Myron Fitzwater show up?" Torrez asked.

Al Fisher looked as if he'd been struck. "Huh?"

"Fitzwater. With the Forest Service."

"I know who he is. What do you mean what time did he show up?"

Torrez' "lizard" stare locked on Al Fisher, the sheriff's heavy-lidded eyes unblinking, not a trace of expression on his face. "He came up here and found you cuttin' up the deer."

Al's mouth opened in company with a frown. "You've been smokin' that funny tobacco, Sheriff. Fitzwater was shoutin' down at the trailer, arguing with Connie, is my guess. But he didn't come up here. Not while I was here, leastways. Who told you that zinger?"

"Traces of his blood says he did."

"His blood? On what?"

"On the staff that probably cracked his skull."

Al Fisher's face wrinkled up as if he'd smelled something rank. "Well, then, you can just go that route. Me, I don't know what you're talking about. You want to get me excited into saying something I shouldn't, you'll have to do a whole lot better than that." He turned to look at Estelle. "Do you know what your friend here is talkin' about?"

"You're a clever guy, Al," she said.

"What's that supposed to mean? Yeah, I illegally shot a deer. I gave it to Lupe. He used his tag. So what? You're not turnin' that into some big deal that it ain't." He shoved his hands in his pockets. "I've had enough of this." He held up an index finger, not quite close enough to be threatening. "And next time you guys come to my house, bring a warrant. Otherwise, I ain't talkin' to you. Same goes for Posey. You tell him that for me."

He turned his back on them like a petulant child and strode

off down the hill, shoulders raked back as if he were right and the rest of the world was wrong. He took the direct line down through the rocks that would take him first to Suarez' backyard before a jog over to his own home.

"That's what I thought," Torrez said. "It ain't easy gettin' the truth out of that pup," he said to Estelle. "I wanted to see what route he'd take down the hill if I got him riled enough."

Chapter Thirty-three

"Hey, you've had fifteen minutes. How much more time at home did you want?"

"I didn't mean to groan audibly," Estelle said. "But actually I did. The kids are down in Tres Santos with *Padrino*. I wanted to be here when they return. But go ahead. What did Mears say?"

The sheriff hesitated, as if he really had to think about the consequences of gratuitously giving out information, even to his own undersheriff. "We got both Darrell Fisher's truck and the Forest Service unit that Fitzwater was drivin' in county impound."

"I knew that."

"Well, okay. Mears has been given both of them the old fine-toothed comb. Somebody always leaves *something*."

"We can hope. But Sarge said earlier that Fitzwater's government vehicle was clean."

"Too clean. He and Craig Stout worked it over, and I mean, it's *clean*. Somebody wiped it down. No prints. The only thing left was marks from the wipe rag, a swipe or two along the windowsill of the driver's door that marked the dust."

"That doesn't do us much good."

"Nope. It just shows intent. That's one thing."

Estelle, who had time to change out of her pants suit and shed several pounds of hardware, looked at the four covered dishes on the kitchen counter. Carlos had evidently been hard at work.

She had been in the process of lifting the foil when the sheriff's call had interrupted her.

"'*That's one thing*' means there's something else."

"Yep. Darrell Fisher's truck *wasn't* wiped."

"We didn't expect that it would be. He was in it, with parts of his chest splattered all over the inside."

"Sure enough. The inside. The slug that blew him apart lodged in the cab metal just below the back window. It didn't break the glass."

"And so…"

"What was in the back?"

"What was in the back?" Estelle asked herself. "Nothing was there. Well, almost nothing. An empty quart oil can, as I recall. A chain saw, chain saw wrench, and file. A small gas can. Lots of wood chips."

"You got a good memory."

"What have I forgotten?"

"Whatever was in the back got pulled out. Smeared along the truckbed. Probably took some of the chips and shit with it."

"Like the deer carcass. Why would they have the deer carcass in Darrell's truck? It's a short carry down the hill to Lupe's. And you can't drive the truck up there to the tank anyway."

"It snowed on the truck a little before whatever it was that was in there was pulled out of the bed."

Estelle didn't respond for a moment, trying to decipher Torrez' mangled syntax. "And you know this how?"

"There's a couple of smear marks. That ain't the important thing. There's a blood smear way over against the fender well. Some of it's in the metal seam there."

"Tom recovered that?"

"Yep."

"And that's where my husband happens to be at the moment." She reached across and picked up the small adhesive note that had waited for her by the phone.

"Perrone's out of town."

"Smart man. Did Francis identify the blood type?"

"First two guesses don't count," Torrez said.

"O-positive."

"Yep. We've been down that road before. Autopsy records show that Darrell's blood type was AB-negative, so it ain't his. He didn't cut himself sharpening that chain saw."

"Prosecutor will laugh us out of court."

"Yep. But it's something," Torrez said with satisfaction. "Francis says that Mears recovered enough blood that the State Police lab can run a DNA test. Compare with the oak staff."

"And if they're the same…"

"Then at some point, after he got himself whacked, Myron Fitzwater's body was put in the back of Darrell Fisher's pickup. Probably wrapped in a tarp."

"And dumped who-knows-where. Let's put a clock on it. The weather got rotten Friday night, but not until after dark. I see Al Fisher shooting the deer sometime around three, maybe four. He's field-dressing it, and Myron Fitzwater walks into the scene. Maybe he and Connie were out for a late afternoon walk. Maybe he happened to hear the twenty-two."

"Could be any number of reasons why Fitzwater went up there. Maybe it was just as simple as him seein' Al walkin' up the hill, gun in hand. Nothin' illegal about that, but Myron butts in anyways."

"And why wouldn't Connie call authorities when Myron didn't come home? Because she was already dead. Al kills Myron, and chases Connie down the hill to her trailer. He took a second to grab Myron's handgun, which the young man was foolish enough to wear. One shot, and Connie's down."

"Could have happened that way."

"Helpful brother comes down for an evening visit. The body goes in the back of his truck, and Al drives the Forest Service truck. By then it's dark or nearly so. Who's to see? Up over the pass, and then up County 14 toward Newton. Pretty clever, and Al Fisher is nothing if not clever, Bobby. Dump the truck a ways out, and investigators are supposed to assume the body is nearby."

"So what's your guess about the body?"

"I wish I had one. The snow's long gone, so we have no tracks. We have no witnesses to step forward. Al knows what happened. That's it."

"But he ain't likely to say."

"Something clever, guaranteed."

"So, after all this, the two of them come back to Al's for the rest of the evening, and watch the snow fly. And all this time, Connie Suarez is lyin' in that trailer, brains blown out. And all this time, Darrell has the little kid with him."

"I don't think so. I think Maria was telling the truth when she said that she spent the evening playing with Derry while the brothers were out and about."

"Then she knows *exactly* what time the two brothers came home."

Estelle fell silent. "Yes. She would know. And I have to wonder what else she knows." She thought about Darrell Fisher, talked into this gruesome undertaking by his brother. Darrell had been a soft-bellied, weak-spined wuss, she had already decided. Could he have kept to himself what the brothers had done? Certainly Darrell might have considered suicide…according to others, he'd been down in the dumps for a long time. And just as likely, his guilty conscience *might* have urged him to tip off the authorities. Al Fisher might have tried to talk his brother out of it, might have argued with him, might have threatened him. Could he have pulled the trigger? By then, he might have had lots of practice.

"We need to talk with Maria," Bob Torrez said. "And it's best if we do it now, before Al takes it into his head to split. She might give us something. When you talked with her last time, did it seem like she was holdin' back?"

"I didn't get that sense. But some folks are better at hiding the truth than others. You're at the office?"

"Yep."

"Let me swing by and pick you up."

"Nah. I don't fit in that bomb of yours. One of the Expeds is here. We'll take that. I'll be by in a few minutes."

Chapter Thirty-four

"You wonderin'?" Sheriff Torrez sat relaxed as he drove his department Expedition, one hand on the steering wheel, his left hand tapping a silent rhythm on the doorsill.

"About a lot of things." Estelle wasn't especially comfortable at the steady ninety-miles-an-hour that Torrez favored with the big SUV, and she had pulled her shoulder harness as tight as she could against the padding of her ballistic vest under her down jacket. "What if Al Fisher really did kill Myron Fitzwater? I could see that happening. Fisher is hard at work dressing out the deer, and Fitzwater arrives and starts throwing his weight around. Al grabs his little twenty-two and bam, bam."

"Except that probably ain't what happened. Somebody clubbed him."

"So it would appear. Maybe *after* Fitzwater got whacked with the oak club. I don't see the point of hitting somebody in the head with a stick *after* shooting the victim a time or three."

"That's what you've been thinkin' on?"

"Yes. A sequence-of-events scenario."

"Who you got swingin' the stick in that scenario?"

"Exactly," Estelle said. "If Fitzwater was haranguing Al for shooting the deer, his back might well be turned on *somebody*. About half of the residents of Regál might be a good fit for not liking Myron Fitzwater."

"Lupe Gabaldon ain't as frail as he makes out to be," Torrez said. "Butchering a deer ain't exactly the hardest chore in the world, but doin' it right—and Lupe does it by the book—that takes some effort, with all the cuttin' and wrappin'." As they crossed the Rio Guijarro, just northeast of the Broken Spur Saloon, Torrez pointed ahead. "Lookit there." He reached down and flipped on all three toggles on the emergency equipment panel, turning the Expedition into a rolling light show. Even as Torrez slowed down, Bill Gastner's cherry red SUV flashed by.

"Take a minute or two and let 'em know what's goin' on," Torrez said. "We ain't going to be long." He swung a hard U-turn to give chase, but Gastner had already pulled off onto the shoulder. Torrez eased the Expedition up a car-length behind, lights still pulsing.

Francisco was the first one out of the SUV, and he hailed his mother before she had both feet on the ground. "Merry Christmas, Undersheriff," Francisco shouted. "Did that guy with you happen to mention that this is a holiday?" He swept Estelle up in a fierce hug. "Dang, you're a walking hardware emporium," he said. "What do you weigh, about two hundred with all that stuff on?"

"The price of law and order." She freed an arm and stretched out to embrace Carlos. "How was Mexico?"

"Desolate," Francisco replied without hesitation. "But it was good to see all the Diaz family again." He put a hand over his mouth. "Too much mulled wine, probably. *Padrino* is our designated driver." He waved at Sheriff Torrez, who lifted a single index finger in acknowledgement.

"It's just so amazing that you're all here." She looked at her watch. "It's just coming up on one now. The sheriff and I have this little excursion that we need to do, but I'll be home for dinner. I hope."

"We'll hold the food until you turn up," Carlos promised.

"And in January? I'm taking a week off before the Aspen concert, and a week after. No more interruptions."

"Sure, Ma," Francisco laughed. "We're headed back to *Padrino's* now for a little bit to talk about things."

"Have your wits about you, *hijo*. He can be very persuasive."

"I hope so."

"Let me say hello, then Bobby and I need to hit the road." As she approached, the driver's side window lowered and Gastner's elbow appeared. "You're a brave man, *Padrino*," she greeted him, and smiled widely at the two young women, the motion-sensitive Tasha riding up front.

"It's been an interesting day," he replied. "It's been way too long since I had time to chat with the Diaz flock. Román's looking good, even." He grimaced. "Hell, what am I saying? He's three years younger than I am."

"I look forward to hearing all about it—all of it. But right now, we need to roll. You'll plan on dinner with us tonight?"

"Absolutely. Are you two making some progress?"

"We think so."

"Then be careful. And save a few minutes out of your day for these guys," and he nodded toward the rear seat as Carlos and Francisco piled in. "And tell Robert to get a life." His smile was only half amused as he reached out and patted her hand. "I can say that because I've been right where you're standing now, with what seems like the whole damn world coming apart. See you this evening. Be careful."

She lifted a hand in a salute more wistful than she would have liked. As she walked back toward the Expedition, she could hear radio traffic, too muffled to understand. As she settled in the seat, she said, "I wonder what a nine-to-five, five-days-a-week job would be like?"

He snorted in amusement. "You wouldn't like it."

"I suppose not."

"Most of the time, anyways, we ain't got nothin' to do. Then something comes down to make up for it."

She watched Gastner's SUV grow smaller in the distance

as Torrez swung the Expedition around. "Christmas Day with unexpected and cherished company would be a nice time to have 'nothin' to do.'"

"You're breakin' my heart," Torrez chuckled.

"Wait until the day that Gabe comes home unexpectedly from college with his beloved in tow."

Torrez laughed again—something of a record for him. More than once, he checked his rearview mirror, and by the time they reached the Regál Pass sign, he nodded in satisfaction. "Company," he said, and picked up the mike.

Chapter Thirty-five

The sheriff drove to the south end of the church parking lot and turned right, just before the fence and its right-of-way. The dirt road jounced west until they reached the complex owned by Danny Rivera and his wife, Irene. In addition to a half-dozen other vehicles in various stages of disrepair scattered about the property, both Danny's one-ton Ford dually pickup and a brawny companion, Al Fisher's diesel Ram with the water tank in back, were parked directly in front of the overhead door.

"That's Al's truck, ain't it?" Torrez said. He twisted around and glanced back at the Riveras' double-wide trailer where a small sedan was parked. "And that's Irene's buggy at home."

Neither Danny Rivera nor Al Fisher were outside the shop, and Torrez didn't slow. A few yards on, they passed an abandoned trailer that had belonged to Danny's grandmother, the late Serefina Roybal. Tumbleweeds had packed around the skirting and in one spot were piled high enough to obscure part of the bathroom window.

"How many illegals you figure spend the night in that place?" he mused.

"There are plenty of other abandoned places in Regál," Estelle said.

"Most of the wrecks don't come completely furnished like this one. I don't know if Danny's even turned the water off or not."

The grapevine-decorated walls of Solomon Apodaca's hacienda passed on the left, and by then Estelle caught sight of two more vehicles coming down off the pass. Torrez reached for the mike.

"Three oh nine, three oh four, park it just beyond Lupe's driveway." Both Pasquale and Jackie Taber acknowledged. "Tom, stay with your unit. Jackie, we'll want you over at Fisher's rock house."

Torrez hung up the mike, and as if reminding himself, added, "The deal today is that everybody goes home in one piece." Estelle looked at him in surprise. "Charge-in Torrez" was being unusually circumspect.

In a hundred yards or so, they reached Fisher's odd little house, looking as if it were being devoured by the boulder behind it. Maria Apodaca's Outback was parked with its nose inches from the boulder, as if trying to push the rock back uphill.

The approaching traffic made just enough noise that White Fang's acute hearing tripped her bark switch, and she stood with her tiny body balanced on her hind legs, front paws up on the large planter beside the front door. The door behind her opened, and the little dog spun around and dashed inside, still yapping. Maria Apodaca appeared, dressed in a bright red sweatshirt over red exercise pants.

"Give me a few minutes," Estelle said. She got out of the truck and saw that Jackie Taber had parked a few yards back down the lane toward Suarez'.

"Al is over at Danny's," Maria greeted. She tried to smile, but her effort looked more pained than anything else. She lifted a hand in greeting as Jackie Taber approached. "Merry Christmas, you all."

"May we come in for a few minutes?"

"Sure. I mean, Al's not here just now."

"Actually, I wanted to talk with you, Maria."

"Oh." She shooed White Fang back with one foot. "Sure. Come on in. You want some coffee or tea or something?"

"No, thanks."

"I kinda knew you would be back, Sheriff."

"Maria, we talked with Al about the deer he shot and then gave to Lupe for butchering. He didn't mention that you were with him up on the hill at the time."

"I mean, I…"

"You were there when Myron Fitzwater showed up." It was not a question, and Maria closed her eyes for a few seconds, then sat down on one of the leather Mexican chairs and clasped her hands between her knees. She said nothing. She looked miserable. Over under the table, White Fang whimpered and shivered but stayed safely put.

"Myron was ready to make an issue of Al's shooting the deer?"

Maria looked down at her hands, and each finger touched the tip of her thumbs as if she were counting to make sure they were all there. Finally, she looked up at Estelle.

"I am so, so sorry," she said. "This whole thing has been a nightmare, from beginning to end."

Giving the girl small rungs to grab as she faced scaling the cliff seemed the most productive approach.

"I can understand that, and I'm sorry, Maria," Estelle said softly. "What you can do right now is help us understand exactly what happened. You were there, you know what passed between Al and Myron." *And Connie Suarez*, she wanted to add, but little admissions first. Estelle pulled her micro recorder from her jacket pocket. "And any conversation we have will be recorded, Maria. For your protection, if nothing else."

The young woman nodded. "Myron said he was going to confiscate the deer carcass, because Al had shot it on federal lands, with an illegal weapon, out of season, all kinds of things. Al told him that he didn't have authority to do any of that, and to stop being such a prick. That's exactly the word he used." She shook her head and frowned. "I don't know why the Forest Service lets Myron do those things. I mean all the enforcement stuff. He can't do that, can he? Why doesn't he get in trouble?"

He did, Estelle thought. "Was Connie Suarez there? Up on the hill with you guys?"

Maria nodded. "She came up the hill with Myron, like the two of them were just hiking or something. When he was arguing with Al, it seemed like Myron was showing off for her. I mean, that's the impression I got. All swaggering macho man. And you know, Al…he's got a little of that himself. The two of them like a couple of roosters, or something. Except Myron was half again Al's size."

"He was wearing a gun?"

Maria sighed wearily. "That was the whole problem. Yes, he was. And he had a pair of handcuffs hooked on the back of his belt, under his jacket. Like he's a cop working undercover or something. He brings those out, and everything went to pieces. Myron's got his hand on his gun, and Al is a couple steps away from where he leaned his little twenty-two. That's when Al maybe did the wrong thing." Maria took a deep breath and held it for a few seconds. "He *laughed* at Myron. Just laughed at him. Then he says something like, 'You are so full of shit,' and tries to turn away. Myron grabs at him and slaps the cuffs on one wrist, you know—like they do in the movies. The cuffs didn't lock, and Al jerked away, lost his balance and tripped over something, and ended up going over backward. Myron had his gun out, and it really looked like he was going to shoot. And then he did."

"He actually fired at Al? When Al was down on the ground?"

Maria bit her lip. "I don't think he meant to. But whatever. The gun went off, and I saw where the bullet hit the ground, about a foot from Al's head."

"Would you be able to show me that exact spot?"

Maria nodded.

"So who actually struck Myron with the stick…the cudgel? The dried piece of scrub oak."

The girl didn't answer, and Estelle waited patiently.

"Maria?"

"I did." She looked beseechingly at Estelle. "They were tussling on the ground, because Al tried to grab his rifle, and Myron was trying to roll Al over on his face and jerk his arms behind his back. It looked like he was going to do it, too. And he still had that gun in his hand, and it was pointing all over the place. *That's* what petrified me the most. I just *knew* that if Al managed to reach his rifle, or something like that…" She lifted her shoulders high in a mighty shrug, then buried her face in her hands. "For a minute it looked as if Myron was going to whack Al in the head with that gun."

"You found the stick?" Estelle asked gently.

Maria nodded. "I mean, it was right there. Somebody's old walking stick or something." Her left hand dropped from her face and clutched at the religious trinket on the fine gold chain around her neck. "When I was little, I used to think it was great stuff to bat rocks with a stick. Thinking I was some great baseball player or something, I guess. Anyway, I swung as hard as I could." She transferred the religious medal from left to right hand, and touched the back of her head behind her ear. "It hit him right there. And I mean, I *really* connected." She shook her head. "It made this awful noise, and Myron just collapsed like a sack of potatoes. His arms and legs were going, like he was trying maybe to crawl away."

"What did Al do then?"

"He twisted loose and yanked Myron's gun away from him. It went off once, 'cause maybe Myron's finger was still on the trigger. I remember seeing wood fly from one of the little trees down below the tank. And then Al twisted the gun loose. I screamed something at him, but it looked like Myron was trying to get back on his feet. That's when Al shot him." She stabbed herself in the side with her left index finger, below the armpit.

"What was Connie doing all this time?"

"She froze. And then she ran back down the hill. 'She'll call the cops,' Al shouted at me, and then *he* took off too, straight down the hill."

"He took Myron's gun with him?"

"Yes."

"And so there you were, left with the dead or dying Myron Fitzwater."

"Oh, my God. He was making little groaning sounds, you know. The way game does after you shoot if they don't die right away. I didn't know what to do. I went to him, but he was out of it. His eyes were already kinda glazed, you know. There wasn't a lot of blood. And then clear as anything, I heard him whisper, 'oh, no.' Just like that. 'Oh, no.' And he was gone."

"You followed Al down the hill?"

"No." As if any tears she had left had been checked and then released, Maria convulsed in sobs. "I couldn't, Sheriff. I just couldn't. I…I got all dizzy, and sat down with my back against the water tank. Just sat there. And there's Myron, curled up on the ground. But I couldn't…I *didn't* want to just leave him, you know? I knew Al would come back, and maybe he'd have figured out how to make things all right again. Then I started thinking that *he* would call the police, because of it all being self-defense and all. I just sat there, arms around my knees, like some little kid all lost and stuff."

"And Al did come back, didn't he?" She nodded. "Did you hear any other shooting?" Maria shook her head. "When he returned, did he have Myron's gun with him?"

"I didn't see it."

"Maria, listen to me carefully now," Estelle said. "When Al ran down the hill after Connie, after saying, 'She'll call the cops,' did he have Myron's gun in his possession?"

Maria nodded. "Yes."

"And when he returned, he did not."

"I don't think so. I didn't see it, unless he had it tucked under his jacket or something."

"All right. Maria, this is what's going to happen now. We'll need for you to make a formal, signed statement. Lieutenant

Taber is going to take you into Posadas to our offices so that you can do that without interruption. All right?"

"I have to do that?"

"Yes. We're asking for your cooperation."

"What if I don't want to? I mean, I've told you everything I know."

Well, not quite, Estelle thought, and glanced at the glacial-faced Jackie Taber, who was probably thinking the same thing.

"Then you will be arrested, afforded the chance to call an attorney, and in all likelihood end up talking to us anyway." Estelle slipped the tiny micro-recorder from her jacket pocket again and held it up for Maria to see. "If you decide to say nothing to anyone, if you refuse to cooperate in any way, then a Grand Jury will listen to all the evidence, and decide what charges the District Attorney might pursue."

Maria closed her eyes and leaned her head back. For a moment, it looked as if she'd fainted.

"Let me talk with Al," she whispered. "He'll know what to do."

"Maria, I'm sorry. That's the one thing that I *guarantee* is not going to happen. Lieutenant?"

Jackie Taber skirted the table and stood beside Maria, one hand on the young woman's upper arm. "Let's do this the easy way, Maria." Taber's voice was quiet and silky.

Maria stood, then immediately collapsed into the chair again. "What about White Fang?"

"She'll be fine. If all goes well, you'll be back here in time to feed her dinner."

When Maria was safely situated in the caged rear seat of Jackie's Expedition, Estelle beckoned the officer to one side, away from the truck. With her back turned to the vehicle, she kept her voice just one notch above a whisper. "When you help her with her deposition, keep her going. Find out what Al did when he returned to the scene of the shooting. What she did. All of that. Lead her through it. I didn't want to take the time to deal with it now, before we round up Al Fisher. The last thing I want to do is deal with that little weasel after dark."

"You got it."

"And keep your recorder running every step of the way back to the office."

"Absolutely. You be careful."

"You said it. Absolutely."

Estelle recounted a condensed version of Maria's story, and Robert Torrez listened without interruption. As Estelle finished, he nodded toward the low, white roofline of Danny Rivera's shop.

"I ain't seen any movement down there, but you ever been inside that shop?"

"Yes."

"Then you know it ain't much for windows. If they were workin' on something, they might not even know we're here. That works for us." He lifted the mike. "Three oh four, I want you to park just between Serefina's place and Rivera's. There's a back door to that shop. Cover that."

"Ten four."

"If Danny has a scanner, he knows we're here."

"That'll work too." Torrez let the Expedition roll quietly down the narrow lane, past Solomon Apodaca's walled hacienda, around the curve in front of the late Serefina Roybal's modest mobile home, and finally drift to a stop in front of Rivera's.

"Let me go in and talk to him," Estelle said as she unlocked her door.

"This ain't no time to be a *heroeen*," Torrez replied.

"But he doesn't think I'm much of a threat, Bobby. You *are* a threat. And if he sees Pasquale at the back door, that's even worse. If Maria's story is true, and I think some of it might be, Al Fisher is going to need some talking down." She twisted in her seat. "We don't know the circumstances of Darrell's death, but now we know what Al did with Fitzwater and Connie…at least Maria's version. And *Maria* doesn't know for sure what went on in Connie's trailer when Al caught up with her."

"Pretty obvious."

"So we think…it's not reasonable to imagine that maybe she wrestled Myron's handgun away from Al, and then turned around and shot herself with it. Right now, Al has to know that there's no way out for him."

"Then we'll get 'em comin', just in case." Estelle knew that the "them" in this case was the whole crime scene team, including the EMTs.

Chapter Thirty-six

Torrez parked the Expedition directly behind Al Fisher's pickup, and Estelle waited for him to finish his radio communication before getting out. She had cleared the front fender, and was walking along the slab side of the pickup when the steel man-door of the garage opened and Danny Rivera stepped out, looking to crush out his cigarette in the metal bucket by the door. He flashed his fetching smile at Estelle, and lifted a hand in salute to Torrez, then froze, one hand on the doorknob, when he saw the shotgun in Torrez' grip.

"Danny, I need to talk with Al."

"Well, sure. He's inside working on the lathe. What's going on?"

She reached out and took him by the elbow. "You need to step away from the building. Wait over by your vehicle so we know where you are."

"Holy shit, what's going on now?"

"Wait by your truck, Danny." When she was sure that the young man would comply, she slipped sideways through the open door, taking cover in the dark shadows. The garage had two grimy windows facing northeast, and a bank of LED shop lights along the opposite wall. About forty-by-eighty feet, the shop was so full of vehicles and vehicle parts that narrow walkways provided the only access across the floor.

Dominating the center of the shop was an older model Oshkosh diesel dump truck with a mammoth snowplow blade. As her eyes adjusted to the dim light, she saw Al Fisher behind a utility trailer, directly under one of the LED lights. His back was turned to her, and he appeared to be concentrating on the lathe in front of him. The big machine was running smoothly, barely a subdued hum, its jawed chuck a bright blur. Like so much else in the shop, the lathe was clearly an antique—the huge, powerful sort of thing that would be adequate to turn the largest workpieces. Al was turned slightly, his left side toward the machine, a pair of calipers in his right hand.

The large figure of the sheriff moved through the door, closing it behind him. As Estelle waited, Torrez crossed over to the rear of the Oshkosh.

For a moment, Estelle watched Al working. The shiny cylinder he was turning was about two inches in diameter and perhaps a foot long. Without moving, she surveyed the interior of the shop. To Al's right was a parts washer, nothing more than a simple metal sink on a wheeled stand where metal parts could be bathed in kerosene or some other solvent. Leaning against the wall behind the parts washer was the small twenty-two rifle that Al had carried up the mountain earlier. To reach it, he would have to take two or three steps, ducking around the end of the lathe in the process.

He was wearing the same tan work jacket as before, and if he carried a handgun concealed under its folds, Estelle couldn't make out its outline.

Estelle turned and signaled to the sheriff that she was going to move toward the headstock end of the lathe, toward Al's left, where she would be in his peripheral vision.

Al turned slightly, his left arm arced over the workpiece. He manipulated the calipers with both hands. The cylinder he was working with was tiny, considering the capacity of the lathe, and that forced him in close. Finally, Estelle had moved far enough that he saw her and looked up quickly. He frowned.

To see exactly what happened next would have required an extra-slow-motion replay. What Estelle saw was a spray of blood, tissue, and bone as Al's body was jerked in hard against the machine, his left arm torn and shredded. His scream was piercing even as Bob Torrez sprinted past Estelle to Al's side, where he punched in the machine's large, red kill button. With his free hand, he reached past the coasting chuck, twisted and then jerked the large plug out of the service box on the wall.

"Get Tom and Danny," he commanded, shucking open the shotgun and dropping it to the floor in front of the lathe. He held Al upright, tight against the machine. "And tell the EMTs to make tracks. Shit, it's got him good." By the time she had reached the door, her radio message had brought Tom Pasquale running, joined by Danny Rivera.

"Look, you got to support him up against the lathe so he don't pull on his arm," Torrez instructed. Al Fisher's head lolled back, his eyes wide and unseeing, blood pouring down from the hamburger that was the left side of his face. Torrez pulled Pasquale's arm to command his attention. "Support him under the hip. Don't let him slide down, don't let him slide back away from the machine."

"Ah, jeez," Danny Rivera groaned. "I shouldn't have left him workin' by himself. And I *told* him to shed that jacket earlier."

"See what you can do," Torrez said to Estelle as soon as she returned. "Come around the backside, maybe. You got to find a way to stop the bleedin'." The blood was a torrent, and it was difficult to tell where torn jacket and shirt fabric ended and tissue began. Torrez cradled Al's head, keeping his face away from the chuck. After grabbing his arm and drawing him in toward the lathe, the polished steel chuck had slammed into the man's left cheek and jaw, peeling away tissue, teeth, and bone.

The sheriff glanced up at Danny, the young man's face ghost-white, and sweat already standing out from his forehead. "Look, pay attention," Torrez barked. "Can you get that chuck off the machine?"

"I…"

"Well, you're going to have to. He's all wrapped up in it, and it sure as hell ain't going to work to unwind him."

Estelle sliced fabric with her knife. "The arm is amputated, Bobby," she said.

Torrez took a moment to peer into the machine. Sure enough, what was left of Al's left hand was stuffed up behind the chuck.

"All right, is all the tissue clear?"

"It looks like it."

"Then cut all the clothing that's hanging him up so we can ease him down to the floor." He looked at Pasquale. "You hear me?"

"Yes, sir."

"Danny, forget the chuck for a minute. Get over here and help support him."

Al Fisher uttered a long, deep gasp, what was left of his mouth falling slack. Torrez twisted so he could check for pulse. "He's still with us. Let's move him while he's out of it."

From deep in the shoulder joint outward, the various parts of Al Fisher's left arm remained in the machine as they eased him away. "Get your blanket," Torrez said, and Pasquale darted away, returning from his Expedition less than a minute later with a thick wool Army blanket.

Estelle stood back, looking hard at Al Fisher. As she did so, she pulled her radio, thought better of trying to reach dispatch with a hand-held in this radio dead-zone, and hustled out to the sheriff's unit. Brent Sutherland was on dispatch, and answered her call immediately.

"Brent, we have a shop accident victim with catastrophic injuries down here at Rivera's, waiting on the ambulance. Contact the hospital and have them start to round up every drop of Type O that they can scrounge. I don't know what type the victim is, but O will work. My husband should be either home or over at Bill Gastner's. Have him come to the ER and start prepping."

"Ten four, three ten. Who's the victim?"

"The victim is Al Fisher, a twenty-eight-year-old male. The injuries are massive to the left side of his body and head, with traumatic amputation of the left arm at the shoulder."

"Ten four." Brent sounded matter of fact. "We'll see if we can find his blood type stats."

"Both the sheriff and I will be ten-six for a while."

"Ten four."

"Who's on emergency rotation now?"

"I don't know, but I can find out."

"If you can, make sure Matty Sheehan is on the response team. She knows where Danny Rivera's shop is."

"Ten four."

She tossed the mike on the seat and jogged back inside. Torrez knelt on the floor beside Al, both hands working in the young man's armpit, blood bright and effusive. "You got smaller hands. See if you can isolate this artery." The bleeder was the size of a pencil, and the gush of blood would drain Al in another couple of minutes.

"Danny, I need a clip. Anything with a narrow bite." She held up one hand, index and thumb half an inch apart. "A paper clip of some kind. Wash it off with something. Gas, kerosene, alcohol, whatever."

Al Fisher's breathing was coming in jerky, spasmodic heaves. "Just stay with us, Al. You're going to make it." She reached up and took the small black steel clip that Danny fetched, the kind secretaries use for heavy folders. "Perfect. Well, maybe not…" She pointed with her chin. "Bobby, see if you can shift that lump of shoulder tissue up and out of the way a little." The clip bit down on the artery, and the stream stopped, but Estelle could see profuse bleeding from a dozen other spots.

"Get me some packing. Clean shop rags, anything."

When he delivered a mound of small flannel rags, she formed a smooth wad and pressed it hard into the gaping wound. "You have big first aid bandages in your kit?" Danny looked flummoxed. "Duck tape will do. Right now."

With Torrez and Pasquale supporting Al Fisher's body, Estelle ripped duck tape around the man's torso and over his left armpit, pulling the wad of flannel rags tight into the wound. Fashioning a smaller pad of shop towels, she covered the huge facial wound.

"Okay. Relax him onto his right side. And Danny, we're going to need that lathe to come apart so we can retrieve whatever we can."

"I can take off the chuck." He didn't sound thrilled about working in the middle of the gore.

"Then do it. Tom, give him a hand if he needs it." With a flurry of clanking chains, the overhead hoist was yanked into position over the lathe, and the chain basket that Danny had fashioned long ago slid into position around the two hundred-pound chuck.

"Oh, Christ," Danny moaned, and turned away, holding a hand across his mouth.

"The problem is that the guy's hand is stuffed into the back of the chuck, in pieces," Deputy Tom Pasquale said matter-of-factly. He reached out and patted the bed of the lathe. "When you get it loose, set it here, real careful."

"It has to unscrew," Danny managed. "I mean the chuck threads itself onto the lathe spindle."

"So unscrew it." Pasquale's brusque tone helped, and Danny reached for a heavy cheater bar that leaned against the lathe.

"He ain't got much of a pulse," Torrez announced. "Little bit, maybe."

The problem for Danny Rivera was that as he manually turned the chuck to back it off the spindle's threads, a fair amount of arm tissue and torn coat came with it. "We got to watch the harness. If that chuck slips, it'll crush your hand."

"I'm clear," Pasquale said. "Okay, take some weight now."

Danny pulled one of the hoist chains, and the overhead winch took weight, but not enough to bind the chuck from rotating. With a few final turns, the chuck came free from the spindle, dragging a fair amount of Al Fisher with it. Pushing the winch away on its overhead track, the chuck hung free a few inches above the lathe bed.

"I would leave it right there until we're done with it, rather than setting it down," Estelle said.

"I got to go outside," Danny moaned, and headed for the door.

"You have him?" Estelle asked Torrez. The sheriff shifted position and nodded. Estelle gently placed a hand on each side of Fisher's neck, on the left side staying below the gigantic, ragged crater that had once been his jaw bone. She closed her eyes and listened with her fingertips. Ever so faintly, blood coursed through his carotids—not a full-blown pulse, but tiny flutterings.

"I need to try and reach my husband," she said. "Stay with him."

"Yup."

Outside, the bright, late afternoon sun was almost annoyingly cheerful. Danny Rivera leaned against the front fender of his truck, his forehead resting on his crossed arms. He looked at her, bleary-eyed. "Use our landline if you have to, Sheriff."

"Thanks. I do."

"Irene went visiting neighbors, but the phone is right on that little table inside the front door."

She sprinted over to the trailer, found the phone, and waited only two rings before Francis Guzman answered.

"*Oso*, we have an incoming patient with massive, life-threatening injuries coming to you."

"Amputation," he interrupted. "They called. We're gearing up."

"Does Matty have Type O on board?"

"I would think that she has some plasma, not whole blood. Is the patient conscious?"

"No. Pulse is feeble and ragged."

"And still losing blood."

"Yes. I have a paper clip on the brachial artery. The torn end of it."

"A clip is better than nothing. If you have something fairly clean, pack it into the wound."

"Done."

"Good. I'll get med-evac coming for a transfer, if he makes it this far."

"Stay tuned."

"Is anything reattachable, by the way?"

"No. Bits and pieces."

"Okay. Be careful."

She hung up and turned to see that Danny Rivera had moved to the back of his truck as if he were walking away from his shop in stages. He leaned against the tailgate, pale and sweaty despite the December chill.

"What was Al making, Danny?" She knew perfectly well that what Al Fisher had been fabricating no longer mattered at this point, but Danny Rivera needed to talk, to force his own blood to move before he fell flat on his face.

"He got this plan off the internet for a suppressor for his rifle…a silencer."

"And you were letting him try to make it on your machine?"

"Well," he said helplessly, "he said he knew how. I mean, he'd come down here once in a while to do little jobs…sometimes to help me with something that I had going that required four hands."

"Lupe tells me that Al was a very helpful neighbor. Good to have around."

Danny nodded, trying for a deep breath that didn't catch in his throat.

Estelle regarded him for a moment. "Danny, let me suggest a large sign for the inside of your shop that says, 'NO.'"

"Is he going to be all right?"

"I'm not feeling especially charitable at the moment, Danny. So, no, he's not going to be all right. Whether he'll enjoy dental implants, a new titanium jawbone, skin grafts, and long-term physical therapy, along with learning to use an artificial left arm and hand…that's the *best* he has to look forward to. If a massive infection doesn't kill him first, that's the best."

"Jeez, I'm sorry."

"Yes, well." While they waited for the ambulance, Deputy Pasquale, now wearing surgical gloves, made himself useful, carefully removing the bone and tissue stuck to, or in, the various surfaces of the lathe. At one point, Danny Rivera tried to approach and help, but his feet and his queasy stomach thought better of it.

"I can't do this," Rivera said, and turned away. The victim's hand had somehow been jammed into the hollow rear framework of the chuck, and riding there as the chuck revolved, had escaped significant injury. But from wrist to shoulder, Al Fisher's left arm was essentially paste.

Estelle grimaced as she used the parts washer to quickly rinse the gore off her hands. So quickly had she and the sheriff been pulled into the rescue efforts that neither one of them had taken the time to don latex gloves. She found a clean shop towel to dry the fragrant kerosene. Then she unlimbered her camera to take detailed photos, including several of Al Fisher himself, still supported by Sheriff Torrez. Every bit of Al Fisher that could be recovered from the lathe went into the transport cooler.

"Been faster to put him in the back of the unit and drive him in ourselves," Torrez observed at one point.

"He's got a ten-minute head start with you calling the EMTs before we went in," Estelle said. "We kinda expected one thing, and got another."

"Three ten, EMT-One." Estelle pulled her hand-held off her belt.

"Go ahead."

"EMT-One is just clearing the pass. ETA six minutes."

"Ten four. I hear you."

State Trooper Hector Dominguez escorted the heavy EMT

vehicle down off the pass so quickly that more than once they could hear the shriek of tire rubber over sirens. Estelle knelt beside Al Fisher. He looked dead, but she was still able to detect the faintest stirring of pulse. "You hang in there, Al," she whispered. She patted his right shoulder almost affectionately.

Chapter Thirty-seven

With Al Fisher and his various body parts safely tucked aboard the ambulance, with plasma flowing along with various other potions and packings, the EMTs flailed the diesel for Posadas, with Trooper Dominguez providing escort, siren wailing.

Estelle forced herself to take another comprehensive batch of photos before leaving Danny Rivera's shop, and then sat down on the front step with the still shaky Rivera as he smoked one cigarette after another, trying to work up the willpower to thoroughly clean the big lathe before the blood ate oceans of corrosion on the polished machine castings.

Interruptions had been a constant stream after the attraction of the ambulance. Estelle saw the neighbors coming, and had Danny lock the shop door. Solomon Apodaca walked over, his bow legs making his footing on the gravel road unsteady. Both Lupe and Flora Gabaldon stopped by. In only a matter of minutes, Estelle supposed, the Regál grapevine would reassure the village residents that it was *not* Danny Rivera, a favorite son, who had been hurt—nor Irene, his live-in girlfriend. "Oh…Al Fisher got tangled up? Huh. Too bad, that one," seemed to be the general consensus. Not surprising, no one wanted a tour of the inside of the shop.

By the time she returned to Posadas, she learned that Al Fisher had survived the road trip from Regál to Posadas General

Hospital, where Drs. Alan Perrone and Francis Guzman waited. By the time the Med-Evac moaned in over Cat Mesa, Fisher had been the recipient of a good share of the blood bank's A-positive blood, as well as plasma. None of the contents in the cooler so carefully packed by Tom Pasquale were of use in the stabilizing process.

The air ambulance cut only the door-side engine during its brief stop in Posadas, and in minutes the unconscious Al Fisher and the cooler of useless parts was Albuquerque-bound…along with the distraught Maria Apodaca, who had learned of her boy-friend's lathe accident just as she was signing the deposition that admitted that she knew Al had never gone hog hunting in Texas.

No surprise there, as Sheriff Torrez pointed out. She did not know what the two brothers had been up to that snowy Friday evening until the obviously upset Darrell Fisher, along with his sleepy, cranky young son, left to drive home.

As she watched the steep climbout by the twin turboprop, Estelle felt a surge of pride in their performance. Al Fisher would receive the best care modern medicine could offer. Hours of surgery awaited him, if he survived long enough. Repeat surgeries, no doubt. Agonizing physical therapy. All provided by the State of New Mexico, along with, eventually, a bed in the state prison.

Estelle turned to Sheriff Robert Torrez, who had joined her at the airport as part of Al Fisher's escort.

"APD says they're going to provide some security at the hospital," he said. "Ain't no use in either one of us makin' that trip."

"Not right away, anyway. I want to go up tomorrow afternoon. Should he survive the trip and the initial surgery, there's a faint possibility of getting some simple yes/no answers from him."

"You're dreamin'."

"Maybe so. But there are so many questions. Myron Fitzwater is still out there somewhere, Bobby. Maria had no reason to lie about that. She admits slugging Myron in the back of the head, and that gave Al time to grab the man's own gun and end the fight right then and there. If she were going to lie about that incident, I can't see her admitting to Al's turning the gun on Myron. And then, if Al talked his brother into helping dispose of the body—"

"Maybe so."

"He left Connie Suarez lying in a puddle of blood, pretty sure we'd think it was a suicide, or maybe that Myron had shot her and then took off."

"Clever guy."

"Too clever. But we have one little bit to work with. Pasquale stopped Darrell Fisher on his way home from Al's just after midnight on Saturday. Let's assume that in reality, Darrel *did* spend the evening at Al's, and now we can guess doing what. They weren't working on greenhouse plumbing, or deer butchering, or anything like that. Their problem was getting rid of Myron Fitzwater's body. No point in trying to bury it on the property. Too many rocks, too many dogs busily digging. Al is anxious to get rid of the Forest Service truck, and figures to shift attention away from Regál." She held up two fingers. "The truck, the body. Al would want them both gone, drawing attention away from the scene."

Estelle could see the little crow's-feet deepen around Bob Torrez' eyes.

"A six-hour window, about," he said.

"Yes."

"So if we was to draw a circle centered in Regál whose radius included where Fitzwater's truck was found up outside of Newton, then somewhere inside that circle is where Fisher hid the body."

She looked at him in mock surprise. "You *didn't* sleep during geometry class," she laughed.

"Nope. But that's a hell of a big circle. You could hide a whole lot of bodies in that much country."

"But the weather was awful. He's not going to go driving off deep into the boonies, looking for a place to dig. But wherever he chose, the weather would cover his tracks, for a little while, at least. And that's why we need to talk to Al." She glanced at the time. "And now I'm due home, or I'll have a revolt on my hands."

He regarded her tan pants suit, now grotesquely splotched with blood and dried gore. "You show up in that outfit..."

"I'll slip in the back door." She made a face. "And don't look at your own self in the mirror, Robert."

"We'd work for Halloween." He pointed with his chin at the hangar looming at the edge of the airport tarmac. "If you get a chance, talk to your son."

"Oh, sure. Your phone works just fine, Bobby. He'd be delighted to have a call from you."

They rode in silence back to the Sheriff's Office, where Estelle picked up the Charger. On Twelfth Street, her husband's SUV was parked in the driveway. She glided the county car to a stop farther down the walk, and when she opened the car door, she could hear the piano.

"Grand entrance," she said, and before sliding out of the car, keyed the mike.

"PCS, three ten is ten seven."

"Three ten, ten four," Ernie Wheeler's familiar voice responded. "Be advised that you have about a dozen messages waiting for you."

"I'm sure there are the same or more on my cell," she said. "Right now, I don't want to talk with anybody."

"Ten four."

She fished out her cell phone, turned it on, and scrolled down the display of all the people who apparently needed something to do on Christmas Day. Even as she scanned the list, a new one popped to lead the board as the phone played its incoming message chord. She pushed *talk*.

"You coming inside, Ma?" To cover the fifty feet from the house to her car, the signal probably had to circle the globe.

"I am, *hijo*." She could see Francisco's figure standing in the light of the window.

He met her at the door, and his eyebrows shot up. "*Ay, caramba!* I hope that's not yours."

She looked down at her bloody, gore-smeared clothing. "No. You should see the other guy." The old joke sounded flat, but she managed to smile at her son. "Who's playing?" She looked around the doorjamb and saw Angie at the keyboard. The young woman stopped abruptly and beamed at Estelle, but her smile of greeting crumpled as she took in the full measure of Estelle's ruined pants suit.

"Dad's in the back getting cleaned up, and everybody else is over at *Padrino*'s. That's where we're supposed to go as soon as you're ready."

"A week or so in the shower should do it."

"Dad said that they had to fly some guy to Albuquerque."

"Yes."

Francisco grinned sympathetically at the cryptic answer. "Angie and I will do some four-hands while you get yourself cleaned up. I kinda like that new kerosene perfume you're wearing."

Back in the bedroom, as she slipped out of her clothes, Dr. Guzman gathered them up and took them to the laundry room, adding only a single "Yuck" as his editorial comment. Half an hour later, after letting the water beat hard on her head and shoulders until the water heater showed signs of protest, she felt almost clean. The surface cleaning was easy; the mental images that remained weren't.

Uproarious laughter floated in from the living room, and she dressed hastily, loath to spend another moment out of the company of people she treasured.

Chapter Thirty-eight

"So what do you think?" Bill Gastner rested his elbows on the table, pushing his dessert plate to safety. The Christmas enchiladas—both red and green chile—had disappeared without leftovers. The dessert—two more sour cherry pies not long out of the oven with designer ice cream melting with the heat—now was just a few crumbs. Gastner made a dismissive gesture. "See, this is the way I look at it." He nodded at Francisco and Angela.

"You two don't need money—you've got a lock on that. What you *do* need is a place to live beyond hotel rooms. Someplace to call home. For those rare moments when you're not traveling. Am I right?" Without waiting for an answer, he added, "That was the whole point of your original notion to buy, renovate, and expand Teresa Reyes' place in Tres Santos. I'm kinda relieved the visit down south today gave the kibosh to that plan. Now, take a long, hard look at this place. It's not St. Moritz, but it's big, it's historical, and it's *expandable*." He reached out and touched the wall behind him. "With eighteen-inch adobe walls, it's quiet as a mausoleum. And you could put a big music wing off the east side, and no one would ever notice. Make it soundproof, as this guy here suggests." He draped a hand on Carlos' shoulder. "And you can play twenty-four hours a day without bothering anybody." He grinned. "And health care is about a hundred steps out the back door. This Francis Guzman guy? He's even got a *dentist* on his clinic staff now."

246 Steven F. Havill

"*Padrino*," Francisco said, "this is your home. You can't just give it away."

"Why the hell not?" The old man folded his arms on the table. One craggy eyebrow drifted upward.

"No, really…"

"Really, schmeely. I'm eighty-four goddamn years old, and I've used up about eleven of my nine lives. So. And, you know, my old man used to say that a fellow was smart to always reserve time to clean up his mess before leaving, if the Fates gave him the chance. Lots of people never get the chance to do that. Those of us who do are the lucky ones. Plus," and he held up both hands, "I'm your *Padrino*, your Godfather. I see that as entailing certain responsibilities."

He frowned hard at Angie. "What the hell is *she* blubbering about?"

Angie burst out laughing, rose, and skirted her fiancé so she could envelope Gastner in a hug. She didn't dab away the tears.

"Careful," Gastner protested. "You're breakin' my neck." He patted her arm as she straightened up. "See, this is the bottom line. I do not need to rattle around in this big old mausoleum all by myself. That's probably why I've got such a case of insomnia. I lay there waiting for some little noise to worry about. You know I never cook for myself, so all I need is my bedroom suite, and I'm happy. Even happier with some company once in a while. And this is what I figure. When I get too old—and I'm damn near that already—these two," and he nodded at Francis and Estelle, "can figure out what to do with me if I can't figure that out for myself. If not them, my eldest daughter, Camille, is just itching for the excuse to be a home care provider—*if* I agree to move to Flint, Michigan—which isn't goddamn likely."

The room fell silent. Gastner pointed at his coffee cup, and Carlos shot out of his seat to do the honors.

"Say yes, and I start on the paperwork tomorrow," Gastner said. "Then the architect here can confab with you, and start *that* process." He turned and regarded the circular, sunken living room behind them that he called his own private kiva. "I figure you'll want your Steinway somewhere in here. Its own room, I'm thinking. But for sure, you know best about that."

"I wonder," Francisco started to say slowly, and he shook his head in bewilderment. "I'm a little bit apprehensive about what your four kids might say."

Gastner smiled and leaned back. "One of 'em is already stinkin' rich, married to her oral surgeon hubby, and she doesn't need the headache. Another lives back east and doesn't even know that New Mexico is part of the United States. My son Buddy is now a colonel in the Air Force, has his own Air Force base in Germany, and has a dozen other things more important to think about. The fourth kid lives in California, has his own life tangled up with computers, and who the hell knows what he might think?" He shrugged. "Anyway, it's my decision to make, not theirs."

He examined the surface of his coffee. "Damn, I wish there was more of that pie. Two pieces just wasn't enough."

"We're going to need to think about all this," Francisco said. "I mean, it's one of those offers that's hard to refuse."

"That's the intent. Give me one good reason why you would."

"Uh…uh." The young man laughed. "Uh…"

"This is what I've done already," Gastner said. "I had the place appraised not long ago. Needed to do that, whether you take me up on the deal or not. And look, I'm not trying to twist arms here. Well, maybe just a little. Look, if it doesn't work out, you can always sell it and pocket the money. While I'm living here, I take care of the utilities and the property taxes. So, no worries there." He took a deep breath. "The appraisal was lowball, to my way of thinking."

He reached out again and took Carlos by the shoulder, rocking him from side to side. "The house was appraised at a bit over three hundred thousand. Three thirty-five, to be exact. So that's the amount of the check that this guy receives as his part of this whole deal."

He turned and leaned toward Carlos. "You're twenty-one, right?"

"Uh, yes, sir."

"Good. Then you don't have to ask permission." He winked at Estelle. "This is fun, you know that? Best Christmas I've had in a long time."

"Back in Berlin, it's going to be really hard to keep my mind on the music," Francisco said. "But *Padrino*, you know—it's really hard just to accept something like this without having worked for it."

"That makes no sense. If I were to croak tomorrow, or even later tonight, much as I've eaten, then they'd read the will and lo and behold! Guess who's named as beneficiaries of the house, and an equal value check to guess who? You wouldn't refuse that, would you?"

"Of course not. Not if that's what you wished."

"Well, then, *this* is sure as hell what I wish, and I don't see why I should be deprived of the pleasure of not *waiting*. I don't buy green bananas, as they say. And you're wrong, my friend. You *have* worked for it. For the past couple of decades."

"Wow."

And Carlos echoed his brother.

"Merry Christmas," Gastner said.

Chapter Thirty-nine

The wind across the asphalt was chilly, but Francisco held back before boarding the Gulfstream jet. He looked hard at his mother. "You know, you never told me what you *really* think about this whole deal."

"That's because all of the decisions are yours, *hijo*. I can't think of anything better than having you all living here, even if it's just a few weeks each year. But *you* have to decide that. *You* have to add up all the pluses and minuses and see what you get. And you guys are young enough. If it doesn't work out…" she shrugged. "There's always St. Moritz or London or Manhattan."

The young man grimaced. "Done deal." He reached out and took his father's hand once again and drew the physician into a tight hug. "We'll see you both in just a few weeks. The Aspen invasion."

"I've cleared my calendar," Estelle said.

"Yeah, right. Until the phone rings. By the way, I called him early this morning."

"Called who?"

"Sheriff Torrez. I told him to pick up the keys to the truck from Jim Bergin. It's no good having that old beast just sit in a dark building, replaying old memories. I'll send him the signed title."

Estelle reached out and touched her son's cheek.

"I've thought about it, and you know, it was just one of those things." Francisco shrugged. "An impulse. We were going to use it here, when we needed it. I had this fanciful vision of us cruising the dusty hills of Mexico." He grinned. "Dumb, huh? At first Bobby said he wouldn't take it. That he'd buy it off me. But I used *Padrino*'s argument and told the sheriff that I was leaving it to him in my will, so he might as well get the enjoyment out of it now."

"What'd he say to that logic?"

"'Wow.'"

She laughed. "Good enough." She hugged him once more. "I wish your visit had been longer, but we'll take what we can get, no? You travel safe, and we'll see you in a few weeks. I wish you smooth air. We love you all."

She clung hard to her husband as the jet's engines spooled up, shrieking and blowing a dust storm out across the highway. Turning tightly, it headed for the eastern end of the taxiway, where it halted as the crew finished the pre-flight. After several moments, with a burst of power, it thrust its nose out onto the runway, then aligned with the center stripe as both engines sent a roar of roiling fumes into the crisp December air. Hands waved at them through Plexiglas as the Grumman Gulfstream shot past, gathering speed, finally rearing up sharply and streaking away, so thunderous that it shook the ground.

"Quite a Christmas," Francis observed. "You know, you could have hooked a fifteen-minute ride to Albuquerque with them." The Grumman was now just a dot, the sun winking on its polished aluminum. "I'm sure they would have been delighted to take a little detour."

"I need my office with me, thanks just the same, not to mention needing a way to come back home. I really like my feet on the ground."

"You're picking up Jackie?" She nodded. "That's good. She's good company. Stop and have a nice dinner somewhere."

"*Oso*, my stomach is tied up in knots at the moment. I'm not sure I could eat anything."

He walked her over to the Charger, his hand gentle on the back of her neck. "Let the lieutenant do some of the driving, *querida*."

"*Sin duda.* I was thinking about letting her do all of it." She looked up at him for a moment and then knocked her forehead against his chest. "She'd make a good undersheriff, too."

"Rough week, wasn't it?"

"*Ay.*"

"And now off to Albuquerque. You know, the odds of him being able to talk are slim to none."

"I know. But we have to try, *Oso*. Right now, Al Fisher is the only person who knows where Myron Fitzwater is." She smiled. "I'll take my thumbscrews and get it out of him."

Four hours later, she and Jackie Taber walked into the Intensive Care ward of University Hospital in Albuquerque. A young Asian American woman in spotless white greeted them with a reserved smile and a light handshake. "I'm Dr. Oromatsu. Dr. Guzman informed us that you would be visiting." Her eyes flicked to Jackie Taber's name tag, then back to Estelle. "Undersheriff Guzman, let's go to the lounge for a little bit," she said. "You've had a long drive. May I get you something?"

"Nothing for me, thanks." Taber declined as well, and Oromatsu led them to a small room with an overstuffed sofa and two recliners.

The physician sat on the edge of the sofa, hands folded primly. "The injuries this young man has suffered are catastrophic. But of course you know that already."

"Yes. Is he conscious?"

"In little bits and snatches, and heavily sedated, of course. In one or two ways, he was very lucky. The machine did considerable damage to his face—the amputated jaw, a complex fracture of the left orbit…it will take several surgeries to reconstruct his face. But his brain was spared. We're seeing no cranial bleeding. And of course, the arm. The damage to the shoulder and upper left chest is severe." She leaned back. "In some ways, his case is remarkable. The time that passed between the initial episode and any kind of medical intervention was excessive, I'm understanding."

"Thirty-five minutes before the ambulance arrived, another hour before any kind of stabilization at Posadas General, then an hour for flight arrangements."

"So we can say at least three hours between the moment of injury and his examination in our ER."

"Yes."

"Most remarkable. In one way, he's most fortunate."

"Maybe he is."

Oromatsu heard the sharpness in Estelle's voice. "From *our* point of view, he is most fortunate," the physician corrected. "I am aware of the two officers from our own APD who have been on the floor since Mr. Fisher's arrival." Her smile was thin. "I assume there is a great deal more to his story than we need to know."

Estelle avoided the fishing excursion. "I need to make every effort to speak with him. And if he cannot speak because of the damage to his face, then we need to communicate somehow. Also, Maria, his girlfriend, rode up in the ambulance with him. We'll need to speak with her again as well."

"That may need to wait. The girl apparently has friends here in the city, and they came and picked her up. I'm sure she'll be back before long. But for Mr. Fisher, there is no telling. As I said, you'll just have to wait."

"It can't wait, Doctor. As I'm sure you're aware by the presence of the officers in your hallway, this is a capital crime case. One of the three victims is still missing, a young man who works with the U.S. Forest Service. We can presume him dead as well, but we don't know with any certainty. The only person who knows for sure is Mr. Fisher, your patient."

"Perhaps just for a moment," Dr. Oromatsu said.

"Doctor, I'm the person who untangled Mr. Fisher from that

lathe. I'm the one who clamped his torn brachial with a file clip and packed the wound with shop rags—the only thing we had at the moment. I supervised the packing of the various severed body parts into the cooler. At Posadas General, my husband, Dr. Francis Guzman, along with Dr. Alan Perrone, did what they could to stabilize Mr. Fisher for the flight to Albuquerque. Now…I *know* what Mr. Fisher's condition is. I *know* exactly how badly he's hurting." She leaned forward and clamped a hand on top of Dr. Oromatsu's. "If he dies without telling us what we need to know, then in all likelihood some hiker will find the victim's bones a year or two from now."

"So what difference does it make, really? Our job is to keep our patient alive, to render whatever medical treatment is indicated. If you know his victim to be dead, of what use are the immediate, extraordinary, and perhaps harmful, measures to communicate with Mr. Fisher? We also must be aware that if the injuries don't kill him, post traumatic infection might well."

Estelle could feel her pulse pounding in her ears. She chose her words carefully. "The young woman who came on the air ambulance—there's every probability that she will eventually be charged with complicity in this incident, Doctor. What Mr. Fisher is able to tell us may make a difference in how she is eventually charged. She may have acted entirely in self-defense, or she may be charged as an accomplice in a double homicide. At this point we have only her version of events."

"I see."

Estelle stood abruptly. "You're welcome to remain in the room with us, with him, at all times."

Dr. Oromatsu rose, obviously deep in thought.

"The entire conversation, if there is one, will be recorded…and witnessed by Lieutenant Taber. I'd like to get started right now."

"You know, he's in and out. You may end up waiting most of the day. And even then…"

"Whatever it takes."

Chapter Forty

Al Fisher was definitely in an "out" phase when Estelle and Lieutenant Taber entered the ICU. Dr. Oromatsu consulted her charts, and nodded at the small epidural pump that hung on its own stand near the bedside. "When he's stabilized a bit more, he'll be on a demand epidural for pain."

"He can give himself a shot," Estelle said.

"Exactly. Strictly controlled. It's a mix of fentanyl citrate and bupivacaine. The machine monitors carefully so there's no way he can over-medicate."

The monitor at the head of the bed reported Fisher's vitals, with the pulse showing a steady fifty-eight with a respiration rate of eighteen. Estelle stepped close to the patient's right side. The heavy bandages swathed most of his head, leaving only his right eye, right ear, and nostrils exposed. His right arm played host to a variety of tubes, and a great mound of bandages covered his left shoulder and chest.

"If you need anything," Dr. Oromatsu said, "just press that buzzer. One of us is always nearby."

"Thank you."

For several moments, she stood at the side of the bed, gazing down at the wreckage. An eyelid flickered.

"Al, it's Undersheriff Reyes-Guzman from Posadas."

The eyelid flickered again. Estelle reached down and took

Fisher's right hand, careful to avoid the taped IV. His flesh was warm and dry. A faint sound issued from behind the bandages, and Estelle felt a slight pressure in his grip.

"You can hear me all right?" The grip tightened again, then relaxed. "Can I get you something?" His fingers moved ever so slightly, forming the grip that would hold a pencil. His index finger and thumb bobbed a little, as if imagining the act of writing. "Just a minute."

"A pad and pencil?" Jackie asked, and Estelle nodded. In a moment, the lieutenant returned with a yellow legal pad and pencil.

Estelle slid the pad under Al's hand and placed the pencil in his hand. His grip was weak, and twice he dropped the pencil. On the third attempt he was able to touch the pencil point to paper, and produced a wandering scrawl as Estelle held the pad steady. She cocked her head and watched as the words appeared.

Give me yr gun for a minut.

"I don't think so, Al. But I'm glad you haven't lost your sense of humor."

The pencil was motionless for long enough that Estelle thought Fisher might have passed out again. Then, one agonizing letter at a time, he managed, *I cant live like this.*

"You'll be all right, Al. They'll take care of you. You have to be tough."

And then jail.

"Most likely, yes. I'm sorry."

A long silence followed before he managed the one word. *Maria?*

"She's in custody. She's given us a statement of her version of the way it happened. She rode up with you, and she may be in later to see you."

Accident, the pencil laboriously managed.

"Which part, Al? What was an accident?" The pencil slipped and rolled across the pad to nestle in the sheets. Estelle retrieved it and slid it back between his fingers, but Al Fisher's grip was limp. The monitor showed that his pulse had increased a couple of beats, and his respiration came more rapidly.

"Uhhhh," he groaned loudly and tried to shift his body. That brought an even louder groan.

Estelle covered his hand with hers, but she felt no motion, no response. She picked up the pad and made a few notations near each one of Al Fisher's, then removed the page. As she did so, Dr. Oromatsu appeared by the curtain.

"Doctor, we'll need to try again in an hour or so. He was able to write answers for us, so that's a help. One more session, maybe two."

"He's in a *lot* of pain," the physician said. "There's nothing we can do, short of inducing a coma, that will relieve all of it. He's going to be in a narcotic fog for quite a while. And there will be further operations to repair the damage to his face and shoulder."

"Weeks?"

"Most certainly. Maybe more. And extensive therapy after that. Months and months."

Estelle lowered her voiced as she moved toward the door. She held the page so the physician could see Al's awkward responses. "A suicide watch would be warranted," she said. "He's hurting, and knows that barring a miracle there's significant jail time waiting for him when and if he gets out of here."

The physician frowned at the faint writing. "He asked for your gun? Is that what this says?"

"And only half kidding, I'm guessing. I'll talk with the officers standing guard, but they need to be careful. What's the schedule for him now?"

"As soon as we're convinced that his condition is stable, he'll be going back into surgery for the first procedure on his face. As you know, a significant portion of his lower jaw was amputated. It's going to be a significant challenge to reconstruct both jaw and cheek. We'll start that process tomorrow morning, if there are no complications today."

"And the shoulder?"

"That's like any serious war wound, Sheriff. Long-term and painful. In several weeks, maybe months, we'll see where we are with an artificial limb. But there's no stump, in addition to which, much of the base musculature and bone support of the shoulder girdle was mangled. Summer, perhaps. We all have to be patient—Mr. Fisher most of all, of course."

"I understand that."

Dr. Oromatsu managed a thin smile. "And the justice system must be patient as well. And all of that is predicated by his winning the battle with infection. That's always a danger...a most significant one."

Chapter Forty-one

i don't have to talk to you, the pencil scratched.

"No, you don't. But you have everything to gain and nothing to lose, Al." She reached out and touched his right cheek, a light stroke to establish sympathetic contact. "Tell us where you and your brother put Myron Fitzwater's body."

Instead, he wrote, *Darel was an accident.*

"But you were there."

so????? The pencil continued drawing progressively larger question marks until he dropped it. Estelle picked it up and slid it between his fingers. *He said hed call the cops.* The pencil paused. *He couldnt take it.*

"Then what happened?"

we both got mad.

"You were in the truck with him? With your brother?"

i follow him from house.

"He had the gun?" There was a long pause, as if Al Fisher was considering how to answer. Finally he groaned and shifted just a little.

In truck. Said he shudnt came with me.

"He helped you with Fitzwater, didn't he? That's what he couldn't face."

wuss. Then he added a string of *ssss* after the word.

"He threatened to shoot himself?"

yes.

"You believed him?"

He was scared.

"Of getting caught?"

Al's fingers bobbled the pencil a little, as if saying "yes" without actually writing the word.

i laugh at him and jab him with the gun. it went off. an acident.

"You jabbed him under the chin?"

so?

"He struggled with you then?"

He's a wuss. He paused after each word, but remained determined. *I nocked him away and jab him in the gut. The gun went off.* Al Fisher flung the pencil away, uttering another agonizing groan.

"Where's Myron, Al? Where did you put him?" She slid the pencil back between his fingers, but for a long time he ignored it.

they got something. for the hurt.

Estelle reached up and pushed the buzzer without taking her eyes off Fisher's face.

"They're coming. Tell me where Myron is, Al."

He grabbed the pencil this time and printed in large block letters, *ASK TORRES.*

Dr. Oromatsu appeared, frowning darkly.

"Just a moment, Doctor. Listen, Al. Listen to me. Are you talking about the sheriff? Sheriff Bob Torrez?"

The pencil drew a series of light circles, just formless doodling, then paused before writing, with a hesitation after each word, *Coyot hotel.* He flicked the pencil away and whimpered. Oromatsu prepped an injection and slipped the needle deftly into the IV plumbing on the back of Al's hand.

"He'll sleep now," she said. Estelle watched Al carefully, and saw the line of tension in his right cheek relax a little. "You need to leave him," Oromatsu directed.

"Thank you, Doctor." Estelle said. "We'll be back in a bit."

She followed Lieutenant Jackie Taber out into the hall. "What do you think?"

Taber took a moment to organize her thoughts, a characteristic Estelle had always appreciated. "I think Al Fisher is the kind of kid who will be clever to the very end." She lowered her voice to a hoarse whisper as one of the APD officers appeared in the ward.

"He isn't worried about Maria, or at least doesn't seem to be. He never has struck me as being overly concerned about losing his brother, and who knows? Maybe it was an accident of sorts. 'Here, you want to kill yourself? Let me show you how.' That sort of thing, and it backfires on him. It's possible that he didn't even know for sure that the handgun was loaded." Taber shrugged.

"Every gun we looked at down in Regál was loaded," Estelle observed.

"Yes, well…now he plays riddles about Fitzwater. Anything to stay center stage for a little longer." She extended her hand to the young Albuquerque cop, whose name tag announced "R.O. Bateson." Without the cop outfit, he could have been a stand-in for a California surfer dude.

"Lieutenant Jackie Taber, Officer Bateson. This is Posadas County Undersheriff Estelle Reyes-Guzman."

"Alan BATson," the cop corrected. "Good to meet you. Dr. Oromatsu said you wanted to talk with me."

"The patient is gravely hurt," Estelle said. "Significantly maimed. He'll be crippled for life—*if* he survives. Even so, Officer, he's a danger to himself and to others. Right now, he's facing three homicide charges, two of which appear to have occurred as a result of a deer poaching incident. The third victim was his brother, and we're given to believe that the brother was contemplating suicide, maybe out of remorse for the other two killings, or for his part in disposing of the bodies…we're not sure. Whether our patient in here *helped* his own brother shoot himself, or whether the brother was simply murdered, we're also not sure yet." She turned and looked toward the portion of the ICU where Al Fisher lay motionless in his opiate fog.

"But to give you some idea of this young man's mental state, the first thing he asked me was if he could borrow my gun for a minute."

"That'll work, won't it? So he can talk okay?"

"No. He manages to write short messages on a pad." She held up the yellow legal pad for Bateson to see. "He has only one arm—his right, and fortunately for him, he's right-handed. You have no reason to approach his bedside, but if you have to, keep *your* right side and your service weapon turned away from him. Pay close attention, every minute."

"Simple enough."

"It is, if everyone pays attention. When you're relieved, pass along these same instructions to the next officer."

"Yes, Ma'am. You two are staying around?"

"For a time, yes. I want at least one more session with our man. He has information that we need. He may—" She broke off when she saw three uniformed officers appear in the ward. "Excuse us."

Craig Stout, who tended to dress down and work in plain-clothes, was this time attired from head to toe in the U.S. Forest Service's best Smokey uniform. He towered over District Ranger Robert Tully, also in full uniform, and a third man in a dark blue business suit whom Estelle recognized immediately.

"Sheriff," Stout said, "I think you know Neil Gentry from our regional office."

"Mr. Gentry, it's nice to see you again," Estelle said. Gentry worked personnel for the Forest Service, and during the fire season—when Estelle had last met him—was a very busy man indeed.

Gentry smiled. "As I get closer and closer to retirement, I get harder and harder to find. How's Bill doing?" As a young Forest Service law enforcement officer, Gentry had worked with Bill Gastner on several occasions, earning Gastner's evaluation that the young Gentry was "a real hotrod."

"He's doing all right. The usual aches and pains and tune-ups that come with being eighty-four. Gentlemen, this is Lieutenant Jackie Taber."

"I've heard about you," Gentry said. "All good things." He grimaced and rumpled his nose with a forefinger. "I hate the smell of these places. Where can we talk?"

"There's a small lounge just down the hall."

"Ranger Tully contacted me when the preliminary search failed to turn up Myron Fitzwater. Am I correct that you're still thinking that Mr. Fitzwater was killed and his body dumped somewhere?"

"Yes. We are now certain of that. We have an individual who claims that she witnessed the killing, one Maria Apodaca, the patient's girlfriend. In fact, she admitted that she participated in the killing by striking Fitzwater in the head with a tree limb. She claims that she was afraid for Al Fisher's welfare as he and Fitzwater struggled, that Fitzwater was attempting to make an illegal arrest, that he possessed both handcuffs and a handgun and was acting in the capacity of a law enforcement officer— which he was not."

"She's in custody?"

"No. She came to the city with the ambulance, and at the moment is staying with friends here." She glanced up at the wall clock. "I would think that she'll be coming by any time now."

Gentry looked amused. "You're such a trusting soul, Under-sheriff Reyes-Guzman."

"She won't run, if that's what you mean."

"You're sure of that?"

"Yes."

He turned to Stout. "That's your understanding, Craig? That Fitzwater might have aggravated this incident in some fashion beyond his authority?"

"I'm afraid that's becoming clear, yes. As I mentioned to you earlier, we have had a conversation with Officer Charles Austin of the New Mexico State Police. On at least one occasion, Officer Austin had a casual roadside conversation with Fitzwater that led him to suspect that Fitzwater might be acting in a capacity inconsistent with his actual position with the Forest Service."

Gentry looked amused. "'Inconsistent.' You mean he was impersonating a police officer."

"Yes."

"That's not the first time you received that sort of report, or complaint about Mr. Fitzwater, is that right?"

"No. Mr. Fitzwater had a letter of reprimand in his file."

Gentry regarded the two Forest Service men with interest. "Why didn't you just fire him? I mean, personnel policies are pretty clear on things like that."

"Until this recent incident, I thought that the violation of policy was an isolated thing. Mr. Fitzwater was reprimanded, he *understood* the reprimand, and clearly knew that any further incident of this nature *would* result in his termination. He's done good work for us in the past. A hard-working young man. Sometimes just a little too gung-ho."

"Catching a poacher in the process was just too much of a temptation, right? Is that what we're saying? That and, as Ranger Tully tells me, the issue of a few gallons of water being stolen from a wildlife tank up in that area."

"Yes."

"It seems to me that we have a situation of a federal employee getting in over his head. Mr. Fitzwater seems to have thought that the shoulder patch," and he touched his own left shoulder, "gave him some sort of authority that he didn't have."

"So it seems," Tully said gloomily.

"And our young poaching friend? What can he tell us?"

"Not much," Estelle said. "He's hurting. Right now he's heavily sedated, and still faces a long string of surgeries to repair the damage. He's still in critical condition."

"A tangle with a lathe, I'm told."

"Yes."

"Must have been a big one."

"It was. A neighbor has a commercial machine shop that the young man was using. He got caught up and the lathe tore his arm off at the shoulder. When it pulled him in, the chuck beat on his face, taking away jawbone and all sorts of other injuries. Under any other circumstance, he would have bled to death."

"But you and the sheriff were there, somehow."

"We had just arrived at Danny Rivera's shop in Regál, where we were told Mr. Fisher was working. In all probability we would have arrested Mr. Fisher, since by then we had substantial information linking Fisher to Fitzwater's disappearance and the murder of Fitzwater's girlfriend, Connie Suarez. We were prepared for that, with backup present. As an added precaution, since we were familiar with Mr. Fisher's volatile temperament, Sheriff Torrez had also requested an ambulance. It was already rolling."

Tully looked perplexed. "Good heavens, you guys can't effect an arrest without having an ambulance standing by?"

"As it turns out…" Estelle said, and then let it slide. "When we arrived, we met outside briefly with the shopowner, Danny Rivera, who told us that Mr. Fisher was inside, using the lathe. When we went inside, Mr. Fisher didn't see or hear us right away. I think that when he did, he startled. That's when the lathe caught him. That little moment of inattention."

"So." Gentry hitched at his trousers and rebuttoned his suit coat. "Any chance we can talk to Mr. Fisher?"

"If you're patient, a slim one."

Dr. Oromatsu looked as if she were more than willing to make the chances even slimmer. She regarded the approach of the five visitors and held up a hand.

"I don't think so," she said curtly. "He's sleeping, and that's the way he can stay." She frowned at Gentry. "And you are?"

"Neil Gentry." He smiled patiently. "We're all with the Forest

Service, one way or another. I'm with the Regional Office. We're all tangled in this together. I see you even have APD here." He grinned at Officer Bateson, who stood off to one side.

"You all believe in miracles, then." Oromatsu's stern expression would have worked well for a primary school teacher faced with lining up twenty-five six-year-olds for lunch.

"If that helps," Gentry said, undeterred. He sighed and looked at Estelle. "Did you manage any progress?"

Estelle handed him the legal pad. "You can see that at one point, when I asked where Fitzwater's body might be, he wrote *ask Torres*. He spelled it with an 's' instead of a 'z' but that's a common mistake." She pointed down the page to another scrawl. "Then he wrote, *Coyot hotel*. That's as far as he got."

Tully shook his head. "Come spring, some hiker will find the bones, I suppose. Unless we can get Fisher to talk."

"You haven't had a chance to confer with the sheriff about that reference?" Gentry asked. "'Coyot hotel.' He should know what that means."

Chapter Forty-two

"I'm sorry, Undersheriff. The District Attorney Schroeder is in conference right now." District Attorney Dan Schroeder's secretary, Kelly Moffitt, was only twenty-four, but already had honed her protective instincts.

"With Sheriff Torrez?"

"Yes, Ma'am."

Estelle kept her tone patient and understanding. "I'm up in Albuquerque at the hospital where they took Al Fisher. I need to speak with the sheriff."

"They should be out shortly. I can have him call you, if you like."

Estelle took a moment to consider her options, then said, "That would be fine." She disconnected and scrolled down through her directory until she found the district attorney's personal cell phone number, and dialed it.

"This is Schroeder."

"Dan, Estelle Reyes-Guzman. Do you have Bobby cloistered with you?"

He laughed. "You want him?"

"Just for a minute. I'm up in Albuquerque at the hospital with three Forest Service guys."

"Uh oh. And how are our Smokey brethren doing?"

"As frustrated as we are. They have a man missing, and are

beyond nervous about that. May I talk with Bobby for just a minute?"

"Sure. Hang on."

In a moment, Bob Torrez' quiet voice came on the line. "Yep?"

"Bobby, I was able to have something of a conversation with Al Fisher before he went back to swim in the drugs. Hurt as he is, drugged as he is, he's still cagey. When I asked him where he hid Myron Fitzwater's body, he said, 'ask Torrez.' And then he added something about the 'Coyot hotel.' That's coyot without the 'e'. Does that mean anything to you?"

The phone fell silent. While she waited, she watched Stout, Tully, and Gentry watching Al Fisher's motionless, sheeted form through the glass partition. APD Officer Bateson watched every-one, including every doctor, nurse, or aide who walked through his territory. If he was bored, he didn't show it.

"Lemme think some more," Torrez said finally. "If I come up with anything, I'll call. What about Maria…anything?"

"Not yet—other than her original story, that she clouted Fitzwater and that Al then was able to gain the upper hand and managed to shoot him."

"She holding up all right?"

The question surprised Estelle, since Bob Torrez didn't often spend much time or energy thinking about how others were doing, or feeling, or coping.

"I think so. She broke away for a little bit and went to spend some time with friends. Right now, we have Stout and Tully from the Forest Service, and Neil Gentry, from the regional office. Remember him?"

"Yep."

"He's upper level brass now, in personnel."

"Whoo-hoo."

"And Maria just came on the floor. I'll check in with you later. In the meantime, hit the old memory files and figure out what a Coyot Hotel is."

"Yep."

She disconnected and beckoned Maria Apodaca, who looked as if she'd been dragged across the city under a bus. Disheveled hair, bloodshot eyes, rumpled clothes…if she'd been looking for rest and peace of mind with her friends, she hadn't found it.

"He's resting," Estelle greeted her. Her hand slipped into her jacket pocket and she turned on the micro-recorder. "They gave him a big dose for the pain. How about you? How are you holding up?"

"Every time I close my eyes," Maria said miserably, "all I see is the blood."

"We think he'll be okay, Maria."

"But his arm?"

"He'll learn to live with that challenge."

"But I mean…" The young woman's shoulders shook. "What will they do to him…after…?" She rubbed hard at her left eye. "I saw the cop in the ward."

"Yes. That's for his own safety."

"Why? Who's going to hurt him any more?"

"Nobody. He needs company now, Maria, that's all. Depression is a natural consequence of a traumatic injury like this." She reached out and rested a hand on Maria's quivering left shoulder. "It's good that you came. He needs you to be here. He shouldn't be alone." Estelle saw that Craig Stout was watching them. "The officers from the Forest Service want to talk with you, Maria. Can you do that?"

"Yes."

"Before you do, let me ask you what I know is on their minds too, all right?"

"Yes."

She walked Maria down the hallway a bit. "After the incident on the hill—after you struck Fitzwater with the club, and after Al shot him, you told me that you *remained* up on the hill, sitting with your back against the tank. You must have been worried sick about what Al would do."

"Yes."

"He pursued Connie down the hill, to her house. *Inside* her house. You didn't hear a gunshot?"

"No, but I was crying so hard, maybe I wasn't able to hear a thing. I couldn't help myself. Do you think that Al killed her?"

"Do you?"

"Sheriff, he couldn't. You know, he liked her. I know that he did."

"But she was going to call authorities. She *witnessed* the killing."

Maria's eyes darted this way and that as if trying to sweep the flood of tears away. "I just don't think he would do that. That's all. I heard that it was suicide, anyway."

"Maybe so. But there you sat, with your back against the tank, and just a few feet away was Myron's body. And the deer carcass. How long was it before Al returned?"

"I don't know. A while."

"A long while, or a short one?"

"Just…just a while."

"And when he returned, what did he say?"

"'We're okay.' That's what he said. 'We're okay.'"

"What do you think he meant by that? What did you take him to mean?"

"That somehow he'd convinced Connie to keep quiet about the whole affair?"

Oh, sure, Estelle thought. *He convinced her, all right.*

"No, really." Maria saw the skepticism on Estelle's face. "Myron and Connie—they weren't getting along very well anymore. So at the time, I believed Al. I believed him when he said everything was okay."

"And later, when you found out that Connie was dead?"

"I…I…I mean, what could I do? Everyone was talkin' about it being a suicide, and so I thought…I thought, just leave it alone. That's what it was. Just leave it alone."

"But that evening—at the time—you believed Al when he said 'We're okay'?"

"Yes. Then he said that Darrell was comin' down to help him. That I should go back to the house and just stay there. Just *stay* there. If Darrell had to bring the little boy, then I was supposed to look after him, 'cause Penny was working nights."

"So Al and Darrell were going to dispose of the body."

"I guess. I mean, they couldn't just leave him lying there."

"A busy afternoon for them."

"What do you mean?"

"Stow Myron Fitzwater somewhere, and then the deer carcass to Lupe's...all kinds of loose ends to clean up, don't you think?" She watched Maria's face and not for the first time saw a glimmer of something other than grief-stricken hysteria. "So that's what you did? Went to the house and stayed there?"

Maria nodded but couldn't meet Estelle's gaze.

"It took the rest of the afternoon and most of the evening, didn't it? Disposing of Myron's truck, his body, the deer? Did you see Darrell and Al drive off at some point?"

Maria's nod was almost imperceptible.

"In Myron's truck? The Forest Service truck? With it gone, anyone might think that if not maybe suicide, maybe Myron killed Connie. One of their many quarrels."

"I don't know. But, yes, Al took the white truck...Myron's government truck. He took that one. Darrell drove his own. I think...I think that Darrell had Myron's body in the back. I know that they got a tarp out of the greenhouse."

"But you're not sure."

"No." She put a hand on each side of her head as if it might be coming apart. "I didn't look. I didn't want to know. All I know is..." and she stopped abruptly.

"Yes?"

"All I know is that Darrell and Al came back and it was close to midnight. Al looked angry, and Darrell looked as if he'd been crying, or upset, or something."

"And then?"

"And then Darrell took little Derry and drove home. I was worried about the snow, but Darrell didn't seem to care."

"Why did Al tell us that he went pig hunting the next day... on Saturday?"

"I don't know."

"He didn't go, did he?"

"No."

"What *did* he do?"

"He worked some in the greenhouse, and then he went down to Danny's for most of the afternoon."

"And you? What did you do?"

"I spent time with Mama and Papa, and that was hard. Mama's got sort of a sixth sense when she thinks something's wrong. I just told her that Darrell was having an awful time with Penny. And he was, you know. I mean, he got stopped by the cops on the way home, and they said he'd kicked Derry out of the truck because he was such a big fuss." The tears turned into gushers. "If he did that, what they said he did, he would have only done it for a couple of minutes. I mean, he would *never* hurt Derry."

"Al thought enough about his brother to provide five hundred dollars bail, right?"

"Well, you know. Al was his *brother*. And then Saturday night, they said he killed himself. Penny called Al, and he went up to their house right away."

Grief strickened. But one less worry, Estelle thought. She looked up and saw Craig Stout approaching. "We need you to talk with the Forest Service folks now, Maria."

"Oh, my God." She wiped at her flooded eyes and snuffled. Estelle handed her a bunch of tissues. Behind Stout, she saw Dr. Oromatsu beckon her with a single index finger.

"Use the lounge," Estelle said. "I need to talk with the physician."

Dr. Oromatsu waited and then fell in step, opening the door

for her. "He's stirring now. You may have a few minutes. I can't guarantee how lucid he'll be."

"Thank you, Doctor."

Al Fisher's single unbandaged eye was open, but wandering. After a moment, he was able to fix on Estelle's face. She slid the pad under his hand, and touched his fingers with the pencil. After a moment, he took it.

They gotta give me something.

"They are, Al. They will. Listen to me, Al. Myron Fitzwater's supervisors are here. From the Forest Service. They want to talk with you."

NO. NO. NO. The scrawls came rapidly.

"Al, if you tell me…just me…where the body is, that's all they want to know. I'll keep them away from you."

I told you. And the pencil stopped. He let it slide, and then lifted his hand, slowly as if powered by hydraulics somehow. Letting out a little whimper as if any motion cost him dearly, he reached out and lightly touched Estelle's left cheek. She didn't draw away, but didn't take his hand in hers. For a handful of seconds, he held his hand there, the softest possible touch.

your a sweet lady he wrote after once more lowering his hand to the legal pad. *you and big bobby*—He stopped and tapped the point of the pencil. *you saved my life.*

"It's fortunate we were there, Al."

yeah. BIG save. look at me now. you should have let…With a spasmodic jerk, he flipped the pencil away. She retrieved it. *i won't talk to them.*

"You don't have to, Al."

dam right. tell bobby…He paused to summon his strength. *to go hunt them coyots.* He flipped the pencil again and groaned as he closed his eye. The jaw muscles on the right side of his face unclenched. Estelle straightened up to find Oromatsu at her elbow.

"I'll be finishing my shift here in a few minutes. Is there anything you need from me? Anything you need to ask me?"

"No, I don't think so. As soon as Maria is finished talking to the Forest Service folks, we're going to be taking her back down to Posadas." She nodded at Al's inert form. "Be careful of this one."

"Oh, yes."

"Make sure the cops don't get careless."

"Dr. Baker—he'll be in most of the evening. I've consulted with him and the nurses. They're all well aware of the situation."

"Wonderful. I may be back tomorrow. May I call you?"

"Any time." Oromatsu pulled a card from her jacket pocket. "Absolutely any time. And that second number is right here in ICU. This evening, you can reach Dr. Baker or one of his staff."

"Thank you."

"You know…" Dr. Oromatsu hesitated.

"Yes?"

"It might be best for the patient if his—young wife, is it?"

"Girlfriend."

"If she were able to remain at his side. For the company, I mean. Just to talk to him and assure him that he's not alone."

"That's not going to happen, Doctor. They can't be left together unattended."

"Well, that's a shame."

"Yes, it is."

Chapter Forty-three

"She needs to be in a cell." Robert Torrez' tone carried not a trace of sympathy. He regarded Estelle without blinking. "What, you're just going to let her sit at home with her pet doggy? She bashed Fitzwater's head in. She gets to walk away from that? From conspiring with Al and Darrell to dump the body? From knowing about Connie Suarez?"

"No, she's not walking away from anything, Bobby." Estelle looked at the uncomfortable straight chair in the sheriff's office, but elected to stand, trying to sort out the kinks from the trip home from Albuquerque. "She's been reasonably cooperative in all this. She knows she has a choice. She stays home, essentially under house arrest, or she is arraigned and jailed here."

"That works for me."

"She's not going anywhere."

"You're going back to Albuquerque tomorrow?"

"Probably. Lots of questions yet. If he has the opportunity, Craig Stout wants to talk with Al. I told him to use a pad. Al can't talk yet. It's going to be a long time before he can do anything other than grunt."

"But he ain't admitted to shooting the girl yet."

"No."

"He knows that Maria thinks he did?"

"I'm sure he does."

"Just hangin' tight."

"He has nothing to lose, Bobby. Yes, he admitted that shooting his brother was just an unfortunate accident." Torrez scoffed. "But Connie's death is out and out murder. That's a whole different story. He's not going to admit to that until he knows he's cornered."

"We can arrange that, too." Torrez stood up and stretched, then stepped to one side to peer at the large county map on the wall. "I've been thinkin'," he said.

"Always good."

He ignored that and jabbed a finger at the dot that represented Regál. "Darrell and Al put Fitzwater's body in Darrell's truck. Just getting the body down off that hill, through all the rocks and shit, had to be tough…and in the dark, or dark comin' on, anyways. Al is drivin' the government truck. It's startin' to snow hard, fixin' to be a miserable night." He turned and looked at Estelle. "Just right for what they want to do."

He turned back to the map. "One road out." He traced the blue line up and over Regál Pass. Then, holding one index finger at the pass, he reached up and touched the spot where Fitzwater's government truck had been found, miles to the north, on the other side of the county. "What's the best way?"

"Most direct is up County Road 14. Right straight up to State 78 toward Newton."

"That's right. Two of 'em together, 'cause when Al dumps the truck, he's got to have a way home. My thinkin' is that the body got dumped *first*. He'd need Darrell's help with that. Then the truck."

"Sure. So where? What do we need? A side road would be handy. Not much traffic that night, and what few there might have been are paying attention to storm driving. So Al and Darrell pull off somewhere."

"We got about forty-five miles between here and Newton."

"That's if they didn't go anywhere else. Skip into Arizona, for instance."

Torrez shook his head slowly. "Truck ends up outside of

Newton." He swept a hand around the county, as if considering a route back through Posadas and then northwest. "Can't believe they'd do that, and risk gettin' stopped. They'd take the nearest, easy way."

"Why Newton at all?"

"Out of the county, number one. Draws attention away, if it's found. *When* it's found. Ain't much traffic up there. Puts the truck and Fitzwater's murder in two different jurisdictions, number two. Like you said, Al is clever. Or thinks he is."

"He hinted about the 'coyot hotel.' He implied that you'd know what he was talking about."

"He's going to have to do a hell of a lot more than hint. I *don't* know what he's talkin' about. All of Posadas County is a coyote hotel, far as I'm concerned. I've seen 'em cruisin' around in downtown Posadas. There's a den of 'em right behind the hospital, out in that arroyo." He almost smiled. "Despite some kids' best efforts."

It had been Carlos, Estelle's younger son, who had had the brainstorm of raising a coyote puppy, and he and a neighbor friend had tried all sorts of brilliant trapping strategies—none of which worked with the cunning canines.

"How long have you known Al Fisher?"

"Since he lived over on McArthur, back when he was in middle school."

"So we're talking more than a decade."

"Yep. Back when his folks were still alive."

"Okay. *Sometime* during all those years, you had something to do with Al Fisher and coyotes. You talked to him about them, maybe you went hunting with him…?"

Torrez snorted in derision. "Not likely."

"Something. He remembers it, even if you don't."

"So we find a hypnotist."

"Just keep thinking, Bobby. Just do what Bill Gastner always used to talk about…going through all your old memory files."

Chapter Forty-four

Her cell phone rang at 5:48 a.m., and it took several Beethoven chord tones before she could find the thing.

"Good morning," she managed.

"Musta woke you." The sheriff sounded alert and almost excited.

"That's all right. I had to get up to answer the phone anyway."

He didn't react to the old joke, but instead said, "I remembered."

"Well, wonderful. Remembered what?"

"Me talkin' with Al Fisher. So I went out to scout around."

She peered at the clock again. "You've been up all night, haven't you?"

"Yep. Anyways, you got time now?"

"To do what that can't wait for daylight?"

"We're going to be busy doing other things come daylight."

A warm hand crept across under the blanket and relaxed on Estelle's shoulder, then moved south along the bumpy road of her ribs to take the rise of her hip.

"Where are you?"

"Down south. How about we meet at Regál Pass as soon as you can? Wear a decent pair of hikin' boots."

She looked at the clock again. 5:52. "This can't wait for seven or eight o'clock, maybe?"

"Nope. I'm thinkin' you have other things going on today?"
Torrez grunted something else that she didn't catch, then added,
"I found Fitzwater. I'm about to call Linda up here, too. We got
us some answers."

"You found him?"

"Yep."

"I'll be there as soon as I can, then."

The warm hand jostled her as she folded the phone and put
it back on the nightstand. "Torrez?"

"Yes." She started to sit up, but the hand made it difficult.

"It didn't sound like an emergency."

"He found Fitzwater."

She looked out through the bedroom window. The two Rus-
sian olives just outside were motionless, with an inky sky still
spangled with fading stars. "It could have been worse," she said.
She selected a pair of lined trousers and a wool shirt, and then
took her time forcing wool-clad feet into her boots.

"You know," she said, sitting still on the edge of the bed after
lacing the last boot, "Gabe Torrez is going to grow up to be a
really interesting kid with Bobby as his father."

"She said, with two such uninteresting kids of her own."

"Yeah, well. With any luck, I'll be back home before…well,
we can hope this doesn't take long."

"Be careful, whatever it is that you're doing."

"Oh, yes."

"And…"

"Wear a vest."

"Yes."

Outside, the ambient air touched thirty-three degrees, but
the mountain would be half a dozen degrees colder, most likely
with a wind as air funneled through the venturi of Regál Pass.
Overdressed, Estelle left the heater off in the Charger as she drove
south. Just before reaching the closed and dark Broken Spur
Saloon, she overtook a sleek little red Honda Accord.

"Merry Christmas, Linda," she said aloud, and touched her siren yelp as she passed. With the Honda pacing her not far behind, she wound up through the switchbacks of the San Cristóbals, finally slowing on the long, straight grade up to the pass. Sure enough, Sheriff Bob Torrez' Expedition was parked just beyond the sign that announced the pass. She parked directly behind his unit, snuggling in close so that Linda Pasquale also had room to pull off the highway.

When she got out of the car, she could feel the lightest of breezes touching her cheeks. She turned and looked across the prairie to the north. True to its policies, *NightZone*, the huge astronomy theme park on Waddell's Mesa, was totally dark—not a single artificial light polluted the night.

"This is soooooo much fun," Linda announced cheerfully as she caught up with Estelle. "I mean *really*."

"Hush," Torrez said in a rare moment of voiced reproof. "See, remember what, maybe seven or eight years ago, we was gettin' reports of a jaguar sighting in these hills?"

"Mountains," Linda corrected dryly. "Cold mountains at night."

"It ain't *night*," Torrez corrected.

"Yes," Estelle said. "And as I recall, one of the folks from down below called you to report that he and a friend had seen one sprint across the highway in front of their car. I remember you talking about that afterward."

"Yep. Octavio Roybal and Fernando Rivera. They was comin' home from a little blow-out at the Broken Spur." He actually smiled, his dark face ghostly in the side-wash of the beams from their LED lights. "I went back and checked that memory, like you said."

"Okay."

"Earlier that day, we'd had a light snow...kinda like we did a day or two ago—Friday night, when Pasquale stopped Darrell Fisher with the kid walkin' along the highway. So back then

I figured, with the snow, if there *was* a jaguar, if Octavio and Fernando weren't just seein' hallucinations, it couldn't be better conditions for trackin'. So I went out to check. If it hadn't snowed, I wouldn't have wasted the time."

He pointed to the north. "Just back there a-ways, where the old forest road comes in? I pulled over and scouted around where they said that they sighted the cat. Didn't take me long to find the tracks, right where Octavio and Fernando said they were."

"Jaguar?"

"Yep. See, a mountain lion has these funny indents on the front of the pads." He patted the base of his hand. "Real characteristic. A jaguar don't. Bigger, blunt foot, more roundy toe pads." He nodded. "And bigger. Way bigger. Front feet are a full inch wider than a cougar."

"This is turning into an episode of *Wild Kingdom*," Linda snarked, and Estelle reached out and clamped a friendly hand on her shoulder.

"A genuine jaguar sighting is a *major* deal," she said. "A major deal. You reported it to the Game and Fish, as I recall. They came out to survey the spot, even though the tracks were long gone."

"That's right. Anyways, I got this little digital camera, and I'm standin' there, tryin' to make it work so I can take pictures."

"Ummmm," Linda observed.

"Yeah, well." He nodded philosophically, well aware of his serious limitations with a camera. "I'm excited, and I can't hold it still. And then the flash won't work. See, I should have called *you* in the middle of the night. Anyways, here comes a car, and guess who it is."

"This has to be related," Estelle said. "So I'm guessing young Al Fisher, our current person of interest."

"That's it. Al and Maria. They'd just started goin' out together, and he's bringin' her home from somewhere. Probably the saloon. They stop, 'cause I guess they thought I was stuck or something." He took a deep breath and let it out slowly. "Now, I *knew* that

Al hunted anything with legs. About the last thing I wanted him doing was blasting a jaguar—maybe also what turns out to be the *only* jaguar in New Mexico? I mean, he'd never believe Octavio or Fernando, either one. Just a couple old drunks. But he'd believe the tracks."

"*Oh sure* you saw a jaguar," Linda said derisively, mimicking the critics. "And I've got a bridge I'll sell you…"

"I told him that something ran across the road and I was sure I hit it. Thought it was probably a coyote. I was gonna see if he managed to crawl back to his den, over there west, in the rocks."

"Al bought that?"

Torrez shrugged. "Sure. He asked if I wanted help findin' it. I said no. As long as the carcass was off the road and all. But then he says, 'You know, I hunt up here all the time. Lots of cover. Lots of coyotes, badgers, skunks.' I agreed with him, 'cause from time to time *I* hunt up here. People think the game is all down on the flat, out on the prairie, but that ain't true. Then Al says something like, 'I even seen a cat a couple times. But mostly coyotes. It's like a big coyote hotel over in those rocks.'" Torrez stopped abruptly and stared hard at Estelle. She reached into her car and tapped the lights off.

"A big coyote hotel."

"That's what he said. I remembered it, 'cause I always thought it was a neat way of describing it." He waited for a reaction, and when he didn't get one, he added, "Remember what we was talkin' about earlier today. What route Al Fisher would take out of Regál. Drivin' two trucks, one with a body in the back, the other they're wantin' to get rid of—throw suspicion somewheres else."

He turned and swung his flashlight up, illuminating the entrance to the rough two-track. The beam was intense, but the dawn light washed it out. "They drove in there a-ways, and then the two of 'em lugged Myron Fitzwater's corpse over to the hotel. Out of sight, lots of critters to help dispose of the body."

"How far in did you have to go?"

"Maybe a hundred yards. Maybe a little more."

"That's quite a tote."

"Maybe drag him on the tarp. There would have been enough snow to make it easier. It wouldn't take much."

"Show me."

"How about I guard the cars?" Linda said helpfully. "If you need me, just shout."

"How about you get your gear and follow us?" Sheriff Torrez said, and it wasn't a suggestion. "He's there, all right."

The sheriff didn't comment on the tracks. Sometime before the snow—or perhaps during it—someone had driven in the narrow two-track, leaving just enough tire impressions to prove they'd been there. Just as easily, so had occasional neckers, drinkers, wood-cutters, and lost tourists. They couldn't have driven far, since the two-track ended in a jumble of boulders that blocked the way, forcing the trail to narrow to a single path. A well-weathered Forest Service sign with a little hopeful arrow announced *Bailey Springs 3½ Mi.*

"Three and a half miles?" Linda mused. "Let us pray they weren't *that* ambitious."

At one point, Torrez had to turn sideways to slip past a rock outcrop, and he stopped abruptly and knelt.

"Light," he said, and Estelle added the blaze of her LED to his, illuminating the rock surface. At this point, Linda Pasquale sidled up close and knelt as well. For long enough that they could feel the cold seeping through clothes, they examined the rock-face. "Something scrubbed by here," Torrez said finally. "Don't see no fibers or nothing. But the mark shows where the lichen was disturbed." Estelle held her flashlight steady to amplify the angled morning light while Linda Pasquale's camera buzzed and clicked, sometimes with the flash, sometimes with available light.

Torrez straightened up. "Cold and snowin' when they done this, dark as the inside of a well, they're not going to hike far." Linda uttered a little sigh of optimistic agreement.

The trail, little more than a path worn by generations of deer and smoothed by a host of soft-footed critters, ducked down a steep incline, and then angled along an impressive overhang. Ahead of them, something heavy crashed through brush, and they heard the knock of hooves on rock. "Somebody's home," Linda said. They saw the flash of a buffy butt that instantly vanished up through the rocks.

"Stop," Torrez snapped. He narrowed the beam of the light and guided it along beneath the overhang. "Photo from here."

"What am I shooting?"

Torrez narrowed the beam some more until it was a pencil point, bright enough in the shade, but just a faint dot on the sun-kissed rocks. "Right there."

"And then an approach series," Estelle added.

"You're telling me that you were up here all last night, tramping around. By yourself?" Linda actually sounded a little concerned. "Absolutely certifiable." She shook her head in wonder. "If you stand to the side just a little," she said to the sheriff, and then to Estelle, "and if you do the same over there, I won't even have to use the flash. Open up your light to give me a nice, even flood."

With the camera clicking away, Linda moved up the slight incline to the overhang. "Do you see any bootprints?" Estelle asked.

"Nope. Just a few scuffs."

"Under the overhang, it's going to be dusty," Torrez reminded her. "Don't disturb it."

"Then maybe they used the old Hollywood trick of brushing their path with a tree bough," Linda said. "'Cause there ain't no footprints here." She took a couple of more shots and stood up. "Okay."

The roof of the overhang was at least three feet high at the front, sloping sharply downward toward the back. Myron Fitzwater's body had been shoved into the space until his face was pressed against the rock. A few scattered tree limbs, sticks, and stones were scattered to camouflage the body. Stretched out on his right side, not curled into a fetal position, Fitzwater's corpse wouldn't have been seen by casual hikers.

Estelle checked her watch. At seven forty-five, rookie hire Tanner Garcia would be finishing up his first rotation as dispatcher for the graveyard shift. Deputy Thomas Pasquale, Linda's husband, would be somewhere out in the county.

On the north slope of the mountain, there was a clear shot back to Posadas. She used her cell phone, dialed, and waited for several seconds before Garcia responded.

"Posadas County Sheriff's Department, Garcia."

"Tanner, the sheriff and I and Linda Pasquale are at a scene on Regál Pass involving one down. It's not an MVA, and we're off the highway several yards. Have Deputy Pasquale respond. He'll see our units parked at the pass. Silent approach, please. As soon as you have Pasquale responding, contact the ME and have him roll this location ASAP. If Dr. Perrone is absolutely unavailable, call Dr. Guzman. We'll also need an EMT unit, but there's no rush on that. Wait for my call, but have them standing by. "

"Got it," Tanner said. "And no lights and siren?"

"You are correct. I don't want the whole neighborhood up here."

"Got it. Pasquale is north on State 78, so he'll be a few minutes."

"That's fine. We're not going anywhere, and neither is the victim."

She pocketed the phone.

"I got coffee," Torrez offered. "We might as well wait in the truck."

"None for me, thanks," Estelle said. "But you're right. Now we wait."

"Might as well let Craig Stout know."

"Merry Christmas to him, too."

Chapter Forty-five

At nine forty-five, Sheriff Robert Torrez and Undersheriff Estelle Reyes-Guzman drove quietly through the tiny village of Regál, with its gentle pillars of smoke rising straight up from each chimney. Deputy Thomas Pasquale headed in the opposite direction for an appointment with District Judge Ralph Tate.

Maria Apodaca opened the front door before either officer reached the steps. Her face was pale. Behind her, White Fang shivered, let out a single yap, and shrank under a chair.

"Oh, is he…?"

"Maria, may we come inside?"

"Of course. Al…is he okay?"

"I called just a few minutes ago. He had a rough night, but he's a tough guy," Estelle said.

Maria visibly relaxed. "Oh, good. I saw you guys driving in, and thought…"

"Al is going to heal, Maria."

"I am *sooo* glad to hear that. I didn't sleep all night. I should go back up to the city." She gestured toward the small couch near the stove. "Please, sit down." She looked nervously at Sheriff Torrez, who had yet to utter a word.

"Maria, tell me again about the moment that Myron Fitzwater was shot. You said he was tussling with Al." She slipped the recorder out of her pocket and laid it conspicuously on the arm of the sofa.

Maria closed her eyes, as if that were the only way to bring the memory back into focus. "They...they were fighting, and Myron had Al down on the ground. He had one handcuff on Al's..." She stopped and looked at Estelle. "His right wrist, but I don't think it was locked. He was trying to manage that, but Al kept punching at him. Then...," Maria stopped again. "Then he...I mean Myron...had his gun out and it went off, and they thrashed around. I was so scared. That's when I hit Myron with the stick. I was so scared. And when I did, Al was able to wrestle the gun away from him. Somehow Al got hold of it."

"And what happened then?"

"He was still struggling to get away, and...and that's when the gun went off again."

"Tell me about that."

"Well, it just went off, somehow."

"Maria, you told me earlier that Mr. Fitzwater was shot once under the left arm. Is that correct? Is that the way you remember it? Do you remember telling me that?"

"Yes."

Estelle fished her camera out of her jacket pocket. No larger than a pack of cigarettes, almost the entire back was the preview screen. She turned it on and thumbed the menu, then scrolled through several photos.

"Maria, I'm going to show you a photo, and I want you to tell me what it shows." The girl started to reach for the camera, but Estelle held up a hand. "Let me hold it for you." For half a dozen seconds, she stared at the photo without breathing. "Maria, is that Myron Fitzwater?"

The girl let out a strangled cry and doubled over, crashing off the sofa onto the floor. She tried to rise, then doubled over again, retching on the pinewood floor.

"I guess that means yes," Torrez observed.

"Get a towel, Bobby." Estelle slid the camera back into her pocket and held Maria by both shoulders, moving her away from the puddle. Torrez strode to the bathroom and returned, handing Estelle a small bath towel. Maria grabbed it, pressing it to her face as she jolted from the first in a string of powerful hiccups.

"Git!" Torrez commanded, blocking White Fang's investigation of the vomit puddle. The dog reacted as if treated to a cattle prod, racing for the sanctuary of the bedroom.

Maria sucked in air, coughed, and hiccupped again. Estelle maintained her grip on the girl's shoulders.

"Tell me what really happened, Maria."

"I…" Another hiccup.

"Take your time."

Maria dabbed at her face once more with the towel. "I think I'll be all right." She leaned over slightly and tossed the towel over the puddle.

"I hit him with the stick. Real hard. I was scared for Al." She stopped as if that were the end of the story as far as she was concerned.

"And then?"

"And then Al wrestled the gun away and kicked loose. Myron was down on his hands and knees." She squinted off into the distance. "I remember that his eyes were closed and he was gasping, like he couldn't get any air. He was making funny little noises, like way down in his throat. Al rolled away and got to his feet. Myron tried to. I mean like he was on his knees, but trying to get up. His hands were on his head."

"And *did* he get up?"

A long silence followed before Maria replied, her voice small and distant. "No. Al fired the gun three times. Real fast, like he does. Myron went down flat on his face."

"Is that when Connie ran away?"

Maria nodded. "She did. I was too scared to move. Al's face was red, like he was going to blow up. Then he took off after her." Estelle waited. "That's what happened."

"Al was standing, Myron was on his knees with his back to Al, and Al then shot him three times in the back."

Maria nodded.

"Maria, think very carefully. Is that the truth?"

The girl nodded.

"I need a verbal answer, Maria."

"Yes, Ma'am, it's the truth."

Estelle glanced over at Torrez, who nodded. They heard a vehicle in the driveway. "Stout's here," Torrez said.

"What will they do to him?" Maria whispered.

"There's no way to predict what a jury will decide," Estelle said.

"But it was all my fault. I hit him."

"That part was your fault," Estelle said. "And maybe you had good reason. What happened next was Al's fault. It's that simple."

"Do I need to find a lawyer?"

"Yes. You do."

Chapter Forty-six

they going to cut on me today. Al Fisher let the pencil fall.

"One day at a time, Al. Whatever it takes. And every day, you'll improve. Just think ahead."

Oh yeah. Funy joke. Think ahead to WHAT. He made a strange growling sound as if he were trying to spit out of the side of his mouth. One of the suction tubes gurgled. *didn't take you long.*

"What, to find Myron Fitzwater? You told Sheriff Torrez where he was. Did you think that Torrez wouldn't remember?"

Al coughed. Eventually he opened his right eye and stared at Estelle. He wrote the next message in three jerky efforts. *dumb as a box of rocks.*

"Many people have made that mistake about Robert Torrez. Are you ready to tell me what really happened with your brother?"

told you.

"You think a Grand Jury will believe it was an accident? Or even suicide?"

dont matter. He paused for a long moment. *one, two, three. it don't matter.*

He tried to shift his body, and pounded one foot on the mattress in frustration. *something you gotta do.*

"Something *I* have to do? What?"

leave danny alone. He didt have anything to do with any of this. and Lupe. he took the deer, but that's all. AND

The capital letters were hard for him, and he stopped, exhausted. "And what, Al?"

maria.

"Al, you know I can't make promises about Maria. There are so many things she *should* have done that she didn't do. The district attorney will review the whole case and after that, it's his call. He'll decide whether or not she's to be charged. We could argue about her hitting Myron in the head with the stick. We could argue that was self-defense, or that she was afraid for your safety. But the law is clear. We have to look beyond that single strike with the stick."

Al's one visible eye was closed, but the bedside monitors said that his vitals were stable. What was going on in his mind was another question.

"She *knew*, Al. She *knew* that you shot Myron Fitzwater three times in the back. That's where it all starts."

The pencil twitched. *He was going…*

"You could have walked away, Al. You and Maria, both. You could have called somebody on your cell phone. You know, after Maria smacked Fitzwater in the head, you could have just walked away. Connie would have been left with a boyfriend with a terrible headache. She had to know that Fitzwater was acting in the wrong. He was no cop, he had no enforcement responsibilities. But your trigger-happy response changed the situation, Al. And Maria knew what you did to Connie. She *knew* what you meant by 'taking care' of the situation. And she kept quiet."

For many seconds, Al lay so quietly that Estelle thought he'd gone to sleep. Eventually his fingers scrabbled with the pencil, and he wrote, slowly and carefully, *i ruint her life, didt i.*

Estelle kept any trace of sympathy out of her voice. "Yes, you did."

The pencil drew circles as if trying to decide what letter to start with, and finally settled on the one he liked best. *i got to help her, then.*

"That's not going to happen, Al. You're not going to lie to cover for her." She watched him digest that. "You think on that now, Al. Hurt as you are, you think on it. And what you decide to do will tell the world a lot about what kind of man Al Fisher really is."

To see more Poisoned Pen Press titles:

Visit our website:
poisonedpenpress.com
Request a digital catalog:
info@poisonedpenpress.com